Praise for the novels of
New York Times bestselling author
DIANA PALMER

"Diana Palmer is a mesmerizing storyteller who captures the essence of what a romance should be."
—*Affaire de Coeur*

"Palmer returns with a splendid Western contemporary novel filled with passion, heartache and small-town life. The story serves as a reminder that life will provide second chances; we just need be brave enough to hold onto them."
—*RT Book Reviews* on *Wyoming Brave* (Top Pick)

"Readers will be moved by this tale of revenge and justice, grief and healing."
—*Booklist* on *Dangerous*

"Diana Palmer is one of those authors whose books are always enjoyable. She throws in romance, suspense and a good story line."
—*The Romance Reader* on *Before Sunrise*

"Lots of passion, thrills, and plenty of suspense... *Protector* is a top-notch read!"
—*Romance Reviews Today*

"A delightful romance with interesting new characters and many familiar faces."
—*RT Book Reviews* on *Wyoming Tough*

**Also available from Diana Palmer
and HQN Books**

Long, Tall Texans

Fearless
Heartless
Dangerous
Merciless
Courageous
Protector
Invincible
Untamed
Defender

The Wyoming Men

Wyoming Tough
Wyoming Fierce
Wyoming Bold
Wyoming Strong
Wyoming Rugged
Wyoming Brave

Morcai Battalion

The Morcai Battalion
The Morcai Battalion: The Recruit
The Morcai Battalion: Invictus
The Morcai Battalion: The Rescue

For a complete list of titles available by Diana Palmer,
please visit www.dianapalmer.com.

DIANA PALMER

DEFENDER

HQN™

HQN™

PLEASE RECYCLE
THIS PRODUCT IS RECYCLABLE

Recycling programs for this product may not exist in your area.

ISBN-13: 978-0-373-80197-8

Defender

Copyright © 2016 by Diana Palmer

Dear Reader,

This book is something different. It has new faces, although it's set in Jacobsville and Comanche Wells, with cameos by old friends. The heroine is the daughter of a multimillionaire. The hero is her father's head of security for his home and racehorses.

But her life of privilege is not what it seems. A tragic decision leads to what seems to be the end of her dream of love. Her employment as a new assistant district attorney in Jacobsville is the beginning of a murder investigation in which she, her younger sister and their former head of security—now with the San Antonio FBI office—are entwined. The end of this book is the beginning of her sister's story, *Wyoming Brave*, which takes place in Wyoming. I loved doing this story. I hope you will enjoy reading it.

This book is dedicated to our nephew. He leaves behind his wife, Heather, his sister, Kathy, his mother, Kathleen, and two great kids, Austin and Tyler. The boys and I play video games together on Xbox One.

As always, thank you for your kindness over the long years, and your friendship. I am your biggest fan.

Love,

Diana Palmer

For our sweet nephew, Tony Woodall, 1965–2015,
who left a hole in our hearts with his passing.
Sweet dreams, sweet boy.

CHAPTER ONE

Isabel Grayling stuck her head around the study door and peered in. The big desk was empty. The chair hadn't been moved from its position, carefully pushed underneath. Everything on the oak surface was neatly placed; not a pencil wasn't neatly in a cup; not a scrap of paper was out of line. She let out a breath. Her father wasn't home, but the desk kept the fanatical order he insisted on, even when he wasn't here.

She darted out of the office with a relieved sigh and pushed back the long tangle of her reddish-gold hair. Blue, blue eyes were filled with relief. She wrinkled her straight nose, where just a tiny line of freckles ran over its bridge. Her name was Isabel, but only Paul Fiore called her that. To everyone else, she was Sari, just as her sister, Meredith, was always called Merrie.

"Well?" her younger sister, Merrie, asked in a whisper.

Sari turned. The other girl was slender, like herself, but Merrie had hair almost platinum blond, straight and to her waist in back. Her eyes, like Sari's, were blue, but paler, more the color of a winter sky. Both girls looked like their late mother, who was pretty but not beautiful.

"Gone!" Sari said with a wicked grin.

Merrie let out a sigh of relief. "Paul said that Daddy was going to Germany for a few weeks. Maybe he'll find some other people to harass once he's in Europe."

Sari went up to the shorter girl and hugged her. "It will be all right."

Merrie fought tears. "I only wanted to have my hair trimmed, not cut. Honestly, Sari, he's so unreasonable…!"

"I know." She didn't dare say more. Paul had told her things in confidence that she couldn't bear to share with her baby sister. Their father was far more dangerous than either of them had known.

To any outsider, the Grayling sisters had everything. Their father was rich beyond any dream. They lived in a gray stone mansion on acres and acres of land in Comanche Wells, Texas, where their father kept Thoroughbred horses. Rather, his foreman kept them. The old man was carefully maneuvered away from the livestock by the foreman, who'd once had to save a horse from the man. Darwin Grayling had beaten animals before. It was rumored that he'd beaten his wife. She died of a massive concussion, but Grayling swore that she'd fallen. Not many people in Comanche Wells or nearby Jacobsville, Texas, wanted to argue with a man who could buy and sell anybody in the state.

That hadn't stopped local physician Jeb "Copper" Coltrain from asking for a coroner's inquest and making accusations that Grayling's description of the accident didn't match the head injuries. But Copper had been called out of town on an emergency by a friend and when he returned, the coroner's inquest was over and accidental death had been put on the death certificate. Case closed.

The Grayling girls didn't know what had truly happened. Sari had been in high school, Merrie in grammar school, when their mother died. They knew only what their father had told them. They were much too afraid of him to ask questions.

Now, Merrie was in her last year of high school and Sari was a senior in college. Sari had majored in history in preparation for a law degree. She went to school in San Antonio, but wasn't allowed to live on campus. Her father had her driven back and forth every day. It was the same with Merrie. Darwin wasn't having either of his daughters around other people. He'd fought and won when Sari tried to move onto the college campus. He was wealthy and his children were targets, he'd said implacably, and they weren't going anywhere without one of his security people.

Which was why Sari and Paul Fiore, head of security for the Grayling Corporation, were such good friends. They'd known each other since Paul moved down from New Jersey to take the job, while Sari was in her last year of high school. Paul drove the girls to school every day.

He'd wondered, but only to Sari, why her father hadn't placed them both in private schools. Sari knew, but she didn't dare say. It was because her father didn't want them out of his sight, where they might say something that he didn't approve of. They knew too much about him, about his business, about the way he treated animals and people.

He was paranoid about his private life. He had

women, Sari was certain of it, but never around the house. He had a mistress. She worked for the federal government. Paul had told her, in confidence. He wasn't afraid of Darwin Grayling—Paul wasn't afraid of anyone. But he liked his job and he didn't want to go back to the FBI. He'd worked for the Bureau years ago. Nobody knew why he'd suddenly given up a lucrative government job to become a rent-a-cop for a Texas millionaire in a small town at the back of beyond. Paul never said, either.

Sari touched Merrie's slightly bruised cheek and winced. "I warned you about talking back, honey," she said worriedly. "I'm so sorry!"

"My mouth and my brain don't stay connected," Merrie laughed, but bitterly. Her blue eyes met her sister's. "If we could just tell somebody!"

"We could, and Daddy would make sure they never worked again," Sari said. "That's why I've never told Paul anything…" She bit her lip.

But Merrie knew already. She hugged the taller girl. "I won't tell him. I know how you feel about Paul."

"I wish he felt something for me," Sari said with a long sigh. "He's always been affectionate with me. He takes good care of me. But it's… I don't know how to say it. Impersonal?" She drew away, her expression sad. "He just doesn't get close to people. He dated that out-of-town auditor two years ago, remember? She called here over and over, and he wouldn't talk to her. He said he just wanted someone to go to the movies with, and she was looking at wedding rings."

She laughed involuntarily. She shook her head. "He won't get involved."

"Maybe he was involved, and something happened," her sister said softly. "He looks like the sort of person who dives into things headfirst. You know, all or nothing. Maybe he lost somebody he loved, Sari."

"I guess that would explain a lot." She moved away, grimacing. "It's just my luck, to go loopy over a man who thinks a special relationship is something you have with a vehicle."

"It's a very nice vehicle," Merrie began.

"It's a truck, Merrie!" she interrupted, throwing up her hands. "Gosh, you'd think it was a child the way he takes care of it. Special mats, taking it to the car wash once a week. He even waxes it himself." She glowered. "It's a truck!"

"I like trucks," Merrie said. "That cowboy who worked for us last year had a fancy black one. He wanted to take me to a movie." She shivered. "I thought Daddy was going to kill him."

"So did I." Sari swallowed, hard. She wrapped her arms around her chest. "The cowboy went all the way to Arizona, they said, to make sure Daddy didn't have him followed. He was scared."

"So was I," Merrie confessed. "You know, I'm eighteen years old and I've never gone on a date with a real boy. I've never been kissed, except on the cheek."

"Join the club," her sister laughed softly. "Well, one day we'll break out of here. We'll escape!" she said dramatically. "I'll hire a team of mercenaries to hide us from Daddy!"

"With what money?" Merrie asked sadly. "Neither of us has a dime. Daddy makes sure we can't even get a part-time job to make money. You can't even live at your college campus. I'll bet that gets you talked about."

"It does," Sari confided. "But they figure our father is just eccentric because he's so rich, and they let it go. I don't have any real friends, anyway."

"Just me," Merrie teased.

Sari hugged her. "Just you. You're my best friend, Merrie."

"You're mine, too, even if you are my sister."

Sari drew back. "One day, things will change."

"You've been saying that since we were in grammar school. It hasn't."

"It will."

Merrie touched her cheek and winced. "I told Paul I fell down the steps," she said, when she noticed her sister's worried expression.

"I wonder if he believed you," Sari replied solemnly. "He's not afraid of Daddy."

"He should be. I've heard Daddy has this friend back East," Merrie told her. "He's in with some underworld group. They say he's killed people, that he'll do anything for money." She bit her lower lip. "I don't want Paul hurt any more than you do. The less he knows about what goes on here when he's off duty, the better. He couldn't save us, anyway. He could only be dragged down with us."

"He wouldn't let Daddy hurt us, if he knew," Sari replied.

"So he won't know."

"Someone else might tell him," Sari began.

"Not anybody who works here," Merrie sighed. "Mandy's kept house for over twenty years, since before you were born. She knows stuff, but she's afraid to tell. She has a brother who does illegal things. Daddy told her he could have her brother sent to prison if she ever opened her mouth. She's afraid of him." She looked up. "I'm afraid of him."

Sari winced. "Yes. Me, too."

"I don't ever want to get married, Sari," the younger woman said huskily. "Not ever!"

"One day, you might, if the right man comes along."

Merrie laughed. "He's not likely to come along while Daddy's around, or he'll be leaving in a body bag in the back of a pickup truck."

The dark humor in that statement sent them both into gales of laughter.

PAUL FIORE WAS ITALIAN. He also had a Greek grandmother. It accounted for his olive complexion and thick, jet-black hair and large brown eyes. He was handsome, too, tall and broad-shouldered, muscular without making a point of it. He walked like a panther, light on his feet, and he had a quick mind. He'd been in law enforcement most of his life until he took the job with the Grayling Corporation. He'd wanted to get as far away from federal work—and New Jersey—as he could. Jacobsville, Texas, came close to his ideal place.

He was fond of the girls, Merrie and Sari, and he took charge of the house when Mr. Grayling was out of the country. He could handle any problem that came up. His main responsibility was to keep the girls safe, but he also kept a close watch on the property, especially the very expensive Thoroughbreds Grayling raised for sale.

The housekeeper, Mandy Swilling, was fond of him. She was always baking him the cinnamon cookies he liked so much, and tucking little surprises into his truck when he had to be away on business.

"You've got me ruined," he accused her one morning. "I'll be so spoiled that I'll never be able to get along in the world if I ever get fired from here."

"Mr. Darwin will never fire you," Mandy said confidently. "You keep your mouth shut and you don't ask questions."

His eyes narrowed. "Odd reason to keep a man on, isn't it?"

"Not around here," she said heavily.

He stared at her, his dark eyes twinkling. "You know where all the bodies are buried, huh? That why you still have work?"

She didn't laugh, as he'd expected her to. She just glanced at him and winced. "Don't even joke about things like that, Mr. Paul."

He groaned at her form of addressing him.

"Now, now," she said. "I've always called the boss Mr. Darwin, just like I call the foreman Mr. Edward. It's a way of speaking that Southern folk are raised with. You, being a Yankee..." She stopped and grinned. "Sorry. I meant to say, you, being a northerner, wouldn't know about that."

"I guess so."

"You still sound like a person born up North."

He shrugged and grinned back at her. "We are what we are."

"I suppose so."

He watched her work at making rolls for lunch. She wasn't much to look at. She was about fifty pounds overweight, had short silver hair and dark eyes, and she was slightly stooped over from years of working in gardens with a hoe. But she could cook! The woman was a magician in the kitchen. Paul remembered his tiny little grandmother, making ravioli and antipasto when he was a child, the scent of flour and oil that always seemed to cling to her. Kitchens were comforting to a child who had no real home. His father had worked for a local mob boss, and done all sorts of illegal things, like most of the rest of his family. His mother had died miserable, watching her husband run around with an endless parade of other women, shuddering every time the big boss or law enforcement came to the front door. After his mother died and his father went to jail for the twentieth time, Paul went to live with his little Greek grandmother. He and his cousin Mikey had stayed with her until they were almost grown. Paul watched Mikey go the same route his father had, attached like a tick to the local big crime boss. His father never came around. In fact, he couldn't remember seeing his father more than a dozen times before the man died in a shootout with a rival mob.

It was why he'd gone into law enforcement at seventeen, fresh out of high school. He hated the hold crime had on his family. He hoped he could make a difference, help clean up his old neighborhood and free it from the talons of organized crime. He went from local police right up into the FBI. He'd felt that he was unstoppable, that he could fight crime and win. Pride had blinded him to the reality of life. It had cost him everything.

Still, he missed the Bureau sometimes. But the memories had been lethal. He couldn't face them, not even now, years after the tragedy that had sent him running from New Jersey to Texas on a job tip from a coworker. He'd given up dreams of a home and all the things that went with it. Now, it was just the job, doing the job. He didn't look forward. Ever. One Day at a Time was his credo.

"Why are you hiding in here?" Mandy asked suddenly, breaking into his thoughts.

"It's that obvious, huh?" he asked, the New Jersey accent still prevalent even after the years he'd spent in Texas.

"Yes, it is."

He sipped the black coffee she'd placed in front of him at the table. "Livestock foreman's got a daughter. She came with him today."

"Oh, dear," Mandy replied.

He shrugged. "I took her to lunch at Barbara's Cafe a few weeks ago. Just a casual thing. I met her at the courthouse. She works there. She decided that I was looking for a meaningful relationship. So now she's over here every Saturday like clockwork, hanging out with her dad."

"That will end when Mr. Darwin comes back," she said with feeling. "He doesn't like strangers on the place, even strangers related to people who work here."

He smiled sadly. "Or it will end when I lose my temper and start cursing in Italian."

"You look Italian," she said, studying him.

He chuckled. "You should see my cousin Mikey. He could have auditioned for *The Godfather*. I've got Greek in me, too. My grandmother was from a little town near Athens. She could barely speak English at all. But could she cook! Kind of like you," he added with twinkling eyes. "She'd have liked you, Mandy."

Her hard face softened. "You never speak of your parents."

"I try not to think about them too much. Funny, how we carry our childhoods around on our backs."

She nodded. She was making rolls for lunch and they had to have time to rise. Her hands were floury as she kneaded the soft dough. She nodded toward the rest of the house. "Neither of those poor girls has had a childhood. He keeps them locked up all the time. No parties, no dancing and especially no boys."

He scowled. "I noticed that. I asked the boss once why he didn't let the girls go out occasionally." He took a sip of his coffee.

"What did he tell you?"

"That the last employee who asked him that question is now waiting tables in a little town in the Yukon Territory."

She shook her head. "That's probably true. A cowboy who tried to take Merrie out on a date once got a job in Arizona. They say he's still looking behind him for hired assassins." Her hands stilled in the dough.

"Don't you ever mention that outside the house," she advised. "Or to Mr. Darwin. I kind of like having you around," she added with a smile and went back to her chore.

"I like this job. No big-city noise, no pressure, no pressing deadlines on cases."

She glanced up at him, then back down to the bowl again. "We've never talked about it, but you were in law enforcement once, weren't you?"

He scowled. "How did you know that?"

"Small towns. Cash Grier let something slip to a friend, who told Barbara at the café, who told her cook, who told me."

"Our police chief knew I was in law enforcement? How?" he wondered aloud, feeling insecure. He didn't want his past widely known here.

She laughed softly. "Nobody knows how he finds out things. But he worked for the government once." She glanced at him. "He was a high-level assassin."

His eyes widened. "The police chief?" he exclaimed.

She nodded. "Then he was a Texas Ranger—that ended when he slugged the temporary captain and got fired. Afterward he worked for the DA in San Antonio and then he came here."

He whistled. "Slugged the captain." He chuckled. "He's still a pretty tough customer, despite the gorgeous wife and two little kids."

"That's what everyone says. We're pretty protective of him. Our late mayor—who was heavily into drug smuggling on the side—tried to fire Chief Grier, and the whole city police force and fire department, and all our city employees, said they'd quit on the spot if he did."

"Obviously he wasn't fired."

She smiled. "Not hardly. It turns out that the state attorney general, Simon Hart, is Cash Grier's cousin. He showed up, along with some reporters, at the hearing they had to discuss the firing of the chief's patrol officers. They arrested a drunk politician and he told the mayor to fire them. The chief said over his dead body."

"I've been here for years, and I heard gossip about it, but that's the first time I've heard the whole story."

"An amazing man, our chief."

"Oh, yes." He finished his coffee. "Nobody makes coffee like you do, Mandy. Never weak and pitiful, always strong and robust!"

"Yes, and the coffee usually comes out that way, too!" she said with a wicked grin.

He laughed as he got up from the table, and went back to work.

THAT NIGHT HE was researching a story about an attempted Texas Thoroughbred kidnapping on the internet when Sari walked in the open door. He was perched on the bed in just his pajama bottoms with the laptop beside him. Sari had on a long blue cotton nightgown with a thick, ruffled matching housecoat buttoned way up to the throat. She jumped onto the bed with him, her long hair in a braid, her eyes twinkling as she crossed her legs under the voluminous garment.

"Do that when your dad comes home, and we'll

both be sitting on the front lawn with the door locked," he teased.

"You know I never do it when he's home. What are you looking up?"

"Remember that story last week about the so-called traveling horse groomer who turned up at the White Stables in Lexington, Kentucky, and walked off with a Thoroughbred in the middle of the night?"

"Yes, I do."

"Well, just in case he headed south when he jumped bail, I'm checking out similar attempts. I found one in Texas that happened two weeks ago. So I'm reading about his possible MO."

She frowned. "MO?"

"Modus operandi," he said. "It's Latin. It means…"

"Please," she said. "I know Latin. It means method of operation."

"Close enough," he said with a gentle smile. His eyes went back to the computer screen. "Generally speaking, once a criminal finds a method that works, he uses it over and over until he's caught. I want to make sure that he doesn't sashay in here while your dad's gone and make off with Grayling's Pride."

"Sashay?" she teased.

He wrinkled his nose. "You're a bad influence on me," he mused, his eyes still on the computer screen. "That's one of your favorite words."

"It's just a useful one. *Snit* is my favorite one."

He raised an eyebrow at her.

"And lately you're in a snit more than you're not," she pointed out.

He managed a smile. "Bad memories. Anniversaries hit hard."

She bit her tongue. She'd never discussed really personal things with him. She'd tried once and he'd closed up immediately. So she smiled impersonally. "So they say," she said instead of posing the question she was dying to.

He admired her tact. He didn't say so, of course. She couldn't know the memories that tormented him, that had him up walking the floor late at night. She couldn't know the guilt that ate at him night and day because he was in the wrong place at the wrong time when it really mattered.

"Are you okay?" she asked suddenly.

His dark eyebrows went up. "What?"

She shrugged. "You looked wounded just then."

She was more perceptive than he'd realized. He scrolled down the story he was reading online. "Wounded. Odd choice of words there, Isabel."

"You're the only person who ever called me that."

"What? Isabel?" He looked up, studying her softly rounded face, her lovely complexion, her blue, blue eyes. "You look like an Isabel."

"Is that a compliment or something else?"

"Definitely a compliment." He looked back at the computer screen. "I used to love to read about your namesake. She was queen of Spain in the fifteenth century. She and her husband led a crusade to push foreigners out of their country. They succeeded in 1492."

Her lips parted. "Isabella la Catolica."

His chiseled lips pursed. "My God. You know your history."

She laughed softly. "I'm a history major," she reminded him. "Also a Spanish scholar. I'm doing a semester of Spanish immersion. English isn't spoken in the classroom, ever. And we read some of the classic novels in Spanish."

He chuckled softly. "My favorite was Pio Baroja. He was Basque, something of a legend in the early twentieth century."

"Mine was *Sangre y Arena*."

"Blasco Ibáñez," he shot back. "*Blood and Sand.* Bullfighting?" he added in a surprised tone.

She laughed. "Yes, well, I didn't realize what the book would be about until I got into it, and then I couldn't put it down."

"They made a movie about it back in the forties, I think it was," he told her. "It starred Tyrone Power and Rita Hayworth. Painful, bittersweet story. He ran around on his saintly wife with a woman who was little more than a prostitute."

"I suppose saintly women weren't much in demand in some circles in those days. And especially not today," she added with a wistful little sigh. "Men want experienced women."

"Not all of them," he said, looking away from her.

"Really?"

He forced himself to keep his eyes on the computer screen. "Think about it. A man would have to be crazy to risk STDs or HIV for an hour's pleasure with a woman who knew her way around bedrooms."

She fought a blush and lost.

He saw it and laughed. "Honey, you aren't worldly at all, are you?"

"I'm alternately backward or unliberated, to hear my classmates tell it. But mostly they tolerate my odd point of view. I think one of them actually feels sorry for me."

"Twenty years down the road, they may wish they'd had your sterling morals," he replied. He looked up, into her eyes, and for a few endless seconds, he didn't look away. She felt her body glowing, burning with sensations she'd never felt before. But just when she thought she'd go crazy if she didn't do something, footsteps sounded in the hall.

"So there you are," Mandy exclaimed. "I've looked everywhere." She stared at them.

Paul made a face. "Do I look like a suicidal man looking for the unemployment line to you?" he asked sourly.

Both women laughed.

"All the same, don't do that when your dad's home," she told Sari firmly.

"I never would, you know that," Sari said gently. "Why were you looking for me?"

"That girl at college who can't ever find her history notes wants to talk to you about tomorrow's test."

"Nancy," she groaned. "Honestly, I don't know how she passed anything until I came along! She actually called up one of our professors at night and asked if he could give her the high points of his lecture. He hung up on her."

"I'm not surprised," Paul said. "Better go answer the questions, tidbit," he added to Sari.

"I guess so," she said. She got off the bed, reluctantly. The way he'd looked at her had made her feel shaky inside. She wanted him to do it again. But he was already buried in his computer screen.

"There was an attempted horse heist just two days ago up near San Antonio," he was muttering. "I think I'll call the DA up there and see if he's made any arrests."

"Good night, Paul," Sari said as she left the room.

"Night, sprout. Sleep well."

"You, too."

MANDY LED HER into the kitchen and pointed to the phone.

"Hello, Nancy?" Sari said.

"Oh, thank goodness," the other girl rushed. "I'm in such a mess! I can't find my notes, and I'll fail the test…!"

"No worries. Let me get mine and I'll read them to you."

"You could fax them…"

"You'd never read my handwriting," Sari laughed. "Besides, it will help me remember what I need for tomorrow's test."

"In that case, thanks," Nancy said.

"You're welcome. Give me your number and I'll call you back. I'll have to hunt up my own notes."

Nancy gave it to her and hung up.

Sari came back down with the notes she'd retrieved from her bulky book bag. She phoned Nancy from the kitchen, where Mandy was cleaning up, and read the notes to her. It didn't take long.

"I'll see you in class," Nancy said. "And thanks! You've saved my life!" She hung up.

"She says I saved her life," Sari said, chuckling.

Mandy gave her a glance. "If you want to save two lives, you'll stay out of Mr. Paul's bedroom."

"Mandy, it's perfectly innocent. The door's always open when I'm in there."

"You don't understand. It's how it looks, that easy familiarity between you two. It will carry over to other times, in daylight. If your father sees it, even *thinks* that there might be something going on…"

"I don't do it when he's here."

"I know that. It's just…" She grimaced. "I don't know where he put all the cameras."

Sari's heart jumped. "What cameras?"

"He had it done while you girls were at school. He had three security cameras installed. He sent me out of the house on an errand while they were put in place. I don't know where they are."

"Surely he wouldn't have them put in our bedrooms," Sari began worriedly.

"There's no telling," Mandy said. "I only know that he didn't put one in here. I'd have noticed if anything was moved or displaced. Nothing was."

Sari chewed on a fingernail. "Gosh, now I'll worry if I talk in my sleep!"

"The cameras are why you should stay out of Mr. Paul's bedroom. Besides that," she added under her breath, "you're tempting fate."

"I am? How?" Sari asked blankly.

"Honey, Mr. Paul takes a woman out for a sandwich or a quick dinner. He never goes home with them."

Sari flushed with sudden pleasure.

"My point is," the older woman went on, "that he's a man starved of…well…satisfaction," she faltered. "You might say something or do something to tempt him, is what I'm trying to say."

Sari sighed and rested her face on her palms, propped on her elbows. "That would be a fine thing," she mused. "He's never even touched me except to help me out of a car," she added on a wistful sigh.

"If he ever did touch you, your father would be sure to hear about it. And I don't like to think of the consequences. He's a violent man, Sari," she added gently.

"I know that." Her face showed her misery. She was too innocent to hide her responses.

"So, don't tempt fate," Mandy said softly. She hugged the younger woman tight. "I know how you feel about him. But if you start something, he'll be out on his ear. And what your father would do to you…" She drew back with a grimace. "I love Mr. Paul," she added. "He's the kindest man I know. You don't want to get him fired."

"Of course I don't," Sari replied. "I promise I'll behave."

"You always have," Mandy said with a tender smile. "It all ends, you know," she said suddenly.

"Ends?"

"Misery. Unrequited love. Even life. It all ends. We live in pieces of emotion. Pieces of life. It doesn't all get put together until we're old and ready for the long sleep."

"Okay, when you get philosophical, I know it's past my bedtime," Sari teased.

Mandy hugged her one last time. "You're a sweet child. Go to bed. Sleep well."

"You, too." She went to the doorway and paused. She turned. "Thanks."

"What for?"

"Caring about me and Merrie," Sari said gently. "Nobody else has, since Mama died."

"It's because I care that I sometimes say things you don't want to hear, my darling."

Sari smiled. "I know." She turned and left the room.

MANDY, OLDER AND WISER, saw what Sari and Paul really felt for each other, and she worried at the possible consequences if that tsunami of emotion ever turned loose in them.

She went back to her chores, closing the kitchen up for the night.

CHAPTER TWO

WHEN ISABEL WALKED past Paul's bedroom after she called Nancy, she noticed his door was closed and the lights were off.

She went into her own room, climbed into bed and extinguished the single bedroom lamp in the room.

She recalled what Mandy had said, about the dangers of getting too close to him, with sadness. Yes, of course, her father would fire him if anything indiscreet came to light. She also recalled the pain she felt when the older woman spoke of Paul going on dates with other women.

He didn't take them to bed, that much was clear. But it also indicated that he wasn't ready to get serious about a woman, that he wasn't interested in marriage and kids. And Isabel was. She'd gladly have given up college to end up in Paul's arms with a baby of her own.

But that seemed more unlikely by the day. She was living in pipe dreams. Paul was content to have her at arm's length. He didn't want her. At least, he didn't want her the way she wanted him. She cared more for him than she'd ever cared for anyone, except her mother and sister.

As Paul liked to remind her, though, she hadn't

been out in the world long enough to know what she really wanted. That amused her. He seemed to think she was still the seventeen-year-old he'd taken to school every day in the limo. She was twenty-one, almost twenty-two now. She'd graduate from college in a few months. That made her, in the eyes of the world, an adult. Not to Paul, though. Never to Paul.

She had to start thinking about what she was going to do with her life after college. Law had always fascinated her. She'd been hanging around the courthouse after school, grilling one of District Attorney Blake Kemp's assistant DAs about what it was like to practice in a courtroom. Glory Ramirez was happy to talk to her, filling her head with thoughts of working in the DA's office.

"Blake knows how much time you spend here, on my lunch hour and after work," Glory teased.

"Oh, no," Sari began.

Glory held up a hand. "He doesn't mind. There aren't that many people blazing paths up the street to the courthouse to solicit work in the DA's office." She sobered. "It's hard work, Sari, with long hours. Sometimes defendants' families target us, because they think we've been unfair. Sometimes the defendants themselves try to attack us when they get out. Those instances are rare, but they do happen. Family life is hard." She smiled gently. "I'm qualified to know that, because my husband and I have a son who's almost four years old. Rodrigo still works for the DEA and I'm at the courthouse all hours. Sometimes we have to have the Pendletons babysit." The Pendletons were Glory's adoptive family. Jason's father had been Glory's, and Gracie's, guardian.

"I don't really think they mind," Sari teased, because it was well-known that although Jason and Gracie Pendleton had a son and daughter of their own now, they still loved to watch their nephew. All the kids had enough toys to stock a nursery.

"Of course not," Glory laughed. "But I'm still missing out on time with my family to do this job. I love it," she added gently. "It's a special thing, to help keep people safe, to make sure people who do terrible things are punished and off the streets. That's why I do it."

"I…would do it for that reason, as well," Sari said, not adding that her terror of a father was one of her own motivations. He was the sort of person who should have been sitting in a jail cell, but never would, because of his wealth. "Justice shouldn't be dealt according to who has money and who hasn't," she added absently.

Glory, who had some idea of Darwin Grayling's illegal dealings, only nodded her head.

"Anyway, what about those courses you mentioned?" she asked, bringing Glory back to the present.

Glory laughed. "Okay. Here's what you need to consider in law school…"

SARI WAS FULL of fire for the fall semester in law school, after she got her undergraduate degree. Her cumulative grades assured her that she would graduate, the finals from each class notwithstanding. She already had a graduate school picked out. Law school in San Antonio.

"You'll have to drive me, of course," Sari told Paul with a sigh when she outlined the courses Glory had told her about. "There's no way Daddy will ever let me drive myself. I don't even have a driver's license."

He scowled. "Surely not."

She shrugged. "He holds the purse strings, you know. Either I do it his way or I don't do it," she said with the complacency of a woman who'd lived such a sheltered life. "So I do it."

"Haven't you ever wanted to break out?" he asked suddenly.

She grinned at him across a plate of cookies, which they were sharing with cups of coffee at the small kitchen table. "You offering to help me?" she teased. "Got a helicopter and a couple of guys wearing ninja suits?"

He chuckled. "Not quite. I used to know a couple of guys like that, though, in the old days."

"Oh, please," she said, munching a cookie. "You aren't old enough to be remembering 'the old days.'"

His eyebrows rose. "You need glasses, kid. I've got gray hair already."

She eyed him. He was so gorgeous. Black wavy hair, deep-set warm brown eyes, high cheekbones, chiseled mouth; he was any woman's dream guy. "Gray hair, my left elbow."

"No kidding. Right here." He indicated a spot at his temple.

"Oh, that one. Sure. You're old, all right. You've got one whole gray hair."

He grinned, as she'd expected him to. "Well, maybe a few more than that. I'm like my grandfather. His hair never turned gray. He had a few silver hairs when he died, at the age of eighty."

"Do you look like him?" she asked, sipping coffee.

"No. I look like my grandmother. Everybody else was Italian. She was tiny and Greek and she had a mouth like a mob boss." He chuckled. "Do something wrong, and that gnarled little hand came out of nowhere to grab your ear." He made a face.

"So that's why your ears are so big," she mused, looking at them.

"Hey, I was never that bad," he argued. He glowered at her. "And my ears aren't that big."

"If you say so," she said, hiding the gleam in her eyes.

"You little termagant," he said, exasperated.

"Where do you get all those big words?" she asked.

"College."

"Really? You never told me you went to college."

He shrugged. "I don't like talking about the past."

"I noticed."

"We could talk about your past," he invited.

"And after those forty-five seconds, we could go back to yours," she teased, blue eyes twinkling. "Come on, what did you study?"

"Law." His face hardened with the memories. "Criminal law."

She frowned. "That was before you came to work for Daddy, yes?"

She was killing him and she didn't know it. His hand, on the thick white mug, was almost white with the pressure he was exerting. "A long time before that."

"Then, what…"

Mandy came into the room like a chubby whirlwind. "Where did you put the ribbons I was saving to wrap the holiday cookies with?" she demanded from Sari.

"Oh, my gosh, I was working on homemade Christmas cards and I borrowed them. I'm sorry!"

"Go get them," Mandy ordered with all the authority of a drill sergeant. "Right now!"

Sari left in a whirlwind, and Mandy turned to Paul, who was paler than normal. His hand, around the mug, was just beginning to loosen its grip.

He gave her a suspicious look.

"Sari doesn't think," Mandy said quietly. "She's curious and she asks questions, because she doesn't think."

He didn't admit anything. He took a deep breath. "Thanks," he bit off.

"We all have dark memories that we never share, Mr. Paul," she said gently. She patted his shoulder as she walked behind him. "Age diminishes the sting a bit. But you're much too young for that just yet," she added with a soft chuckle.

"You're a tonic, girl."

"I haven't been a girl for forty years, you sweet man, but now I feel like one!"

He laughed, the pain washing away in good humor.

"There. That's better," she said, smiling at him. "You just keep putting one foot in front of the other, and it gets easier."

"It's been almost five years."

"Thirty years for me," Mandy said surprisingly. "And it's much easier now."

He drew in a breath and finished his coffee. "Maybe in twenty-five years, I'll forget it all, then."

She looked at him with a somber little smile. "It would do an injustice to the people we love to forget them," she said softly. "Pain comes with the memories, sure. But the memories become less painful in time."

He scowled. "You should have been a philosopher."

"And then who'd bake cookies for you and Miss Sari and Miss Merrie?" she asked.

"Well, if we had to depend on Isabel's cooking, I expect we'd all starve," he said deliberately when he heard Sari coming.

She stopped in the doorway, gasping and glaring. "That is so unfair!" she exclaimed. "Heavens, I made an almost-edible, barely scorched potato casserole just last week!"

"That's true," Mandy agreed.

Paul glowered. "*Almost* being the operative word."

"And I didn't even mention that I saw you pushing yours out the back door while I was trying to pry open one of my biscuits so I could butter it!"

Sari sighed. "I guess they were a pretty good substitute for bricks," she added. "Maybe I'll learn to cook one day."

"You're doing just fine, darlin'," Mandy said encouragingly. "It takes time to learn." She shot Paul a glance. "And a lot of encouragement."

"Damn, Isabel, I almost got one of those biscuits

pried open to put butter in!" He glanced at Mandy. "How's that?"

"Why don't you go patrol the backyard?" Sari muttered.

"She's picking on me again, Mandy," he complained.

"Don't you be mean to Mr. Paul, young lady." Mandy took his part at once.

"He says terrible things about me, and you never chastise him!" Sari accused.

"Well, darlin', I may be old, but I can still appreciate a handsome man." She grinned at them.

Sari threw up her hands. Paul made her a handsome bow, winked and walked out the back door.

"You always take his side," Sari groaned.

Mandy chuckled. "He really is handsome," she said defensively.

"Yes. Too handsome. And too standoffish. He'll never look at me as anything but the kid I was when he came here."

"You've got law school to get through," Mandy reminded her. She sobered. "And you know how your dad feels about you getting involved with anyone."

"Yes, I know," Sari said miserably. "Especially anybody who works for him." Shivering softly, she said, "It's just, I'm getting older. I'm a grown woman. And I can't even drive myself to San Antonio to go shopping or invite friends over."

"You don't have any friends," Mandy countered.

"I don't dare. Neither does Merrie," she added solemnly. "We're young, with the whole world out there waiting for us, and we have to get permission to leave the house. Why?" she exclaimed.

Mandy ground her teeth. "You know how your dad guards his privacy. He's afraid one of you might let something slip."

"Like what? We don't know anything about his business, or even his private life," Sari exclaimed.

"And you're both safe as long as it's kept that way," Mandy said without thinking, then slapped a hand across her mouth.

Sari bit her lower lip. She moved closer. "What do *you* know?"

"Things I'll die before I'll tell you," the older woman replied, turning pale.

"How do you know them?"

Mandy ignored her.

"Your brother, right?" she whispered. "He knows people who know things."

"Don't you ever say that out loud," she cautioned the younger woman, looking hunted until Sari reassured her that she'd never do any such thing.

"It's like living in a combat zone," Sari muttered.

"A satin-cushioned one," came the droll reply. "If you want an apple pie, here's a do-it-yourself kit." She put a basin of apples in front of the younger woman. "So get busy and peel."

Sari started to argue. But then she recalled the delicious pies Mandy could make, so she shut up and started peeling.

GRADUATION CAME ALL too soon. The household, except for Darwin Grayling, who was in Europe at the time, went to Merrie's first at the high school and took enough pictures to fill an album. Then, only a few days later, it was Isabel's graduation from college. Merrie kept fussing with Sari's high collar.

"It's okay," her older sibling protested.

"It's not! There's a wrinkle, and I can't get it smoothed out!" Merrie grumbled.

"It will be hidden under my robes," Sari said gently, turning. She smiled at her younger sister. She shook her head. With her long blond hair like a curtain down her back, wearing a fluffy blue dress, Merrie looked like a picture of Alice in Wonderland that Sari had seen in a book. "I like your hair like that," she said.

Merrie laughed, her pale blue eyes lighting up. "I look like Alice. Go ahead. Say it. You're thinking it," she accused.

Sari wrinkled her nose.

Merrie sighed. "He decides what we'll wear, where we'll go, what we do when we get there," she said under her breath, her eyes on their father, standing with Paul near the front door. "Sari, normal women don't live like this! The girls I go to school with have dates, go shopping…!"

"Stop, or I won't get to graduate at all," the older sister muttered under her breath when Darwin Grayling shot an irritated glance toward them at Merrie's slightly raised tone.

Merrie drew in a deep breath. "It's Sari's collar," she called to her father. "I can't get the wrinkle out!"

"Leave it be," he shot back. He looked at his watch.

"We need to leave now. I have meetings with my board of directors in Dallas in three hours."

"That's your graduation, sandwiched in between breakfast and a board meeting," Merrie teased under her breath. "At least he came home for your graduation," she added a little bitterly.

Sari kissed her sister's cheek. "I was there at yours. So were Mandy and Paul. Now shut up or I'll never graduate," came the whispered reply. "Let's go!" She smoothed down her very discreet black dress, regardless of her own wishes, and started toward the door. She noticed Paul's faint wince as he saw how she was dressed, like someone out of a very old Bette Davis movie instead of a young woman ready to start graduate school.

She didn't answer that look. It might have been fatal to his employment if she had.

GRADUATION WAS BOISTEROUS and fun, despite her father, who sat through the entire ceremony texting on his phone and then conducting a business call the minute the graduates filed out into the spring sunshine.

"Maybe it's glued to him," Merrie teased as she and Sari were briefly alone.

"Attached by invisible cords," Sari replied. "Hi, Grace, happy graduation!" Sari called to a fellow graduate.

"Thanks, Sari! You off to law school in the fall?" she asked.

"Yes. You?"

"I'm moving in with my boyfriend," Grace sighed,

indicating a tall, gangly boy talking to another boy. "We're both going to the University of Tennessee."

"Oh, I see," Sari said, still not comfortable with modern ideas and choices.

Grace made a face. "Honestly, Sari, you need to buy normal clothes and go out with boys," Grace said, loud enough for Sari's father to hear.

He hung up his phone and moved to join them, looking expensive and coldly angry. "Are you ready to go, Isabel?" he asked curtly. His eyes never left Grace. He looked at her as if she were some disease he was afraid his daughters might catch.

"Uh, congrats, Sari. See you around," Grace said, red-faced, and went back to her boyfriend.

"Slut," Darwin said, just loud enough for his voice to carry and Grace to look both ruffled and insulted. "Let's go." He took Sari by the arm and almost dragged her to the waiting limousine, with a flustered Merrie running to catch up.

"I'll have Paul watching," Darwin said as Paul put the girls into the back of the limo and stood aside, holding the door, so that Darwin could slide into the seat facing them. The door closed. "I'll expect you to associate with decent girls. Do you understand? That goes for you, too, Meredith!"

"Yes, Daddy," Sari said.

"I understand," Merrie added with a sigh.

The sisters didn't dare look at each other. It would have been fatal.

THE DINNER DARWIN had referred to was obviously going to be prepared by Mandy and just for the two women. Darwin had Paul drive him to the airport, where his corporate jet was waiting. Sari and Merrie sat down to a lovely chicken casserole with homemade rolls and even a chocolate cake.

"It's delicious, Mandy," Sari said halfway through the meal. "Thanks!"

"Yes, it's wonderful!" Merrie enthused.

"Some graduation," Mandy muttered. "Should have gone out with your classmates and had fun, not be stuck here with me and an empty house."

"You know how Daddy is," Sari said quietly. "He doesn't think…"

"He doesn't care," Merrie interrupted coolly. "It's the truth, Sari, you just don't want to admit it. He doesn't want us going out with men because we might get involved and tell somebody something he doesn't want known. He doesn't want us getting married because we'd be out from under his thumb! Besides, some of that money might go outside the family!"

"I suppose you're right," Sari said, tasting her cake. "It's just, you get used to a routine. You don't even realize that it really is a routine." Her eyes twinkled. "Honestly, I thought Daddy was going to have a coronary when Grace talked about moving in with her boyfriend!"

Merrie chuckled. "I know! At least four of my classmates live with boys. They say it's very exciting…"

"Don't you even think about it," Mandy told them, waving a spoon in their direction. "There's enough wild-eyed girls out there already. You two are going to get married and live happily ever after."

"You make it sound like a fairy tale," Sari accused.

"Maybe, but I want more for you than being some man's temporary bed partner while he climbs the ladder to success," Mandy murmured. "Your mother wanted that, too. She went to church every Sunday. She believed that people have a purpose, that life has a purpose. She was an idealist."

"Yes, well, she waited to get married and she found Daddy," Sari said quietly. "So there goes your fairy-tale ending. I remember her more than Merrie does. She was unhappy. She tried not to let it show, but it did. Sometimes I found her crying when she thought nobody was looking. And she had bruises…"

"Don't ever speak of that where Mr. Darwin or even Mr. Paul could hear you," Mandy cautioned, looking frightened.

"I never would," Sari assured her. She grimaced. "But it's like living in prison," she muttered.

"A prison with silk hangings and Persian carpets," Mandy said mischievously.

"You know what she means, Mandy," Merrie piped in as she finished the last of her cake. "We aren't even allowed to date. One of my friends thinks our father is nuts."

"Merrie!"

"It's okay, he's from Wyoming," Merrie said, grinning. "He's in private school up north somewhere, but he visits a cousin here during the summer. His name is Randall. He's really nice."

"Don't you dare," Mandy began.

"Oh, it's not like that. We're just *friends*." She emphasized the word. "He goes through girls like some people go through candy. I'd never want somebody like that! But he's very easy to talk to, and he listens to me. I like him a lot."

"As long as you don't tell him things you shouldn't," Mandy replied.

Merrie's eyes fell. "I'd never do that."

Sari put down her fork with a sigh. "Well, it was a very nice lunch, even if it didn't come with scores of well-wishers and dancing." She frowned. "Come to think of it, I don't know how to dance. I've never been anywhere that I could learn."

"We went to that Latin restaurant once, where they had the flamenco dancers," Merrie said, tongue in cheek.

"Oh, sure, and I could have gotten up on a table and practiced the steps," came the sardonic reply.

Suddenly a door slammed. Paul came into the dining room with his hands deep in his pockets. His thick, wavy black hair was damp and there were droplets on the shoulders of his suit coat. "Well, it's raining," he sighed. "At least it held off until after the graduation ceremony."

"At least," Sari replied. "There's plenty left." She indicated the remnants of the lovely meal. "And lots of cake."

He chuckled. "I'm sorry."

"About what?" Sari asked.

"You should have gone out with your friends for a real celebration," he said, dropping into a chair. "With balloons and music and drinks…"

"Drinks?" Sari asked with raised eyebrows. "What are those?"

"I had balloons at my fifth birthday party, when Mama was still alive," Merrie added.

"Music. Hmm," Mandy said, thinking. "I went to a concert in the park last week. They had tubas and saxophones..."

Paul threw up his hands. "You people are hopeless!"

"We live in hopeless times," Sari said. She stood up and adopted a pose. "But someday, people will put aside their differences and raise balloons in tribute to those who have given their all so that we can have drinks and tubas..."

The rest of them started laughing.

She chuckled and sat back down. "Well, it was a nice thought. Daddy doesn't like us being around normal people, Paul," she added. "He thinks we'll be corrupted."

"That would be a choice," he replied. "I don't think you get one if you live here."

"Shh!" Sari said at once. "Don't say that out loud or they'll find you floating down some river in an oil drum!"

His eyes twinkled. "We found a guy like that once, back when I was a kid. Me and some other guys were goofing off near the river, in Jersey, and we saw this oil drum just floating, near the shore. One of the older boys was curious. He and a friend went and pried off the lid." He made a horrible face. "We set new land speed records getting out of there! It was a body inside!"

"Did you get the police?" Merrie asked curiously.

He gave her a long look. "Honey, if we'd done that,

we'd probably have ended up in matching oil drums ourselves! You don't mess with the mob."

"Mob? You mean, real mob…mobsters?" Merrie asked, her eyes as big as saucers.

"Yeah," he replied, grinning. "I grew up in a rough neighborhood. Almost all of the kids I knew back then ended up in prison."

"But not you," Sari said, with more tenderness in her tone than she realized.

"Not me," Paul agreed. He smiled. "How about a plate?" he asked Mandy. "I've fought traffic all the way from San Antonio and I'm starved!"

"You had the nice big breakfast that I made you this morning," Mandy taunted.

"Yeah, but all of it got used up listening to that guy who spoke at Sari's graduation ceremony. Who was he again?" he teased.

"That was one of the finer politicians this state has produced," Sari informed him haughtily. "In fact, he's your US senator."

"In that case, may he return to Washington, DC, with best possible speed and stay there from now on!" he said. "Gosh, imagine having to listen to him drone on for hours in Congress!"

"It beats having him drone on at somebody's graduation," Merrie said under her breath. "Oh, sorry!" she told her sister, but she ruined her apologetic tone by grinning.

Sari laughed, too. "I think there's some basic rule that people who speak at graduation ceremonies have to bore people to death."

"It would seem so."

"Who spoke at your graduation?" Sari asked Paul.

"The director of the FBI," he replied without thinking. His fingers, on the fork he was holding, went white.

"That must have been an interesting speech," Sari said. Not looking at Paul, she didn't see the effect the words were having on him.

"I'll bet he bored Paul out of his mind," Merrie teased.

Paul snapped out of it. He glanced at her and laughed. "Well, not completely. He had a sense of humor, at least."

"What did he…oh!"

Mandy turned over the cream pitcher as Sari was about to ask Paul something else about his graduation.

"I'm getting so clumsy in my old age! My poor fingers just won't hold things anymore! Get us a rag, will you, darlin'?" she asked Sari.

"Of course." She paused to hug the older woman. "And you're not getting old!"

After Mandy mopped up the spill, the girls went to change out of their finery into casual clothes.

"Saved my bacon. Again. Thanks," Paul said to Mandy when they were alone.

She sat down beside him. "Whatever it is, you haven't really faced it, have you, dear?" she asked gently, laying a hand over his big one.

His lips compressed. "I came south," he said. "I couldn't stay where I was, doing the job I was doing. I wanted to get away, do something different, be around people I didn't know." He shrugged. "It seemed the best thing at the time, but I'm not sure it was. You don't face problems by running away from them."

"No," she said softly. "You never do. They just come along for the ride." She patted his hand again and got up. "But, that being said, there's no need to go rushing back to deal with them, either," she added with a smile. "We've gotten used to having you around."

"I like it here," he confessed, leaning back in his chair. "I didn't expect to. I mean, a south Texas ranch, cowboys all over the place, people with thick accents who wouldn't know a dissertation from a dessert." He glanced at her. "I got a surprise."

She laughed. "A lot of those drawling people with accents have degrees, in all sorts of surprising subjects," she translated. "And a slow voice doesn't equate to a slow mind."

He nodded. "The Grier boys changed my mind about a lot of things. You don't expect to find somebody like Cash Grier working as a small-town police chief. Or a guy who worked with the FBI's Hostage Rescue Team, like his brother Garon, heading up a local FBI office."

"Cash has been a constant surprise," Mandy said. "None of us really expected him to settle down here. He was going around with Christabel Gaines before she married his friend Judd Dunn. Then, all of a sudden, he's married to a former supermodel and he's got two kids."

He laughed. "I know what you mean." He leaned over his coffee cup. "But the big surprise was finding Eb Scott here with a counterterrorism school. I knew him years ago. He worked as an independent contractor when I was overseas, in the Middle East."

"In the military?"

He nodded. "Spec ops. Green Berets," he added with twinkling eyes. "Eb saved my life. He went on to bigger and better things."

"So did you."

"Me? No, I'm just private security," he said, pausing to sip coffee.

"Not what you were before, though," Mandy said.

He glanced at her, frowning.

"My brother." She averted her eyes. "He…pretty much stays in trouble. He lived in New Jersey for a long time, working for some…well, some people you probably knew in the old days. I mentioned your name. Not deliberately, just in passing." She swallowed. "He knew about you."

His face went hard. Very hard. He looked up at her with cold dark eyes.

"I never tell anything I know to anybody, Mr. Paul," she said quietly. "And shame on you for thinking I would."

He grimaced. "Sorry."

"You don't know me. Not really." She sat back down beside him. "Our parents died when we were young. Grady took care of me. He worked odd jobs, did some questionable things, but he kept us together and put food on the table. When I graduated high school, I got a job working for Mr. Darwin, here. Grady figured I could take care of myself, so he went north, looking for better pay. He found it." She drew in a breath. "I keep thinking I'll hear one day that he's been found in an oil drum," she added with a wan smile. "I can't stop him from doing what he pleases. The best I can hope for is to make sure Mr. Darwin doesn't ever have a reason to turn him in to the authorities."

He scowled. "Would he?"

"You know he would," she replied quietly. Her eyes met his levelly. "It's why I never tell anything I know. And you'd better make sure you do the same. You may not have people he can blackmail you with, but Mr. Darwin could plant evidence and have you put away. It wouldn't be the first time," she added in a whisper, her eyes looking all around.

"There's no surveillance equipment in here," he whispered back.

"Would you care to bet on it?" she returned.

He hesitated. Then he pulled out a small electronic device and turned it on. His eyes, when they met Mandy's, were furious.

CHAPTER THREE

PAUL FOLLOWED THE small device's signature to a hidden microphone in a potted plant. He traced the signal into Darwin's study, to a small recording device in a drawer. Holding his finger to his lips, he cautioned Mandy not to say anything. He pulled out the recorder, made an adjustment and put it back, careful to wipe his prints first.

He led her outside. "I wiped it," he said quietly. "But make sure you don't say anything in the dining room that you wouldn't like to share with the world. And tell the girls."

"Maybe you should sweep their bedrooms, too, just in case," she said worriedly.

"Good God, it's like living in a camp of some sort!" he exclaimed. "What the hell is he so afraid of?" he added. "What does he think you might say?"

Mandy's green eyes were old and wise. "I can't tell you. But I don't want to see my brother go to federal prison, and I'd rather not see you there, either. Just pretend you know nothing and do your job."

He grimaced. "Those poor girls," he sighed. "They have no life at all. No social life. How long does he think he can keep them prisoner like this?"

"As long as he wants to," she said. "He does have

a point, in one respect. He's one of the richest men in the world, and there have been kidnapping attempts before. You foiled one yourself. The girls don't have any street sense, especially Merrie. They'd be sheep among wolves, literally, if they had the kind of freedom you're advocating."

"They're young and pretty. Surely they'll want families one day," he said, and his eyes darkened as he said it.

"Sari wants a career right now," she said evasively. "And Merrie's just graduated high school. She doesn't know what she wants to do just yet."

"It's not a normal life," he replied.

"It wouldn't be, under the best of circumstances. They're worth millions. Mr. Darwin would have problems if they ever wanted to marry, depending on who they wanted to marry. He'd be wary of men who wanted the money instead of the girls."

He knew that. But he wouldn't permit himself to think about it. Isabel wanted a career. She wouldn't be interested in a future with anyone just yet, anyway. Not yet. It was…a relief, although he wouldn't let himself wonder why.

He found the other two surveillance cameras. One was at the back door, one at the front door and the only bug had been the one in the dining room. Paul took note of where they were.

DARWIN FLEW HOME a few days later. He called Paul into his office and closed the door.

"I want to know who's been in this office since I was away," he said at once.

Paul raised both cycbrows. "Just me and the girls, when they had to use the encyclopedia—" he indicated volumes on a bookshelf "—or the computer." He nodded toward the desktop computer. "Nobody else."

Darwin glared at him. "Somebody wiped part of a surveillance log I was keeping."

Paul frowned and managed to look completely innocent. "A surveillance log?"

Darwin realized his mistake at once and backtracked. Paul was head of security. He should have known about the cameras.

"I meant to tell you that I'd installed a new set of cameras," he said, averting his eyes. "I've had a threat just recently, one I didn't tell you about. I ordered the cameras installed and forgot to tell you. Sorry."

"No harm done, sir, it's your house and your equipment. But it helps if I know what you're doing, so that I don't duplicate efforts and cost you money."

"Yes, of course." Darwin hesitated. "I'm involved…with a woman," he confessed, his back to Paul. "She works for the federal government. Just lately, there have been people following her." He turned and caught the surprised expression on his security chief's face. "The girls don't know, and they're not to know," he added firmly. "It's a long-standing relationship. I don't want to remarry, but I'm a man. I have needs." He shrugged, averting his eyes.

"That's your personal business, sir," Paul said respectfully.

Darwin cleared his throat and seemed to relax. "Yes, it is. However, I can't rule out the possibility that we might have a threat here. I don't want my daughters involved, but I want you to be aware of the threat."

"What sort of threat is it, sir?"

Darwin looked briefly uncertain. He hesitated, running a hand over his balding head. "She has contact with some unsavory people, in the course of her job."

Paul's eyes narrowed. "Unsavory."

"Yes. Her superiors don't know. She's doing some groundwork for a...regional director."

Paul just watched him. "I still have contacts at the agency..."

"No!" Darwin lowered his voice. "No. I don't want any federal involvement. She's in enough danger as it is. You won't mention this to anyone. But you'll add on more security, especially in the house. More hidden cameras, microphones, whatever it takes."

"Yes, sir. I'll get on it today," Paul promised.

Darwin drew in a breath. "More security. Yes. Many more cameras. Put them everywhere!"

Paul was hesitant.

"Not in the bathrooms, obviously," the older man said when he read the consternation on Paul's features. He grimaced. "And not in the girls' bedrooms. Or yours or mine or Mandy's. Obviously, nothing going on there that will affect them." He hesitated. "We can leave the ones at both front and back doors, although you can remove the one in the dining room. But get those cameras installed outside the house, everywhere. Today."

Paul relaxed. He managed a faint smile. "Yes, sir. I'll get to work."

"Monitor the cell phones, too," he added curtly. "The girls' especially."

That would be dead space, Paul thought, because the girls had no friends to call. But he didn't say so. He just nodded.

Darwin hesitated. He drew in a breath and put a hand to his head. He swayed a little, but caught himself. "Funny, these dizzy spells," he murmured, drawing in a breath. "Drives me out of my mind." He turned to Paul, and seemed oddly disoriented. He wiped at his eyes. "Forget what I said about putting more cameras in the house. I don't know why I wanted them in the house in the first place," he said suddenly. "Nobody needs to know what goes on in here, anyway. Get rid of the bugs and the indoor cameras. There are only three cameras, actually—one at the front and back doors and in the dining room," he added. "I had the other two put outside at the stables. In fact, we only need them outside, to monitor who comes and goes. No need to give up my privacy for an external threat," he added, and Paul relaxed even more.

Darwin's eyes narrowed. "Cameras can be hacked. I don't want men staring at my daughters. Any men."

"Of course not, sir."

"They'll make good marriages eventually, when I decide on their husbands," he continued absently. "Not for years, though. They're just children."

Isabel was twenty-one, Merrie was eighteen. And Darwin still thought of them as children, Paul wondered.

"They won't have the freedom their mother did,"

he said to himself. "Tried to sell me out. Damned slut, running to another man with information…" He caught himself and glanced at Paul. "You didn't hear that."

"I only hear what you tell me to hear, sir, and I never repeat anything," Paul said.

Darwin nodded. "I know that. It's why you've lasted here so long. Never had a security chief before who could keep his mouth shut."

Paul just nodded.

Darwin stared at him. "You don't mention anything about me to any of those contacts you still have. Got that?"

"Why would I, sir?" Paul asked, frowning.

"Well, of course. No reason to, after all." He checked his watch. "Have Danny fuel up the Learjet and do the walkaround. I have to be in Denver tonight for a meeting with some…contacts."

"Yes, sir. I'll get right on it."

"Good man."

Paul went to make the arrangements, giving a silent thanks for small blessings. He'd wondered how he'd ever manage to do his job with cameras watching every move he made. He wouldn't admit that having Isabel come in and sit on his bed at night to chat was one of his few guilty pleasures. He'd have hated sacrificing that in the name of extra security.

Meanwhile, he wondered why Darwin Grayling was such a fanatic about his privacy. The man obviously had things he was trying to hide. Paul wondered if he was involved in anything illegal. But he didn't pursue that question, even in his own mind.

"Do you think he might be paranoid?" Paul asked Mandy outside a few days later, when Darwin had jetted off to a European conference.

"I don't think it, I know it," Mandy replied in a hushed tone. She wrapped her arms around her ample figure. Despite her sweater, she was chilled. "He hasn't ever been exactly right in the head," she said. "But after the girls' mother died…" She bit off the rest.

"You might as well tell me," Paul said. "You know I don't talk about anything I know."

She glanced up at him in the semidarkness, because it was dusk. "She fell and hit her head, he said. But Dr. Coltrain demanded an autopsy, because he didn't believe her injuries were consistent with a fall."

"And…?" Paul was remembering with cold chills what Darwin had said about his wife selling him out to someone.

"And he was called out of town to consult in a case with a former patient," she continued. "While he was gone, Mr. Darwin called in a favor and had the autopsy rushed through. Accidental death was what they put on the death certificate. By the time Dr. Coltrain got back, she was buried, and Mr. Darwin threatened legal action if the doctor tried to interfere further." She shook her head. "Dr. Coltrain has a really nasty temper, but Mr. Darwin is so rich that he could… well, there were strange things that started happening around Dr. Coltrain's house, around his little boy. He realized what could happen, and he stepped back." She looked up at Paul. "Mr. Darwin has done some things that I'd rather die than tell you about. He holds my brother over me like a sword. He'll find something to hold over you, too, Mr. Paul, if he can. He likes having people who work for him over a barrel."

Paul smiled ruefully. "If there was anything in my past that could be used against me, it would have come out years ago, when I was...when I worked in another field."

Her old face softened. "You're wasted here," she said gently. "I mean it. You're smart. You could be anything you wanted to be. Hired private security is, well, it's..."

"I keep you and the girls safe," he interrupted with a grin. "Not to mention the racehorses. Imagine how the jockeys would mourn if one of the horses got an infected foot or something!"

She laughed, as she was meant to.

"He wanted cameras set up," he added. "But he had me take out the one he'd put in the dining room, along with the bug he had in his office. I'll tell the girls. I was afraid I'd have to watch every word I said. And the girls have been worried." He sighed. "Merrie's really afraid of him. Sari...not so much, but she doesn't go against him." He turned to her. "Why are they so afraid of him?"

Mandy wanted to tell him, but she was too afraid for her brother. "He got physical with them when they were younger," she compromised. "He believed in that 'spare the rod, spoil the child' thing."

He scowled. "He didn't abuse them?"

"Not the way you're thinking," she said easily.

He let out a breath. "Thank God."

"It would have been like living in jail, having cameras all over the house," Mandy said quietly. "I didn't even know where they were until you told me he'd only put one in the dining room and had his office bugged. We'd have had to watch every word we said." She hesitated. "And you'd never have been able to let Sari come into your room anymore," she added with an amused smile.

He chuckled. "Don't tell her, but I'd have missed that. I enjoy our chats. She's a sweet child."

"It's such a shame," Mandy said. "Sari and Merrie are two of the sweetest kids I've ever known. I was hoping they'd meet someone, get married, have families. I should have realized that Mr. Darwin would fight against that to his last breath."

"Surely he wants an heir from them, to carry on the line, to inherit what he has."

She bit her lower lip, hard. "I asked him that, once. He said that he wasn't sharing his fortune with anybody, and no men were going to trick his daughters into marriage so they could live like kings."

Paul felt his face tauten. "What if they fell in love?"

"Fat chance," she replied. "They aren't allowed to go anywhere that they could meet men. Sari wasn't even allowed to go to a graduation party. Neither was Merrie. He keeps them under lock and key. They're only let out to go to school for the most part, although Sari has a little more freedom now. But whether you know it or not, they're watched every second they're away from here, even at school."

"What?"

"I didn't think you knew that," she said, walking back toward the house. "He has a couple of men trail behind them when they're not here. Supposedly it's to make sure nobody tries to abduct them for ransom. But it's really to make sure they don't get involved with boys. Merrie tried to go on a date once…" She let that thought trail away. "It's getting chilly out here!"

"Wait." He moved between her and the door. "Merrie tried to go on a date…?"

She looked up at him with real fear. "I can't say. You can't ask. Please! You'll cause problems that you can't imagine. He's not…normal."

"Why do you stay?" he asked.

"Because I'm all they've got. It isn't much, but sometimes I can head off trouble."

He drew in a long breath. "I thought it was a peach of a job when I first got it. More and more, I think I made a huge mistake."

"The girls don't think so. They're both very fond of you. So am I, but you know that." She chuckled.

"I know that." He smiled gently.

"Video cameras in the house," she said, shaking her head. "I'd have been afraid to open my mouth."

"Oh, it wouldn't have been so bad," he said facetiously. "There's a community college with a theatrical department," he teased. "We could have asked somebody to write us a script, and we'd have performed it at every meal. He'd have gotten bored watching it all the time."

She burst out laughing. "Now, there's a thought!"

"Send Isabel out, could you? I need to talk to her." He grimaced. "Just in case he put a bug in that I didn't find, it's safer out here. I'll sweep the house again later."

"I'll do it. Want Merrie, too?"

"Just Isabel," he said, smiling.

"Okay."

HE PACED BETWEEN the light from the house and the distant fence and ranch gate that led to the stables. He was uneasy. He didn't like being under surveillance, and he didn't buy Darwin Grayling's explanation of why it was necessary. He wondered if Darwin had learned about Sari's visits to Paul's room. He knew Mandy hadn't sold him out, but what if there were other cameras and bugs that Paul didn't know about? He was going to make a thorough search later.

The back door opened. Sari came out, wearing a long blue-checked dress with a white blouse under it. The garment covered her from neck to ankles, but it fit in just the right places to give Paul an uncomfortable ache. She had pert little breasts and a narrow waist that led down to softly curving full hips and long legs. Her reddish-gold hair was piled on top of her head, curling wildly down from a ponytail clip, and her blue, blue eyes twinkled at him in the pale light from the house.

"Mandy said you wanted to talk to me. Are we going to get bulletproof vests issued? Maybe a gun?" she teased.

He shrugged. "Beats me. I feel like some of those guys used to on a show called *Candid Camera*. That's before your time, tidbit," he added with a grin.

"It is not. I watch it on YouTube."

He shook his head.

"Don't knock it," she chided. "All the best programming is on YouTube. I can watch shows from fifty years ago. I can travel all over the world in somebody's backpack," she added with a chuckle. "I was just touring the Incan ruins in Peru."

"I'd love to see that," he mused. "I never miss an archaeological special on TV."

"Me, neither," she agreed. "I used to think I'd get to see the sites in person one day, but Daddy says it's too dangerous to let us travel outside the country."

"It probably is," he said noncommittally.

"So, what do you want to talk to me about?" she asked. She cocked her head. "Are you going to ask me to run away with you and live in sin somewhere in Kansas?"

He was disconcerted. "Why Kansas?"

"Well, it's probably the last place on earth Daddy would think to look for us," she sighed. She tilted her face up to his. "Sure you don't want to run away with me? We could get jobs working in a convenience store and live on doughnuts and Slurpees."

He burst out laughing. "Honest to God, Isabel…!"

"I like it when you laugh," she observed, smiling. "You almost never do."

He sobered. "It doesn't really go with the job description," he said. He studied her quietly. "Your father has had me update all the security systems. He had the dining room bugged and you were on camera wherever you went that was in sight of the doors, except to the head."

"The who?"

He scowled. "The head. Sorry. The bathroom."

"You said it was wired?" she asked worriedly.

He nodded. "I wiped the recordings."

Sari was catching her breath. She'd been sitting on Paul's bed...

"I wiped everything," he repeated. "Just in case there were bugs in other places besides in the dining room. I couldn't be sure."

"Why was everything wired?" she wondered.

"I'm not sure. He gave me some pretty wild reasons. But the only security cameras left are the two at the front and back doors and the ones on the outside. So you can still come bouncing into my room and sit on my bed in your pajamas." He grinned. "As long as I make doubly sure he hasn't put any hidden cameras or bugs up there."

"Oh, dear." She glanced at him. "Imagine if Daddy saw *that* on YouTube," she mused.

"Then imagine me lying in a dark alley with parts missing," he returned.

"He wouldn't dare," she said simply. "I'd avenge you."

"Your allowance is a little over a hundred dollars a month. I think guys in ninja suits cost a bit more than that," he mused, his dark eyes twinkling.

"I'm saving up," she promised.

He chuckled and started walking back toward the house, hands in his pockets. "He says there's a threat. Something external, and to do with someone he knows."

"That woman he sees," Sari said. She looked up at Paul's surprised expression. "Merrie and I know about her," she added. "Her name is Betty Leeds. She came here once, driving a new Mercedes, all decked out in expensive clothes with a purse that cost more than my leather coat. She looked down her nose at me and Merrie, went into Daddy's study with him and closed the door."

He frowned. "She can afford all that on a government salary?"

She scowled. "I didn't think about that. I don't think the government pays salaried workers that much, and I overheard Daddy tell somebody that she worked in an office as an analyst or something."

He let out a breath. "Best not advertise that news, tidbit."

"I wouldn't. Daddy has an unpredictable temper." Her whole body went taut. "Neither of us wants to make him mad, ever."

He turned to her in the shadow of the porch, out of range of the security cameras. "Why are you afraid of him, honey?" he asked softly, his voice unconsciously tender.

Sari's heart jumped. She wasn't used to endearments from anyone except Mandy. Paul never used them. She looked up at him with quiet, soft eyes, searching over his hard face. "He's just volatile," she hedged. "We never know how he's going to react to anything we say. It's almost like he's two different people, especially when he has those dizzy spells." She wrapped her arms around herself. "Merrie and I learned early not to make him mad."

"He wouldn't really hurt you, would he?"

"Oh, of course not," she lied, managing a smile. "It's not like that. He just yells and stuff."

"I see."

"Where are the cameras?" she asked suddenly.

He pointed to one at the corner of the house that had the security light, and to another camera just over their heads, pointing away from the house.

"Do they have microphones?" she worried.

"They do." He pulled a little device out of his pocket. "But that one—" he indicated the one overhead "—has had a slight malfunction." He showed her the device and grinned.

She grinned back. "Devious."

"Very. I'm going to turn it back on. Watch what you say."

She nodded. He pointed the device at the camera and clicked it.

"I wonder what Mandy's got in mind for supper?" he asked conversationally. "I'm starved."

"Me, too. Thanks for showing me the new foal, Mr. Fiore," she lied. She'd seen it much earlier, but it was for the sake of the recording, in case her father saw it.

"My pleasure, Miss Grayling," he replied, and went to hold the door open for her.

LATER, PAUL WAS reading Herodotus when Isabel came through the door and jumped onto the bed with him. She was wearing a gown this time, a pink silk one with a matching peignoir. She was nicely covered, but the silk slithered over her firm, pretty little breasts and it dipped down so that just the tops of them showed. It was a modest gown. The problem was that little sliver of pretty, pale, freckled flesh. Paul had to drag his eyes away from it, especially when he saw quite suddenly two little peaks on either side of the bodice.

She liked his eyes on her, and it was visible in a way she didn't even seem to know.

The girls didn't date. They had no knowledge of men, or even their own bodies. Isabel was very likely a virgin. It made him react unexpectedly, in a very masculine way. He leaned forward carefully so that his reaction was less noticeable in the folds of his black silk pajama bottoms.

"You're reading that man again," she noted, looking at the book in front of him on the bed. "Wouldn't it be easier to read him in English?"

"You lose something in the translation," he said easily, smiling.

"How did you learn Greek?"

He smiled. "From my grandmother. She was a firecracker. I never saw anything or anyone she was afraid of." He shook his head. "She went after a mob boss once with a length of salami. Damn, she had spunk!"

"A mob boss? A real one?" Isabel asked, fascinated.

He nodded. "Most of our family worked for, shall we say, underworld elements. One of them was a mob boss with a real attitude problem. He came to a family gathering and insulted one of her grandsons. She took after him with a salami and damned near unmanned him with it. He actually apologized to her." His eyes were far away and thoughtful. "After that, he sent her a present every Christmas. Shocked us all. He wasn't the type, you see."

She smiled. "I never knew my grandparents, on either side," she recalled sadly. "Mama's people originally came from Georgia. Her parents were pretty old when I was born and they died when I was a baby. Mama was worth millions. Her people were a founding family in Jacobs County. My father never talked about his people much. His father was very wealthy—that's where Daddy's money came from. He inherited after he married my mother. His mother died when he was a baby. He didn't have brothers or sisters."

"That's sad, not to have family."

"Do you have any?" she asked softly.

He averted his eyes. The question hurt, but she didn't realize it. "No. Not anymore," he said tautly. "Except for a cousin."

He didn't like remembering it. His grandmother had died years ago. He'd had a brother, but when he was in his teens, his sibling had died in a particularly horrible way, and not one he felt comfortable telling an innocent girl about. The others, well, he had a lot of guilt about the way they went, and the memories tore at his heart like talons.

"I'm sorry," she said gently, touching his muscular arm.

He looked up, surprised at her empathy.

She shrugged. "You never talk about your past. I guess you have some memories that are pretty bad, huh?"

He nodded. "Yeah. Pretty bad."

She drew her hand back. "I've never had the opportunity to make any real memories," she said on a sigh. "I go to school and come home, do class work, eat, sleep, get up and do it all again, except in the summer."

"I get up, work, eat, sleep, go to bed." He chuckled.

"I suppose there's some sort of comfort in the routine. No great shocks. No big surprises."

"It's tedious, isn't it?" she asked suddenly, surprising an odd look in his large brown eyes. "We don't do much except go through the motions of living."

He cocked his head. "You're pretty clued in, for a sheltered little chick."

"I listen," she said simply. "I don't have much experience of my own, but women talk. I overhear things I don't really understand, but once in a while, a woman is nice enough to explain it to me without making it sound vulgar."

Both thick eyebrows went up. "Now I'm intrigued."

She cleared her throat. "It's nothing I could talk about in mixed company," she said, lowering her eyes.

"I see. It's that sort of conversation, is it?" he teased.

She flushed. "Well, books and movies and television sort of hint at things, but you don't really know, do you? It's just secondhand."

"So is hearsay evidence," he mused.

"Now you sound like a policeman," she accused.

His eyes narrowed. "And you'd know that how?"

"There's this nice policeman who works for Chief Grier," she said. "I have lunch in Barbara's Cafe every Friday with Blake Kemp's assistant. The policeman is usually having lunch there, too, with a couple of his friends. They sit next to us and we talk." She laughed. "He's really funny. I like him."

He felt an unreasonable surge of jealousy. He fought it down and even managed a convincing smile. "Your age?"

"Oh, no, he's closer to your age. At least, to what I think is your age," she added, because Paul had never told her how old he was.

"Is he new here?"

She nodded. She leaned toward him. "There's some gossip about him," she said in a stealthy, mischievous tone.

"Is there? What is it?" he asked.

"You remember Kilraven, who was supposed to be working for the chief, but was really an undercover Fed?"

"I remember. He married Winnie Sinclair."

She nodded. "Well, our policeman is apparently an undercover Fed, too, working on some mob-related criminal activity."

Paul's heart jumped. He had an inkling of what that might be, but he didn't dare tell Isabel. He still had contacts inside—well, actually, on both sides of that issue—and he didn't want to have to admit to them. He was still raw from the past, despite the years of distance.

"Know what it is?" he asked.

"No," she returned. "He isn't telling anybody about that. I heard all about it from Mr. Kemp's paralegal, who's friends with the chief's secretary, Carlie Farwalker."

He let out a breath. "Isabel, is there anybody you don't know?"

"Well, Jacobsville is a very small town. And Comanche Wells, where we live, is even smaller. I've lived here all my life. I know everybody. Is it like that, where you come from?" she asked, curious. "I mean, did you come from a small town?"

He burst out laughing. "I came from Jersey," he said. "Nothing small about New Jersey, kid."

"But don't you have neighborhoods there, where people live for a long time together?"

He thought back to his childhood, to the place he grew up. "I suppose we did. My grandmother had lived in the same house since she was married. She knew everybody in the neighborhood, and I mean everybody."

"So it was like here?"

"Only if everybody here was Greek or Italian," he said with a grin. "On my mother's side, mostly Italian. My grandmother and her father were the only Greek blood in the family."

"I guess you speak Italian, too," she said softly.

"Italian, Greek and an odd little dialect of Farsi."

"Farsi?" She frowned. "Our police chief speaks that. So does Wolf Patterson's wife, Sara. In fact, he speaks it, too. They had some extraordinary arguments in Farsi before they married." She grinned. "I heard about it from Bonnie, who works in the pharmacy in Jacobsville."

"I'll have to watch my back, so people don't tell you girls anything about me," he chided with twinkling brown eyes. But he wasn't mentioning his time in Afghanistan in Special Forces.

"Nobody knows anything about you, Paul. You're a mystery," she said with a sigh.

The way she said his name made something inside him wake up. He didn't want that.

"I don't talk about my past. Ever," he said absently.

"Oh? Were you, like, a hit man for the mob?" she teased with twinkling blue eyes.

His face tautened to steel. His eyes blazed for an instant, and he seemed made of stone.

"I was kidding!" she said at once, shocked at the reaction she'd provoked. "I'm sorry, really I am...!"

He forced the anguish out of his face. It wasn't her fault. It was nothing to do with her. She'd simply made a joke, hitting a tender spot without even knowing it.

"No sweat," he said, and forced a smile. "Hey, I'm Italian. We get too many mob jokes," he added.

"Sorry," she said again, her voice softening. "It was a dumb remark."

"It's okay." He reached out and tweaked a long, curly strand of red-gold hair. It was the first time he'd really touched her. "I guess you get Irish jokes all the time, huh?"

"Irish?"

"You're redheaded, kid," he teased.

His hand in her hair was provoking some very unusual stirrings in her untried body, and she was trying to pretend she felt nothing. She wasn't successful. Paul, with his greater experience, could see everything she felt. It flattered him, that she could find him attractive.

"Oh. Redheaded. Irish. I get it." She laughed nervously. "No, it isn't Irish. My father's people were from Wales."

"Wales!" He laughed. "I never knew a single person from Wales."

"Me, neither," she confessed. "I did try to learn a

word or two of the language, but I think I sprained my tongue, so I never tried again."

"Sprained your tongue." He smiled and let his attention drift down her softly rounded face, over her lightly freckled straight nose, to the pretty bow-shaped mouth under it. His gaze lingered there for a long time. So long, in fact, that he heard her breathing change.

His eyes narrowed. His chest rose and fell quickly. It had been a long time since he'd felt this way; years, in fact, and he felt the stirring of his body with fascination and regret. But she was off-limits. Period. He didn't dare touch her. Her father would string him up.

He let go of her hair with a grin. "Better get some sleep, kid. I've got an early appointment."

"Okay." She jumped up from the bed, and then hesitated beside it, frowning. "Paul, you're sure about the cameras? That there aren't any around here?" She looked around worriedly.

"I swept the whole house myself twice," he assured her. "No cameras. No bugs. Nothing."

"All right, then." She hesitated. "I wouldn't want to get you into trouble with my father. We're just friends, but if he saw us together like this… I mean, he might get ideas."

"No cameras, no bugs," he repeated gently. "On my honor."

She smiled at him. "Okay."

"Go to bed."

She sighed and turned toward the door. She paused at the doorway. "And I'm sorry again."

"For what?"

She made a face. "Bringing back bad memories for you. Good night."

She was gone before he could protest, in a whirl of pink froth.

He lay awake in the dark, memories haunting him. Memories of blood. So much blood. Blond hair, darkened with it, spread on the bare floor, and a smaller form...

He rolled over and buried his face in the pillow. *Don't think, don't remember, it's gone, it's over.* He closed his eyes. Eventually, he slept.

CHAPTER FOUR

PAUL WAS RESTLESS after his conversation with Isabel the night before. He kept seeing her sitting close to him, her pretty pert breasts straining at the silky fabric of her nightgown, hard little points pushing up and out. She wanted him. She might not realize it yet, but he knew.

Sari didn't know her body had betrayed her, but she remembered the way Paul had touched her hair, the way he'd looked at her mouth. She might be innocent, but she knew what he'd been thinking. He'd thought about kissing her. His eyes had clung to her lips like a bee to honey. It made her wild, thinking about how it would have felt if he'd moved toward her, just a few inches...

She stopped herself. If he ever moved toward her, her father would find out and fire him. He might do more than that. She kept remembering the cowboy who'd moved all the way to Arizona hoping Mr. Grayling wouldn't come after him for trying to date Merrie.

"You're so unsettled lately," Merrie chided when they were alone in her room. "What's wrong with you?"

"Daddy," Sari said miserably. "We're never going

to have the opportunity to get married and have families."

"That's not quite true," Merrie said miserably. "I overheard him talking to Paul. He said he'd find husbands for us."

Sari clenched her teeth. "Oh, that's just great. I can imagine what sort of man he'd have in mind!"

"So can I," Merrie groaned. "But what can we do? If we try to run away, he'll have his bodyguards catch us before we can get to the bus station or the airport. We'd never get away! He could have us brought back. He owns people in all sorts of shady professions."

"Paul would help us."

"Paul could be fired and hunted," Merrie reminded her. "He's just as vulnerable as anybody else who works for Daddy. I'd hate to see him gone," she added. "He and Mandy are all we have!"

Sari nodded sadly. She and her younger sister exchanged despondent looks.

"We could try to run away," Merrie suggested suddenly.

"Where? There's no place on earth Daddy couldn't find us."

"I'm not so sure of that," Merrie said. "My friend Randall has an older brother who has this huge ranch in Wyoming. He's almost as rich as Daddy. Randall said that if things got too bad, he could hide me up there. I know he'd let you go, too."

Sweet Merrie. So kind. And so clueless. "Merrie, I have law school starting up in August," she reminded her. "It might be practical for you to run, but I have responsibilities. If I want a career, this is the only way I can afford it. Daddy won't even let us get part-time jobs!"

"Sorry," Merrie said, grimacing. "I keep forgetting about law school." She drew in a long breath. "I wanted to go to college, but it looks like a few art classes at Jacobsville Community College are going to be what I end up with."

"Your paintings are exhibition quality," Sari chided. "You do the most lifelike portraits of anyone I've ever known. Your landscapes are exquisite, whatever medium you work in. You have genius in your hands, Merrie. College won't matter."

"Thanks," Merri replied. She hugged her sister. "I'm glad you think so." She smiled wryly. "It's just as well, really. I don't see myself as a doctor or a lawyer. But you'll be a natural," she added with twinkling eyes. "Lawbreakers, beware! Assistant DA Sari Grayling will nail you to the wall with her legal briefs!"

Sari laughed. "As if!" she teased. "I talked to Mr. Kemp this week. He said I'd have a job waiting when I graduate law school, if I still want it."

"If Daddy will let you take it," Merrie said miserably.

"I'll cross that bridge when water runs under it," the older woman replied. "If worse comes to worst, I might let Mr. Kemp plead my case. Daddy respects him. Well, as much as he respects anybody."

Merrie nodded. "You might marry."

"And elephants might fly," Sari returned whimsically.

"You must have thought about it. You love children so much," she added softly. "Don't you want a family?"

Sari hardened her heart. "It's no good wanting something you can't have," she replied.

"You don't know you can't have it if you haven't tried to grab it with both hands," her sister argued.

Sari dreamed about Paul's hard mouth on her own and got goose bumps. She rubbed her arms and laughed. Talk about the impossible dream!

"Are you cold?" Merrie asked, frowning.

"No. Somebody just walked over my grave," she laughed, using the old folk saying.

"Don't say things like that!" Merrie blurted out. She hugged her sister, laying her head on Sari's shoulder. "Don't ever say that. All we have is each other."

Sari hugged her back tightly. "I know. I'm sorry. I was only kidding." She didn't add that she'd had an uneasy feeling lately, one that was puzzling as well as worrying. It felt as if she were sitting on top of a stick of dynamite, waiting for the fuse to run out. Which was absurd. Her life was as tranquil as a pond in the woods, without even a water skimmer to touch it.

She let Merrie go. "Stop worrying," she chided. "I'm healthy and happy and I plan to live for years. At least long enough to get every single lawbreaker in Jacobsville behind bars!"

"That would take about two days," her sister said with a droll smile. "I mean, there are like, what, two criminals in town and they're both locked up."

"Chief Grier finds more every day. We're growing."

"Yes, we actually had an increase of five people

this year in our population!" Merrie exclaimed. "We'll have to expand the water system!"

Sari picked up a newspaper and threw it at her.

"Overcrowding in the schools!" Merrie called after her as she left the room. "Increased traffic jams…!"

"I'm not listening!" Sari called back.

Soft laughter followed her down the staircase.

Paul was standing just inside the front door. He looked up. "What in the world was that all about?" he asked.

"We had a huge population increase, it seems," Sari told him. "Merrie says we've gained five whole people in Jacobsville this year."

"The jails will be full!" Merrie called over the banister.

"Will you go paint something, please?" Sari called back, exasperated.

"Paint a sign, telling people to move to Dallas," Paul suggested.

Merrie laughed gleefully.

"Don't you encourage her," Sari told him firmly.

"I only told her what she could paint," he defended himself.

"Paint a wildflower," Sari suggested. "You're great at those. Maybe a wildflower and a log. How about a morning glory curling around a dead stump in a forest clearing…"

"Great idea! Thanks!" Merrie rushed back into her room.

"Nice," Paul mused.

Sari chuckled. "She really does draw well."

"I know."

"Merrie's shy about her work. I wasn't sure you knew that she painted."

"I had her do a portrait of my grandmother," he said, surprising her. "I had a few photos. She truly brought them to life." He shook his head. "She should be showing her work in a gallery somewhere."

"You never showed me the painting," she said.

He hesitated. "I...sent it to my cousin, in New Jersey, for a Christmas present last year," he explained. "My grandmother raised both of us. We were like brothers."

"You never talk about him."

He shrugged. "No reason to. We don't see each other. We talk once in a while, maybe text when there's something to say."

"What does he do?"

He glanced at her. "Dangerous things. And that's all I'm saying."

She flushed. "Sorry."

He caught her arm as she started to leave the room. "Don't get your feelings hurt," he said. "I can't tell anyone. It's not just you."

She swallowed, embarrassed. "Sorry."

"And stop apologizing every second word," he chided. "I notice that Merrie does the same thing."

"We've done a lot of it, over the years," she said.

He frowned. "Why?"

She averted her face. "I have to start the yeast for Mandy. She's making homemade rolls and beef stew for supper."

"Homemade rolls." He closed his eyes. "I think

I've died and gone to heaven," he teased. "I can almost smell them. Nobody makes rolls like she does."

She grinned. "Mandy has a friend who still makes fresh butter the old-fashioned way, with a churn and a wooden mold. We're having some with the rolls."

"What's a churn?" he asked.

"City boy," she teased. "It's a round, oblong container, usually made of thick ceramic. You put fresh milk in it, then you use a dasher—a long stick with a crosspiece on the bottom—to churn the milk until it finally starts to make butter. Then you scoop the butter out and salt it and put it in a mold."

"Wow. That sounds complicated."

"It is complicated," she agreed. "Especially when you're the person who does the churning." She grimaced. "Whenever it was churning time, no matter where I hid, my mother would always find me." She smiled sadly. "But she was sweet about it. I got a whole quarter for my efforts. That was a lot of money to a seven-year-old. I could buy a comic book or an ice cream cone with it."

"Good luck finding a comic book for that price today," he scoffed.

"I know."

"Well, I'll go scout the perimeter and make sure all the surveillance systems are up and running," he said. "Call me when there's food."

"I will."

She watched him go out the back door with quiet, faintly worshipping eyes. After last night, she thought they might be closer. But he was as distant as ever. In fact, he seemed even more distant than before.

She went into the kitchen and started taking out ingredients for the rolls. Well, Rome wasn't built in a day. She had time. Paul wasn't going anywhere. And she was patient. She smiled and sang to herself as she put yeast and sugar into the mixing bowl and added warm milk to start the yeast rising for Mandy.

THEY ATE SILENTLY. Paul went through the rolls like mad, even forgoing extra stew for them. "You have a gift," he told Mandy when he was sipping his second cup of black coffee.

"Thanks," she replied, beaming with pride.

"Who taught you to make rolls?" he asked. "Couldn't have been her." He indicated Sari with a grin. "She can only make biscuits."

"Biscuit bigot," Sari muttered.

He burst out laughing. So did Merrie and Mandy.

"It was a trainer who came to work with one of the Thoroughbreds," Mandy said with a smile.

"A horse trainer?" he exclaimed.

She nodded. "He was Australian. Before he became a trainer, he worked in a bakery with his parents, who owned it. He could make anything. He taught me how to make rolls and breads and cakes and even French pastries. You remember, Sari, he had that hunky son who was your age. He spent some time with you while his dad was teaching me new recipes."

Paul frowned. He didn't like the sound of that. He was jealous, and furious with himself because he was. "When was this?" he asked abruptly.

"I don't remember," Sari said, oblivious to Paul's expression.

Mandy saw it and winced. "Oh, it was years ago. You were fifteen," Mandy said. "And I had to make the boy stay in the kitchen with his dad the whole time I was learning, because your father was afraid the boy might make a pass at you."

"That's right," Sari said. She sighed. "The trainer was so nice. Blond and big and handsome."

"And married," Merrie added gleefully.

"Yes. And married." Mandy laughed as she finished her own coffee. "Besides that, he and his wife had two little girls, much younger than the son who came with him to work with the horses. He had photos of them. They were so beautiful."

Paul had pushed back his chair. "Sorry, I have to make one last pass around the stables. Back in a jiffy."

Sari frowned and exchanged glances with Mandy and her sister. "Did we say something wrong?" she asked.

Mandy had a suspicion, but she didn't dare voice it. "You know how he is," she laughed. "It's hard for him to sit still."

"I guess so," Sari replied. She smiled and asked Merrie about the art classes she was taking, the subject of the handsome horse trainer and his family quickly forgotten.

OUTSIDE, PAUL LIFTED his face to the cool air, and his eyes were closed as he fought back memories that terrified him. Sari hadn't known, hadn't meant to resurrect the past, but it came sometimes without warning.

He stuck his hands in his pockets and moved toward the stables, pushing the memories away, locking them back into a compartment where they were harder to access. It had been four years, but he couldn't escape them. The Bureau had offered psychological counseling. He should have taken it and stayed where he was, not tried to run away from it. The pain had been so severe, the trauma so reaching, that he couldn't think past it. He'd thought running was the answer. In retrospect, he realized it wasn't. Memories were portable, invincible, eternal.

He kicked at a rock and sighed. Maybe he'd done the wrong thing, but he couldn't really regret it. He loved it here, with the girls, with Mandy. It was the only peace he'd ever found in his turbulent life. He was reluctant to think of giving it up.

But he was thinking of it. The job, while nice, was a dead end. Not only that, Darwin Grayling's behavior was deteriorating to the point that it made Paul wary of him. The man had issues, and his paranoia was getting worse. Someday, Paul might be required to take action, and that would only hurt the girls.

He kept remembering Sari's pert little breasts under that silky gown, and his physical reaction to it. She was almost twenty-two. Years too young for him, he told himself, at thirty-two. But one day, maybe, the years wouldn't matter so much. It was possible...

No. He had to stop thinking that way. She was a Grayling. She was already worth millions. One day she'd inherit half the money her father had, and she'd be worth even more. It, like this job, was a dead end. He couldn't let himself be tempted. It would only lead to tragedy. Darwin Grayling planned to arrange his daughters' marriages to other wealthy men so that the fortune wouldn't be squandered. While the girls didn't like the idea, and he didn't blame them, it was sensible to make sure the money stayed in the family.

Money. His nose twitched. He'd hated his relatives' greedy planning and plotting as they searched for ways to get instant wealth. Most of their plots were outside the law and they were lucky that they hesitated to put anything into motion. Because Paul would have turned them in, and they knew it.

The absolute worst was his cousin Mikey. The man, younger than him by a few years, would do almost anything for money. His thirst for it had led to tragedy. Paul wished he could blame his own tragedy on Mikey, but it was his own fault. He'd prodded the wrong man, trying to make a name for himself, trying to prove that just because his whole damned family was on the wrong side of the law, he wasn't. That decision had produced devastating results.

In the end, he'd brought the mobster down. But the cost. Dear God, the cost! The Bureau had lauded him, rewarded him. But he'd walked through the accolades like a zombie, his heart broken. His grandmother had comforted him, stayed with him. But so soon afterward, he'd lost her, too. Now there was just him and his cousin left. Out of respect for family loyalty, he kept in touch with Mikey. Who knew; one day there might be a good reason for it.

ANY OUTING, REGARDLESS of its routine, required Paul to accompany whichever of the girls had to make it. Today, it was a trip to the law school in San Antonio to register. Sari already had her letter of acceptance, but registration was required.

Paul went with her and waited while she filled out forms, learned the campus and spoke with a faculty advisor about courses she had to take in the fall semester.

When she was finished, he was still waiting, his eyes on a black anvil cloud in the sky nearby. He didn't like the look of it. Texas was notorious for tornado outbreaks in the spring, and his cell phone had already flashed a tornado watch alert.

"You look worried," she accused, holding a sheaf of papers in one hand. "What's up?"

"That." He indicated the black clouds gathering. "There's a tornado watch."

"Nothing unusual for here, sadly." She cocked her head. "How about lunch before we go home? There's a nice little place beside the River Walk."

"Suits me. I'm starved."

He drove them to the touristy area and parked the car. It was hard to find a spot, because traffic was teeming.

"How about that one?" he asked, nodding toward a small café with tables overlooking the river.

"Perfect," she replied.

They ordered sandwiches and coffee and waited for them to be brought out. Paul's eyes were still on the clouds, worried.

"Will you relax?" she chided. "It's just storms."

"I don't know," he mused. "I've got a bad feeling."

He had them infrequently. Mostly about weather. He'd predicted the last very unusual snow that fell on San Antonio, and a downburst that had destroyed trees nearby in an earlier storm.

"You're a weather magnet, that's what you are," Sari chided. "Like that guy in the movie about tornadoes."

He chuckled. "Maybe I am." He shook his head. "I guess I watch too much TV."

"You should surf the internet, like I do," she replied, biting into a thick roast beef sandwich. "I learn things."

"Such as?" he asked with twinkling dark eyes.

"How to bathe a cat, for one thing."

"You don't have a cat, so why would you need to know how to bathe one?"

"Oh, cat ownership is an impossible dream of mine," she confessed. "We've never been allowed to have animals inside. Or outside."

"Why not?"

Her mind avoided the memory of why not. She forced a smile. "Daddy's allergic to fur," she lied. "Anyway, if I ever get a cat, and I might one day, I need to know things like that."

He finished a bite of his own sandwich and washed it down with coffee. "Okay. So how do you bathe a cat?"

"First you put on a raincoat and galoshes and one of those scuba diving thingies, with a scuba mask and a snorkel."

He stopped eating, blinked and stared at her. "Excuse me?"

She was laughing uproariously. "I read it on a website. I could barely get through it all. It doubled me over."

He chuckled. "I think I read that one, too," he mused. "No sane person would even attempt to bathe a cat, though," he added. "They have groomers who do that."

"Groomers?"

He nodded. "They do cats as well as dogs, didn't you know?"

"No. How did you?"

"We… I had a cat once."

She forced herself to ignore the slip. She sipped her coffee while she tried not to think about what it implied. "There was this other video," she continued, "about goats." She grinned, putting on an act so that he wouldn't realize she was reacting to his statement.

"Goats?" he asked.

She nodded. "Here. Let me show you." She pulled out her phone, went through a few screens, hit a button and handed it to him. There was a goat. But when he opened his mouth, he screamed like a human.

Caught by surprise, Paul burst out laughing.

Sari watched him, smiling. She loved to see him laugh.

He handed her back the phone and caught his breath. "I can see that YouTube has a lot to recommend it," he confessed.

"It's so much fun." She put up the phone. "I don't have a social life, so I hang out on YouTube to see what the rest of the world is up to. Some of it is just hilarious."

"It is." He shook his head. "I never heard a goat scream."

"Me, neither," she said, grinning.

His dark eyes went over her face like searching hands. Something inside him clenched. She was beautiful. Not in a conventional way, perhaps, but what was inside her was beautiful. She had a soul like a poet.

Her reddish-gold hair caught the light and shone like gold touched by sunlight as she bent over her cell phone. Paul watched her, aching inside for something he knew he could never have.

"What are you looking for?" he asked.

She looked up and grimaced. "It's a text from Daddy. He wants to know why we haven't come back home yet."

Which meant Darwin Grayling was tracking them. It made him furious, but he had to hide it. He smiled. "Tell him there's a storm and I don't want to get caught on the road in it."

She nodded and typed some more. Then she drew in a sharp breath. "He says come home anyway, he has to speak to you about something." Her blue eyes narrowed with concern.

"Okay. His call. But if that storm hits, I'm getting off the road and to hell with being a little late getting home. Tell him that," he dared, dark eyes glittering.

She bit her lip. "Will you send flowers, if I do?" she asked with graveyard humor. "Okay. But I'm editing that a little," she added, as she started typing again.

"Chicken," he taunted.

She laughed hollowly. "Paul, you haven't ever really seen Daddy in a temper," she told him when she was putting the phone in her purse. "If you had, you'd think twice about making him angry."

"Why?" he asked innocently as he drained the last of his coffee. "Does he start turning green and burst out of his clothes?"

She didn't get it at first. Then she did, and she exploded with laughter.

He leaned forward and said in a ghostly voice, "You wouldn't like me if I was angry!"

The laughter increased. She wiped tears from her eyes.

He grinned and got up to pay the bill, beating her to it.

"I was going to get that," she protested.

"I might not be a millionaire, but I can afford lunch," he said with apparent good humor, but there was hurt pride beneath it. He was painfully aware of the differences between them.

She glanced at him, with his hands deep in his pockets as they walked, his lifted chin as eloquent as a eulogy.

"It bothers you, doesn't it?" she asked.

He frowned. "What does?"

"That I'm…that I stand to inherit millions," she blurted out.

"Nah," he said, passing it off. "I like you in spite of it."

"Oh, you!" she laughed, punching his muscular arm.

"All the same, your dad's going to be particular about any man who comes into your life," he added.

"That would be pure luck," she said with a sigh.

"We're wrapped in cotton and packed in a box when we aren't studying. I had to beg and plead just to get to go to college in San Antonio. And he only made that concession because he knew you'd be driving me both ways."

He stopped walking, aware of boats going by on the river in front of the businesses, draped in bright colors and packed with tourists despite the summer heat. "Don't you feel like breaking out of that satin prison? Ever?"

She looked up at him with her heart in her eyes. Of course she did. With him. She wanted to run away with him, live with him, love him, take care of him. And that would never be possible. Her father would kill him, even if he actually wanted her. Which he didn't.

She smiled faintly and turned away, walking again. "There's not really any way to get out, unless Daddy loses his millions. Then it wouldn't worry him if I got involved with someone, because he'd have nothing to lose."

"Not much chance of that ever happening," he said in a neutral tone.

"Not much," she agreed.

"He won't let you date, will he?" he asked suddenly.

"No."

He glanced at her. "I don't like that note in your voice, Isabel," he said quietly.

"What note?"

"Fear."

She swallowed. He couldn't know how her father reacted to threats of male interaction with his girls.

She couldn't tell him, for fear of what he might do. He'd lose his job and she'd never see him again. Or even worse.

"Can't you talk to me?" he asked softly.

She hated that deep, tender tone. It made her toes curl, made her hungry for things that had no real physical expression. "I wouldn't dare," she said, and then laughed as if to make a joke out of it.

He didn't realize that she wasn't kidding. He'd never seen her father raise a hand to her or Merrie. In fact, all he saw was that he was overly protective of them.

"I read somewhere that millionaires marry among their own, to keep the money in the families that have it," he said as they reached the car.

"It's pretty much true," she had to confess. "Two of my friends at college married men their parents picked out for them." She made a face. "Neither of them was happy about it. One girl even tried to run away, but her parents' security team caught her at the airport and brought her home."

He unlocked the car with his smart key and put her inside. He was quiet, uncommunicative. He'd just recalled what he'd learned about the bodyguards that watched Sari and Merrie any time they were away from the ranch, even when they were with Paul. It made him angry, as it had when he heard about it. It was as if Mr. Grayling didn't trust Paul to take care of his daughters.

Unless, he thought irritably, the man thought he might get fresh with one of them, Isabel in particular. He knew Mandy wouldn't give them away, but there might have been a hidden camera somewhere that he hadn't known about. Mr. Grayling might know that Isabel often came into his room at night and sat on his bed, talking to him.

"You're positively morose," Isabel teased. "What's the matter with you?"

"Did you know…?" His foot hit the brake and he turned suddenly into the parking lot of a closed business.

"What's wrong?" Isabel asked.

"That." He pointed to the rearview mirror.

She turned in her seat and saw it coming. The sky was a nasty green color. A whirling mass was coming toward them. "Paul! What do we do?"

"We can't outrun it, honey, and there's no ditch. Get down." He pushed her down and covered her with his body as the winds hit the car with the force of a bulldozer.

She heard shattering glass and felt the impact of something besides wind, probably a huge limb off one of the nearby trees. She felt the heat and power of Paul's fit body all along hers on the seat as he covered her, protecting her.

"Not much longer," he whispered huskily. His body was reacting to the closeness of hers in a way he couldn't help. She was warm and soft and she smelled of wildflowers. One of Paul's hands was braced on the seat, keeping them from pitching into the floorboard; the other was around her waist, pressed hard against her stomach. That hand began to move, softly, involuntarily, as the pitch of the wind decreased and the car stopped rocking.

Paul felt his heartbeat racing. It had been a long time since he'd had a woman, and his dreams of Isabel lately had been hot and graphic. He couldn't get the picture of her in that pink silk nightgown out of his mind.

"Is it over?" she whispered. She sounded almost normal, but her body was tense, her back arching as he touched her, trying to get closer to him.

"Mostly," he whispered back. His hand was openly caressing her, moving up from her belly to the soft underside of her breasts and back again, sensuous, taunting.

"Was it…a tornado?" she managed, because her voice, like her body, began to shake.

"A little one, maybe," he murmured. His face nuzzled against hers until it made its way under her hair to her neck. His lips moved into the soft, warm flesh. "Move back a little," he groaned at her ear. "Closer, honey…"

She was dreaming. She knew she was. Because his hand was insistent, forcing her pliant young body back into the changed contours of his, letting her feel the raging arousal that was making him hot all over.

Those searching fingers moved up suddenly, right over the thrust of one small, pert breast, swallowing it whole while his forefinger nudged the nipple and made it go hard and sensitive.

He made a rough sound in his throat. It wasn't enough. Not nearly enough. His hand moved again, under her blouse, up to the bra's clasp. He unfastened it with one hand, and then he was touching her, caressing her bare flesh hungrily, feeling her helpless response to his expert touch as she arched her body and moaned out loud.

"Baby…" he groaned.

He moved her, turned her over, so that he could see her flushed, hungry expression, see the turmoil in her blue eyes. Her whole body was trembling as she looked up at him, helpless to protest as his hand started up again, taking the hem of the shirt with it.

"I want to look at you," he said huskily. "I want to put my mouth over your nipple and suckle you until you cry out…!"

She gasped at his graphic words, but she didn't try to get away or catch his wrist. She shivered and her body moved restlessly on the seat.

"Oh, baby," he whispered, his face taut with desire as the fabric moved slowly, slowly, up past her rib cage toward the unfastened band of the bra. "I've dreamed about this…!"

She arched toward him, her eyes closed, her body taut and tingling with new sensations, with new hungers that made her helpless, with an anguished, unfamiliar need. She poised there, her body arched, waiting, waiting…

CHAPTER FIVE

JUST AS PAUL'S hand moved the soft cotton fabric of her shirt higher, his mouth poised over hers, his dark eyes burning with desire, sirens became audible, moving closer to them.

He felt as if he were coming out of a trance. He looked down at what he'd done and flinched. What the hell had he been about to do? His face contorted as he pushed Isabel up from the seat and turned away while she frantically worked at putting her bra back on.

A police car pulled up beside them and a tall policeman got out, noting the shattered glass of the back window and the small limb that had done the damage.

"Are you folks okay?" he asked with concern.

"Yeah, thanks," Paul said, breathing in deeply. "I thought we'd bought the farm," he added on a chuckle while he tried to divert the officer's attention so that his hunger for Isabel wouldn't be visible. He turned to her. "You okay, Miss Grayling?" he asked formally.

"I'm...fine," she said. "A little shaken, that's all." She smiled for the policeman and looked around at the shattered back glass. "We were lucky," she added when she noticed the devastation all around them.

"Very lucky. NOAA's calling it a downburst," the policeman said. "Did a lot of damage on this city block and just swept right over everything else." He shook his head. "Go figure."

Paul got out of the car, his hunger finally tamed by doing math problems in his head. He grimaced when he saw the back windshield.

"I guess I'd better get her home and call the insurance company," Paul said. "She'd just signed up for law school, too."

The policeman smiled at her. "I've got a son who just graduated from it," he confessed. "He's going into corporate law."

"I'm going to get a job with the Jacobsville district attorney's office when I graduate," Isabel said shyly. "I've been plaguing them for years."

He laughed. "Not a job many people want. But good luck to you." He shook his head as he surveyed the damage. "Need to go to the emergency room? We can take you over, if you want," he added, indicating his partner, who was standing by the patrol car.

"I'm fine. Not a scratch," Isabel said. She couldn't look at Paul. "My nerves are pretty raw, that's all."

"Mine, too," Paul said with a grin. "The car should be fine, once I remove the tree from it," he added with pursed lips.

"Let us help you with that."

The men got the limb out of the back window and one of the officers wrote up some notes on the damage for the insurance company. Paul said he'd get back with them about a copy of the report in a few days. Then he got Isabel back into the car, cranked it, waved to the police officers and started back toward Jacobsville.

Isabel was too shocked and uncertain to speak, and Paul was too angry at himself.

He turned on the radio to listen to the news, which was just reporting the damage in the small area where the downburst had happened. He kept it on and remained doggedly silent all the way back to Comanche Wells while Isabel stared out the window and ground her teeth at a moment that would live in her mind and her heart as long as she drew breath.

He only wanted to forget it had happened. She knew that. He knew the difficulties and he wasn't rushing to involve himself with a woman worth millions whose father would have him roasted on a spit if he knew he'd even touched her.

But she was suddenly awake and aware in a way she never had been before. Her body knew passion, knew pleasure, knew the siren song of desire. Paul had touched her. He'd wanted her. She knew nothing of men, but her friends at college were open about their relationships. She knew what happened when a man felt desire. Paul's body, at her back, had been raging with it. His hands on her had been hungry, out of control.

But that was only desire. He was fond of her, but that was as far as it went. Today had been a spur-of-the-moment thing, a result, surely, of the burst of wind and the shattering of the windshield. It had been a moment of shared fear that had just gotten out of hand.

For him. But for her, it had been a revelation. She'd loved Paul forever, it seemed. But he'd never touched her, not even when she'd tempted him by showing up on his bed in that slinky pale pink nightgown with her robe unfastened. She'd given up hope that he was ever going to give her anything except grudging affection.

Then he'd pushed her down in the car to shelter her. His voice, deep and soft as velvet, had been as caressing as those big, warm, rough hands on her untried body. In her whole life, no man had ever touched her like that, so intimately, so hungrily, without the slightest hint of restraint.

She wondered how long it had been since he'd really been with a woman physically, because it had felt very much as if he'd been starving to death. She knew he dated; he'd made no secret of it. But if he didn't have a steady girl, he was going without. Had that prompted his loss of control? Or had it been something else, something more...

"Don't sit over there and make love's eternal dream out of what happened when the wind hit us," Paul said curtly as he turned into the long driveway that led to Grayling's. He glanced at her with cold dark eyes. "I haven't had a woman in a while. I just lost my head. It was purely physical, Isabel. Nothing more."

Her knuckles were white where she clenched her purse to stop herself with crying out from the pain of what he was saying. She forced a smile and even looked at him with a calm face. "I know that, Paul. I won't read anything more into it. Honest. We were lucky," she added, glancing behind them at the broken glass all over the backseat where the limb had blown through it. "Just a foot or so more and it would have gotten us as well as the back glass."

"Yeah, I noticed," he replied with a clipped smile.

"I'll get the insurance company on it first thing. They'll send someone out to the house to fix it."

"Classes start next week," she said, her eyes straight ahead. "I'll have plenty to do."

He didn't answer her. He pulled up at the front door and stopped. He started to get out and open the door for her, but she was quicker.

"Thanks for driving me up to the school," she said and smiled as she ran quickly to the front door.

He could see through her. She was hurting, upset, shocked by what had happened, and he'd treated it more like a joke than like the trauma it probably was to her. She had no experience with men. He should have explained it better than that. But he couldn't take the chance that she'd see it as a beginning. He'd had one relationship, before his life was shattered. He wanted no more of them. Ever.

He parked the car at the back door and walked into the house. Darwin Grayling was waiting there. He saw the car and exploded.

"What the hell happened? Is Isabel all right?" he burst out.

"We got caught in a downburst. At least that's what the weather guys called it. A limb came right through the back windshield. It stopped short of us, but Miss Grayling is pretty upset." He never used her name or her nickname with her father.

"Thank God." Darwin let out a breath. "You'll handle all that…?" He waved a hand at the car.

"Yes, sir. I'll get the insurance company right on it."

"Let that wait. I need to speak to you. Come into my study, please."

Paul followed him, his teeth grinding together. Surely the man didn't have cameras in the car, or upstairs, that Paul didn't know about. If he did, this was going to be a very short trip. He'd be grilled and fired on the spot if Grayling had any inkling of what had really gone on inside that car after the downburst hit. Or if there was a hidden camera in Paul's bedroom. He could picture Grayling's reaction if he knew that Isabel often spent time in Paul's bedroom—on Paul's bed—to talk to him late at night in just a gown and a robe...

Darwin closed the door with a snap and turned to Paul. He wasn't smiling. "How much do you know about that police officer who's been flirting with Isabel in Barbara's Cafe?" he asked at once.

Paul's mind was in limbo. The question came out of left field and he was unprepared for it. "There's nothing going on there, sir. He has lunch at the café and Isabel's talked to him a time or two when she had lunch in town with one of Blake Kemp's employees. That's all it is. I don't think she's been around him more than once or twice."

"You don't think," Darwin said angrily. "You make sure he keeps his distance," he added curtly. "My daughter is off-limits to any man, but especially one who's an undercover federal officer!"

"A Fed?" Paul feigned surprise.

"Yes, a Fed," came the short reply. "I had him checked out." His eyes narrowed. "Something you should have thought to do the minute you heard Isabel was letting him flirt with her!"

He caught his breath. "Sir, if I'd thought he was a threat..."

"He *is* a threat, Fiore!" he returned, his face reddening. "Any man I don't choose for my daughters is a threat! I'm not losing one penny of what I own to some grubby little lawman who looks at my daughter and sees himself set for life! They're mine! I've spent a small fortune keeping them safe from fortune hunters while I find the right husbands for them! Merrie's too young, but Isabel will be married when she's twenty-five. I have a prince picked out for her. He's wealthy and his brothers have all produced sons, so he's a good match. I must have heirs, so that Graylings doesn't go into the ground with me."

Paul was shocked. He didn't know how to react. He just stared at the older man while he searched for a reply that wouldn't get him fired.

Darwin looked at his watch and grimaced. "I have to be in Finland for trade talks. I'll be away for at least two weeks. Don't delegate your responsibility to any other security person. You take Isabel anywhere she wants to go, but you watch her! And if that Fed shows any more interest in her, you get her out of that café if you have to carry her out, is that clear?"

"Yes, sir," Paul said curtly.

"I'll hold you responsible if she gets involved with anyone, too," Darwin added.

"I'll remember, sir," Paul said.

"See that you do. Have Morris drive me to the airport. You keep an eye on Isabel," he added curtly.

"I'll do that."

Darwin waved a hand, indicating that his security chief was dismissed. Paul left the room, hiding his expression. He wanted to tear the man apart with his bare hands. Marry Isabel to some foreign prince as breeding stock for the next generation? The man was insane!

He walked outside to get some fresh air and lifted his face to the breeze. Grubby little Fed, he'd called the lawman in town. Grubby. That was how Darwin Grayling pictured anyone without money. That included Paul. No commoner was good enough for his daughters. No, they must marry money. It didn't matter what the man who had the money looked like, either. He could be old and fat and bald and it wouldn't matter. Isabel must marry within her class.

Why did it bother him so much to know that? He was aware of the differences. He wasn't lining up to court Isabel, to win her, to marry her. *Marry.* He closed his eyes and shivered. He couldn't bear to think about marriage again.

So why was he picturing Isabel in white? Because she'd be walking down the aisle in it, looking like a fairy princess. Isabel had a white dress that she often wore to church—one of the few venues that the girls were allowed to attend. The dress had a tight bodice and a full skirt, and it drifted around Isabel's long legs when she walked, giving teasing glimpses of the long, beautiful legs underneath. He loved her in white. It emphasized the amazing color of those long, curly red-gold locks and her blue, blue eyes.

He wanted to deck Darwin Grayling.

HE WAS STILL wearing that cold, angry expression when Mandy started putting supper on the table, several hours later.

"And what's the matter with you?" Mandy chided.

"A man who's escaped certain death should look happier."

"It's listening to that man talk about auctioning Isabel off to some foreign prince as breeding stock," he muttered. "Merrie, too, of course," he added, so that he didn't give her the idea that it was only Isabel for whose welfare he was concerned.

"Money marries money," she said simply. "That's the way the world is, Mr. Paul."

He drew in a long breath and picked up a piece of celery from the appetizers she'd just put on the table. He shoved it into his mouth.

"Don't spoil your appetite," she chided.

He chuckled. "You sound like my grandmother," he replied. "I was forever stealing little bits of food from the table when she set it. Of course, at our house it was bread and olive oil rather than raw veggies."

"You miss your grandmother a lot, don't you?" she asked kindly.

He drew in a long breath and crunched the celery before he answered. "Mandy, in my whole life, she's the only human being who ever really loved me," he confessed. He smiled wistfully. "None of the ones who came after did, except..." He stopped there. He couldn't bear the memory. Blood. So much blood! His eyes closed, trying to shut out the memory.

He felt a soft hand on his arm. "I made a nice supper," she said, drawing him back. "You have to stop looking back, Mr. Paul. The world is bright and beautiful. The path ahead is sweet."

He made a face. "Sweet. Sure. Sweet like vinegar."

She hit him. "Cut that out. You'll curdle the milk in my nice pudding."

He laughed. "Mandy, you're a tonic."

"Glad you think so." She went back into the kitchen and returned with a pan of rolls and a small plate with butter.

"Rolls!" he exclaimed. "You sweetheart!"

"After your close call, I thought you and Miss Isabel might like something special. I made macaroni and cheese, too." She indicated the big square dish on the table.

"I have truly died and gone to heaven," he assured her. "Uh, could you wait a bit to call the others?" he added, tugging the casserole toward him.

Mandy laughed out loud. "Oh, Mr. Paul, shame on you!"

She went to call the girls down to the supper table, still laughing.

"NOT NICE," ISABEL chided him when she sat down. "Trying to hog all the macaroni and cheese."

"Villain," Merrie agreed with twinkling gray eyes. "We love it, too! Nobody makes it like Mandy does."

Mandy made them a nice curtsy before she brought the coffeepot to the table and put it down in the center, next to the cream and sugar on the silver tray.

They ate in a pleasant silence until Mandy brought in the pound cake, sliced and served it with coffee.

"What did the insurance company say about the car?" Sari asked.

"I've got a guy coming out tomorrow to replace the back window, and a cleaning crew to get out all the glass and other debris from the car," he said without looking at her.

"Glass?" Merrie asked, puzzled. "What glass?"

"Didn't your sister tell you?" Paul asked. "We got caught in a downburst in San Antonio and a tree came through the back windshield. Part of one at least," he added, forking into his slice of cake. His face was carefully schooled to show no emotion whatsoever as he spoke.

"You didn't tell me!" Merrie exclaimed. "Were either of you hurt?"

"Not a scratch," Isabel assured her. She ate cake mechanically, while her heart raced madly and her breath caught in her throat. "We were lucky."

"My gosh! I'd have been terrified!" Merrie said, shaking her head. She glanced at her sister. "I wondered why you looked so shaken when I passed you in the hall. And you never said a word!"

It was an indication of just how badly Isabel had been shaken, Paul thought sadly. He couldn't do anything about it. He had to let her think he was unconcerned. It was something that never should have happened. He had to make sure it never happened again.

"The cake is great, Mandy," he enthused when he was having a second cup of coffee.

The girls echoed the praise.

Mandy grinned at them. "Aw, shucks, t'waren't nothin'," she drawled in her best Texas backcountry accent.

"It's a miracle I don't weigh three hundred pounds,

with food like this," Paul sighed. His dark eyes twinkled at her.

"It's a miracle we don't all weigh that much," Merrie teased.

"Where was Daddy going?" Sari asked without looking at Paul.

"Finland," he said. "To some economic conference. He does know his way around the world of high finance."

"Yes, he does," she agreed.

"How long is he going to be gone?" Merrie asked.

"Two weeks, he said." Paul remembered all that Darwin had said to him and his dark eyes glittered as he finished his coffee. "I'd better do a quick recon outside," he said, "and check in with the rest of my staff, to make sure they're on the ball."

"Is Daddy getting jumpy again?" Merrie asked. "The last time he got jumpy, one of the racehorses was stolen. We got him back, but Daddy was furious. He talked to some people about the man who stole the horse…"

"And the police got him on other charges," Sari interrupted with a sharp glance at her sister. It was dangerous for Paul to know what they knew. "Daddy didn't even have to testify."

"When was this?" Paul asked.

"Just before you came to work for us," Sari replied. "It was a long time ago."

"But Daddy has lots of people watching the horses now," Merrie added.

And watching Darwin Grayling's daughters, too,

he thought irritably. He wasn't going to mention that, but it irked him that the man didn't think Paul could protect them. If he had, he wouldn't have whole sets of bodyguards following them every time they left the house.

"I'll make another pot of coffee if you like, before I go to my church meeting," Mandy offered, glancing at the clock on the wall.

"You go ahead. I can make myself coffee if I want it," Paul said with a warm smile. "Get Morris to drive you. We've got three other men watching the house and the horses. It will be all right."

"That's nice of you, Mr. Paul," she said. "Thanks."

"Have to take care of you," he mused. "We'd starve if you got carried off by martians or anything."

She laughed. "So you might!"

"I'm going to watch that new fantasy movie," Merrie said. "Want to watch it with me, Sari?"

"No," she replied. "Thanks, but I've got some textbooks to find for my classes. I'm going to get them online."

"Going to do digital ones again?" Merrie asked.

Her sister nodded. "Except for one that's only available in paperback."

"Dry old law books," Merrie teased. "You'll gather dust like they will."

"Virtual dust," Sari said, waving her hands. "Witchy things!"

"Careful, somebody might throw water on you," the younger woman mused, tongue in cheek.

Sari's mind went to the *Wizard of Oz* scene where

the green-faced witch melted after being doused with water, and she laughed. "Wicked," she said.

Merrie just smiled.

Paul smiled, too, but not with any enthusiasm at the byplay. He went out the back door, grateful for the cool night air that might help him forget Isabel's hungry eyes begging for his mouth as they lay together in the car.

HE PACED IN his bedroom, his mind going back again and again to the downburst, to the car, to Isabel in his arms, hungry, responsive, wanting him.

His mind told him that he was crazy to think he could ever have her. If he showed the least personal interest in her, Darwin Grayling would have him skinned alive and grilled, just before he fired him. Of course there were plenty of other security people who could replace him, but none with the history he had with Isabel and Merrie. They were family to him. He went above and beyond to keep them safe, because he genuinely cared about them. Another man might be careless, might not bother with the tiny details that never escaped Paul. Well, there was Morris, his second-in-command. The man had been working for Grayling for several years. He seemed to be fond of the girls, but he did anything that Grayling told him to. He never questioned an order.

On the other hand, Paul knew he was coming to the end of his time with the Graylings. Merrie was out of high school, Isabel was in law school. Sure, they still needed protecting from possible kidnappers or people with a grudge against their father. But he couldn't stay here much longer. The genie was out of the bottle as far as Isabel went. They were physically aware of each other. That situation was only going to get worse. The tension would grow as they denied the hunger; it would build to a flash point and then explode.

He didn't know how he was going to stay alive with no glimpses of curly reddish-gold hair and blue, blue eyes in a gamine little face with freckles just over the nose. He didn't know how long ago Isabel had wormed her way into his heart, but she had possession of it now. And he couldn't have her. He could never have her.

He groaned out loud. He stood at the darkened window, looking out toward the stables, where security lights burned near the accommodations for the boss's Thoroughbreds. He had three men out there full-time, just to make sure nothing happened to the horses. Inside, the girls were safe with him. He didn't have cameras in the house, but he had the doors and windows wired. Nothing—no one—would get in without his knowing about it.

He perched his hands on his lean hips over the black silk pajama bottoms as he contemplated his next move. When the boss came back, he was going to have to put in his notice. It was for Isabel's protection as well as his own. Her father had an unpredictable temper. He didn't know much of what had gone on before he started watching the girls, but he'd heard gossip. He didn't want Isabel to get in trouble because he'd gone too long without a woman and couldn't keep his hands off her.

The tap at the door was so soft that he didn't hear it until it came again. He frowned as he went to open it.

Isabel was wearing pajamas with a thick cotton robe. No way was she going to be accused of tempting him.

"I won't come in," she said, eyes downcast. "I just wanted to apologize."

He drew her inside and closed the door. "Apologize for what, baby?" he asked softly.

The tenderness in his voice ground into her heart like broken glass. "For…what happened. I shouldn't have… I should have…"

He pulled her into his arms and wrapped her up tight, his face in her warm throat. "You didn't do anything. It was me. I've been too long without… Well, I let things get out of control."

She drew back and looked up at his handsome face. She searched his dark eyes quietly. "Too long without a woman." She finished the sentence for him.

His face hardened. "Yeah."

"How…how long?" she asked daringly.

He drew in a rough breath. His hands slid up under the wide sleeves of her robe onto her bare, soft arms. "Years."

Her heart jumped. She hadn't realized that men could go without sex for years. She didn't dare ask the question, but her eyes did.

"It's something I can't talk about," he told her. "Not even to you."

Her eyes scanned the hard lines of his face like

an artist, drawing a picture, memorizing the subject. "I… I would…" she begun.

He put his fingers over her soft mouth. "And what do you think would happen then, Isabel?" he asked solemnly. "You know how your father thinks. He'll want someone with a title for you, at least someone with a wealthy background like yours."

Why, he'd considered a future with her, she thought in amazement. "There are these places in the Amazon jungle where people go and are never heard from again," she began.

He chuckled softly. His eyes lit up, dark and soft. "Sure. We'd be eaten by bugs and used for target practice by the people who live there."

She grimaced. "It was just a thought."

His big hands framed her face. He searched her eyes and groaned inwardly. "I can't have you, baby," he whispered. His head bent, despite his will, until his hard mouth was poised right over her soft one. "I can't ever have you, Isabel…"

Her name went into her mouth. His lips parted hers, burrowing softly into them and then hesitating, as a surge of pleasure like a shock of lightning froze him in place for just a few seconds. Then he groaned and wrapped her up in his arms, his mouth hard and slow and insistent.

She didn't know anything, but she melted into him and let him do what he wanted to her mouth. The sensations he aroused in her were shocking, shattering, to a woman who'd never even been kissed before.

Her arms started up around his neck, but he stopped

them. He smoothed the robe away from her body, still in the thin silky blue pajamas, and he bent and lifted her, his mouth hungry on hers.

"This is a big mistake," he said through his teeth, but he didn't stop kissing her.

"I don't care," she sobbed. "Paul…!"

He put her on the bed and followed her down, his legs tangling with hers as he made a meal of her soft, responsive mouth. His hands were busy unbuttoning the pajama jacket. In seconds, it was gone and his mouth was on her white, soft, freckled breasts.

She was unprepared for the shock of his lips on her bare skin and she jumped. He lifted his head, amused at her tiny start of surprise.

"Men do it to women," he said softly. "It's okay. Honest."

"All…all right."

He chuckled as he bent back to her body and drew his lips slowly over the soft mound of her breast, teasing around the nipple until it went hard and rosy, then swallowing it with a soft, slow suction that made her arch and shiver.

Her nails dug into his shoulders as she moaned, her mind in limbo, her body shivering with its first taste of sensual pleasure.

The sound went right to Paul's head. His mouth traveled down her body, to the place where her belly and her leg were joined and then over her soft stomach and back up the other side. She smelled of some soft, floral cologne and she tasted like heaven. He was drunk on her already, and he'd barely started.

She lifted to his mouth, guided his head back to her breasts, her eyes wild and excited as each stab of pleasure was replaced by one even more intense.

"Oh, baby," he whispered against her soft skin. "You taste like whipped cream!"

"I don't know...how to do...anything," she whispered.

He smiled against her soft skin. "What do you want to know how to do?"

"How to make you feel...what I'm feeling."

"I already do." He lifted himself above her, so that his eyes looked down into hers. "I'm on fire for you, honey. I ache all over."

"Me...me, too." Her eyes dropped to his bare, hair-roughened chest and she arched expressively.

"Is this what you want?"

He eased down over her, so that his chest rubbed against her taut nipples.

She gasped and clutched at him.

"It is, isn't it?" he said, almost to himself. His eyes darkened as he moved, levering himself between her long legs so that only two layers of cloth separated them from each other in an intimacy she'd never yet shared with a man.

Her nails bit into him. She was willing, it was in her eyes. But she was also afraid.

"Don't panic," he whispered as he moved slowly against her. "We can't go all the way. But we can go... this...far...!"

He thought, he really thought, he could control what he felt. But he couldn't. He drove against her helplessly, so hungry that he was dying for her.

She shifted under him, her earlier fears forgotten in the heat and hunger he aroused in her. She moved again, her long legs starting to curl around his hips.

Her father. Pregnancy. The past. Blood. So…much… blood…!

He jackknifed away from her and rolled over onto his stomach, gripping the pillows so hard that he almost tore them as he fought his hunger for her. It had been close. So close. Too close. He shuddered.

Isabel watched him and felt the guilt all the way to her soul. He was in agony. And it was her fault. She'd come in here and tempted him. She'd known on some level how very hungry he was for her. She should never have tempted him. The pain he was feeling was so obvious that she groaned inside.

She got up off the bed, fastened her pajama jacket, and searched for her robe. She took her time putting it back on. By the time she closed it, Paul was breathing easier. He was still lying on his stomach, cursing his own weakness.

"I'm sorry," she whispered. "I really just came to apologize."

He heard the guilt and shame in her voice. He rolled over, his body still aroused but the killing heat slowly draining out of him.

He got to his feet and moved toward her, but he stopped an arm's length away.

"That was a near thing," he said quietly.

She nodded miserably.

He drew in a shaky breath. "This can't happen again. I can't control it. Do you understand?"

She nodded. "The Amazon jungle probably wouldn't

be far enough away, anyhow. Daddy's got people all over the world."

"I know."

She searched his eyes, pain in her own. "If only," she began huskily.

He managed a taut smile. "If only." He reached out and barely touched her tousled curly reddish-gold hair. "He has plans for you, honey," he said after a minute. "Try not to let him force you into something you don't want. Life is too short to live by other people's rules."

She smiled back. "It's a little harder than it seems to talk back to people you're scared of," she replied.

He shrugged. "I talked back to my father," he said. He chuckled. "I was missing a tooth or two the first time I did it, but I didn't stop. He had ideas about what he wanted me to do with my life, too," he added. "I wasn't willing."

"Life is so hard," she bit off.

Something flashed in his dark eyes. He drew back his hand and let it drop to his side. "You can make book on that. Now go to bed."

She nodded. She turned and glanced back at him over her shoulder, loving the slight swell of his lower lip where hers had pressed so hard against it, loving his tousled black wavy hair, his dark eyes, his beautiful chest.

"Go on," he said, forcing a smile, because he wanted to throw her down on the bed and go into her, so hard…!

"Good night, Paul."

She went out the door and closed it behind her. He stared at it for a long time before he turned off the light and lay down in bed. He knew what he was going to have to do. It wasn't going to be pleasant. But he no longer had a choice.

CHAPTER SIX

PAUL WAS POLITE and courteous to Isabel and not much more in the days that followed. He had Morris go with him when he transported Isabel up to San Antonio for her first days of classes in law school. Isabel realized why he was doing it. She pretended not to care that it tore the heart out of her that Paul was going to draw back.

Realistically, she knew she couldn't have him. He wasn't rich or titled, and she was worth millions. It shouldn't have mattered. But it did. Her father could have him killed, if he ever found out how close she and her bodyguard had grown. She didn't want Paul hurt. On the other hand, it was killing her to know how sweet it was to be held and kissed and touched by him. She wanted it all the time, but Paul never even looked at her now.

She was businesslike with him now, because it hurt so much, what she'd lost. It was a change that was noticed by Paul's associate who rode along with them to San Antonio.

"Boy, has she changed," Morris remarked when he and Paul were on their way back to the ranch after dropping Isabel off at school. "She was crazy about you for a while there."

"She's an heiress," Paul said noncommittally.

"What does that matter?" The man chuckled. "Hey, you could marry her and be set for life, right? You'd never have to work another day as long as you lived. You could fly all over the world, rub elbows with famous people, have fancy cars and clothes. Man, what I wouldn't give for that!"

"Money isn't everything."

"It is when you're poor," the man sighed. "I can't even afford a decent suit. I buy mine in chain stores." He shook his head. "You really ought to play up to that girl…"

"Her father would have me killed for even thinking of it, and he'd fire you for talking about her that way," he said suddenly.

"Hey, no harm done," the man said at once, holding up both hands. "I was just thinking out loud. Say, what do you think about that new city ordinance they're trying to pass in Jacobsville…?"

The man's voice droned on. Paul nodded his head in the appropriate places, but he wasn't paying attention. He was hearing another man assume that he wanted Isabel for what she had. She was a sweet, kind, loving woman, and all the other man could see was her fortune.

But that was what most men would think of him if he went crazy and tried to get Isabel to marry him. They'd think he only wanted her for her money.

Her father would never let a "grubby little lawman" like Paul have her. He'd marry her off to some prince or millionaire and never care that she was miserable, as long as he had an heir with the right bloodlines.

Paul felt the despair in the pit of his stomach like acid. Isabel was putting on a good act so far, not letting on how physical things had gotten between them. But she could slip. Or Paul could. It would mean disaster for both of them.

So he kept up the cool and courteous front until Darwin Grayling came back from his trip to Finland. Then he asked to speak to the man. They went into the study and closed the door.

"My daughter...did what?" Darwin exploded.

Paul held up a hand. He was already regretting the words. "She was just flirting, and it was only the one time," he said firmly. "But..." He drew in a breath. "Mr. Grayling, I haven't been entirely honest with you. I know you did a background check on me, but I sort of controlled a little bit of the information you were given. A cousin owed me a favor." He rammed his hands into his pockets. His teeth clenched. "I have a wife and daughter in New Jersey," he said. "I go home often enough to see them, and I send them money," he added. "But I thought a family man might not be acceptable for this job, so I concealed that part of my life."

"You have a family," Darwin said.

"Yes, sir." He bit his lip. He was lying through his teeth. But he couldn't let it show. "So I know Isabel was just sort of cutting her teeth on me. She doesn't know about my family." He shrugged. "But I don't want to be the cause of any embarrassment to her. Or to you. So I think it would be better if I went back to New Jersey."

Darwin Grayling didn't say anything for a minute. He stared at Paul, hiding an explosive reaction to the man's surprising statement. "Isabel was flirting with you."

Paul laughed. "Picking at me, not really flirting," he lied. "I don't think she even knows how to flirt, honestly. And it was just the one time. You know how young girls are."

Darwin drew in a breath. "Yes. I do."

"So, I'm going to put in my two weeks' notice…"

"No need for that," Darwin said. He forced a laugh. "Young women do have these little quirks. No, you don't need to work the next few weeks. I'll have Rosalee cut a check for you and you can pick it up in our San Antonio office on your way to the airport. Just tell her where you want to go, she'll make sure you have an e-ticket, as well. I'll have your Christmas bonus enclosed, even though you won't be working for us then."

"Sir, that's very kind of you, under the circumstances," Paul said, trying to deal with the guilt he felt at betraying Isabel. It wasn't even her fault.

"You've been a good security chief. The best I've ever had." Darwin put a friendly arm around his shoulders. "You get packed and I'll have Morris drive you up to San Antonio. Thank you for all you've done for us, Paul. I'll miss you."

"Thank you, sir."

Darwin smiled. "Have a safe trip home."

Paul nodded.

Darwin closed his office door.

PAUL PACKED AND HAD Morris take his bags to the car while he said his goodbyes. But only Mandy was in the kitchen.

She was shocked and started crying when Paul told her he was leaving.

"He found out about Sari sitting on your bed at night, didn't he?" she asked glumly.

"No. I just told him she was flirting with me. And that...well, something else," he added. He couldn't bring himself to tell her the truth. He hugged her. "I'll miss you, girl."

"I'll miss you, too, Mr. Paul." She winced. "The girls went into town to have lunch with Mr. Kemp's assistant district attorney," she said. "Can't you wait until they get back?"

"Not a good idea," Paul said tersely, but with a smile. "Hug them for me and tell them I'll miss them, will you?"

She nodded. "Why?" she asked sadly.

Paul couldn't tell her. He just smiled again. "Nothing lasts forever. I need a change, that's all. You take care, Mandy."

"You, too."

He looked around the room, taking it all in, smiled once more and went out to the car where Morris was waiting.

ISABEL'S FACE WHEN Mandy told her was a study in shock and grief.

"He's gone? And he didn't wait to say goodbye to us?" she asked, aghast.

"He was in a hurry," Mandy said, trying to come up with a good reason for his haste.

"I'll miss him so much," Merrie said. "He was so kind to us." Tears ran down her cheeks.

Isabel was crying, too. Mandy hugged them both close. She didn't understand what was going on, either, but she knew something had been growing between Paul and Isabel for months. It wouldn't show to outsiders, but she knew them both very well.

A STORM WAS COMING. Nobody knew, because Darwin Grayling had a poker face. But he sent Mandy to Dallas for several days to see a play she'd been raving about, and paid for a luxury hotel room and a shopping spree, as well.

"You need some new things, and you've been talking about that play," Darwin said with a smile. "You'll have a good time."

"Thank you, Mr. Darwin. Thank you so much!" she said, almost in tears at his generosity.

"It's little enough to do. You take wonderful care of all of us." He stopped and put a hand to his head. He winced.

"It's that headache again, isn't it? You should see the doctor, Mr. Darwin," she worried.

"I'm all right. It comes and goes. You go get packed. I'll have Morris drive you," he said.

"Okay, then. But who'll cook for you?" she worried.

"I've hired a relief cook," he lied. "She's arriving this afternoon. Just go."

She laughed. "Yes, sir!" She packed, hugged the girls and went out to the car.

The house was very quiet when Darwin called Sari into his study and closed the door.

He put a hand to his head and winced. He had a horrible headache, but that wasn't going to save Isabel.

"Paul said you were flirting with him," he said at once.

She gasped, but her face flushed. It told him all he needed to know.

"You little slut," he raged. "Just like your mother! She wanted lots of men, too!"

"She never...!" Sari returned.

"Shut up! Strutting around here with your fancy college degree, so sure men will climb all over you if you just bat your eyes! And him a married man!"

"M-married?" she said, shocked. "Paul?"

"Yes! Married!" he shot back. "He has a wife and daughter back in New Jersey!"

Sari thought she'd never felt such shame in her entire life. She closed her eyes and groaned inwardly. She'd kissed him, loved him, wanted him, almost gone too far with him. And he was married! He'd never said that, never even hinted about it. He'd wanted her, so desperately...

Darwin was pulling his belt out of the loops of his pants while she agonized mentally. He halved it and snapped it, making a sound like a whip. He'd always done that before he went for the girls, to heighten their fear of him. Just the sound was enough to send poor Merrie running.

Sari lifted her head. Misery gave her courage she'd never realized she had. "You're not hitting me...!"

"The hell I'm not! You little slut!"

He brought the belt down on her shoulders, hard enough to knock her to her knees. He was behind her then, slamming the thick leather against her back, not relenting even when she started screaming and trying to get away. He put his foot on her and pushed her down again while he went at her with the belt. Blood flew up everywhere.

The door opened suddenly and Merrie ran at her father.

"No!" she screamed. "Stop! You're going to kill her, Daddy, you have to stop!"

But the only thing Merrie accomplished was to have him turn on her, and he did. He threw her to the floor and brought the belt down on her, shredding her T-shirt as it hit her back again and again and again.

Only when he was too exhausted to lift it over his head again did he finally stop and drop back down onto a leather chair to suck in air. He could barely get his breath and his head was splitting.

He leaned forward, coming back to himself. The girls were both on the floor, barely conscious. Blood was all over their backs, all over the carpet.

He was tempted to let them die, but then who would inherit the money he'd worked so hard to make? No, he couldn't do that, not even if they deserved it for defying him. Isabel, flirting with his security man! It shamed and disgusted him. A married security man, at that. Well, she'd be watched. She'd never get the chance to do it again. Neither would Merrie.

But for the moment, they'd need some medical attention. He couldn't take them to Jacobsville General. That suspicious redheaded doctor, Coltrain, would surely involve the law, and Darwin wasn't so sure he could buy off Cash Grier as he'd bought off other lawmen in the past. No, he'd have to handle this at home.

He had a physician on his payroll, one who'd lost his license for getting drunk before he operated on patients. There had been two deaths. But that didn't concern Darwin. The man could keep his mouth shut. He picked up the phone and dialed.

PAUL, ON HIS way back to New Jersey, was relieved at the way Darwin Grayling had taken his comment about Isabel flirting with him. He'd laughed. The girls would be okay. Even if Darwin got angry, Mandy would be there to make sure Darwin didn't hurt them.

He laid his head back against the headrest and closed his eyes. The hard part would come now, trying to live every day without a glimpse of eyes the blue of the open sea. He had to find a new job as well, but that would be easier. He'd already been in touch with a former FBI colleague who was now a senior agent in charge in New Jersey. He'd go back with the Bureau. He could face it now, years after the tragedy that had sent him south. He'd have a new job, new surroundings and no temptation from a woman he could never have.

If only he'd been a prince, he thought wistfully. He could have had Isabel. He'd have given up a kingdom and all its wealth, just to live with her in some humble little cottage in the woods. And chance would be a fine thing, too.

He groaned inwardly when he remembered her arms around him, her hungry mouth under his as she felt the reality of a man's desire for the first time in her life. He'd had the first sweet taste of her innocence. But he hadn't taken it. That privilege would belong to another man, a richer man. He hoped it would be a man she could love.

He wanted her. She wanted him, too. But it was surely just desire on her part, he reasoned. She wasn't mature enough to know what love was. He closed his eyes. He'd known love once. Now his memory of it was forever wrapped in guilt. Blood. So much blood...

He opened his eyes and saw the seat-belt light come on. They were landing in Newark very soon. He sat up and thought ahead, to the logistics of getting a place to stay. Of getting his life back on track, without Isabel in it.

SARI COULD BARELY MOVE. Her back felt like shredded meat. It hurt even to breathe. Some doctor she didn't know had given her injections, after which he'd cleaned the deep wounds and sutured some of them. Apparently he'd done the same to Merrie, poor Merrie, who'd tried to save her.

Darwin had stayed at home while his daughters were healing from the effects of his brutality. He didn't want to take the chance that they might be tempted to call the sheriff or an attorney.

He paused beside Sari's bed. She was too sick to say much, but he reminded her that Paul could still meet with an unexpected accident if she dared to say anything about what had happened to her.

Until that minute, she'd seriously thought about calling someone. It would have been difficult, since he'd taken away the phone in her room and her cell phone, her computer and her iPad.

He'd done the same to Merrie.

She wanted not to care what happened to Paul. He'd lied to her, left her without even a word. But there were years of companionship behind her pain. Paul had been part of her life since she was a senior in high school. She still cared about him. And her father knew it.

Days after the brutal beating, Mandy came home. They'd been warned about telling her. She could easily disappear, Darwin had told them with a cold smile. He'd done it before. He knew how to make a suspicious death look like an accident and he'd gotten away with it. He was fairly sure that even if Isabel didn't care about Paul, she did care about Mandy. It would be enough to stop her from telling anyone what he'd done.

Sari knew that Cash Grier wouldn't mind how much money her father had; he'd go after him in a heartbeat if he knew what the man had done to his daughters. But the threat of losing poor Mandy was enough, without the reminder that Paul could also be "disappeared."

She hated herself for caring what happened to Paul after what he'd done to her. She might have risked it, if that was the only threat. But sweet Mandy was irreplaceable. She didn't dare call her father's bluff.

So she told her professors that she'd been in an accident and would miss a few days of classes. She got permission to use her cell phone, in her father's presence, and asked a classmate to take notes for her in each of her classes. The cell phone was taken away from her afterward.

Mandy was told that the girls had been in a car wreck, but that a private physician had taken care of them. They were careful not to let her see their backs.

The physician came a few days after Mandy returned, to remove the sutures. Darwin reminded the girls about what would happen to Mandy if they talked, and he left on another mysterious trip. Isabel went back to law school with a dead heart. Merrie painted strange, violent subjects. Mandy cooked and cleaned and worried, because it seemed that everything had changed in her absence.

CHAPTER SEVEN

THREE YEARS PASSED. Sari graduated from law school, with Merrie and Mandy in attendance. The girls' father had been gone for several weeks on some private business. When he came home, he'd searched through his desk for papers he couldn't find and accused the girls of taking them.

They'd denied it. He had Morris check the security cameras, which showed a telephone repairman in Darwin's study. Except there was nothing wrong with the phone. Morris checked and the phone company hadn't sent anybody out.

Darwin had gone out, cursing and raving mad. He'd come home quiet and worried and hadn't spoken to the girls at all. Sari hadn't mentioned her graduation ceremony to him. She didn't frankly care if he attended or not.

The dean handed her diploma to her, shook her hand, and she went to Mandy and Merrie to have photos taken with her iPhone and candid shots with her college friends who had also graduated. There were no close friends. Darwin made sure of it.

Nobody mentioned that Darwin didn't attend. They didn't discuss it in the limo, either, because they didn't trust Morris. He wasn't like Paul, who shared things with them and protected them. He was Darwin's man all the way. If he overheard anything, he'd go straight to his boss with it.

But back home, Sari went into Merrie's room with a small device a classmate had helped her obtain. He'd taught her how to use it, too. She turned it on before she spoke.

"What's that?" Merrie asked.

"A jammer," Sari said coldly. "It keeps bugs from listening or recording us. I overheard something."

"What? Where?" Merrie asked worriedly.

Sari sat down on the bed with her. "One of my classmates is going with the FBI when he graduates. His older brother is a special agent in Houston. He said that some millionaire from Comanche Wells has his fingers in a statewide money-laundering operation with ties to organized crime."

Merrie drew in a breath. "There are only two millionaires in Comanche Wells, and I don't think Jason Pendleton would ever…!"

"He wouldn't," Sari cut her off. "It's our father. From what I heard, I'm sure of it." She leaned forward. "They say that he's working with some woman with ties to the federal government, that she has access to confidential information."

"Oh, no," Merrie said heavily. "It's got to be that woman he keeps," she added bitterly.

"It must be," Sari agreed. "Morris doesn't say much, but he let slip the other day that he had to drive Daddy over to her house urgently, because she'd phoned him and made threats."

Merrie's pretty face drew up. "Unwise, making threats to Daddy."

Sari nodded. She toyed with the hem of her skirt. "Life is so hard."

Merrie put a hand over hers. "You still miss Paul, don't you?"

Sari's face hardened. "Why would I miss a man who made me out to be a slut, who left without a single word? What happened to us was his fault. It was all his fault!"

"You loved him."

Sari closed her eyes and shivered. "I thought I did," she confessed. "But he had a wife and child and he didn't tell me. He let me go on hoping, wishing..." She stopped and bit her lip. "He didn't seem like that kind of man."

"No, he didn't." Merrie cocked her head. "You know, Paul was very proud. He wouldn't even let us buy him a coffee when we were in San Antonio. He paid for his, and for ours."

Sari blinked. "Yes, he used to do that."

"He would have told you," Merrie insisted. "I don't know why he said that to Daddy, but I think I have some idea. Morris was talking to that new man Daddy hired, and he said that any man who married one of us would be set for life. Maybe he said that to Paul. It would have hurt his pride, if another man even thought he was getting involved with one of us. And, sorry, but the way you looked at Paul was pretty easy to read. You were crazy about him. And everyone could tell."

Sari just grimaced. "I didn't know."

"You were in love. Of course you didn't know," she said softly. "But he was a proud man. He knew Daddy would never let you marry him…"

"He was married already," Sari interrupted, and her face closed up. "Married, with a little girl…!" She got up from the bed and wrapped her arms around her chest. "You can't imagine how ashamed I was. I felt like a potential home wrecker. Not that many women care anymore about breaking up families," she added bitterly. "You wouldn't believe the stories I hear from some of my classmates. And when I mention that we go to church, they laugh. They laugh, like it's a joke to believe in a higher power!"

Merrie got up and hugged her sister. "I just do what I please and ignore what other people think. You should, too. You can't go through life worrying about other people's opinions."

Sari smiled at her. "You're so open, Merrie. You love the whole world. After what we've been through here, you should be like me, cynical and cold and calculating."

"You're only like that on the outside, so you won't be hurt anymore," Merrie said sadly. "Inside, you're the same marshmallow you always were."

"Lies."

Merrie grinned.

Sari drew in a long breath and let it out. "Well, I'd better get my clothes laid out for tomorrow. Big day. My first day in court!"

"My sister, Perry Mason," Merrie said proudly.

"Wrong gender."

Merrie just grinned again.

"Ah, well, I might actually do some good. Mr. Kemp is just letting me observe at first, so that I can get the feel of court cases. I will get to help with voir dire, though."

"You're going to be famous one day, and everybody will be impressed when I tell them I'm your sister!"

Sari was looking at a painting on the wall, one Merrie had done of her when she was younger and madly in love with Paul. Her eyes in the painting were so full of love and hope that they made her want to cry.

"You're the one who'll be famous," Sari corrected. "Merrie, you have such genius in your hands. Your portraits are like photographs!"

"Aw, shucks," Merrie said, mimicking what Mandy said when she was praised.

"I'm not kidding. You should take some of your canvases up to San Antonio to an art dealer and talk about having a one-woman show."

"I could never do that," Merrie said gently. "I'm too shy. I'd fumble and stammer and they'd just put me on the sidewalk and shut the door."

"I very much doubt it."

"Besides, Daddy wouldn't like it," Merrie added. She shivered. "What are we going to do?" she added, almost in a panic. "Daddy said that we need to think about getting married. He's got some prince picked out for you."

"He can pick out all the men he likes. I'm not getting married. Ever."

"He wants somebody to inherit Graylings," Merrie said sadly.

"He can adopt a son and give him everything, for all I care. I've lived in a golden cage all my life, twenty-five years," she said with growing anger. "I'm tired of not having a life!"

"So am I," Merrie said. "But bad things happen to people who go against Daddy."

Sari turned. "Maybe it's time bad things happened to Daddy," she said shortly.

"What do you mean?"

"I mean, somebody came into the house and walked off with some confidential information and Daddy went ballistic. Don't you wonder what they got?" she asked. "He's got his fingers in some nasty things, and not everybody is scared of him, despite his millions."

"He'll never get caught, no matter what he does," Merrie said miserably. "We'll be shoved at titled Europeans and our lives will never be our own, no matter what we do."

"No," Sari replied. "No. We're getting out. One way or another."

"Whatever you say," Merrie replied. "Just don't let Daddy hear you say that," she added with a whimsical smile.

BLAKE KEMP CALLED Sari into his office after her first day in court. He closed the door, hit the intercom button and told his secretary to hold all his calls.

Then he motioned Sari into a chair and sat down behind his desk.

"You want to know how I did such a magnificent job at voir dire, I just know it," Sari said with bright, laughing eyes.

But Blake didn't smile. "A woman was killed just outside Jacobsville three days ago," he said.

"Oh. And we're prosecuting the killer?"

"They don't have a suspect," he said coldly. "The woman was trampled, supposedly by two of her own horses. The coroner doing the autopsy said that it was probably an accident, but the injuries were suspicious. He called in Hayes Carson."

"Our sheriff," she said, nodding.

"Hayes thinks it's a homicide and he's proceeding in that direction." He cocked his head, his gray eyes narrowing. "You won't like what I'm going to say next."

She swallowed and looked around the room. She held up a hand and brought her jammer out of her purse. She put it on his desk and turned it on.

"You think someone could have bugged my office?" he exclaimed. "I'm the district attorney!"

"My father has men who would dare anything," she said. "I know the woman who died. It was on the radio. Her name is Betty Leeds. She's been involved with my father for years. They say she's his mistress. I don't know for sure. She has the coldest eyes I've ever seen, and her meetings with him were always clandestine." She paused. "Some man posing as a telephone repairman took some files out of Daddy's office. He went crazy. He had surveillance tapes." She paused again. "Daddy left the house rather suddenly three nights ago, and he didn't have Morris drive him, as he always does. He drove himself. I think he went to see the woman. When he came home he was sweating and nervous and his head was hurting. It usually hurts when he does something violent to people."

"Something you know for a fact, Miss Grayling?" Blake asked.

"I wouldn't dare admit it, even if it's true, Mr. Kemp."

He measured her proud look with the faint traces of fear in her eyes and drew a conclusion. He leaned back in his chair. "Well, even if he's involved, we'd have to have an investigator go out to inspect the car he was driving, and before we could do that, we'd have to have probable cause. The fact that he knew the woman and she died violently doesn't give us enough evidence to get a search warrant out of any judge in Jacobs County."

"I know that. But I might be able to help."

He read the growing unease in her face even as she offered. "No," he said after a minute. "If he'd been involved with the woman for a long time and he killed her, it speaks of a total lack of emotion on his part."

"You don't know the half of it," she said under her breath.

"I don't imagine I do. So you steer clear. But you may need to talk to Hayes Carson. I can bring him over here on the pretext of discussing a court case and you can come in with your sturdy little spy gadget and we'll have a discussion."

She grinned. "I had a friend whose brother was in the FBI. He taught me about covert surveillance."

"Nice. But I have Cash Grier right downtown and

he's even the most dangerous criminal's worst nightmare. He also has friends with mob connections," he added, "although I certainly wouldn't condone having him contact them."

"I'm sure they're all legit," she drawled, her blue eyes twinkling. "One of them was Marcus Carrera. He was the epitome of a dangerous crime boss, but he got out, and now he and his wife have two little boys."

He chuckled. "They still live in the Bahamas, although she comes home to visit occasionally. She's from here."

"I heard that."

He stared at her. "If your father has ties to this case, it will go hard for him. The FBI will certainly pursue the case, since it involves a federal agent. I understand that they have someone going over files right now to look for evidence of money laundering."

"That would be Secret Service…"

He shook his head. "That's tampering with money. This is hiding money from the government, cleaning it so that underworld elements can get to it legally. There's talk that over a billion dollars has been funneled through the operation. Big money. Somebody is going to do time for that. A lot of time. And if murder was involved…"

Sari's face paled. She was remembering something her father had said when he'd beaten her and Merrie.

"What is it?"

She bit her lower lip. "Daddy admitted once that he'd killed someone and made it look like an accident."

"Did you ask him anything about it?" he asked.

She smiled jerkily. "I was bleeding pretty badly at the time. He'd just beaten me and Merrie..." Her eyes closed on his murderous expression. "You mustn't ever let that get out. He'd kill us..."

"Not in my town," Blake said coldly. "Not if I have to get help from Eb Scott's whole damned operation. I promise you that."

She felt relief, but only for a minute. "Mr. Kemp, he's richer than you realize, and he can buy people."

"He won't buy me."

"Of course not. But he can buy European talent. Do you know what I mean?" she added. "Plus, you have a wife and children."

She let the insinuation sink in.

"So that's how he does it?" he asked coldly.

She nodded. "Everyone has a weakness that can be exploited. He keeps me and Merrie by threatening our housekeeper, Mandy. She has a brother who works for somebody in the mob up north. Daddy keeps her in line by threatening her brother." She closed her eyes. "Fear is a powerful incentive to keep quiet."

Blake was pensive. He did know what evil men could accomplish. He'd have to make certain that Isabel and Merrie were safe, before he acted.

"Surely your own father wouldn't kill you," he said shortly.

"I wouldn't bet the farm on that," she said. She leaned forward. "There have been rumors for years that he killed our mother," she added with emotion in her voice. "I don't know. Merrie and I weren't home when it happened. But Dr. Coltrain thought her death was suspicious. He insisted on a complete autopsy, but he was called out of town and when he got back, the coroner listed her death as natural causes. Dr. Coltrain was furious, but he couldn't do a thing about it."

"If Coltrain thought it was suspicious, it was," Blake replied.

Sari drew in a breath. It was such a relief just to have his confirmation, just to have any of it out in the open.

"You had a security chief who was formerly with the FBI," Blake said suddenly, curious at the way Sari's face flushed. "Would he know anything about your father's dealings and would he be willing to talk?"

"Paul left three years ago," she said coldly. "None of us have heard from him since. Nor do we care to," she added when he started to speak. "I would walk on the other side of the street just to make sure I didn't have to speak to him."

He let out a whistle. "I see."

"When do you want me to talk to the sheriff?"

"I'll try to get him over here tomorrow."

"Thanks."

He glanced at the device on the desk. "And be sure you bring that gadget with you tomorrow."

She smiled. "Yes, sir."

CHAPTER EIGHT

SARI FINISHED UP at her desk and called Morris to drive her home. Her colleague Glory Ramirez was curious about the woman's closed expression.

"You've been morose all day," she said to Sari. "Can I help?"

Sari was touched. She smiled. "I'm just tired. I'm not used to standing on my feet all day," she added with a grin. "But thanks. I mean it. I'm not used to people being concerned for me. Well, except for my sister. And Mandy. She's our housekeeper."

"I don't believe that." The other woman chuckled.

It was pretty much the truth, just the same.

"We're having a birthday party for Mr. Kemp tomorrow night at Barbara's Cafe," she said suddenly. "My husband and half the government agents in Jacobs County will be there. Don't you want to come?"

Sari smiled sadly. "I would love to. But I can't."

"You never go out. You never date. I don't mean to get personal, but could I ask why?"

"I'm down on men, that's all."

The older woman sobered. "I see."

"Life happens," Sari replied, smiling. "Besides, I have all these files to go through for you," she added. "Do you really want me to put them off to eat a buffet dinner and dance with some man whose name I don't even know?"

Glory laughed. "I guess not. But you really should get out and have fun. The Fourth of July is coming up fast," she added. "We'll have concerts in the park and dancing…"

"I love concerts," she said.

"Me, too." She leaned closer. "And we get a whole three-day holiday weekend! I can play with my son. Rodrigo and I are still amazed that we even have him. He's such a joy!"

Sari would never have a child, or a husband. But she smiled and said something appropriate in response.

She had no holidays in her poor heart. She was dead inside. She only went through the motions of living since Paul's defection. "Well, there's Morris," she said, glancing out at the street where the immaculate black stretch limo was pulling up to the curb. "I have to go. See you tomorrow."

"You lucky devil," the woman said, shaking her head. "You get to ride around in stretch limos all the time."

Sari laughed. "And you ride around in a racing green Jaguar XK," she said with pursed lips. "You could ride in stretch limos if you liked."

"I guess so," Glory said, smiling gently. "Jason and Gracie took care of me until I married, and Rodrigo's family was very wealthy. We're luckier than most, to have money at a time when most people can barely pay the bills at all."

"All the money in the world won't buy happiness," Sari said wistfully.

The other woman gave her a curious stare. "No, it won't. But it makes misery easier to bear," she added with a wicked grin.

Sari laughed. "Just the same, you can ride in the limo with me whenever you like," she added with twinkling blue eyes.

"I heard that," their paralegal, Tera Caldwell, broke in. "How about me?" she asked. "I drive a ten-year-old Ford with a straight stick shift. How pathetic is that?"

Sari chuckled. "Okay. I'll take you out to lunch in it one day."

"Really? You would?"

"I really would. Friday?"

"Oh, yes, Friday. I'll bring my camera!" Tera enthused. "Thanks!"

"You're welcome. But just don't post pictures on Facebook," she pleaded. "My father would be upset about it. He…values his privacy."

"I've heard that. No problem. Thanks for the offer!"

Sari laughed. "You're very welcome. See you tomorrow."

"So long."

"That was nice," Glory said when the paralegal was gone. "She struggles just to pay for gas."

"I like her," Sari replied. "I've heard that she spent the night in the law library once trying to find a legal precedent for Mr. Kemp. She couldn't make search strings work for what she needed online, so she did it the hard way, with real law books."

"Yes, she did," Glory acknowledged. "He won the

case, thanks to her legwork. She's like a bloodhound when she's on the trail of something."

"Well, see you later."

"Have a good evening," Glory said gently.

Sari just smiled.

SARI WORRIED ABOUT the possibility that her father might be arrested and charged with murder. Despite everything he'd done in the past, he was still her father. But she was an officer of the court now. She couldn't afford to overlook a murder, even if her father had committed it.

When she got home from work, he was in his study, yelling at someone on the telephone. She couldn't make out what he was saying, and she didn't want to get caught eavesdropping. She put her purse and coat down and went into the kitchen, where Merrie was helping Mandy with supper.

"Something smells really good," Sari said with forced brightness.

"It's liver and onions," Merrie said with an evil smile.

"Liar." Mandy chuckled. "It's that Sussex Stewed Steak you love so much, the kind that King Henry VIII liked, if history got the recipe right. It's in that medieval cookbook you girls got me for Christmas last year."

"A five-hundred-year-old recipe," Sari mused. She sat down at the table. "Well, maybe we won't start spouting Tudor history when we eat it."

"And lemon meringue pie for dessert," Merrie

sighed, nodding toward it in the heavy plastic container on the counter.

"It sounds lovely."

"You look tired," Merrie noted. "Hard day?"

"Yes," Sari said, and didn't dare say why. "I've got a lot to learn about the routine in the DA's office. I'm the new kid."

"Glory Barnes—excuse me, Ramirez—works for Mr. Kemp," Mandy added. "She'll steer you right. She worked for the San Antonio district attorney's office before she married Rodrigo and moved down here."

"She never had to work at all, since she was an adoptive child of the Pendletons," Merrie recalled. "Jason Pendleton's stepsister, in fact."

"Like Gracie, but he married Gracie," Mandy recalled. "They live on the ranch down here in Comanche Wells with their son and daughter."

"Children must be nice," Sari said, and then remembered Paul's little girl and winced.

"I suppose," Mandy said with a sad smile. "I was never able to have any while my husband was alive. But I have you two," she added, her eyes twinkling.

"And we have you," Merrie said. She hugged Mandy. "I don't know what we'd do without you."

"That's the truth," Sari said. "In fact…"

"Sari, I want to talk to you," Darwin Grayling interrupted curtly. "In my study. Now."

"Yes, sir." She got up automatically and followed him, not daring to meet the curious glances of Mandy and her sister. She knew things they didn't. She had to hope she could keep her nerve, because she knew the subject at hand was going to be her job.

Darwin closed the door.

"Have you heard anything about an investigation into Betty Leeds's death?" he asked abruptly.

Her eyes widened. She managed to look shocked. "Betty Leeds? The woman who used to come here with you? She's dead?" she exclaimed.

He stared at her. Trying to size her up, she thought bitterly.

"Yes, that Betty. Have you heard anything?" he insisted.

"No, I haven't," she lied with a straight face. "Why would they investigate it? Was she murdered or something?"

"No," he said heavily. "She was killed by two of her horses, when she was trying to get them out of the barn during that storm that hit three days ago. It was an accident. A terrible accident."

"Oh. What a terrible thing," Sari said.

"Yes. Terrible." He pulled out a handkerchief and mopped his forehead. He was sweating. "I went to see her... I found her..." He hesitated. "She'd been dead for a while, I think. She was cold. I called the sheriff's department myself."

"That must have been difficult for you," she said.

"Very difficult. I was fond of her. We'd been together for a long time." He drew in a long breath and turned to Sari. "If you hear anything, anything at all at work, you're to tell me at once, do you understand?"

"Yes. But surely they wouldn't need to investigate an accidental death. I mean, beyond the autopsy and having the investigator verify the cause of death," she said, looking surprised.

"I don't know," he bit off. "I have no idea. It's that sheriff, Hayes Carson," he added angrily. "He was a very young deputy sheriff when your mother died," he said. "He thought I'd done something to her." His face tightened and his hand went to his head. He winced. "Ridiculous! I talked to his boss and that lunatic idea was put to rest," he said coldly. "Now he's the county sheriff. He's got a little power and it's gone to his head!"

Sari's heart jumped. She'd heard once that her mother's death was suspicious. She hadn't doubted that her father was capable of violence. She herself had been subject to it, like poor Merrie. But she schooled her face to show nothing of her inner turmoil.

"I'm sure he was just young and overenthusiastic," she said.

"He's just as unreasonable now," he said angrily. "But he's not going to do anything to me. I can take care of it. I know people. I can have someone from Europe come over and handle it."

She remembered that Hayes and his wife had just had a little girl. She knew what her father was talking about. He'd already told her that he'd committed murder. If he'd also killed his paramour, he wouldn't hesitate to go after Sheriff Carson's family.

"It's routine to investigate a sudden death of any sort," she said, hoping she sounded nonchalant. "You remember when old Miss Murphy down the road had a stroke and died on her front porch? They still had to investigate and do an autopsy to make sure there was no foul play. It's just routine."

"Routine?" He looked hunted as he turned to her. "You're sure?"

"Of course," she lied. "It's nothing to concern yourself with. I'm sure they know it was accidental by now."

He drew in another breath. He rubbed his head.

"Another headache?" she asked.

"Yes. They get worse…" He stopped and turned to her. "You can go. By the way, I have visitors coming next month. A Middle Eastern prince with ties to the British monarchy." He smiled coldly. "We have business dealings together. It will be a fine merger." His eyes dared her to say a word.

She didn't dare. There was too much at stake. "I see," was all she said.

"You're old enough to marry."

"I do have a job…"

"Expendable." He cut her off. "It's just something to keep you busy. You'll learn court manners from his mother and sister. And the money will stay in the family."

She didn't know what to say to that, so she said nothing.

He waved her away. "I won't be in for supper. Tell Mandy. And remember what I said, about anything you hear at work," he added with a cold threat in his voice.

"Of course, Daddy," she said, forcing a smile.

She opened the door and left him. She felt as if she were shaking from her head to her toes, but she maintained her poise all the way into the kitchen.

"What did he want?" Merrie asked covertly.

"Nothing," she lied. "He just wanted to know how I was liking my job. Oh, Mandy, he won't be in for supper, so can we all eat in here?"

"Suits me," Mandy said. "I hate setting the table in the dining room. I'll get the plates!"

WHEN THEY WERE sure their father had gone, Sari pulled out her jammer and activated it.

"Just in case there are bugs," she told the other women. "Daddy said that he found that Leeds woman dead at her home three days ago, trampled to death by two of her horses. He called the sheriff's department himself."

"I heard about it on the radio," Merrie replied solemnly, "but I didn't want to say anything."

"She died?" Mandy asked, shocked. She bit her lip. "Convenient timing."

Sari's heart jumped. "What do you mean?"

"You can't repeat this," Mandy said.

"You know we won't," Sari told her, and Merrie nodded her agreement.

She leaned forward. "My brother has a friend. His cousin's with the Bureau. They're investigating a money-laundering operation that has ties to organized crime…"

"I know," Sari said heavily. "Mr. Kemp told me this afternoon." She winced. "He says they think our father is involved."

"Well, the Leeds woman worked for the government, and what my brother told me is that she was an agent assigned to investigate money laundering in south Texas. But she switched sides and started working for your father. She was helping him process the funds by covering up the transactions in collusion with a bank employee at one of the larger national banks in San Antonio. But she got cold feet, or something Mr. Darwin did spooked her, because my brother says she suddenly went to the US attorney in San Antonio and spilled her guts."

"Oh, dear," Sari said, grimacing.

"Mr. Darwin found out," Mandy continued. "That's why she had an accident."

"They'll call in the FBI," Sari said. "And the Department of Homeland Security. A federal employee's death involves government intervention. You can bet your life that Hayes Carson has already called them."

Merrie bit her lip. "What will they do to Daddy?"

"They'll seize any illegal funds he has and arrest him," Sari replied.

"He'll buy off anybody he has to," Mandy said.

"He's already threatened to call in outside talent to take care of Sheriff Carson," Sari told them.

"No!" Merrie exclaimed. "He and his wife have a little girl. And they have her little stepbrother and stepsister...!"

Sari held up a hand. "I won't let that happen, no matter what I have to do," she said. Her face was very pale. She swallowed. "Any way it ends, it's going to be a mess."

"There's something more," Mandy said quietly.

"What?"

"Betty Leeds has a son. He's Merrie's age," Mandy said. "And unstable. He's been in and out of facilities. They say he loves his mother insanely. She doted on him, spoiled him, bought him things. In fact, they say the reason she went in with your father in the first place was that she wanted to have enough money to leave for her son's care, if she died."

"She never seemed that sort of woman," Merrie said. "She was incredibly rude to us."

"She didn't like girls, apparently," Mandy said. "But she loved her son. She took care of him. He was in and out of therapy for years and there was talk of an attempted murder charge once. Now she's gone and he's on his own. No other relatives."

"Poor guy," Sari murmured.

"Poor us, if they put Daddy in jail," Merrie added. "Nobody will be safe. He can buy anybody. He can hunt anybody." She shivered.

"We'll be okay," Sari said. "If it comes down to it, the authorities will look out for us. And we can hire some people to protect us."

"With what?" Merrie asked.

Sari grimaced. Merrie was right. They had no means of their own, no money that they had access to. Darwin had made sure that his daughters were kept poor, so that they couldn't leave him or ask for help to get away from him.

"We're stuck," Merrie concluded. "We can't get away. Ever."

Sari drew in a breath. She didn't mention the Middle Eastern prince. Rather than marry a stranger, she'd run away, even if she had to hide at Eb Scott's place and beg work there. Then she laughed. Fat chance about that. She couldn't even shoot a gun.

"What's funny?" Merrie asked.

"I was thinking maybe I could hire on at Eb Scott's place," Sari laughed. "Now I'm just getting silly."

"We could learn to be mercs," Merrie mused. "I'll bet we'd be the terror of the Texas plains."

"No doubt about that, if somebody gave you guns," Mandy said and gave them a mock shudder. "There wouldn't be a streetlight left in Comanche Wells!"

"I could shoot if I wanted to," Sari said haughtily.

"Honey, you couldn't. Trust me," Mandy said. "Remember the slingshot?"

"I'm trying to forget it," Sari returned, wincing.

"It was only two windows." Merrie defended her sister.

"I might have learned to aim properly if you hadn't taken it away from me," Sari said with a mischievous glance at Mandy.

"Or not. Okay, there it is." Mandy indicated the casserole and accompanying dishes she placed on the table. "Dig in!"

HAYES CARSON CAME into Blake Kemp's office the next afternoon, shook hands with Blake and Sari, and took a seat, crossing his long legs. Sari had the jammer on Mr. Kemp's desk, turned on, just in case.

"I hear you might know something about a case I'm working on," Hayes said to Sari.

"I'm afraid I do," she replied. "My father told me that he found Mrs. Leeds and called in the police about the accident."

"That's true," Hayes said. His face hardened. "Except that it was no accident. Dr. Copper Coltrain, our county medical examiner, performed the autopsy last night. He said that her injuries were not compatible with such an accident. She was beaten with a blunt instrument, most likely a tire iron found propped against the wall at the scene of the crime. He's put it down as a homicide and the coroner is calling an inquest. That means your department will be assigned investigative duties as well, with an eye to local charges. Not that federal charges won't supersede those, if they're made."

Sari leaned forward, sick to her stomach. "So, now what?" she asked miserably.

"So now we gather evidence. Since Mrs. Leeds was a federal employee, the Bureau is sending down an agent from San Antonio to aid with the investigation."

"But Garon Grier lives here…"

"He's giving a class at the FBI Academy in Quantico," Hayes replied, "and he won't be back for a while. In fact, you might know the agent they're sending," he added, watching her. "It's a man named Paul Fiore. I believe he once worked for your father."

Every ounce of blood drained out of Sari's face. Her hands on the chair she was sitting in were clenched so tight on the arms that her fingers were white.

Hayes's eyes narrowed. "He didn't want the case," he added, his voice softening when he noted her violent reaction to the news. "He said that there were some personal issues involved. But they didn't have another agent available. So he's coming tomorrow."

"I won't talk to him," she said in a driven tone. "I won't see him. I'll give any information I have to you," she told Hayes, "and you can relay it. But there

is no way that any member of my household will even
speak to Mr. Fiore."

Hayes wasn't surprised. He just nodded. "He said
that."

"We'll work around it," Blake assured her. "It's
all right, Sari."

She was breathing as if she'd been running a mar-
athon. Her face was flushed now, her body so tense
that it felt trapped.

"Sari, we'll handle it," Blake repeated. He looked
concerned. "Are you all right?"

She wasn't all right. She'd never be all right again.
Paul was married. He had a wife and child. He'd be-
trayed her. Her father had beaten her. Because of Paul.
Because she'd loved him...

"Sari!" Blake repeated.

"I'm sorry, what?" She was buried in the past, re-
living the trauma. She pulled herself back to the present. She felt her heartbeat shaking her. She could see
each beat in her eyes, behind her eyelids if she closed
them. A gray static had already started to fill one eye.
She groaned and put her hand to her eye. The aura
led to throbbing pain.

Both men were watching her, but Sheriff Carson
seemed puzzled. Blake wasn't.

"Tera!" Blake called.

His paralegal came running. "Yes, sir?"

"Go rummage in Sari's purse and bring her migraine capsules and a bottle of water. Hurry."

"Migraine capsules...?" Hayes asked.

Blake grimaced. "I have two assistants who both
have cardiovascular issues," he explained to Hayes

with a smile. "Glory has high blood pressure and Sari gets migraines. It's okay. As long as Sari and Glory keep their meds handy," he added.

"Sorry, boss," Sari said, swallowing hard. "I only get them once in a while. But I've had a lot on my mind lately. I guess that's what brought it on."

"I know that."

Tera was back with the pills and the water. She handed the prescription bottle to Sari, who shook out a capsule and swallowed it down with water from the bottle. She took a long breath. "It will work. It just takes a little while. Sorry again for all the drama," she told Blake.

He smiled gently. "No need for apologies. But keep up with those meds. I can't afford to lose you. Not many people line up to do this job," he added with a grin.

She laughed. "I guess not. I applied when I started law school and the job was still open when I got here."

"Not quite," he mused. "We had Barkley White working for us for a while. But then he decided that Austin was a better place for an up-and-coming lawyer. He's working for the Hart boys' brother Simon, our state attorney general."

"Nice job," she said.

"Don't you dare," he returned shortly. "Don't you even think about going to Austin. This is a great job. You're doing valuable work. Local crime will be stemmed forever because you work here," he added.

She grinned as she began to calm down. "Actually, it'll be reduced forever because of him—" she pointed at Hayes "—and Cash Grier."

"They're good," Blake conceded. "But I'm the best DA in Texas. You remember that," he told Sari, who chuckled.

"Yes, sir, I will," she promised. The pain finally began to ease. She relaxed visibly.

"Do you know where your father is right now?" Hayes asked Sari.

"I'm sorry, I don't," she replied. She noticed the look Hayes was giving her. "I really don't," she added. "Sheriff Carson, we loved our mother very much. You've surely heard the gossip about her death being suspicious?"

"I have," he replied. "In fact, I was involved at the time. I'd just started with the sheriff's department. I never thought her death was accidental."

She stared at him. "I don't think it was, either. If you knew my father, you wouldn't doubt that he's capable of murder." She swallowed. She didn't want to admit it, but she was going to have to. It had bearing on the matter at hand. "You see, my sister and I have been the victims of...well, of beatings, since we were in grammar school. Anything could set him off. Our mother pulled him off me when I was ten. I'd left a wet towel on the floor of my bathroom. He hit me..." She broke off, swallowing, aware of the furious looks on the men. "He liked perfect order, everywhere. It wasn't too many years after that when our mother died. She fell and hit her head. So he said."

Hayes winced. "Good God, why didn't you tell somebody about what he was doing to you?"

"I tried," she said. "But Daddy had us watched 24/7. We're still watched," she added worriedly. "By tonight, he'll know that I talked to you." She wrapped her arms around her body. "He'll be wild..."

"We'll get some protection for you, before tonight," Hayes told her firmly. "He'll never hit you again."

She fought back tears. It had been so long that she and Merrie had lived with the pain and the terror. "We've been like prisoners all our lives," she said tautly. "He wouldn't let us get jobs, or earn money, so we'd have no means to get away from him. Mama left us half of the house and its contents, but he's made sure we can't claim them by tying them up as collateral for loans. And in case that didn't work, he threatened us with people we loved." She looked up. "He knows you have a family, Sheriff Carson. That's how he'll try to stop this investigation. You must take precautions..."

Hayes just smiled. "I have two of Eb Scott's men living in the house with us."

"Oh," she said.

"And by tonight, you'll have two of them guarding you."

"Daddy will have them arrested for trespassing, or he'll have Morris or one of his men shoot them," she worried aloud.

"No, he won't," Hayes said flatly.

"I don't understand."

"You will," Hayes said. "For now, do what you normally do. When you go home, you'll have company."

"How will I know who they are?"

"Oh, you'll know," Hayes said amusedly.

"Whatever you say," Sari replied. "Poor Merrie. She can't even leave the house except to go to art classes. When Mandy goes to get groceries, she's followed. We're always followed."

"It will end," Hayes told her. "I promise you, it will all end soon."

She swallowed. "I hope so," was as far as she'd go.

THAT AFTERNOON, SHE TOLD her coworkers goodbye and went outside to get into the limo. Morris was standing, dumbfounded, beside two tall, muscular men dressed in camo and carrying small automatic weapons.

"What the hell is going on, Miss Grayling?" Morris asked.

"Retribution," Sari said. She looked at the two men and smiled. "Thanks," she said quietly.

They only nodded. They opened the door for her, giving Morris a look that sent him quickly to the driver's seat, and then they climbed in on the seat facing her.

She didn't speak all the way home. She worried. Her companions were equally quiet. She worried about what the authorities were going to do to her father. But she worried more about what her father was going to do to them. They were underestimating his ability to protect himself. He had a fortune and he knew how to intimidate people at the highest levels. Once he saw her protectors here, he was going to go ballistic. She dreaded the thought of what he might do to her, and to poor Merrie.

And then there was Paul. What in the world was he doing back in Texas? He'd left without a word three years ago, gone back to his family up north. Had he brought them with him?

At least he knew that Sari wanted nothing to do with him, that none of them wanted him around. Maybe they'd have another agent, perhaps the one with Homeland Security, question her and Merrie and Mandy. She didn't even want to see Paul ever again.

She thought of the deep scars on her back, still felt the blows, the pain, the horror of her father's attack. Because of Paul. Because he'd gone to her father and accused her of coming on to him, a married man.

She would never have let him touch her if she'd known he was married. It made her sick, remembering how much she'd loved him, the dreams she'd built around a future with him. Even if it had been unrealistic, the dreams had been sweet. He'd held her and kissed her, hungered for her. Probably because he was missing his wife, she thought bitterly.

Paul had turned her whole life into one long misery. She didn't want to see him. It would bring back all the memories that still tormented her.

"Mr. Grayling isn't going to like this," Morris said as he parked the car, glancing through the open window at Sari's companions.

"You know what, Morris?" she asked coldly. "I don't give a damn!"

MORRIS ACTUALLY CAUGHT his breath. He'd never heard her talk like that, in all the years he'd worked for the boss. Now he wondered if he'd lose his job, because he didn't call and warn Mr. Grayling about these guys. But how could he? They carried small automatic weapons, and he had no doubt that they knew how to use them. Maybe he could use that as an excuse. He did wonder what Miss Grayling was up to. The boss was going to be mad. Really mad.

SARI WENT INTO the house, accompanied by her two bodyguards. Merrie, coming down the stairs, just stopped and gaped at them.

"Where's Daddy?" Sari asked coldly.

Merrie took a minute to compose herself. "He came home and went into the study and made some phone calls. That was before they got here."

"They?" Sari asked.

"Yes. The FBI, Homeland Security, Mr. Kemp and Sheriff Carson and a handful of deputy sheriffs. They arrested Daddy on suspicion of murder and took him away."

Sari caught her breath. Nobody had told her about it, and they surely knew. Did they think she'd warn her father?

"Who…?" Merrie asked worriedly, nodding toward Sari's companions.

"Eb Scott let us borrow them," Sari said, catching her breath. She looked up at them with a smile. "They're not going to let Daddy hurt us anymore."

"Well, only if you feed us," the broader one of the two men said, shrugging. "Eb starves us. We'd do almost anything for good food. And dessert," he added.

"Eb doesn't starve us," the taller one returned. "We had fried snake just last week."

The broader one made a face. "Living off the land isn't what it's cracked up to be. I had better food when I was stationed in Iraq."

"Sheep's eyes!" The taller one grimaced.

"Hey, they're good!" his companion objected. "It's an acquired taste."

"I could acquire a taste for pie, if you've got any." He nodded toward the girls.

Mandy came out of the kitchen and gaped at the two men dressed in camouflage. "Are you the A-Team?" she asked.

"Wrong generation," the broader one said with a grin. "We're the Avengers."

"Don't tell me," Mandy quipped. "You're Hawkeye and he's Captain America."

"I told you people would recognize us," the broader one told his companion with a grin.

The taller one just shook his head.

"If you feed them, they'll take care of us," Sari told the housekeeper.

"In that case, you can have pie. But only if you eat your peas and carrots first," Mandy said sternly.

"Beats snake any day," the broader one said.

"Sure beats sheep's eyes," the taller one said disdainfully.

"Come on in," Mandy invited.

"When did they take Daddy away?" Sari asked.

"About four o'clock this afternoon," Mandy said. She glanced around the table. "He'll make bail any minute and come through that door looking for blood."

"If he does, he'll find some," the taller of the visitors said grimly. "Nobody's hurting women on my watch."

"Mine, either," the other one added.

Sari smiled gently. "Thanks, guys."

"Thanks a lot," Merrie added. "It's been scary, living here. He's unpredictable and he hits us."

"He gets even, when people go against him," Sari worried aloud.

"So do we," the taller of the two said, and his face was dead serious when he said it.

"Don't worry," the broader one told them in a quiet tone. "We know what we're doing. The Feds briefed us. They're shorthanded, and they know Eb. We're sanctioned to do whatever we need to do to protect all of you."

"You don't know how grateful we are," Sari began.

The front door opened and slammed shut.

"Where are those damned girls!" Darwin Grayling roared.

CHAPTER NINE

SARI AND MERRIE JUMPED. The men got to their feet and slung their weapons. They turned as Darwin came through the door.

He stopped short at the sight of them. "What the hell are you doing in my home?" he demanded. "Get out!"

"You're within your rights to ask us to leave, sir," the taller one said. "But your daughters have asked us to stay."

"Tell him that's a lie, Isabel," he said to his eldest, daring her to argue.

She stared back at him. "It isn't. Merrie and I asked for protection. These gentlemen work for Eb Scott. He had them come home with us."

Darwin seemed stymied. He was shocked that Isabel would defy him.

"This is still my home," he began.

"And my home. And Merrie's and Mandy's," Sari said, gaining strength. "I will not live in fear any longer."

"Neither will I," Merrie said quietly.

"The Feds are asking about you, Daddy," Sari added. "They have a lot of questions for you to answer."

"You're all against me!" Darwin raged. "You want me in prison so you can spend my money! Well, you'll never get it. Never, do you hear me? I'll disinherit you both!"

"So what?" Sari asked. "It will beat living as a virtual prisoner for years."

"We can make our own money," Merrie agreed. "We don't need yours."

Darwin was absolutely shocked. He stared at them without a comeback. He blinked. "Then you can get out of my house!"

"Not today," Sari replied, regaining her wits. "Mother left us half ownership of the house. You may have all the money, but we have half the house and we aren't leaving. Neither are our bodyguards," she added.

Darwin clenched his fists at his hips. He was red in the face, absolutely raging. "People will regret ever having charged me in this matter. It was an accident. An accident! I called an ambulance. I called the law! I tried to save her!"

"You can tell that to your very expensive defense attorney, Daddy," Sari replied. "I'm sure he'll move mountains to prove your innocence."

"It will never go to trial," Darwin said coldly. "And you will regret what you've done today, Isabel. You will regret it bitterly."

He went upstairs into his bedroom and slammed the door.

Sari let out the breath she'd been holding. She was shaking. But she managed a smile. "First time," she said, when the men gave her curious looks.

"First time for what?" the taller one prodded.

"First time in my life I ever talked back to him." She laughed shakily. "It felt good."

"It did, didn't it?" Merrie seconded, smiling from a pale face. "Now all we have to do is keep him from killing us because we did it."

"Nobody's going to hurt you," the broader one said. His companion nodded. "Ever again. It will be all right. We promise."

THEIR FATHER WENT back out that night with Morris. The girls heard them talking, muffled speech that they didn't understand. The door slammed behind them and soon there was the sound of the limousine being started up and driven away.

Sari propped herself up on Merrie's bed. "He'll hurt us, if he can. He'll find a way to intimidate everybody connected with this."

"He's welcome to try," Merrie replied. "I don't think he'll get very far in Comanche Wells or Jacobsville. Not now. He's on the defensive, isn't he, for the first time. Even with the best attorney, he might not be able to beat a murder charge."

"I'll have to testify," Sari said miserably. "I saw him come in, the night the woman died, all upset and sweating, and his head hurting. I heard him say he'd gotten away with murder once, the night Paul left, when Daddy beat us."

"I heard it, too. I'll testify with you." Merrie hugged her. "If he disinherits us, I don't care," she said. "Oh, Sari, imagine being able to live without people following you all the time, without being locked up in a house and never let out to go to dances or concerts…!"

"I know." Sari hugged her back. "It would be worth making our own way in the world. I don't care about the money, either." She drew back. "And we still own half the house," she reminded her sister with a short laugh. "He can't really throw us out."

"If our bodyguards weren't here, he could do that, and much worse," Merrie reminded her. "What's he going to do now?" she worried. "Where do you think he went?"

"I don't know," Sari said. She drew in a long breath. "And I'm not sure I want to know."

In fact, Darwin Grayling was on his way to a secret meeting with two of his coconspirators, men who had helped him and Betty Leeds launder billions in revenue from gambling casinos and prostitution rackets in half a dozen states. If he went down, he was taking them all with him.

But it wouldn't come to that, he was certain of it. His overlords would have to save him, in order to save themselves. He wouldn't think of the other possibility, that of having his accounts suspended, held by the government while they tried to prove him guilty. If he was charged under the RICO statutes, his bail would be almost a billion dollars. Even Darwin Grayling would have had a problem coming up with that much cash. Racketeering was a federal crime of some magnitude and his arrest on suspicion of murder paled in comparison with the money laundering that could hold him accountable for what he'd sent his people out to do. He could go to prison for the rest of his life on those charges alone. If his assets were frozen, he could no longer hire men to take care of his enemies.

His blood ran cold at the thought of losing all that money, the accumulation of years of illegal enterprises. Betty Leeds had been most useful. But she'd betrayed him to the government in order to save herself. She should never have confessed it. One of the mobsters they dealt with had threatened her precious son, and she had to do it to save him. He was only misunderstood, he would never really hurt anyone, she'd exclaimed. She'd moved her private savings over to his accounts, just in time to save that part of her fortune from the Feds. Her son would be taken care of, even if the worst happened.

Darwin had showered her with an outpouring of rage. He'd touched his throbbing head and threatened fatal retribution. She tried to put him off. She claimed she wouldn't have turned the files over to the FBI except to save her son. She was sorry for Darwin, but he was much wealthier than she was, he could get attorneys to prove him innocent. Everything would be all right, she was sure of it.

That was when his hand had gone to the tire tool one of the men at her farm had left leaning against the barn wall. Outraged, betrayed, bent on revenge, he loomed toward her with it. She raised her hands, still protesting. She screamed, but only once.

Afterward, he cleaned the tire tool with kerosene and dragged her body to the small corral where her horse trainer worked with two new breeding stallions she'd purchased with her ill-gotten gains. He opened the gates of their stalls and moved them into the corral. Then he waved his jacket to upset them. Highly strung already, upset by the violent storm that was raging, they ran crazily around the muddy ring. One of them avoided the woman's body, but the other, younger one, was too unsettled to care that he was walking over his mistress in his fear.

At first sight, it did seem that the woman had been working with her horses and they'd gotten out of control. Hopefully, the authorities would think the storm had frightened them into attacking her. That's what Darwin told them he was certain had happened, although he'd arrived too late to witness the start of the tragedy. Those horses were dangerous, he'd added, convinced that they should both be put down as quickly as possible.

But Dr. Copper Coltrain, the medical examiner, remembered the death of Darwin's wife. He also remembered the barriers that had been placed in the way of his investigation of what had seemed like a suspicious death.

This time, there was no way he was going to get put off by the seeming coincidence of Grayling's involvement. A horseman himself, he questioned the sanity of any horse owner putting two breeding stallions together in a small corral. Then, when he performed the autopsy, any remaining suspicions he'd had were crystallized into a verdict of homicide.

"This was no accident," he told Sheriff Hayes Carson when he finished the autopsy. "There was blunt force trauma, but it wasn't consistent with trampling by horses."

"And no sane human being would have two breeding stallions together in a confined space," Carson replied. He kept horses himself. He knew what would and wouldn't be done with them. His eyes had narrowed. "It was a sloppy setup," he added. "Stupid of a man who owned Thoroughbreds to slip up like that."

"Probably an unexpected confrontation that ended in a crime of passion, followed by a hasty and fumbled cover-up," Copper mused.

"Yes, and not very well done."

"You're not letting them put those horses down?" Copper added.

Hayes shook his head. "I had them taken to my place and guards put on them, for the time being. The woman's son is barely coherent, but he said she loved her horses. He wasn't agreeing to them being euthanized for a crime he doesn't think they even committed. He said Darwin Grayling killed his mother for something she knew," he added curtly.

"Did he say what?"

Hayes shook his head. "He's too distraught to say much. Emotionally brittle and drinking a lot, as well. He's hanging out in a bar over near San Antonio nightly, we're told. Raging about Grayling and swearing bloody revenge."

Copper sighed. "Not much he can do about it, I'm sorry to say."

"His mother left him a bundle," Hayes replied. "Over a million in ready cash. Money can buy retribution, if you know where to look. And one of the Feds said that bar has some unique and deadly customers."

"I hope somebody's watching him," Copper replied.

"So do I." Hayes shifted his shoulder. He was still favoring the arm that had been shot in an assassination attempt some time back. He'd regained most of the use of it, but it still pained him. "Grayling has some health issues, doesn't he?"

"He has violent headaches, his eldest daughter told me, and he goes crazy when he gets them. I doubt he'd let a physician near him, but his behavior is consistent with some sort of mental issue. Perhaps with an organic cause."

Carson nodded. "I've wondered about that myself. His daughters seem traumatized to me, and it's not a new thing."

Copper nodded. "I treated the eldest for a fractured arm once, when she was about eight," he said. "I never thought it was from a fall, but she swore it was. So did her father, who came with her and stayed with her while I reduced the fracture."

It was left unsaid that he probably did that to keep Sari from letting anything slip about the true nature of the "accident."

"Her mother died under unusual circumstances, as well," Carson said. He'd helped with the investigation, as had Copper.

"Interesting how so many members of his family have suffered falls over the years," Copper replied. "Even the youngest, with sprains and pulled muscles and, once, a compound fracture of the lower leg."

"Amazing, how clumsy they are," Carson said coldly. "I'd love to get their father in front of a judge."

"Stand in line and take a number," Copper said icily. He let out an angry breath. "Well, this goes down as a homicide, and I hope you're putting the suspect under a microscope."

"You'd better believe I am."

SEVERAL DAYS LATER, a small group of assorted lawmen in San Antonio, Texas, were going over a printout of Darwin Grayling's financial transactions with a large northern bank. A federal judge had agreed to issue a warrant for the information, overruling threats from both Grayling and his attorneys.

One of the lawmen had ties to the family. Paul Fiore, a special agent with the local FBI office, had once worked for Grayling.

"You know the man," assistant FBI special agent in charge Jon Blackhawk remarked, glancing at a tall, dark man bending over the desk where the printout was placed.

"I know him," Paul replied coldly. "I worked for him for several years."

Jon shook his head. "This is one hell of an amount of money he's passed through his various holdings for the mob. I don't think I've ever seen so much."

"I have," Paul mused with a hollow laugh. "I led a bust in Jersey years ago, with a dollar figure even larger than this."

"At least we caught him in time, before he was able to process even more. His lover, Betty Leeds, helped him," Jon added. He shook his head. "She had an excellent record with the Bureau before she allied herself with Grayling. But at the end, she turned on her shady friends. We hear it was because of her son. Poor guy. He's got some mental issues, and he's taking it hard. She was the only family he had. He blames Grayling for the whole thing. He said she was a good woman."

"Probably was, in the beginning," a Texas Ranger working the case concurred. He was Colter Banks, now heading up the cold-case unit in San Antonio. His black eyes narrowed. "Money corrupts."

"Grayling's involvement is less understandable to me than hers," Jon said. "He had millions already."

"Only about ten million, from what we know," Paul said. He schooled his face not to show any emotion. "He kept his daughters on a short leash, never let them get jobs to earn a dime. And he never spent any money on them that he didn't have to spend. I guess even millionaires can get greedy."

"One of the attorneys he uses got drunk at Shea's Roadhouse near Jacobsville one night and spilled his guts," Jon returned. "He said that the girls were supposed to get a flat amount in their mother's will, besides half the house and its furnishings, but Grayling had done something to prevent it. He wanted to make sure they never got a penny, so that they couldn't leave home. He had a Middle Eastern prince lined up to marry the oldest girl—what was her name?—Isabel, I think. Imagine that, he was going to force her to marry some guy so he could get even more money into the family."

"You'd know about money, Blackhawk," another agent teased. "You and your brother, Kilraven, own half a county in Oklahoma."

"That's the government's fault," Jon returned,

tongue in cheek. "When they moved my family out of Montana and into Oklahoma, oil was discovered on the bare little patch of land where they settled us."

"I wish the government would move me onto some scrubland with oil on it," another agent sighed. "I can barely meet my car payment, let alone my rent."

"You'd have to go back over a hundred years and change your ethnicity first, Gaines." Jon chuckled. "I'm mostly Lakota, with a hint of Cherokee."

"I think one of my ancestors shook hands with Geronimo once," the agent sighed wistfully. "That's as close as I come to being Native American."

Paul listened to the banter between the agents halfheartedly. What he heard about Isabel hurt him. A prince. Her father had found her a prince. Had it gone further than negotiations? Did she care for the man? Or was she just being forced into something she didn't want?

He knew that her father kept her from working until she graduated from college. But he'd assumed that was because the man was paranoid about kidnapping attempts. He grimaced as he thought back to things he'd seen and dismissed. His mind had been elsewhere, on the past. Blood. So much blood…!

He shook off the memories. It was getting easier, with the passage of time, to come to terms with what had happened. In the three long years he'd been away, he'd missed Isabel badly. He wanted to see her again. Time after time, he'd wanted to call her, to apologize, to explain why he'd done what he'd done. But he got cold feet. Despite how he felt, despite everything, she stood to inherit millions and he was just a wage earner. That gulf would never be closed, no matter what he did. Not that old man Grayling would have let Paul near his daughter.

"Fiore, I said, what about the wiretap warrant?" Colter prodded him gently.

"Sorry. Lost in thought." Paul excused himself with a grim smile. "I talked to a judge about the wiretap, but he was less than enthusiastic about it."

"He may be in Grayling's corner," Jon said. "Try another judge. Try one in Jacobsville," he added firmly.

"I'll drive down there this afternoon," Paul promised.

"Judge Comer is sitting today, on a drug case in circuit court. She'll be in her offices at the Jacobs County Courthouse around five o'clock, if court recesses by then. She's not afraid of millionaires."

His heart jumped. Isabel worked for the Jacobs County district attorney, whose own offices were in the courthouse. He might see her on her way out of the building. It was stupid, to hunger for just the sight of her. He knew she didn't want to see him. The district attorney he'd talked to, Blake Kemp, had made a point of saying that to him. But a glimpse of her, just one, would feed his starving soul.

"I'll work it out," Paul said.

"All right. Now, who's on surveillance?" Jon asked.

"Me," Gaines groaned. "Along with Phillips, from San Antonio PD." He made a face. "Sir, couldn't you possibly ask Lieutenant Marquez if he could spare anybody besides Phillips?" he asked Jon.

"What's wrong with Phillips?" he asked.

"He's got this stupid game on his cell phone," he muttered. "He's addicted to it. If I hear one more laser being shot off, one more scream from a human victim being eaten by aliens…"

"Tell him to turn his phone off," Jon replied.

"He can't."

"Why not?"

"His girlfriend wouldn't be able to get in touch with him, constantly, in between the munching aliens," Gaines muttered.

"I'll speak to Marquez," Jon said in a long-suffering tone.

"Thanks, sir!"

Jon waved him away. He turned back to the charts.

THE TOWN OF Jacobsville was busier than it had been when Paul was working for Darwin Grayling. He remembered the small town with pleasure. Most of the familiar landmarks were still there.

There was a summer festival just getting started, he noted. There was a band in the park, playing its heart out in the big gazebo, while people lounged nearby on blankets or quilts spread over the green grass. Despite the heat, they seemed to be having a good time.

Paul checked his watch. Quitting time. People would start pouring out of the courthouse soon. If he hoped to get to Judge Comer before she left, he needed to hurry.

He ran up the steps and walked in the front door. He almost collided with Isabel Grayling.

His heart jumped as he looked down at her. He

scowled. This wasn't the laughing, teasing Isabel he'd
known three years ago. Her long reddish-gold hair
was pulled into a tight bun at the back of her neck.
She wore no makeup at all. Her face was thinner, and
there were dark circles under her blue, blue eyes. She
looked at him with blatant hostility before she turned
away and started to walk out.

"Not even a hello, Isabel, after all this time?" he
asked softly.

She didn't even reply. She just kept walking.

He ground his teeth together. Well, what had he expected? He'd walked out without a word. Presumably,
her father had told her about his family back home.
It was a lie, but she wouldn't know that. She'd think
he'd betrayed her. She'd be right; he had.

But he'd hoped for…well, he'd hoped for more than
the very cold shoulder she'd given him. He turned the
corner and kept walking, toward the judge's quarters.

ISABEL WAS BARELY BREATHING. Paul, here in town, in
the flesh. It had been a shock. Of course she knew he
was back in Texas, working out of San Antonio, but
she hadn't been prepared for walking into him like
that, without warning.

She knew that her heartbeat was pounding a mile
a minute, and her body must be shaking. She went
quickly toward the waiting limousine. Her two bodyguards were inside. It was sad that she had to be protected from her own father, who was now blatantly
on the run from the authorities.

She climbed into the limousine, nodded at her companions and instructed Morris to take them home.

"I SAW PAUL at the courthouse today," she told Merrie and Mandy while they were eating supper.

"How was he?" Merrie asked.

"I don't know. I didn't speak to him," Sari said coldly.

"He'll be working on the case, I don't doubt," Mandy said without lifting her head. "He knows so much about Mr. Darwin, he'd be the proper person to do the investigating."

"I guess so," Sari said.

"Where was he?" Mandy asked.

"Going into the courthouse," Sari replied.

"Well, he'd need to talk to Mr. Kemp, certainly," Mandy said.

"He might need to speak to the judge about a warrant," Sari added, picking at her food. "They have to be very specific about what they ask a warrant to search for. If they don't specify, they can't touch anything they find, even if it's stark evidence of malfeasance."

"Doesn't she sound like an officer of the court?" Merrie teased. "It's so impressive, Sari!"

"Stop or I'll hit you with my radish," she threatened, forking it to hold it under her sister's eyes.

"I'll hit you back with my pepper," Merrie taunted, raising it on her own fork. She studied it. "It's a jalapeño, too," she said.

"No food wars at the dinner table, if you please," Mandy said firmly. "Don't play with your food."

They both made faces at her.

"Anyway, he'll need all the tools he can find to try to get evidence on Daddy," Sari replied. "I feel sorry for Betty Leeds's son," she added. "She might have been unpleasant to us, but I hear that she doted on her son, spoiled him rotten. He loved her very much."

"Poor guy," Merrie agreed.

"He has some sort of problem that he's been in therapy for," Sari continued. "He's furious at Daddy. He knows it wasn't an accident. He told someone that he was going to get even with Daddy, no matter what it took."

"Good luck to him," Mandy replied. "People have been trying to do that for years."

"Without any success at all," Sari finished for her. She put down her fork. "Has anybody seen Daddy?" she asked.

Mandy shook her head. "He's in hiding, I understand. Everybody's after him now, from the Feds to the local sheriff, even the big guys up north," she added heavily.

"What about us?" Merrie asked worriedly. "We're his daughters. If anybody wants revenge on him for what he's done, we might be prime targets."

"I've thought about that," Sari said reluctantly. "But we have the bodyguards to protect us. They'll know that. And they'll know where the bodyguards came from, as well," she added. "Eb Scott was just interviewed by one of the major news agencies for his perspective on that latest terrorist attack, too."

"That helps," Merrie said. She propped her elbows on the table and her chin on her hands. "Maybe we'll be safe from Daddy as well as the dozens of potential assassins who want to get even with him."

"Hope is all we have," Sari said with twinkling

eyes. She sat up straight. "Listen, life is a dream. I heard it in a song, once. That means none of this is real and we can stop worrying."

"Life is not a dream," Mandy told her firmly.

"But it was in a song," Sari insisted.

"Lies." Mandy finished her coffee. "If it was a dream, I wouldn't be stuck in here with the dishwasher," she concluded, getting to her feet.

"We can help you put the dishes into the dishwasher," Merrie offered.

Mandy hugged her. "I'm kidding," she said with a grin. "Maybe," she added to Sari, "life *is* a dream."

Sari pursed her lips and smiled. "Nah," she scoffed, and walked out of the room.

LATER, SHE SAT on her bed in her nightgown and thought back to the way things had been three years ago, when she'd come into Paul's bedroom each night and perched on his bed to chat.

Life had been easier then, sweet and full of hope and dreams. So soon, that optimism had given way to agony. Paul had a family. He'd never told her, never told anybody. Even worse, he'd walked out without a word.

After the friendship and companionship and, finally, the mutual hunger he'd shared with Sari. It had been dishonest. Why hadn't he ever told her?

She'd believed he was such an honest, honorable man. If he was given to lies, why hadn't they found him out in over four years of daily contact? Surely, even if he'd hidden knowledge of it from everyone else, he'd have been honest with Sari.

She sat up straighter. That thought had never been allowed into her mind before. He knew she was innocent, that she wasn't the sort of woman to play around with a man, even lightly. So why had he given in to his hunger for her without saying anything?

Her chest rose and fell. Why not? Men were men. He'd been hungry for her, almost starving. Would he really have said something to make her turn away from him?

On the other hand, he'd been away from his family for a long time. She remembered he'd taken very infrequent vacations, which meant that his wife and daughter hadn't seen him often. Perhaps he'd just been missing them and things had gotten out of hand.

The worst part of it was that Sari had constantly tempted him. She'd been infatuated with him from the beginning, and made it obvious. Even an honorable man could be tempted. There was no getting past that.

But she still blamed him for what had happened. No matter how she sugarcoated it, he'd sold her out to her crazy father. And here she was, three years later, just as vulnerable, just as helpless. If he came near her again, she wouldn't be able to resist him. So they couldn't see each other again. She had to make sure of that.

JUDGE COMER WAS more than willing to give Paul a warrant for a wiretap.

"I can't comment on an ongoing case, but I remember Wisteria Grayling's death very well," the judge said as she signed the warrant for the wiretap and handed it to him. "She was my friend."

That was the first time Paul had heard the late Mrs. Grayling's first name. "Wisteria?" he asked.

She smiled sadly. "Her mother was as crazy about flowers as she was. She had two daughters. She named them Wisteria and Camellia. But Camellia was killed when she was very young by a drunk driver." Her smile faded. "Wisteria was young and innocent, and Darwin Grayling was unscrupulous. She was an heiress. His family was wealthy, too, but he wanted more money." She sighed. "Wisteria wanted children. He didn't, but in the end he decided that sons would be useful to inherit the money. Wisteria only had girls. He hated them from the day they were born. He'd have kept her pregnant and having more babies if it had been possible, but she'd had high blood pressure and the doctor insisted that another child would kill her."

"I thought Grayling had all the money."

She shook her head. "He had some. But Wisteria had more. Her family dates all the way back to the Civil War here in south Texas. In fact, she was distantly related to Big John Jacobs, the founder of Jacobsville."

"Do her daughters look like her?" he asked, because he'd never even seen a photo of the woman.

"Isabel is the spitting image of her," the judge replied. "She's going to make her mark in the district attorney's office, if her health permits."

"Her health…"

The phone rang before the judge could elaborate. "Sorry, this is a call I have to take," she told him.

"Thank you for the warrant, Your Honor," he said formally.

"You're most welcome."

Paul walked out of the courthouse worried. What health problems? Was there something wrong with Isabel? Surely not! She'd been perfectly healthy when he'd known her.

The worry about her father must have some bearing on it, he decided. No doubt it was something brought on by stress. He went back to his car, but he sat in it for several minutes lost in thought. Poor girls, to have their father arrested for a federal crime. It was already big news on all the media outlets. The tabloids would be on the scent next.

So it was Isabel and Merrie's mother who had the most wealth. Ironic, that even with all that money, Darwin Grayling had gone outside the law to add to the family fortune. It would all be for nothing, too, because his ill-gotten gains would be confiscated. Darwin would lose every penny of it. With luck, some of the illegal money would go to law enforcement, to help them shut down similar venues.

He thought of Isabel and Merrie, so wealthy, who would now be without money. That put Isabel on equal footing with him, wouldn't it? His heart jumped. He might actually have a chance with her now, with the money that had been such a bone of contention out of the way forever.

But he'd hurt her so badly that she wouldn't even speak to him in public. It would take time and effort to get past that prickly exterior, to the woman inside it. He had so many regrets that he couldn't count them all. He should have handled it differently. He should have spoken to her about it, admitted his feelings, his doubts, his concerns. If he'd been honest in the first place, he might not have had to leave town to spare himself the heartache.

Not that he'd spared her anything. He was sure that she'd been in agony about the news of his family, his defection without even a goodbye.

But at least he'd soft-pedaled his reasons for leaving with her father. He would have died to keep her from getting in trouble with Darwin. So he'd spared her that.

Now he had to investigate the extent of Grayling's involvement with money laundering, ferret out the root of it and the persons involved. He spared a thought for the girls, who might become a target for disgruntled criminals who wanted revenge on their father.

He felt a chill go through him. No. Not again. He couldn't go through it again in one lifetime. The mob got even in ways that decent folk couldn't even talk about in polite conversation. He knew it all too well.

There had to be a way to save Isabel and Merrie from retribution. He could call Mikey and see how things stood. Maybe he could get him to bargain with the higher-ups, to explain what the girls had already gone through at the hands of their father. The big guys were human. If you didn't poke them with sticks, they were remarkably merciful sometimes. He'd made mistakes that had been costly, because he'd poked them. But he was older and wiser now. He couldn't bear the thought of Isabel in the hands of people who meant her harm.

He'd talk to the other agents and see if something

could be done about protection for them, and for Mandy.

Yes. He could do that. He *would* do that.

"PROTECTION?" JON BLACKHAWK asked blankly.

"Yes, protection," Paul said, his eyes intent. "You know how organized crime works. They get even with the people who cross them. If they can't find the main guy, some of them have no qualms about going after the soft targets, the families of people who go against them."

"I understand that."

"So there has to be some way we can get protection for Isabel and Merrie and Mandy," he insisted.

"I guess nobody told you," Jon sighed.

"Told me what?" Paul asked.

"That Eb Scott loaned them a couple of his guys. Barton and Rogers. They're experts in counterespionage. In fact, they both were with secret squads overseas in that capacity. They're trainers, for Eb's organization. He sends them as consultants for paramilitary organizations all over the world."

"Thank God," Paul said heavily.

"I guess you were close to the women. You worked for Grayling for several years," Jon said.

Paul nodded. "Yeah, I wouldn't want anything to happen to them."

"Neither would we. How did it go with the wiretap?"

"I've got two guys in a storeroom near the Grayling properties listening to every word that comes in or goes out over their telephone line," he said. "They hate each other. I get calls from them, complaining like hell, every two hours."

"I know the guys. Pizza," Jon said.

Paul's eyebrows arched. "Pizza?"

He nodded. "It's the only thing they both like, and when they're not hungry, they get along."

"Pizza." He grinned. "What sort do they like?"

CHAPTER TEN

ISABEL WAS KNEE-DEEP in a file on an upcoming case when she heard footsteps outside in the corridor. Mr. Kemp was in consultation with police chief Cash Grier in his office, along with Sheriff Carson and an agent for Homeland Security. Tera was at lunch with Glory. The administrative assistant who handled all the secretarial work had gone along with them. It was just Isabel in the outer office, at her desk. There were two other assistant district attorneys, but one was at a crime scene and the other was at a local defense attorney's office, taking a deposition.

She didn't look up when the door opened, creaking because the courthouse was almost a hundred years old and the doors were just as old. People came and went all the time. She saved the file she was looking at and lifted her eyes.

Her face went stark white.

Paul Fiore was standing there with his hands in his pockets, his black eyes narrow and quiet, focusing on her face. His hair was thick and black, with a few gray hairs tucked in on the sides. His face had a healthy olive tan. He was clean shaven and he looked very neat in his gray suit and patterned red tie. Very FBI. She hated him.

He shrugged. "I have to see the DA," he said almost apologetically as he noted the changes time had made in her face. "You're thinner."

She lowered her eyes to the screen. Her hands were trembling on the keyboard. She was frightened. The sight of him upset her. She couldn't bear to speak to him, to look at him.

"He's in conference right now," she said curtly.

"Yeah. I noticed." He stopped beside her desk, solemn and quiet. "Listen, I know it's too late for an apology..."

"I don't want apologies."

His heart jumped. "What do you want?"

She looked up with cold blue eyes, with nothing in them save vengeance. "I want you, with your heart cut out, hanging from a pike."

Both eyebrows shot up to his hairline.

She'd embarrassed herself. She lowered her eyes to the screen, flushed. She was an officer of the court. She couldn't believe she'd said such a thing, and to an FBI agent no less, which he was, even if she hated him. And she did.

He didn't react. "For what it's worth, I made a joke out of it. I told him it was just a little flirting..."

"Because of what you told him, the doctor put in about eighteen stitches," she said in a voice like death warmed over. "Merrie had sixteen."

He didn't get it. He was scowling. "What?"

She looked up at him with ice-cold loathing. "A doubled-up belt. He almost killed me. Merrie came running in to try and stop him, and he started on her." She swallowed, shivering. "He said...that sluts deserved to have the sin beaten out of them," she added, looking up at him. "He said that no decent woman... would try to entice a married man with a child." She managed a shaky smile. "Spare the rod and spoil the child, is what they call it. Although I was no child, and neither was Merrie."

"They arrested him, right?" he asked, shaken and not reacting well to what he'd just learned.

"Nobody knew," she bit off. "He had an unlicensed doctor on the payroll who came in and treated us. Mandy had been sent off on a vacation first, so she wouldn't know. Wouldn't have mattered if she had. She loves her brother. Daddy threatened to have him killed."

He'd never felt such rage. He'd caused that! "He laughed it off...!" He closed his eyes. "Dear God," he ground out.

His reaction surprised her. Paul hadn't cared. She knew he hadn't. He'd only been playing around with her, after all. He had a family. A wife and child.

"Isabel," he said huskily, trying to find the words.

Before he could, Blake Kemp's door opened suddenly and several men came out. Blake shook hands with them, his keen eyes going quickly to Isabel's pale face and Paul's distorted one. He said his good-byes and walked over to Isabel, casting a cold glance at Paul.

"Have you taken your meds today?" he asked her. He knew she took a new preventative for migraine, a drug that usually worked wonders. She had other meds for the times when it didn't work.

She drew in several steadying breaths, her cheeks

flushed with color. "Yes, sir." She forced a smile. "I haven't forgotten."

"See that you don't. Between you and Glory, I'm going to have gray hair in no time. Mr. Fiore, what can I do for you today?" he asked, addressing the FBI agent.

"I need to speak to you about the Grayling case," he said, his mind obviously not on what he was saying. He stared at Isabel with horror. She lowered her eyes and went back to work.

Blake motioned Paul into his office and closed the door.

"What meds is she taking?" Paul asked at once.

Blake searched the other man's wild eyes. "She has migraine headaches. They've grown worse with all the stress she's been under lately. The preventative ones don't always work, so please don't upset her if you don't have to," he added abruptly as he sat down at his desk. "Good assistant DAs aren't thick on the ground around here."

Paul sat down in the chair Blake indicated. He leaned forward, his head in his hands, his mind reeling from what Isabel had just told him.

"What about Grayling?" Blake prompted.

Paul had forgotten why he came. His mind was whirling with the images of what he'd caused. "Her father beat her," he said in a haunted tone. "I'd just told him I was leaving. I said I had a family up north, that Isabel was just flirting with me—you know, like young girls do. He laughed. He said it was nothing, that he understood. He paid me two weeks' salary and didn't ask me to work the rest of the time. He even paid for my plane ticket. He was smiling…" His eyes closed. "He beat her! Because of me!"

Blake was shocked. The FBI agent seemed supremely cool and collected. He was melting down right there, in Blake's chair.

Blake grimaced. He knew things about the FBI agent that Paul wasn't aware of. Which made what had happened to Isabel all the more tragic.

"You should have told her the truth," Blake said quietly.

"How?" Paul asked, lifting his head. His face was contorted with rage, with grief. "Do you know what Grayling's worth? One of her father's men said I had a great thing going because Isabel liked me," he added with hot distaste. "He said I'd be set for life, that I'd never have to work another day." His black eyes pinned Blake's blue-gray ones. "How would you like that? How would you like to be thought of as some woman's toy boy, even if she didn't look at you that way?"

Blake drew in a breath. "I'd run."

"Yeah. So I ran." He scowled. Blake didn't look threatening or angry. In fact, there was quiet compassion in his eyes. "You know, don't you?" he added.

Blake nodded.

Paul closed his eyes and shivered. "I was new to the Bureau. I was going to clean up the streets of my town. Trenton isn't large, you know, not like a lot of eastern cities. There was a particular mob boss. I hated his guts, for what he'd done to my family. So I went after him." He laughed hollowly. "You know, there are consequences for every action you take. I was young and hot-blooded, and I thought I was invincible. Well, maybe I was. But they...weren't." His head bent. "Blood," he whispered. "So much blood. I have nightmares, still, after all this time. I dream they're calling to me, and I can't get to them in time..."

"I served in Iraq," Blake replied quietly. "A captain, in a special ops unit, on the front lines. My men were like my family." He hesitated when Paul's head lifted. "So I know."

Paul swallowed. He took a breath and sat up straighter. "I never told her," he said. "You can't, either," he added, his black eyes pinning the other man's. "I'll never really get over her. But I'm still not in the market to be any woman's boy toy."

Blake nodded. "It's a hell of a shame."

"Yeah." Paul smiled sadly. "But I don't think I'd have the guts to try again, so it's just as well."

Blake didn't believe him, but he didn't comment. He leaned back. "So. What did you want to tell me about the Grayling case?"

"We have a CI in San Antonio who hangs out in bars. You know, where there's always some stupid guy who wants to off his wife, and he's eager to hire an undercover FBI agent to do the dirty work for him?"

Blake chuckled. "I've prosecuted at least one of those."

"Well, this Confidential Informant overheard a young man discussing business with a known member of the local mob."

"What sort of business?"

"He wanted to hire a cleaner."

Blake whistled. "Not surprising, really. There are

plenty of men who'd rather kill a woman than pay years of child support..."

"No. Not a woman. He was talking about having Grayling killed."

"He'll need more money," Blake said drily.

Paul shook his head. "There's more. He thinks Grayling is crazy about his daughters. His mother told him how he protected them from everything," he said, and Blake's expression went very still. "The CI said he was drunk and raging about doing away with Grayling, but doing away with his kids first."

Blake caught his breath. "Of all the damned cold, stupid things to do...! I hope you've got him under twenty-four-hour surveillance!"

"That's the thing," Paul replied. "He slipped out the back with the man he was talking to. The CI didn't have a legitimate reason to follow him, and he didn't want to blow his cover. He was working on another job for us. He didn't realize until he reported in that what he'd overheard was essential information in a murder investigation."

"Damn!" Blake exploded.

"There's a good chance that we can pick him back up before he scores," Paul returned. "But in the meantime, just in case, we need to have somebody watching the women."

"They have bodyguards that Eb Scott provided," Blake began.

"You don't understand. We need to have somebody here, in town, with them and somebody at the ranch with Mandy," Paul emphasized. "She could just as easily be a target."

Blake frowned. He was only beginning to realize how unsettled Fiore was. The man was obviously emotionally involved with all three women. It wasn't just a job to him.

"You think of them as family, don't you?" Blake asked abruptly.

Paul hesitated. Then he drew in a long breath and shrugged. "Yeah. I've got nobody left except a cousin in Jersey." He lowered his eyes. "I spent several years with them. Mr. Grayling was away on business most of the time. I got close to all three of the women." He looked at Blake. "They were the only family I had. Until I left." He averted his eyes. "God, if I'd had any idea what sort of person Grayling was behind that mask…!"

"We all wear masks of one sort or another," Blake replied. "Grayling had all of us fooled. Well, not Hayes. He and Copper Coltrain knew there was something fishy about Mrs. Grayling's death, but they were both stonewalled by Grayling and his money." His pale eyes glittered. "He won't be stonewalling anyone, ever again. We'll have his bank accounts enjoined and his property entailed very soon. He won't have the money to buy any more public officials or stop investigations into his activities. If he's guilty, and I can't pronounce judgment on a man who's only been charged with malfeasance, he'll pay the price."

"We'll get him on racketeering charges, if that investigation pans out, and federal crimes carry a higher penalty than state or local ones do."

"Yes. There's also the murder investigation," Blake added.

"How's that going?" Paul asked.

"Copper ruled it a homicide. We've got investigators on it already."

"How did you know so quickly?" Paul wanted to know.

"The victim allegedly had two breeding stallions in the same corral in a thunderstorm to work them."

Paul rolled his eyes. "I don't know much about breeding stock, but even I know that you don't put two stallions in the same ring. And nobody sane puts any horse out to work in a corral during a thunderstorm."

"Grayling owns breeding horses, doesn't he?" Blake asked.

"Thoroughbreds," Paul said. "Funny, I never connected it when I worked for him. The trainers always made sure the horses were taken care of and plenty of stable boys were around when Mr. Grayling went out to inspect them."

"There was one incident that we know of, from years ago," Blake recalled. "A horse had to be put down. We heard about it from a man who used to work for Grayling. He said it was badly injured. The rumor was that somebody had taken a blunt object to it. Hayes tried to investigate but nobody would talk to him. In fact, the man who talked about it disappeared. Nobody knows where he went."

"Maybe he never went anywhere," Paul replied.

"That's what we thought. But a man with three hundred million dollars can buy a lot of silence from people in authority," Blake muttered.

"Not down here he couldn't." Paul chuckled.

Blake smiled. "Yes, Jacobs County has some of

the most incorruptible public officials in Texas," he agreed. "Hayes hated to see that investigation come to nothing. He runs horses at his own place. He and Minette have palominos. They love them."

"I used to see them from the road," Paul recalled. "I had to go by their place sometimes on my way to pick up Merrie at school."

"She could be famous if her father would let her exhibit her artwork," Blake said quietly. "She's incredibly talented."

"Yes, she is." He stared at the floor. "What about Isabel?" he added, looking up. "Migraines and a job like this are a bad mix."

Blake sighed. "Glory has high blood pressure, but it doesn't stop her from coming in to work every day. In fact, she used to work for the DA in San Antonio. This is less stressful than that job. And she doesn't have to hide out from drug dealers trying to kill her."

"Not many of those left, from what I hear, thanks to Eb Scott and Hayes Carson."

Blake smiled. "Well, Hayes is married to Minette, whose real father is known to one and all as El Jefe, one of the biggest drug dealers in the country. Not that he ever breaks the law in south Texas," he added with a grin. "He wouldn't be able to visit his new granddaughter."

Paul smiled. "Little girls are sweet." His face closed up. He was remembering his own little girl. He stood up. "I have to get back to work. We'll be keeping an eye on Mrs. Leeds's son. But if you have any contact with Eb Scott, ask him as a personal favor to me to send somebody to take care of Mandy." He swallowed. "She's one of a kind."

"I'll do that."

PAUL STOPPED AT Isabel's desk on his way out. There were two other women in the office now, as well as a man.

"Could I see you for a minute?" he asked.

Her teeth ground together. "I'm sorry. I'm quite busy."

"Sorry," he said, as he bent down and picked her up in his arms. He started out of the room, carrying her. He glanced at the other workers, whose jaws were dropping. "No problem, I'm just practicing hostage rescue. It's just a drill. Pay no attention."

There was muffled laughter as he carried her out of the office and down the hall.

"You…put me down…this instant!" she panted, struggling in his arms.

"You're going to make me drop you, then I'll have to arrest myself for battery," he muttered. "I just want to talk. All you had to do was say yes."

"I don't want to talk to you!"

"Yeah, I know. I pretty much screwed up everything." His jaw was taut. His teeth were clenched so hard that he hoped he didn't crack them as he walked out of the courthouse toward his car.

Two men in camo stepped in front of him.

"Sir," the broader one began.

"Special Agent Paul Fiore, FBI," he interrupted. "My ID's in my left inside jacket pocket, next to my sidearm. But if you reach for it, you'll cause me to drop Miss Grayling." He gave the men a long stare. "She's a material witness in a murder investigation and I need to interrogate her."

"Sir," the broader one began again, visibly confused, "there's a conference room in the DA's office…"

"They're conferring in it," Paul said. "Besides, their air-conditioning sucks. My car's much cooler. Look at this poor woman—she's sweating!"

Which drew their eyes to a fuming Isabel, who was actually doing exactly what Paul said she was.

"Put me down!" she told Paul.

"Yes, ma'am," Paul agreed. He started walking again.

"Put her down, sir," the broader man ordered.

"Didn't we just have that argument?" Paul asked over his shoulder. "Come on, guys. Ten minutes. I just want to eat a little crow. It's going to taste bad enough. Don't make things worse, okay?"

The men followed them, still unsettled.

"Look, just stand out here and make sure nobody tries to hurt her while we talk. That's not so much to ask, right?" Paul murmured. He opened the back door and slid Isabel into the seat. Then he slid in beside her.

"You're not going anywhere, right?" the taller man asked.

"Not one step," Paul assured him. "And if she screams, you're right here. Of course, I belong to the FBI. No funny business here." And he slammed the door.

"You are the most maddening…" Isabel began, exasperated.

Paul leaned back and stared at her, all the humor gone out of his face. "I made some damned stupid decisions," he said abruptly. "You paid for them and so did I. I never meant for your father to hurt you. I never thought he would. I was trying to find an easy way out for both of us." He looked away. "I thought I had."

"Sure you did," she muttered, sweeping back loose strands of red-gold hair that had escaped from her tight bun. Her blue eyes were icy. "You were married…!"

"That was a lie. My wife and I…are no longer together," he replied quietly. "There was no chance of my going back to her. Ever."

She was at a loss for words. She just sat there, stunned.

He glanced at her. "I didn't want to hurt you, Isabel, but I couldn't stay. We were too volatile together. You were painfully naive, honey," he added quietly. "And I still have a little honor left. I don't seduce virgins."

Her face flamed. She averted her eyes.

He drew in a long breath. "I thought I was doing the right thing. After what happened in my room that night…" He swallowed. "I had to have a reason to leave suddenly. So I told your father a lie. A little white lie. I never dreamed that he'd hurt you and Merrie." His eyes closed. "God, I'm sorry. So sorry!"

She was shaken. She couldn't find the words she wanted to say. "You had a child…"

He turned to her, his eyes so full of pain. "I don't talk about her."

"Oh. I'm so sorry." *It must have been a painful di-*

vorce, she thought. Maybe he didn't have visitation rights for his child.

"I hope your damned father resists arrest when they take him back in for trial," he said through his teeth.

"Paul!"

He couldn't bear the thought of Isabel being beaten, almost killed, because of what he'd said to Darwin. "We go through life from tragedy to tragedy, picking up the pieces in between. But we never get to put them back together again. Life is so damned hard."

She shifted on the edge of her seat. "Yes."

He glanced at her. "And Merrie. God love her." He smiled sadly. "Of course she'd have tried to save you."

She nodded. "Mandy didn't know until weeks later. We were afraid to tell her, because he made threats to us, about what he'd do to her if we talked." She bit her lower lip. "He actually told me when he was… beating me…that he'd killed people before and made it look like an accident. He said that everybody has people they'd do anything to protect. It's how he controls people who work for him."

"I never saw that side of him," Paul said quietly.

"He wears a mask," Isabel returned curtly. "Most people never see what's beneath it, unless they cross him. Like that Leeds woman did. They say her poor son is out of his mind with grief."

"So we hear." He wasn't going to tell her the rest. She'd have enough protection that the boy would never be able to harm her or Merrie or Mandy.

"He brought the Leeds woman to the house from time to time. They'd go in his office and talk. She never liked us. But they say she loved her son very much."

"She must have. She made sure he had money, apart from what was seized when her part in the money-laundering cover-up was discovered."

"Are they doing that to Daddy's money, too?" she asked.

"Trying to," he replied. "It takes time to build a case."

"Meanwhile, he's on the loose somewhere, thinking up ways to hurt more people," Isabel said darkly.

"He isn't at the house?" he asked.

"No. We haven't seen him for days. He came raging in and ran headlong into Eb Scott's two guys." She laughed softly. "He made a sudden stop, then left."

"I imagine there was more between the sudden stop and him leaving," Paul noted.

"Yes. He told me and Merrie to get out and I told him we weren't going anywhere," she recalled.

"What?" He smiled, almost tenderly. "You actually talked back to him?"

She smiled back. It was almost like old times, exchanging confidences. "I did. I reminded him that Mama left us half the house and its furnishings. It's worth quite a lot of money. He does have control of it. He used it for collateral in loans and made us sign papers to give permission. But that means he can't sell it, either. Mama wouldn't have liked what he did with the money she left us."

"What did he do?"

"He said he put it in a trust until we're thirty years old. So we had no way to run from him, no way to escape. Merrie and I thought how wonderful it would be, to just go for a walk and not have bodyguards watching every step we took." She looked up at him. "We've been under surveillance our whole lives."

"Under surveillance." He suddenly pulled out his cell phone. He punched in numbers and waited. "Gaines. It's Fiore. Listen, did anybody check if there was a memory stick in those surveillance cameras at Grayling's house and at the Leeds woman's house?... Not yet? How about having somebody go out there and look, before Grayling thinks to check it himself?"

He nodded and smiled. "Good man... What?... Yeah, it worked. I bought two pizzas. Well, the guys didn't like the same stuff. One didn't even want cheese... I know, right? Insane!... Thanks. You, too."

He hung up.

"Pizza?" Isabel asked.

"We've got these two guys doing surveillance. They hate each other. They hate each other more when they're hungry. So you buy pizzas for them and they get along."

She laughed.

"Remember that," he instructed. "It might come in handy one day, if you have to send people to stake out suspects for you."

"I'm just the new kid right now," she protested. "There's plenty of stuff to learn."

"You'll do fine. But you remember to take those meds," he said firmly. "Merrie's got nobody but you. Neither does Mandy."

"I will. But migraines aren't fatal, you know. They're just uncomfortable." She didn't add that people who had migraines were much more susceptible to strokes. He probably knew. She'd had only one migraine while he was working for her father, and it hadn't been a bad one. Since she'd graduated from law school, and gotten this job, they'd been worse and closer together.

He looked down at her hand on her skirt. It was thin, like she was. He wanted desperately to clasp it in his and bring it to his mouth. But it was far too soon for anything like that. He had to go slowly, carefully. She was still a millionaire heiress and he was still a penniless kid from the streets of Jersey.

"Nice ring," he commented when she seemed puzzled by his scrutiny of her hand.

"This?" She smoothed her other hand over it. "It belonged to my great-great-grandmother. She came to Texas in a covered wagon in 1901 with her husband and two little boys. She left a diary, which I also have. Mama willed them to me. She wanted Merrie to have the diary, but Merrie said it went with the ring and I should have it, since she had our great-great-grandfather's pocket watch." She looked up at him. "He was a Texas Ranger."

"Well!" he said, impressed.

"We had another great-great-grandfather who was a horse thief," she followed up. "They hanged him on one of those big oak trees in downtown Jacobsville. It's over a hundred years old."

"I think I have a couple of horse thieves in my ancestry, too. And at least one pirate."

"Was he Greek?"

He smiled. It flattered him that she remembered

details about his family. "Yeah. He ended up with fishing boats. Never was sure if they were really his to begin with," he added with a grin.

Suddenly, there was a tap at the window.

Paul opened the door. The key was in his pocket, and it wouldn't lower the power window without being in the ignition first.

"Yeah?" he said.

The taller bodyguard bent down. "Mr. Kemp says that you have to give his assistant back or he's calling Cash Grier back here to talk to you."

Paul chuckled. "Hey, I'm not that brave. She can go."

He got out of the car and helped Isabel out. He held her hand just a few seconds too long. The look on his face was one she wondered if she'd ever puzzle out. He looked…anguished, for those few seconds.

"If you hear anything at all…" he began.

"I know what to do," she replied.

"And thanks for the tip," he added, smiling. "Even us hotshot FBI agents overlook a few minor details."

She smiled back. "Okay."

He watched her go back inside with eyes that absolutely ate her up, every step of the way.

The bodyguards exchanged glances.

Paul turned to them. "I hope your boss owes the DA a favor," he said heavily. "Because Mandy won't have anybody watching out for her."

They were both laughing.

"What?" Paul asked.

"We have a newbie who just joined. Eb's mad at

him. So he sent him over to Grayling's to keep an eye on Mandy."

"Mad at him? Why?"

"He bought Eb's daughter a rabbit."

"So?"

The broader one chuckled. "So Eb's allergic to rabbits. And she wanted it to live in the house. No way was he going to refuse her."

"Did he know Eb was allergic?"

"He does now," the taller one said, laughing.

Paul smiled sadly. "My kid had a rabbit..." He broke off, then checked his watch. "I'll get back to San Antonio. Thanks."

"For what?"

"Keeping her safe," he said, with a glance toward the courthouse. He gave them a wry smile and got in his car.

He was driving away before the tall bodyguard spoke. "You hear about what happened to his kid?"

"Yeah," the broader one said. His face was drawn. "Hell of a thing."

"Hell of a thing," his partner agreed.

ISABEL FLUSHED AS she sat back down at her desk, keenly aware of the interest Paul had evoked by carrying her out of the building.

Blake Kemp didn't say a word. He just lifted an eyebrow and smiled. Isabel ignored him.

When she got home, she changed into jeans and a T-shirt, then went down to the kitchen to see if she could help Merrie and Mandy with the evening meal. They were all in there, the bodyguards, as well. They all stared at her and grinned when she walked into the room.

Isabel threw up her hands. "Is nothing sacred?" she asked, exasperated, as she glared at the two men. "You told them, didn't you?"

"Hey," the taller one said, "we don't get out much."

"He carried you out of the building?" Merrie exclaimed.

"I wouldn't talk to him," Isabel replied.

"I guess he does need to know things. For the case, I mean," Mandy agreed. She tried not to look pleased. She loved Paul. She'd been talking to him all along, unbeknownst to the girls. She didn't want them to think she was a traitor, but she was very fond of the ex-bodyguard.

"Yes, that's right," Isabel said at once.

"Have they found Daddy?" Merrie asked.

Isabel had a sudden thought. She held up her hand and ran for her purse. She pulled the jammer out and put it on the table.

"Where did you get that thing?" the taller bodyguard asked, surprised.

"I could tell you, but..." she added.

Everybody knew what the rest of that sentence would be. "Hey, you wouldn't have to kill me! I've got top secret clearance," the tall one said.

"Me, too," the broader one added.

"I got it from a questionable source," she finally admitted to them.

The two men exchanged glances. "The prisoner the Feds picked up," the taller one guessed.

"The one who was nabbed for industrial espionage."

Isabel gaped at them. "Well, it isn't as if it was evidence in a case," she said, defending herself. "And an acquaintance gave it to me, and then taught me how to use it. If Mr. Kemp thought it was illegal, he'd have given it back!"

"Bribery," the tall one said.

"Exactly," his companion agreed. "Or extortion."

They both stared at Isabel.

"I have not bribed or extorted anyone!"

"A likely story," Merric said with glee. "You tried to bribe me with Lindt chocolates so I wouldn't tell Mandy what happened to that last piece of chocolate meringue pie!"

"Aha!" Mandy burst out. "So that's where it went!"

"Bribery and petty theft," the taller one mused.

"You'd have thefted it, too, if you'd ever tasted it." Isabel mangled the English language in her own defense. "Thick milk chocolate. Two-inch-high creamy meringue." Her eyes were closed and she was smiling. "Flaky, perfect crust." She opened her eyes. "I'd have gladly done time for it. You didn't need it anyway," she said to Merrie. "You've gained a whole ounce since your last doctor's visit." She smiled smugly. "I was saving you."

"If you save me again, so help me, you'll need a good defense," Merrie told her. "And you blamed it on them!" she added, pointing to the bodyguards.

They both looked comically shocked.

"Us?"

"We'd never...!"

"Liars," Isabel said with a haughty smile. "I have it on good authority that a whole plate of chocolate-chip cookies vanished mysteriously while Mandy was at the grocery store last Thursday."

Mandy looked sheepish. "Well, actually, I gave them the cookies."

"You did?" Merrie exclaimed.

"Why?" Isabel asked.

"Go on. Show her. I dare you," the broader one said, grinning.

Mandy sighed. She reached into a nearby drawer and brought out a huge knife in a black sheath.

"What in the world is that?" Merrie exclaimed.

"It's a Ka-Bar," Isabel said before the men could. "A commando knife."

"And how in the world would you know that?" Merrie asked.

"Because I've seen one just like it in Sheriff Carson's evidence room," Isabel returned.

"Where did he get it?" Merrie asked.

"It was sticking out of a drug dealer's arm when it was recovered." Isabel chuckled.

"Yes, and Cy Parks put it there," the taller man added, smiling. "Hell of an aim he's got. Of course, that was a while back, before he married."

"Marriage tames men," Merrie teased, glancing at the bodyguards meaningfully.

"Nobody's taming me," the taller one said.

"I'm not housebroken," the broader one said in a hushed whisper.

Isabel broke up. It had been a very eventful day, she thought. Paul had told her things she'd never known about him. She wasn't sharing that information just yet. She wasn't sure that they'd ever have a future, but at least he hadn't meant to get her in trouble with her father.

Not that it would remove the scars she and Merrie carried. Those were going to be a lot harder to forget.

CHAPTER ELEVEN

THE NEXT DAY, there was news. It wasn't good.

Paul cursed under his breath as Jon Blackhawk laid it out for the task force working on the money-laundering operation.

"The Leeds boy went to bury his mother. She's from Brooklyn." Jon ground his teeth together. "He won't have to look far for a cleaner in all of New York City. Especially if his acquaintance from the bar in town here told him where to go."

"The CI said he talked to the go-between," Paul told him. "He said he didn't know any cleaners locally, but he knew somebody in Brooklyn who might be able to steer him toward a contract man. Works for a guy who runs a bar over near Fifth Street. Bar owner had a father, I think he said, who fought bulls in Spain."

Jon scowled, deep in thought. "Cash Grier had a contact in Brooklyn, a guy who used to work for Micah Steele, in the days when he was still doing merc jobs. He might have some ideas. You need to go talk to Grier, Paul."

"Grier has a lot of contacts," Paul said with a grin. "Most of them don't carry badges. And some of them are, shall we say, fugitives from justice."

"You can think of my brother as a CI," Garon Grier

said, sticking his head in the door. "He has friends in some really low places," he added with a grin. "I have to get back to my office. Grace and I have to take Tory for his checkup. I like to go, too." Garon was the SAC at the Jacobsville satellite office, but he'd worked for the San Antonio branch of the Bureau as ASAC before that.

"Our little girl, Gwen, has a checkup upcoming, as well." Jon chuckled. "Markie's crazy about his baby sister."

Garon sighed. "I'm glad Joceline didn't decide to give up working here completely," he told Jon. "I mean, who'd threaten to feed my legislative proposals to the paper shredder and water the ficus plant with undrinkable coffee the agents have to make because *she's liberated and she won't make coffee!*" he yelled out toward the hallway.

Joceline Blackhawk, Jon's wife, sailed by the open door with a handful of papers. "Oh, SAC Grier, so sorry to tell you that those letters you dictated for those visiting dignitaries are about to meet with an unspeakable act of gratuitous violence," she called back. "Tough luck that your secretary in Jacobsville got sick and I had to do them for you!"

"Speak English!" Garon called after her.

"Shouldn't insult administrative assistants," she trolled.

"Quick, go tell her I'm sorry," Garon told Jon.

"Why do I have to go?" Jon wanted to know.

"Because if I go, she'll know I'm lying," he said. Jon shook his head. "Let me get these guys out of here and I'll do my best for you. I only hope it will be enough," he added with a chuckle.

Garon threw up his hand and went out the back door.

Jon turned back to his task force. "Paul, go see Cash. Phillips, talk to the bank's loan officer and lean on him just a little. Banks." He stared at Texas Ranger Colter Banks, who was lounging back in his chair with the two front legs off the floor, his big booted feet on the desk.

"Hmm?" A deep voice emerged from under the broad brim of a white Stetson propped over his eyes.

"You said you knew one of the Leeds woman's friends," Jon continued.

"I do." Banks leaned forward, getting to his feet in a graceful motion. He adjusted the tilt of his Stetson. "I'll see what I can find out about her schedule for the past few weeks."

"Good. And, Mack," he said, glancing at the financial officer.

"I know," Mack said good-naturedly, "see how many recent transactions I can trace that have the Leeds woman's cyber footprints. I'll enlist some help from other agencies and get back to you."

"I hate money laundering."

They all looked at the Treasury guy, Al Butrell. He was glaring at the table.

"We all do, Butrell," Jon began.

"I hate it more. Every time I have to track down one of these unscrupulous guys, my wife starts feeding me hot dogs. Every night. Hot dogs, with mustard."

"Why?" Jon asked.

"Because I talk in my sleep. She says I'm good for two hours a night about how to follow the money trail. She hates it when I talk in my sleep. And I hate hot dogs. So…"

"There's a simple solution," Paul advised. "Eat out!"

Jon chuckled. "And that's my advice, too. Okay. Let's meet back here in a couple of days, same time. Hopefully, we'll have more information by then and a plan of action."

CASH GRIER WAS sitting on Carlie Farwalker's desk dictating letters. She was typing them at the computer. They both looked up when Paul entered the room.

"No," Cash said without preamble.

Paul's dark eyebrows went up. "I haven't asked you for a thing yet," he protested.

"Well, the answer's no, when you do ask for something."

Paul glanced at Carlie, who was trying to choke back laughter.

Cash glared at her. "That's right, give me away! Honestly, why do I even keep you around here?"

"Because I laugh at your jokes and I'm the only person in town who can read your handwriting," she said smugly.

Cash just shook his head and grinned. He turned his attention to Paul. "All right. You want me to tell you where to find somebody in a case you're dealing with."

"Are you psychic?" Paul asked, fascinated.

"My wife is, but that's another story," Cash said. The grin got bigger. "Jon called me. Come on in. Carlie, coffee please?"

"Coming right up, Chief."

"You make him coffee?" Paul asked, stunned. "We have to make our own in San Antonio."

"You could always replace Joceline with a coffeemaker," Cash suggested. "Of course, you'd have to find one who could type and deal with unpleasant visitors."

"We've pretty much given up having drinkable coffee, unless we can find somebody to do away with Special Agent Murdock, who makes it," Paul confessed. He shrugged. "On a happier note, the ficus tree seems to thrive on caffeine, except that it shakes all the time now." He scowled. "I wonder if a ficus tree can have a nervous breakdown?"

Cash chuckled. "Come in and have a seat," he said, motioning him into the office. He closed the door.

"Who do you want to find?" Cash asked when they were seated.

"A guy who works in a bar in Brooklyn," Paul said. "The bar's owner had a father who fought bulls in Spain…"

"Viejo," Cash said at once. His dark eyes narrowed with angry memories. "That's what we called him. His son helped kidnap my wife and almost got her killed. The boy's doing twenty years for kidnapping and assault and battery."

Paul let out a breath. "I didn't think you'd know which bar I was talking about. Heavy stuff."

"Very." He stared at Paul. "Why do you want to talk to Viejo?"

"I know you're aware of the Grayling case."

"Isabel could get you for kidnapping, while we're on the subject," Cash chided. "And you an officer of the law, too," he added with twinkling dark eyes.

"Don't start," Paul muttered. "She wouldn't talk to me and she had information I needed. I just carried her out to my car to talk to her about her father…" He stopped, averted his eyes and fought down rage. "I didn't know he was hurting those girls. I swear to God, I never saw him lift a hand to them!"

"Nobody knew, except a local physician," Cash replied coldly. "He talked to Hayes Carson, but they couldn't prove anything. Grayling had some damned good lawyers. The upshot was a threatened lawsuit that the county wouldn't risk if they pushed it. Isabel swore it was an accident."

"I guess she'd learned to be afraid of him. She and Merrie both," Paul replied. He shook his head. "Mandy wanted to tell me, but she said she'd land her brother in prison if she opened her mouth. Grayling can buy just about anybody."

"Not in here, he can't," Cash replied. He leaned back with his boots propped on his desk. "Not in Hayes Carson's office now, either, since he's the sheriff and not just a deputy." He pursed his lips. "Besides that, my cousin Simon Hart just got reelected."

"State attorney general, wasn't it?" the other man asked.

Cash nodded. "And if that isn't enough, my family owns half of El Paso."

Paul sighed. "It's always about money, isn't it?" he asked with more rancor than he realized.

Cash saw a lot. He knew about Paul's sudden exodus from Jacobsville three years before, and he had a pretty good idea why Isabel hadn't wanted to talk to the FBI agent.

"Money shouldn't stop people from going after things they want."

Paul laughed coldly. "Sure." He met Cash's eyes. "Suppose your gorgeous wife was worth two hundred million and you had to live on a police chief's salary, before you married her."

Cash didn't speak. He winced.

"See?" Paul replied.

"It's a shame."

Paul averted his eyes. "Life is a series of tragedies, followed by death. I just do my job and go home to complete control of the TV remote. There are people worse off."

There was a knock and the door opened. Carlie came in with two mugs of coffee. "I hope you don't want cream," she told Paul. "One of the patrol officers used the last of it and I haven't had time to go shopping for more."

"I'm no sissy," Paul scoffed. "I like my coffee straight up."

Cash chuckled. She grinned at him, left the coffee and closed the door behind her.

"Why are you looking for Viejo?" Cash repeated.

"Not him, just a guy who works for him," Paul replied, sipping coffee. "His bar is where the Leeds woman's son was sent to look for local talent. He's after a cleaner."

"Oh, my God," Cash ground out. "For Grayling?"

"Nobody knows. He was pretty drunk when he approached a local hood in San Antonio about the name of a cleaner for a job. But he mentioned something about taking out Grayling's daughters first. He thinks the man loves his daughters because he's so protective of them. Loves them, the devil," he said harshly. "He wanted to marry Isabel off to a Middle Eastern prince so he could keep the money in the family, and get even more." His face tautened. "He even told me once to watch her around one of the local cops here who was flirting with her. He didn't want his daughter to get mixed up with, as he put it, 'a grubby little lawman.'"

Cash grimaced. He could see the pain in the other man's face. He wondered if Isabel Grayling even knew the man was crazy for her. Probably not, if Paul had to carry her out of the courthouse just to get her to talk to him.

"I never cared about how much the job paid," Paul said quietly. "I loved my job. I loved it too much, once."

Cash leaned forward. "Any job that requires guns brings scars with it."

Paul looked up. "I guess my past is an open secret around here," he said when he noted the compassion in the dark eyes that met his.

"Just in law enforcement circles."

"I was going to clean up Trenton," Paul said with a sad smile.

"You got one major killer off the streets," Cash replied quietly.

"I did. But the cost was almost unbearable."

"For what it's worth, life gets a little easier down the road."

"You don't know what it's like to lose a child!"

"The hell I don't!" Cash shot back.

The men exchanged long glances. Paul grimaced. "Sorry. I didn't know."

"It was a long time ago. I have a gorgeous wife and a little girl and a brand-new son," Cash said. "I moved on, because I had to. I still have nightmares about some of the things I've done in my life. But not as many."

Paul cocked his head. "I've heard some stuff about you. Not sure I believed it."

Cash just smiled. "Whatever it was, these days I'm just a small-town police chief."

"Yeah. Like Putin was just a cop."

Cash got the reference and burst out laughing. "I know where that smart remark came from. Where the hell did you see Marc Brannon? He used to work with me when I was a Texas Ranger," Cash replied. "I worked with him again when I was with the DA's office in San Antonio a few years ago, doing cyber-crime."

"He told Colter Banks what he said, and Colter told us." Paul chuckled. "He's part of the task force we put together to track down Grayling's associates."

"Colter. He's my cousin."

"So he said."

"I haven't seen Marc for a while. He and Josette

sold their ranch and moved to Wyoming with the kids. Marc said Jacobs County was getting too crowded to suit him. He's running purebred Black Angus now, and he says he doesn't miss law enforcement," Cash recalled.

"I don't like cattle. I like horses," Paul replied. "I didn't know much about them, but I had to learn. When the girls went riding, I had to go along. One of the Thoroughbred trainers felt sorry for me and taught me how."

"Shame about Grayling," Cash said. "If he gets convicted, he'll lose everything."

"The girls will still have the house and what's in it," Paul said. His eyes narrowed. "After what he did to Isabel and Merrie, I'll be at every damned parole hearing he gets for the rest of my life."

"So will they, I imagine," Cash said. "The difference is that he won't have money to buy high-powered attorneys."

"Poetic justice."

"Exactly."

"Jon Blackhawk said he thought you also knew a guy who does merc work in Brooklyn, and that he might talk to us if you asked him. I don't want to spook a potential hit man by walking into a bar and asking questions."

"Peter Stone," Cash said. "He's still with Micah Steele's old group. He knows the territory and he's got contacts of his own. I'll give you his phone number. And I'll call him myself and ask him to talk to you."

"Thanks," Paul said.

"We're both on the same side," Cash reminded him.

"The bottom line is to get criminals off the street before they commit crimes. I'd hate like hell to have either of the Grayling women hurt any more than they've already been hurt."

"That makes two of us."

SARI AND GLORY were leaning over a table, studying a map that was involved in a criminal case Blake Kemp's office was trying in the next session of superior court, when Paul walked in the door.

Glory saw him first and smiled. "Mr. Kemp's out..." she began.

"That's okay, I can come back," he said.

"He won't be back till tomorrow," she told him.

He shrugged. "I'll catch him later in the week, then. I should have called first, but I had to talk to the police chief. Miss Grayling," he added formally, when Sari glanced at him, "could I have a word with you?"

"Only if you promise not to carry me out the door again," she said haughtily.

He pursed his lips. "Spoilsport," he said.

She flushed. Glory coughed.

Sari walked over to where he was standing, and folded her arms over her breasts defensively. "Yes?"

He stuck his hands in his pockets. He was somber. "We're tracking the Leeds woman's son," he said under his breath. "He's gone to Brooklyn to bury his mother. We think he's going to look for a cleaner."

"A cleaner." She wasn't getting it.

"A contract killer," he said.

Her breath caught. "For Daddy?" she asked.

"We're not sure."

"Oh." She wasn't sure what he was saying.

"You've got bodyguards. Make sure they know what I've told you. They'll understand what they need to do. That guy, Morris, he still work for your dad?"

"Yes." She said it with pure ice in her voice.

"Is he with your dad, or at the house?"

She swallowed. "He's still driving for me."

His teeth clenched.

"I can't fire him," she said. "I'd like to. He's strictly my father's man. But I don't pay his salary."

"I'll talk to Eb Scott," he said.

She looked up into his drawn face. She felt a cold chill go up her spine. "It isn't just Daddy you think he's after, is it?"

He didn't answer the question, except indirectly. "Nobody's hurting you or Merrie, or Mandy," he said tightly. "No matter what it takes, we'll protect you."

The emotion he couldn't hide was adding new lines to his face. His dark eyes were glittery with it.

"All right," Sari said. She searched his eyes. "Thanks."

He averted his gaze. "Tell your bodyguards I said to keep an eye on Morris, just in case." He didn't add that he was going to talk to Eb Scott and repeat what he'd told Cash.

"I will."

He turned to go.

"Why, Paul?"

He hesitated. Then turned back to her. "Why, what?" he asked curtly.

"Why do you care what happens to us now?" she

asked tautly. "You just walked off and left us years ago, and never looked back."

His heart ached, just looking at her. "I like my life, just as it is," he said. "No entanglements. No emotional ties. I do the job and go home."

"Is the job really enough?"

He smiled sadly. "It's all I have."

He walked away while she was struggling to find a reply.

PAUL CALLED EB SCOTT the moment he got back to San Antonio.

"Morris is one of those guys who'll do damned near anything he's told if he's paid enough," he said. "He's driving Isabel and, I assume, Merrie. But he needs to be watched. There's another complication."

"What?" Eb asked.

"The woman who was helping Grayling launder mob money had a son. He's gone to Brooklyn to arrange her funeral, but we think he may be arranging a contract killer for Grayling and his daughters, as well. He's mentally unstable and apparently drunk most of the time trying to deal with the loss."

"Damn," Eb muttered.

"I can't get on the house or grounds without an invitation, and the girls can't give me that. Grayling would love having me hauled up in court for trespassing on his property. But if professionals are brought in, the surveillance I assume Grayling still has won't be adequate. There's nothing to stop a killer from calling one of the women and saying another one has been hurt, or needs help, to lure her out of a safe zone."

"That was done not too long ago. Jake Blair's daughter Carlie was kidnapped by just such a ploy," Eb said.

"Blair. The minister?"

"Yes."

"Damn!"

"She was rescued in time. The boss was actually after Jake, not her. But if they aren't warned, it could work. How certain are you that the woman's son has the daughters and not the father in his sights?"

"We're not certain of anything right now. I just want them safe." He hesitated. "Look, I don't have family. Well, I've got a cousin in the mob in Jersey, but he doesn't really count. Isabel and Merrie and Mandy, they're my family. Things were done to the girls because I left. I didn't know about it. But even if all three of them hate me, I have to do everything I can to keep them safe."

"They won't be harmed. You have my word. The men I've got watching them are the best I have."

"Grayling always had other people watching them, even when I was head of security for him," Paul cautioned. "I don't know if that's still the case, but I imagine it is. And the men he'd hire won't be like yours. They'll come from the backstreets."

Eb chuckled.

"Okay, what's that about?" Paul wanted to know.

"Rogers and Barton spotted them the first day," Eb replied. "We got intel. The first move they make toward the women, they'll be sitting over at the detention center with Hayes Carson. They're both on parole. One false step…"

"God, I like the way you roll." Paul chuckled.

"Come work for me," Eb said. "I'll make you a legend in your own time."

"Thanks, but I like where I'm at," Paul said lazily. "If I ever get old enough to retire, the benefits will be nice."

"Well, to each his own, I guess. Don't worry about Isabel and Merrie and Mandy. I've got it covered."

"Thanks. I feel better."

"If you need help, you know where I am."

"I appreciate it. Grier gave me the name of a merc he knows in Brooklyn. That's going to be my starting point."

"Good luck."

"I'm going to need a little of that," Paul replied.

HE GOT ON a plane to Newark the next day. Betty Leeds's son had shown up in the bar Cash told Paul about. Peter Stone had staked it out and had a photo of the man on his cell phone to compare. He pegged him talking to a known mob figure.

With that information, Paul went to the US Marshals office and sat down with old friend Bryan Moss.

"What can I help you with?" Moss asked warmly.

"This guy." He pushed his cell phone across to the man, who grimaced when he saw the photo that Peter Stone had texted him from the bar.

"Anthony Cross," Moss replied. He shook his head. "If Justice could just get one conviction on this guy… I guess we live on hope." He pushed the cell phone back across to Paul. "He's only been arrested once in connection with a hit. He doesn't do them himself. Too dirty for his little hands. He subcontracts. There's one main guy he uses. Tony Barca. He's got half a dozen arrests, but there's always a witness who disappears or a technicality he gets off on. He belongs to the East Riders. They've got great lawyers."

"East Riders?" Paul asked.

"Local gang. They harbored a fugitive we had to take down a few months ago. Get this, the turkeys actually targeted one of my squad leaders!"

Paul smiled. "I'll bet that didn't go the way they planned."

"Are you kidding?" Moss scoffed. "Justice got two of them on attempted murder, and they didn't walk. We got one hell of a US attorney here. He nailed them to the wall, and the witnesses were our own guys—incorruptible."

"At least somebody's sweeping up the trash."

Moss gave him a warm smile. "You did a great job yourself. You were, and are, one hell of a lawman. Incorruptible, like us."

"Lot of good it did me, personally," he said. "I still feel the guilt, all these years down the road. I was so hotheaded in those days."

"You didn't know, Paul," he replied quietly. "Nobody could have guessed what would happen. LaCarta was a minor mob boss. He didn't even have much of a rep in Trenton."

"Yes, but he was the kid brother of the guy I sent up," Paul reminded him. "And he got even."

"Not without cost," Moss said. "He paid the price."

"Ten years, with good behavior," Paul said coldly.

"Ten years! He'll be eligible for parole in… Why are you looking at me like that?"

Moss's eyebrows arched. "You didn't hear?"

"Hear what?"

"I know somebody from the local DA's office was supposed to contact you about that. Listen, LaCarta got a shiv in the heart last month."

Paul's eyes widened. "He live?"

"No, he didn't live." Moss lowered his voice. "Rumor is that your cousin had a pal do him. I don't know if it's true. Mikey never got over what happened, either."

"Me and Mikey are all that's left of my whole family," Paul said. "Yeah, he was tight with… Well, I won't pretend to mourn LaCarta. God's mill grinds slowly but relentlessly, they say."

"They're right. What's Mikey doing these days?"

"Still working for Leo, I guess," Paul told him. "I talk to him occasionally. We got together in Newark a couple of months ago. I was on my way back to Texas." He hesitated then he looked up. "We talked about the past."

"I guess he talked about the past to someone else," Moss mused. "Just as well. LaCarta is one less piece of trash to sweep off the street."

"So he is."

"You were crazy about that guy's daughter in Texas," the older man said. "Why didn't you stay?"

Paul's face closed up. "Money."

"Money?"

"She had two hundred million and I work for the government," Paul replied. Pride almost choked him.

"You take things too seriously, pal," Moss sighed. "If she wanted you, she could have given it up, you know? Put it in a trust, donated it to charity. She could have found a way."

"She's had money her whole life, Moss," Paul replied. "How could I ask her to sacrifice her way of life, to live in a tiny apartment and do her own cooking?"

"If she loved you, it wouldn't be a sacrifice."

Paul lowered his eyes. "Yeah, well, I made a stupid decision and now I'm stuck with the consequences. It's a lot more than money now." He thought of the scars she must be carrying, both she and Merrie, from what he'd said to her father. It wounded him. "I can't ever have her. She hates my guts. But I'll protect her, any way I can."

"Tell Mikey to have a talk with the Leeds woman's son," Moss chided.

"Oh, sure, that'll work. Hell, the guy loved his mother. Maybe he's just nuts from grief and he's talking through his hat."

"If you believed that, you wouldn't be sitting in my office."

Paul grimaced. "Well, no, I guess I wouldn't. So, where can I find this go-between guy?" he added, and pulled up the notes app on his cell phone.

ISABEL FELT SICK at what Paul had told her. She pulled her bodyguards to the side before they got into the limousine that Morris was driving.

"Paul said that Morris would do anything for money, and he works for my father," she began.

The tall one held up a hand. "Eb's already talked to us," he reassured her. "We also know about the other bodyguards your father assigned to follow you."

"Yes, we do," the broader one said with a cold smile. "They have priors and they're on parole. One little slip and the sheriff's going to have some new boarders in his detention center."

Isabel smiled. "Thanks, guys. I feel much better."

"We're not letting anything happen to you," the tall one told her.

"We wouldn't dare," his companion agreed. "Eb would skin us alive!"

"He seems like a very nice man," Isabel said, having seen him and his wife at community get-togethers.

"That's exactly how he seems until you see him at the other end of an automatic weapon," the tall one replied.

"I'm just grateful for the help," she told them. "My father is scary."

"Not to us," the broad one said gently. "So just relax."

Which seemed like good advice. Except that when they got to the mansion, Darwin Grayling was standing in the hall, waiting for them.

"Isabel," Darwin said coldly. He looked from one of her bodyguards to the other. "I'd like to speak to you in private for a moment, please," he said, his voice soft and nonthreatening. "It's about the house and the furnishings. I've made a decision about them."

"The house?" Sari asked.

"Yes. Your mother left some papers in the safety-deposit box for you. I'd like to discuss them with you. I have a meeting with my attorneys, so it won't take long."

Isabel glanced at the bodyguards, who were unusually tense. But her father seemed all right. Surely he wouldn't hit her in front of witnesses. And she could always scream if she had to.

"All right," she said. She smiled at her companions. "I'll just be a minute."

The taller one stared pointedly at Darwin Grayling, who simply ignored him. He opened the study door. Isabel walked through it. He reached behind him, unseen, and locked it quietly.

"Did you know that Timothy Leeds wants me dead?" her father asked conversationally. "He's got it in his head that I killed his mother."

She turned toward him. "Did you?" she asked boldly.

He smiled coldly. "I'd hardly admit it to an assistant district attorney, even if I had."

"Hardly. What was it you wanted to talk to me about?"

"I want you to get on a plane to Saudi Arabia tonight," he said, still smiling. "I have the private jet waiting at the San Antonio airport. Morris is going to drive you."

"Wh…what?" she exclaimed.

"The government is about to confiscate all my bank accounts," he said. "I have to have money to pay my attorney. The prince I spoke to you about is willing to marry you right away. He'll advance me several million…"

"I am not marrying some man I've never met!" Sari exclaimed.

"You'll do it," he said. "You won't refuse."

"The devil I won't...!"

While she was protesting, he jerked his belt out of his trousers and folded it, snapping it loudly.

The sound paralyzed her for several seconds, bringing back memories of intolerable pain, physical anguish, fear.

She backed away from him, white in the face, too startled to open her mouth.

"You'll go, or you'll die, damn you!"

He raised his hand and brought the belt down on her shoulders. She screamed at the top of her lungs and ran behind the desk, holding her arm, which was bleeding from contact with the belt buckle.

Two things happened at once. The door behind Darwin Grayling burst open, and Grayling grabbed his head, screamed once and fell down dead.

CHAPTER TWELVE

PAUL MET PETER STONE in a Japanese restaurant near the bar where the younger man had photographed the go-between criminal.

"I love sushi," Paul commented as he dug into his own platter of it. "I found a little Korean place that makes Japanese-style sushi in San Antonio."

"It's one of my favorites, too," Peter said. He looked up. "Cash Grier sounds like a man who's got the world lately," he added on a chuckle.

"A little girl and a new son, and a wife who makes models look ugly by comparison. What's not to be happy about?" the older man said with a smile.

"He's still got an edge over most men, but in his day, he was unique," Peter said. "They tell stories about him even now. He's done things most of us only dream about. You know, he went through the British SAS's Fan Dance on the first attempt."

"That, I had heard," Paul replied. He smiled. "The assassin thing. True or false?"

"True," Peter said. "He rarely even worked with a spotter. Did black ops jobs all over the world."

"Hard to imagine a man like that settling down to be a police chief in a small town."

"Even harder to see a man like Jake Blair do it." Peter chuckled.

"The minister?" Paul exclaimed.

"Yes. He was black ops, too. They called him 'Snake.' He's pretty legendary himself, although he has a different mindset these days."

"Quite a change from what he did, all right."

Peter nodded. "I have a few free days. I'll shadow your go-between and see what I can find out. He doesn't know me and he'll have no idea I'm connected in any way to his new project."

"Nice of you."

"Hey, I'm from Brooklyn," Peter said. "We're all nice!"

Paul just smiled.

He was on his way to the airport when his phone rang.

"Fiore," he answered.

"When are you coming back to Texas?" Jon Blackhawk asked curtly.

"I'm on my way to the airport now. I've got a volunteer watching the potential go-between for action on the Leeds man's part. Why?"

"Darwin Grayling's dead."

His heart jumped. "When? How?"

"He wanted to talk to Isabel in private, he told her bodyguards. She thought it was all right. She went into the study with him and he locked the door."

Paul was holding his breath. "Is she all right? Did he hurt her?"

"He got in a pretty hard blow before her bodyguards kicked in the door. She needed stitches. But she's all right. It's just that he died while he was using the belt on her. She's taking it pretty hard. Mandy called me and asked if you were coming back soon."

The hairs on the back of his neck stood up. "Why did they want to know?"

"Well, you see, after she got back from the hospital, Isabel locked herself in her room and she won't come out for anybody, even for Merrie. She thinks she killed her father."

"I'll be there as soon as I can," Paul assured him. "I won't come in to the office, I'll head straight down to Jacobsville."

"There's more."

"Good God, what?"

"Somebody took a shot at her."

SARI WAS ALMOST in shock. She held her arm, felt the throbbing pain where the pale flesh was patched back together. The belt buckle had bitten into her like a knife with her father wielding it.

She'd hated him. She and Merrie had both hated him. But he was their flesh and blood, and she'd killed him. If she'd done things differently, he'd still be alive. He might have spent the rest of his life in federal prison, but at least Sari wouldn't have had to bear the guilt for his death.

That worried her far more than the gunshot that had grazed the porch where she'd stood waiting for the police and the ambulance to come.

Her bodyguards had herded her back inside and given chase, but the sound of a distant car driving away was the only indication that someone had been nearby.

Sari hadn't cared overmuch at the time. Her arm had been bleeding, and hurting, and the shock of watching her father die had numbed her. She remembered Merrie hugging her close and telling her everything was going to be all right, felt Mandy's arms around her, as well. But nothing would ever be all right again.

She heard them calling to her through the door. She wouldn't answer. She sat on the bed with her eyes closed, hating herself, hating her life. She just wanted to forget everything that had happened.

A LONG TIME LATER, the murmur of voices outside her door got louder. There was a pause, then a series of clicks and her door opened.

Paul came into the room, closing it behind him. He put a small kit of some sort back into his suit jacket and approached her.

"Hi," he said. "How's it going?"

The sight of him brought back so many memories. Paul, teasing her when she was a teenager. Paul, her constant companion on the daily trip to San Antonio to college. Paul, in his bed while she sat next to him every night to gossip. Paul, holding her so close that she felt like she was a part of him in the car, during the storm, in San Antonio. Paul, gone in a heartbeat, without a word.

Her eyes were dead as they met his. "I killed my father," she said simply.

"He tried to kill you, don't you remember?" he

asked gently. He sat down beside her on the bed. "You can't stay in here and hide from the world. You have to give the sheriff a statement about what happened, so he and his investigator can go home. They've been here a long time waiting for you to come out."

She searched his eyes. "I don't want to remember," she said in a haunted tone.

He caught her hand in his and linked his strong fingers into hers. "I'll be right there with you. The whole time."

She swallowed, fighting tears. "How's Merrie? And Mandy?"

"Downstairs, worrying about you," he said. He tugged her up from the bed, fighting the urge to drag her into his arms and rock her, hold her so close that she felt like part of his own body.

"They took me to the hospital. My arm hurts. I was there a long time," she added numbly. "It's Friday night. They had a lot of accidents, because of the rain."

"It's pretty wet outside," he agreed.

She hesitated for a minute, frowning up at him. "Were you here, when it happened?" she asked.

"I was in Brooklyn," he replied.

"New York?"

He nodded. "I got a flight to San Antonio and came straight here. Jon Blackhawk called me. Mandy called him, because she couldn't get you to come out of your room. You scared her."

"I'm sorry," she said. "I'm… I was just…shaken."

"No wonder." He grimaced at the evidence of the blow she'd taken on her arm.

"My back looks like that, where he hit me," she said dully. "So many scars. So many whippings. I never knew why. Mama tried to stop him. He hit her, too." She bit her lower lip.

His face was like stone. He was remembering why her father had left scars on her back. Because of him.

"What do they want me to do?" she asked again. "I feel...foggy."

"They gave you something for pain, didn't they?"

She nodded. "It made me dizzy. I'm still dizzy."

"I won't let you fall," he promised. "Come on."

She started for the door, in a daze. "Have you ever killed anybody?" she asked suddenly.

"Yes," he bit off.

She looked up at him. "Bad people?"

"Some were."

He opened the door before she could ask any more questions. He didn't want to tell her the truth yet. But one day, he might have to.

SHE SAT DOWN with Hayes Carson and his investigator and went over what had happened in the study when her father came home.

Hayes grimaced. He hated having to make her re-live it, but he had no choice. There would be a coroner's inquest, following the autopsy. It was a pretty obvious case, although because of who Darwin Grayling was, protocol had to be followed exactly. The media was already camped outside the gates. Bad news traveled fast.

"He had headaches," Sari said wearily. "Violent headaches. He got dizzy and his eyes glazed over and he hit us and hit us," she droned. "Nothing we did or said made any difference when he got like that. Once Merrie accepted a date with a boy, and Daddy fractured her arm." She winced. "It was worse, later, after…" She looked at Paul and stopped suddenly. She averted her eyes from his agonized expression. "He was like that when he came home, the night Betty Leeds died. He was complaining of a headache…"

"Copper Coltrain thought there might be a medical reason for the violence in him," Hayes said softly. "They'll do a thorough examination during the autopsy."

Sari drew in a long breath. "He was so greedy," she recalled. "He was never satisfied with what he had. Mama was rich. She left him a lot of money, millions, but he wanted more, always more." She looked up at Hayes. "Why is money so important to people?" she wanted to know.

Hayes managed a smile. "I wish I knew."

She finished giving her statement, which the investigator took down word for word on his small laptop. When she finished, he turned the screen and let her read it. She made a correction in two places and confirmed that the statements were accurate to the best of her memory. He printed them out and had her sign and date them.

"We'll go home and get out of your hair," Hayes told her. "But there's one other thing. The shot that was fired…"

"I can fill you in on that, I think," Paul told him. "I've been in New York, getting evidence."

"Okay."

"Let me get Isabel back upstairs first," he said, drawing her to her feet. "Bed for you, kid. You've had a hell of a day."

She smiled weakly. "Feels like it."

"Merrie, can you stay with her?" he asked the younger woman. "She shouldn't be alone."

"Of course I can," she said. She smiled. "Thanks, Paul."

He smiled back. "It was little enough to do. Where's Mandy?"

"In the kitchen, making more coffee," Merrie said. "She figured we were going to need it."

"Not me," Hayes said. "I've got to get up early and go to work."

"Same here," his investigator said.

They made their goodbyes and left.

Mandy came back into the living room as Paul went outside with Hayes. "Doesn't anybody want coffee?" she wondered aloud.

"I'll take a cup," the taller bodyguard said.

"Me, too." The broader one nodded. "Thanks, Mandy. It's going to be a long night."

"We called Eb," the taller one added. "He's sending over one of our guys with some sensitive surveillance equipment."

"Infrared," his companion said somberly. "And a couple of drones with night vision. We're going to have this place covered like clouds."

"Thanks," Mandy said, her eyes going to the staircase Merrie was helping Sari up. "I have a feeling we're going to need it."

"Do you have any idea where the Leeds man is?" Hayes asked Paul on the porch.

"We've got people hunting him," Paul said. "We lost him in Brooklyn, but one of Cash Grier's friends is helping with that. So is the local US Marshals office. I've got a buddy there."

"If he set Sari up, it's quick timing," Hayes remarked.

"Very quick. And if he missed, he's sloppy," Paul added. "It's been my experience that when you hire a contract killer, he very rarely misses. If you do the work, you have to have the rep or nobody wants you."

Hayes raised an eyebrow. "Know a lot about that, do you?"

Paul laughed hollowly. "Too much. My family was heavily involved in organized crime when I was a kid. Most of them are dead now. I have a cousin who's still thick with the local crime bosses. I was the only one who managed to escape going to prison."

"My dad was sheriff before I was," Hayes replied. "But my little brother got mixed up with drugs and died young."

"I'll bet you never even smoked a joint," Paul ventured, smiling when the sheriff admitted that he hadn't. "Me, neither," Paul added. "I like my brain the way it is. I don't even drink."

"It's a bad habit to get into," the investigator remarked. "My father drank like a fish his whole life. Died of cirrhosis of the liver when he was my age."

"Addictions are unwise," Paul commented. "Addictions of any sort."

"Well, we'll be on our way," Hayes said. "Let us

know what you find out, and we'll let you know what we find out."

"Deal," Paul said.

"Considering how easily an assailant got onto the property tonight, some additional security measures might be wise," Hayes said.

"Lot of good that did you when the drug cartel sent a hit man after you," Hayes's investigator said, tongue in cheek.

"That is sadly true," Hayes said. "Got me on my own front porch, and nobody knew he was even on the property. I had surveillance measures in place, too."

"No protection is foolproof," Paul said.

"It isn't, but you might see if Eb Scott's got anything new he could lend Sari and Merrie," Hayes said. "This guy missed one time. He may not miss again."

"With a little luck, we may be able to find out who the Leeds man hired," Paul said. "If he's known, his methodology will also be known. It could give us an edge." It chilled his blood to think a contract killer had Isabel in his sights. He was going to do whatever it took to keep her safe.

"I'll see what's needed," Paul assured him. "Good night."

"Good night."

PAUL WENT BACK INSIDE. "Any coffee going?" he asked the bodyguards.

"Mandy just made a pot," the taller one said. "Eb's sending Sarkey over with some infrared stuff and a couple of night-vision drones." His face was hard.

"We thought we had all our bases covered, but that coyote got under the wires."

Paul's eyes were old and sad. "Contract killers are wily," he said.

"I guess you run into them in your line of work a lot," the taller bodyguard said.

Paul laughed curtly. "I grew up around them in Jersey," he corrected. "My old man was a small-time crime boss. He had his own cleaner."

The bodyguards stared at him in surprise.

He shrugged. "I joined the Trenton police force when I was seventeen, straight out of high school. My old man disowned me and none of the rest of my family except my cousin ever spoke to me again," he recalled. "They said I'd dishonored my blood."

The bodyguards chuckled.

"It was just as well," Paul confided. "They were a bunch of losers, most of them."

"You ever have to arrest any of them?"

Paul's eyes became haunted. His face tautened. "One."

"Hey, man, I'm sorry," the tall one replied solemnly. "Shouldn't have gone there."

Paul scowled and looked him in the eye.

The man grimaced. "Yeah, I know," he said heavily. "We both do." He indicated the broader one. "Hell of a thing to happen to somebody. Just trying to do the right thing."

"It felt like the right thing when I started out," Paul said. "It didn't end that way."

"Nobody gets out of the world without a few nightmares along the way," the broad one said softly. "We just do the job and keep on going. Right?"

Paul smiled. The man had the sunniest damned disposition for a merc. "Right." He sipped coffee. "I'm going up to say goodbye to the girls, then I'm headed back to San Antonio. We've got a task force meeting."

"The Leeds man, right?" the tall one asked.

He nodded. "I feel sorry for him. His mother shouldn't have had to die for what she did. But killing other people isn't going to bring her back, and it's going to land him in federal prison."

"Better he's off the streets before he hurts someone else," the broad one said. "Where did he find somebody so quick, though?"

Paul frowned. "You know, that thought just occurred to me, too."

"Odd coincidence. He goes up to Brooklyn to bury his mother, and this happens even before the funeral. Nobody works that fast. Not even a contract killer."

"Especially a contract killer," Paul replied. "I know how they work. They stalk. They plan. They outline what they're going to do. Sort of like a squad leader in the army, planning a snatch and grab."

The broad one grinned. "That sounds like something from personal experience."

Paul chuckled. "There was this Iraqi general, and they wanted him real bad at HQ. So me and a few of the guys stole a jeep, hid out in a native village for three days, made friends, won hearts and found out that the general had a son who'd married somebody local. There was a wedding that he attended. Except he didn't get to stay for dessert."

"Remind me never to tick you off," the tall one said.

Paul smiled. "I just catch crooks now. Big difference."

"Yeah." The broader one chuckled. "Less sand, no camels."

Paul laughed heartily as he went up the staircase toward Isabel's room.

He knocked gently. Merrie came to the door. She looked worn out.

"How is she?" he asked.

Merrie opened the door. Sari was still crying, facedown in the pillow, clutching it with her hands.

"I'll go downstairs and make some chamomile tea for her," Merrie said. "It calms her down."

"Has she taken her migraine meds today?" he asked. "This kind of stress is more than likely to bring one on." He smiled sadly. "My cousin Mikey used to get them."

Merrie nodded. "She did take her meds. I made sure of it." She managed a smile. "Thanks for coming, Paul."

"I'm sorry, about what happened to you two when I quit," he said grimly. "I had no idea…"

"You didn't know," Merrie said gently. "It's okay. Really. You didn't do it. Daddy did." She drew in a breath. "He was a sick man. Really sick. I'm sorry he died like that, but I'm not sorry he's gone," she added. "It's like being sprung from a prison cell. That's exactly what it feels like. No more people watching us night and day, every step we take… Oh." She was watching Paul's face. "They'll still be watching us, right?"

"For a while, honey," he said gently. "The Leeds woman's got a son..."

"The bodyguards told us. I doubt Sari even heard, she was almost in shock. But they told us he'd gone up north to try and find a hit man. I thought it was for Daddy, because he was responsible for Betty's death." Her pale blue eyes looked up into his. "But they said he wants to kill Sari and me, to hurt Daddy. He won't know Daddy's dead, will he, Paul?"

"Not yet," he agreed.

"So if he's hired somebody to kill us..." She drew in a sharp breath. "Can you call off a hit?" she asked.

"Not if money's already changed hands," Paul said coldly. "It's a matter of personal honor, for the man who contracts to do it."

Her eyes were soft and searching. She knew he was holding back something. Something very personal.

"Why?" she asked suddenly.

"Why, what?"

She grimaced. "I wasn't blind, you know. Sari might as well have been wearing a sign. They said you were married and had a child. But that's not you, Paul," she added with keen insight that left him shivering inside. "You're much too honorable to behave like that."

"Smart girl," he replied.

"Morris said it was the money," she returned quietly.

"The money?" he asked, surprised.

"Yes. Sari and I are worth millions and you work for wages. So you left."

"Damn!" he bit off.

"I won't tell her," Merrie said softly. She shook her head. "They'll confiscate everything Daddy had. Sari and I will be left with the house and what's in it, but that's not worth millions. Not exactly."

"You see deep, don't you, kid?" he asked quietly.

"I'm an artist," she said simply. "I have to see deep or I can't paint." She smiled sadly. "She cried for days when you left. Please don't hurt her like that again."

"I never wanted to hurt her," he interrupted. "But I couldn't stay. I had another life, before this one. Bad things happened to the people I loved." He grimaced, looking into the room where Sari was still buried in her pillow, out of earshot. "I didn't want to go through it again. I got cold feet and I ran." He looked down at her with a whimsical smile. "It's been a long three years. Sometimes when we do the right thing, it all goes wrong."

She put a hand on his arm. "Sometimes people get second chances, too." She turned and went downstairs.

Paul went into the bedroom and sat down beside Sari, smoothing a big hand over her soft, disheveled red-gold hair.

"Don't do that," he coaxed. "I can't stand to watch you cry."

"You never could," she recalled, wiping at her tears.

"It makes guys feel helpless. We hate that. Come on, now, Merrie's gone to make tea for you."

She dragged herself into a sitting position. She was wearing a yellow nightgown with lacy panels. Under the bodice, her beautiful, firm little breasts were artfully displayed. He looked at them and remembered, and hurt all the way to his soul.

She realized how she must look. She grimaced and pulled up the covers. "Sorry," she said. "I wasn't expecting company."

"I didn't mean to stare. It's hard to turn away from something so beautiful and pretend it doesn't affect me," he added with a warm, tender smile. "You really are gorgeous. I'd give anything to…" He caught himself. "Sorry."

She drew in a shaky breath. She was vulnerable and he was married and had a child, even if he and his wife were separated. She had to remember that. "No problem. It's been a hard night."

"You didn't kill your father," he said firmly. "Get that through your head. The medical examiner and the coroner will find out what did. But I guarantee it wasn't you."

"Maybe if I hadn't gone to the sheriff, if I hadn't told what I knew about the night Betty Leeds died…!"

"Isabel," he interrupted gently, "you're an officer of the court. You did what the job required. Personal privilege isn't an option when murder is involved. You did what you had to. Period."

Her wide blue eyes sought his, sought comfort. "Did I?"

"Yes." He smoothed the hair back from her wet cheek. "You have the most beautiful skin," he said involuntarily.

"I have freckles," she muttered.

"What's wrong with freckles? I think they suit you." He smiled tenderly.

She bit her lower lip to stop it from trembling. She'd loved him insanely three years ago. It was hard not to fall back into those emotions. She remembered so many times in the past that Paul had been the only comfort she had. It wasn't quite the same with Merrie and Mandy.

"You always knew what to say, to calm me down," she recalled.

"I cared about you. A lot." He averted his eyes. "God, I'm so sorry for what happened! I was only thinking of myself. I never even suspected what consequences would follow that decision."

"You didn't want to get involved with me," Sari replied quietly. "I understood it, when I finally knew the truth about you. It even made sense. You were too honorable to get involved with someone when you were married. I just didn't know..."

He groaned, scooping her up against him, burying his face in her throat, his heart beating hard as he felt the softness of her breasts against his chest, smelled the familiar floral fragrance that was so much a part of her. "Do you think I wanted to go?" he ground out. "Dear God!"

She didn't know what to say, what to think. He sounded absolutely grief stricken.

She let her cheek go against his shoulder and she closed her eyes while he rocked her in his arms. It was like old times. Paul kissing the hurt places.

Merrie came to the door with a cup of tea in a saucer and froze in place.

"It's okay," Sari said, pulling away from Paul. "He was kissing the bruises," she added on a laugh.

Paul drew in a steadying breath and got to his feet. "So many bruises," he replied, glancing at her with a pained expression.

"I'm all better now. Thanks," Sari added, but she didn't quite meet his eyes. She had to steel herself to take the tea from Merrie, so that nobody noticed her hands shaking.

"The bodyguards said that you were in Brooklyn," Merrie said, glancing at him.

"Yes. I followed a lead to a bar in Manhattan," he replied. "Cash Grier had a friend there who helped me track down Leeds's contract. I called in a couple of markers and I've got some friends of my own checking out modus operandi."

"Ooh, Latin," Merrie exclaimed with twinkling eyes. "Method of operation!" She glanced at her sister. "I know big words like that in Latin. I should have gone to law school, too."

"You'd never make a lawyer, sweetie." Sari chuckled. "The perp's mother or sister would come in and cry all over you and you'd go find a public defender to get him off."

"She's right," Paul mused, grinning at the younger woman.

Merrie sighed. "I suppose one lawyer in the family is all that's needed." She sobered. "Somebody shot at Sari. They chased the guy, but they didn't catch him."

"Leeds went to New York yesterday," Paul said. "Nobody gets a contract killer on the job that quickly."

Sari looked up over the rim of the teacup she was sipping from. She drew back. "What are you saying?"

"That somebody here has been bought off."

Her lips fell open. "No. No, not the bodyguards," she said at once. "I don't know them well, but Eb Scott does."

Paul held up a hand. "I checked them out. No way was I trusting your safety to men I didn't know," he added firmly when she glared at him.

"It could have been one of Daddy's so-called bodyguards," Merrie added coldly. "I know that one of them was in trouble with the law. He actually got arrested on the campus of our local community college, where I had that art class last semester, remember?" she asked her sister, who nodded. "One of the campus security guards had been with the police department just briefly, but he recognized the man from a wanted poster that the chief had."

"Daddy was furious," Sari recalled, swallowing. "He bailed his employee out personally and made threats against the security guard."

"He had to know the guy was dirty," Paul began.

"He did. But it was a man he used for dirty jobs," Sari said. "Daddy really couldn't do without him."

"We'll check out everybody on the place," Paul said. "I know a couple of the guys who still do security here, but there are new ones that I don't know."

"If we had any money, we could hire a private investigator to do background checks on them," Merrie said wistfully.

"I know," Sari added miserably.

They both looked up at Paul's astonished expression.

"Daddy didn't want to risk having us leave, so he kept us poor," Sari told him. "We only got enough pocket money to pay for lunch at school and a meal at Barbara's Cafe once in a blue moon. We don't even have bank accounts."

"My God," Paul said. "I didn't know."

"You'll also notice that we never wore designer clothes," Merrie said. "He didn't want us selling the clothes off our backs to get pocket money. We were kept poor, and threatened about talking to anyone about what life was like inside this house."

"He was very thorough," Sari added. She glanced at Merrie and her eyes softened. "That nice man Merrie tried to date went all the way to Arizona to get a job. He was afraid Daddy would have him followed or maybe killed." She shivered. "Poor Merrie only wanted to go out on one real date."

"Daddy didn't want us even talking to men," Merrie said softly. "That was another escape route he was determined to keep closed. You see, he was going to pick men for us. Rich men, who could add to his fortune. He was going to sell us to Middle Eastern princes who were filthy rich."

"What a piece of work," Paul exclaimed harshly.

"But he can't ever try to do it again. No more threats. No more beatings. No more fear." Sari's eyes moistened again. "I'm so ashamed. I can't even be sorry that he's dead. Although I am very sorry that I helped kill him."

"Isabel, I told you, you had nothing to do with it," Paul said gently. "Nothing at all. He made his choices and they led to terrible endings. And now you have your own life to live."

"Assuming we can keep me alive long enough to enjoy it," Sari said with faint irony.

"Nobody's killing you on my watch," Paul assured her. "Eb Scott's got a guy coming over with drones and infrared gear. Nothing's going to happen around here without our knowledge for the immediate future."

"I feel like we're in the military," Merrie sighed.

"Don't knock it. We'll wrap you both up tight and wait for the man Leeds hired to make his move. When he does, we'll nab him."

"I like that part," Merrie said, smiling.

"Me, too, honey," Paul agreed. He checked his watch. "I have to get back to my apartment. I've got a task force meeting early tomorrow. Keep the doors locked, the windows shut and your bodyguards within screaming distance," he added.

"We will," Merrie said.

"Thanks, Paul," Sari said. She smiled, but she still couldn't quite meet his eyes. She felt guilty for the way she felt when he held her. Nothing had changed. She was as vulnerable as she'd ever been.

"You're welcome. I'll be back tomorrow to check on things," he told them. "Try to get some sleep."

"Easier said than done," Sari confided.

"I know," he replied. "I've had bad nights, too. See you tomorrow."

He went out and closed the door.

"Are you going to be all right?" Merrie asked her sister.

Sari nodded. "Thanks for the tea. Are you staying?"

"You're my sister. Of course I'm staying," Merrie teased. "Now try to sleep."

Sari put the cup and saucer on the bedside table and got back under the covers. "I guess I can try."

Merrie smoothed her hair. "It's all over, Sari," she said with faint wonder. "We're free. We're finally free."

"Free," Sari seconded. She was asleep almost before she got the word out.

CHAPTER THIRTEEN

TIMOTHY LEEDS HAD BEEN traced to a funeral home in Brooklyn, where he arranged the final services for his mother. He wasn't really surprised when two federal agents came and sat down beside him in the funeral home chapel office, where he was waiting for the director to come and talk to him.

"It's about that bar, isn't it?" he asked solemnly, seeming both guilt-ridden and resigned.

"Bar?" one of the Feds asked.

"The one where I hired the hit man. Contract killer. Whatever." He waved it away. "I figured you guys would be onto me pretty soon. I mean, I told everybody I was going to get even with Grayling. He killed my mother," he added, fighting tears. "She was all I had in the world. She took care of me. Now I'm all alone, because of him!"

"We know that. We're very sorry."

The other agent produced a paper. "We're sorry about this, too, Mr. Leeds. You're under arrest for conspiring to commit murder. You have the right to remain silent. Anything you say can and will be used against you in a court of law. You have the right to an attorney and have him present while you are being questioned. If you cannot afford an attorney, one will be appointed to represent you before any questioning if you wish. You can decide at any time to exercise these rights and not answer any questions or make any statements. Do you understand each of these rights I've explained to you?" he added, quoting the Miranda Law.

"Yes," Leeds said solemnly.

"Do you wish to give up the right to remain silent?"

Leeds just shrugged. "What does it matter now?" he asked miserably. "My mama's gone. I got nobody else in the world. Yes, I hired a contract killer." He frowned. "Maybe I hired two. I can't remember. I've been so drunk ever since she died." He turned his head. "You guys ever lose anybody close like that?"

"Lost my dad," the first agent said.

"Lost my wife," the second one replied.

Leeds sighed. "Then you know how it is, right? Well, I guess you didn't hire someone to kill people. I shouldn't have. I didn't mean to. I was just so angry!" he added, reddening. "That Grayling man! All he ever thought about was money, money, money! Mama said he had millions that he inherited from his wife. He even cheated his daughters out of it. But it wasn't enough. So he started laundering money for people in organized crime. He talked Mama into helping him. God knows why she loved him. But she loved me more. When one of his cohorts threatened to do something to me, she got scared and went to a man she knew at the Department of Justice."

"We heard about that," the first agent said.

Leeds nodded. "She told him what Grayling was doing. He found out what she said. He had all these security guys who planted bugs and video cameras. Anyway, she said he was coming over to her place. There was a storm. She was always scared of storms..." He stopped and choked up again. He wiped his eyes. "So I get a visit from the police in San Antonio, where I live, and they say my mama's dead and her horses killed her. Bull! They found her in the corral with two stallions! No horseman in the world would believe that she went out in a thunderstorm to work with two stallions at once in a corral!"

"Do you know where the video cameras were placed?" the first agent asked.

"Yes. Most of them. Actually, Mama had a guy come out to add a couple more. Grayling didn't know about them. Nobody did."

"Can you tell us where they are?"

"Sure." He outlined the locations and one of the agents pulled up a Google Earth map of his mother's house, so that they could identify the placement of the units. Leeds also told them the location of the bugs Grayling had placed in the house, and a secret file his mother had kept on her dealings with Grayling, hidden in a drawer of her desk with a fake bottom. "If you can't find those things, I can go out there with you and show you exactly where they are. But first I got to bury my mama," he added. He teared up. "You won't lock me up before the funeral, will you?" he added, his face so tormented that one of the agents winced.

"Listen, we have to take you in," the first one said gently. "But we'll make sure you get to go to the funeral. We won't have the marshals take you to San Antonio until after the burial."

"You promise?" he asked.

"We promise."

"Okay."

"If you cooperate, you might be able to plea-bargain for a lesser sentence," the first agent said. "Do you have an attorney?"

"Yes, in San Antonio. He was Mama's lawyer." He sniffed. "I'll call him. I get a phone call, right?"

"Right. Now, you said Grayling had the phones bugged. Do you know where the recording equipment was?"

"Yes. It was in her filing cabinet, in her study at the house. But he probably found it already and got rid of it," he said miserably. His face hardened. "I shouldn't have done it. I shouldn't have tried to have his daughters killed. I should have sent the guy after him instead!"

The agents didn't say anything.

He wiped angrily at a tear that escaped his eye. "I just wanted him to hurt like I was hurting. I figured his daughters were precious to him, the way he had them watched all the time. So I thought, if I killed his kids—or had them killed—he'd suffer. He'd really suffer!"

The Feds exchanged solemn glances.

Leeds wiped angrily at his eyes. "I found somebody in San Antonio with contacts. He made a few phone calls and I gave him some money. He said he knew a guy who could do it. But I wanted to be sure it was done right, so I asked him about a professional for the other girl. He said he knew somebody in New York. I was going to Brooklyn to bury my mother, so he gave me a place to find the guy. A bar. Guy named Viejo ran it."

"We know about that," the first agent said impatiently. "It's the second bar. What was the name of the second bar?"

"If I knew, I'd tell you," he said heavily. "I don't have anything left, not with my mama dead." He looked up at them. "I'm really sorry. Do you think you can stop them in time?"

"We'll do our best," the first agent said.

"Grayling will have to know that I sent killers after his daughters," he said, his eyes blazing. "He'll have hundreds of security people guarding them, but maybe it will shake him up a little bit anyway, that I tried. He'll never get convicted. He's killed people before and got away with it. He killed his wife. He told Mama. She was scared of him, finally, when he told her that. He said he'd kill her, too, if she ever crossed him. And he did." He looked up. "Don't let him get away with it! He threatens jurors' families! That's how he got off the first time he killed a man."

"Do you know who he killed?" one agent asked.

"I wrote it all down. Everything Mama told me." He groaned. "He killed her. Over money! What good is money?"

"Where did you write it down?" the first agent asked him.

"On the notes, on my iPhone." He produced it. One agent took the phone, pulled up the file and emailed it to himself at the local FBI office. He kept the phone. A record of recent calls from it would be invaluable in the investigation.

"Are you guys at least going to arrest Grayling?" Leeds asked plaintively.

They hesitated just a minute. Finally, they told him, "Darwin Grayling is dead. He had some sort of attack and died in his own home, night before last. We've kept it from the media so far."

Timothy Leeds opened his mouth and gaped at them. His round face grew redder by the second. "He's…dead?"

"Yes."

"Oh, my God. Oh, my God! I only wanted to hurt the girls to hurt him! What have I done?" he exclaimed.

"You have to tell us who you got to kill the girls," the Feds asked grimly.

"Who I got… He's dead! He's dead!" He was so shocked, he was lost for words.

"Mr. Leeds, who did you hire to kill the Grayling women?" he was asked again.

The small tape recorder under one Fed's arm was whirling happily away.

"I don't know," Timothy said dully.

"What?"

"I don't know!" he repeated. His teeth ground together. "I was so drunk that I don't remember anything except going to the bar and handing out a bag of money. I paid cash. He wanted a lot of money, so I gave him everything I had. I didn't care about money. I just wanted Grayling to pay for killing my mother!"

"Who?"

"I don't know," he said for the third time. "I was drunk. High as a kite on alcohol and drugs." He bit his lip as he stared at them. "I had a name from somebody in that Spanish guy's bar. So I went to another bar, somewhere in Brooklyn. The man in the bar told the cabbie where to go. I didn't hear what he said. When I got there, I didn't care about what it was, I didn't look at the name. I went inside, and a man sat down at the table with me. We talked for a little while, I gave him the money, then he left. I can't even describe him! I was almost passed out by then. Alcohol helps numb the pain. I don't want to remember that she's gone!" He started crying. "I woke up in my hotel room. I don't even know how I got back there."

The Feds looked at each other with veiled horror. This man had hired someone to kill two innocent women, and he had no idea who. It was going to take a lot of investigation just to pinpoint somebody who'd seen him with the go-between or the killer. Right now they didn't even know the name of the second bar he went to. That would involve interviewing patrons of the first bar, cabdrivers, dozens of people. It was going to take time, and time was the one thing they didn't have.

WHEN PAUL GOT the call from the Brooklyn FBI office, he was livid. Even Jon Blackhawk hesitated to go in the room with him until he calmed down.

"What is it?" Jon asked after a few minutes.

Paul was pale. "They found Leeds and took him into custody. He hired men in Brooklyn to kill the girls. But he doesn't remember who. He was drunk. The go-between at Viejo's bar sent him to another bar—the man told the cabbie where to go. Leeds didn't hear the name of the bar, and he was too drunk to notice much by the time he got there. A man sat down beside him, he gave the information out, the man took the bag of money and left. Leeds woke up in his own hotel room the next day with a massive hangover and doesn't remember anything about the man he hired."

"Dear God," Jon said quietly.

"We can go through cab companies and find someone who took a fare to another bar from Viejo's bar, if we're lucky, but it will take time. Lots of time. Our best starting point is the bar in San Antonio where he talked to a go-between. I can't walk in there," he added. "I'm known here. We need an undercover officer to pursue what the CI already told us."

"I know a man," Jon replied.

"Meanwhile, Betty Leeds had installed security cameras Grayling didn't know about. Timothy Leeds told the agents in New York where they were. He's cooperating, at least. After his mother's funeral, the marshals service will bring him down here and we can question him more." He drew a hand over his face. He was pale. "The immediate thing is to keep the girls safe while all this is going on. A professional is going to be hard to stop." He looked at Jon. "You know what I mean."

"I know." He stuck his hands in his pockets. "Well, the Grayling women are as protected as it's humanly possible to protect anyone."

"At home," Paul qualified. "We can't plant bugs and security cameras in every place Isabel might go in Jacobsville, especially when she's working on a trial."

"I'll talk to Blake Kemp," Jon said. "We can put men there. Security cameras are already in place. We can situate a couple of bugs in Blake's office. He won't mind, under the circumstances."

Paul ran his hand through his thick hair. He couldn't hide his concern.

Jon put a hand on his shoulder. "Go take a couple of hours off," he said. "You have to pull yourself together. I should never have assigned you to this case. I didn't realize how closely connected you were to Isabel and Merrie."

Paul looked up, his dark eyes solemn. "I thought I was doing the right thing, when I left. If I'd had any idea of the tragedy I was about to provoke..." He ground his teeth together. Jon didn't know about the aftermath of his resignation and he couldn't bear to tell him. "I'm not sorry Grayling is gone. The girls will be free for the first time in their lives. But their lives are in danger and it's his fault. Damn him, it's his fault!"

"Go see Garon Grier. He's SAC in the Jacobsville office. He'll help any way he can."

"I know. He's a good guy." Paul smiled sheepishly. "Sorry for all the drama. This is all such a shock."

"The capacity of people for irrational actions constantly amazes me. Who hires a hit man to go after a murderer's daughters? It isn't even sane."

"Neither is Timothy Leeds, from what we hear," Paul confided. "He's always been ten degrees off normal, apparently from a congenital condition. It's a shame, and I'm sorry for him. But he's threatened the lives of women I care about. He'll have to pay a price for it in court."

"Yes. In court." Jon shook a finger at him. "You remember that. No vigilante justice."

"Not me, boss." Paul sighed. He indicated the badge on his belt. "I've been in law enforcement too long to go rogue. But I'll be sitting in court when they try him, I swear I will."

"Let me know what you find out."

"Count on it."

PAUL STOPPED BY Garon Grier's small office in Jacobsville, but he was out.

"When will he be back, do you know?" Paul asked the receptionist.

"Not sure, sir. There was an attempted shooting at the Grayling mansion…"

She only got half the statement out before Paul ran out the door.

He had to get past Eb Scott's men and Hayes Carson's deputies to even get to the house. He managed to talk his way in, then he rushed inside.

"What's going on?" he asked Garon.

The older man glanced at him. "Someone took another shot at Isabel," he said.

"Where is she? Is she all right?" Paul asked quickly.

"She's fine. The guy is no professional," he added roughly. "He hit the porch column beside her. We've tracked the trajectory and there was a tire impression and two bullet casings where a car was parked."

Paul relaxed a little. "Gold. Pure gold," he said with a smile. "From that, you can tell his name, his football allegiance and the color of his shorts," he added facetiously.

"Maybe not the football thing," Garon said with a rare smile. "Isabel's in the kitchen."

"Thanks."

Paul went to find her, his concern far more visible than he realized.

She looked up and seemed to relax a little when she saw him.

"You okay?" he asked softly.

She nodded. "Just a little shaken."

"Listen, the guy missed you by half a foot. Some hit man!" he scoffed. "My old man's cleaner never needed a second shot."

Sari stared at him curiously. "Your father was in the mob?"

He nodded. "My whole family," he replied. "Everybody except me. They said I had bad blood," he added with twinkling dark eyes.

She smiled back. "Did you find Mr. Leeds?" she added.

"How do you know I was looking for him?"

She gave him a droll look.

"We had a couple of guys at our Brooklyn office go hunting him. He confessed. He was horrified that your father was dead. He only sent a man after you and Merrie to hurt your dad, to make him pay for killing his mother."

"What a joke on him," Sari replied. "Our father never cared about us. We weren't boys," she added bitterly. "He said we were worthless. Mama couldn't have any more children after Merrie. He hated her for that. He said if they could have had other children, he'd have had his son. But he couldn't divorce her, you see. She had most of the money."

Paul sat down in a chair facing hers. "Leeds didn't know any of that. He didn't know about your dad, either. The agents said he was sorry."

"They can put that on my tombstone."

"Stop that," he chided. "You're not going anywhere. You have case files halfway to the ceiling waiting for triage."

She burst out laughing. "What a way to put it!"

"I work with ADAs all the time," he replied. "Most of them are great at what they do. We have them out at crime scenes, too." He cocked his head. "You had the initiation yet?"

"You mean did they lure me to a bloody murder scene and wait for me to throw up?" she asked.

He nodded, smiling.

"The only recent murder we've had is Mrs. Leeds, and it wasn't my case." She lowered her eyes. "My father was…"

"He was not murdered," Paul said firmly, grasping her hands tight in his. "And you weren't responsible," he added. "Wait until the medical examiner has time to write up his report. I guarantee you'll see some medical reason for his death. Some underlying and probably long-standing medical reason."

"You always could make me feel better when the world was crumbling around me," Sari told him. She searched his eyes, then quickly dropped hers before he could read the hunger in them. "It was hard for me and Merrie, after you left three years ago."

His hands tightened. "I thought I was sparing us both more heartache," he said bluntly. "I didn't want to get involved again, Isabel," he added. "I've been down that road before. I lost my family..."

She looked up, shocked.

He bit his lower lip. "I didn't mean to say that."

She didn't say a word. She just waited silently for him to continue.

He looked up into her eyes. They were a soft, compassionate blue, full of feeling.

"I had a wife, Lucy, and a little girl, Marie," he said heavily. "I was new at the Bureau and I felt I had something to prove, like even if every other member of my family was involved in criminal activity, I wasn't. So I went after our biggest local crime boss with everything I had. I never considered that there might be personal consequences. But the night they indicted him, after I celebrated with my colleagues, I went home. The house was surrounded by ambulances, police, crime scene technicians." He swallowed, hard. His hands were bruising, but Sari hardly felt them. "Blood," he said huskily. "So much blood. It was everywhere, even on the damned ceiling. I managed to get past the police who were guarding the crime scene. I saw..."

His eyes closed. The memory was almost physically painful. "They dragged me back outside. I remember fighting them trying to get back in. They tackled me and stuffed me into a patrol car. I was taken into the emergency room and a doctor injected me with some sort of tranquillizer. It was so bad that I woke up in the hospital the next morning." He forced himself back to the present and looked into Sari's soft eyes. "The crime boss had flowers delivered. They came with a card. One word. 'Congratulations.'" He smiled sadly. "I won. But I lost." He smoothed his hands over hers. "Afterward, I couldn't bear to even be in the same city where it happened. I heard about the job Grayling was offering, and I left the Bureau to take it. I thought the change of scenery, the change of jobs, would help me forget."

"You should have told me," she said quietly.

"I guess so. It might have helped you understand why I was so reluctant to get involved with you. That was one reason I left. The other..." He held her eyes. "You're worth how much, honey, two hundred million? I work for wages. I wear suits that come from department stores. I buy shoes off the rack."

"I'm not worth two hundred million," she pointed out. "I own half the house and half its contents. Well, Merrie and I have half of that. It won't amount to even half a million in today's dollars."

He managed a smile. "It seemed like an obstacle I couldn't overcome three years ago," he concluded. "I thought if I just left, it would solve the problem." His eyes closed and his face contorted. "I had no idea that Grayling was that crazy. I never realized he was hurting you!"

She relaxed a little. At least he felt something for her. "He was always unpredictable," she said. "He'd laugh at something you said one day, and rip his belt off and hit you the next. Mama tried to protect us while she was alive. After she died, I protected Merrie as much as I could and tried to just stay out of his way.

He traveled a lot, so that helped. He was very careful not to let his temper show around people who worked for him," she added. "He wore a mask in public."

"It was a good mask. I used to be a good judge of people, but I never saw through it."

"You were dealing with your own tragedy. I'm so sorry, Paul."

He drew in a breath. "I've been living with ghosts. I couldn't let go." He laughed shortly. "I spent the last three years trying not to regret walking out on you. It was a good thing, in one way. I was so job oriented that I got back with the Bureau and made a name for myself in violent-crime investigation." He toyed with one of her soft hands, teasing the palm with his forefinger. "But I missed you and Merrie and Mandy. So much. It was like giving up the only family I had left."

She was silent. She didn't want to make it worse than it was.

He realized that. He looked up into her eyes. "Yes, I know. You didn't miss me. You and Merrie had every reason in the world to hate me, after what your father did to you. I wish I'd been here. I wish I'd known. I'd have broken his neck…!"

"Don't even think it," she interrupted. "You're an officer of the law and I'm an officer of the court. We aren't vigilantes."

"If I could find the guy who shot at you, I might be tempted to become one," he confessed.

"We'll find him," she assured him. "We have all sorts of evidence."

"There was one other thing Timothy Leeds told our agents."

"What's that?"

He let go of her hand. "He said that your father defrauded you and Merrie out of an inheritance your mother meant for the two of you. If that money still exists, it belongs to you."

Her heart sank. Money again. He was going to let it stand between them, if it was true that she and Merrie had inherited their mother's fortune.

She managed a wan smile. "I could give it all to Merrie," she suggested, only half joking.

"You are who you are, Isabel," he replied. "I'm not cut out to be a boy toy."

For the first time, she realized just what she'd been up against three years ago. Someone had said something to Paul. Her feelings for him were so intense that she couldn't really hide them. Boy toy. Paul's pride would never let him assume that position. Money didn't mean anything to him. Unlike her father, he wouldn't do anything to acquire it. He was happy with his life as it was.

She leaned back in her chair and managed a smile for him. "I understand."

"If you were working for wages, however, Miss Grayling," he added with a sad smile, "I'd be on your doorstep nightly with flowers and candy and invitations to the movies."

She smiled back. "Life is an obstacle course."

"Indeed it is. And I've got another obstacle to attack," he added. "I'm going to see what our investigators have turned up. You be careful where you go and what you do. Make sure your bodyguards are with you at all times."

"Because that worked so well an hour ago," she returned with faint sarcasm.

"Nobody can see a bullet coming," he told her. "We can assume we know who might be shooting at you, but we can't be everywhere." He didn't add what President Kennedy had once said about assassins.

"John Kennedy said that if a man was willing to trade his life for yours, he couldn't be stopped," she said for him.

His eyebrows arched. "Reading my mind? Naughty, naughty, you might see some really bad things."

"Really?" She gave him a rakish grin.

He chuckled. That sounded like the woman he remembered. He reached out and touched her flushed cheek gently, his eyes warm and quiet with regret and something more, something far deeper.

"You're old enough now to know that life isn't what we have, it's what we make do with."

"I have money, you don't, so I guess we'll just be good friends," she translated.

He drew his hand back with a sigh, shaking his head. "If you were me, you'd understand it better."

"If I were you, we wouldn't be having this conversation," she pointed out.

He just shrugged. "I'll go detect. If you go lawyering, take help."

"I'd curtsy, but I misplaced my skirt," she murmured.

He chuckled as he walked out. He hesitated and looked back at the doorway. She was just sitting there, watching him leave, her heart in her eyes. He actually winced as he turned away.

SARI SIPPED COFFEE with Merrie and Mandy.

"They'll find out who did it. I'm sure of it," Merrie assured her sister.

"I know that. But this makes twice now I've been shot at," Sari reminded her. She frowned. "He's a really lousy shot, isn't he?"

"I was thinking the same thing," Mandy interjected.

"Odd. Nobody knew he was here, and he had a clear target. But he missed. Twice." She pursed her lips. "If somebody paid him to kill me, they'd be appalled at how bad he is at his job."

"Call Paul," Merrie suggested.

"What for?" Sari asked absently. "He doesn't want me. I'm too rich for him."

"How do you know that?" Merrie asked, surprised.

"He told me so."

"Idiot," Mandy murmured.

"This, from his greatest fan?" Sari asked. "I'm shocked!"

"He's crazy about you, and he's letting money come between you."

"Morris helped him," Sari said sourly. "He didn't say it was Morris who was teasing him about having it made if he married me. But I know it was. Who else did he talk to? He didn't even like most of the other security men Daddy had hired."

Merrie frowned. "Morris sure hasn't been around much since Daddy died," she commented.

"He's probably ashamed," Mandy told them. "After all, he was Daddy's pet. He always said he'd do anything for money. That's why Mr. Darwin kept him around. Morris was useful."

"Not so useful anymore," Merrie returned with cold eyes.

"When the will is probated, he's going to be looking for work," Sari said firmly. "Along with most of Daddy's other hired men. And anybody who was keeping an eye on us is going to join them."

"I feel the same way," Merrie said. "I can hardly believe I'm able to make a decision on my own, talk to boys, go on a date if I like, go anywhere I want to go."

"Well, not just yet," Sari advised. "Neither of us is safe without being guarded right now."

"Good point," Merrie conceded. "But when this is all over," she amended, "we'll have actual lives, like other people!"

"I won't know how to handle it. We've lived in fear for so long," Sari commented.

"All of us," Mandy agreed. "My poor brother." She shook her head. "He never knew how close he came to federal prison just because I worked for Mr. Darwin."

"Paul said his whole family was involved in organized crime, except for him." She didn't add what Paul had told her about his wife and child. That was private information and she wasn't sharing it.

"He turned out well," Merrie said. She grimaced. "It really wasn't his fault, what Daddy did to us three years ago. It wasn't right that we blamed him for it."

"He understood," Sari said. She drew in a long breath. "I wish I was poor."

"We are what we are," Mandy said. "And we have

to accept people as they are. Mr. Paul will realize that one day."

"Think so?" Sari asked. "I wouldn't bet on it."

"Where are our bodyguards?" Merrie asked suddenly, looking around.

"Communing," Mandy said with twinkling eyes.

"Communing with whom?" Sari returned.

"A large group of people in law enforcement. I have no idea what's being said, but they seem to have found out something new to add to the confusion," Mandy said.

"Maybe they found the contract killer," Sari said hopefully.

"That could be a possibility," Mandy replied. "I've hardly ever seen so many law enforcement people gathered in one place before in my life."

"I guess I'll find out tomorrow when I go to work," Sari said. "Weekends are nice, but they put me off my schedule."

"You can't work 24/7," Merrie said. "It will make you dull and spooky."

"Only to an artist," Sari retorted, smiling. "Which brings to mind something else. You can go to college now, anywhere you want to go, when this is all over."

Merrie pushed back her long blond hair, and her pale blue eyes were thoughtful. "I don't know. I really like the idea of painting and maybe working in a gallery."

"We have a local one," Sari pointed out.

"Yes, but the owner, Brand Taylor, is trying to retire," Merrie said. "It will be sad, to have our only art supply store closed. Not to mention our own gallery."

Sari's eyes widened. "Merrie, you could buy it!"

"What?"

"You could buy it! Once the will's through probate and we get back at least some of Mama's money, you could buy the art store!"

Merrie looked as if she'd won the lottery. "You wouldn't mind? If I spent the money, I mean? Businesses are iffy, and I don't have any real business experience."

"I do. And we can find a good CPA to advise you. Well? What do you think?"

Merrie brightened. "I'll think about it."

"There," Mandy said, smiling. "Something to look forward to. We all need that, you know, even if it's only looking forward to a movie, or reading a new book. Goals keep us going through hard times."

"I think we're due some good times," Sari said.

"That Leeds man," Merrie mused, shaking her head. "I know he loved his mother. But hiring someone to kill two women who never did a thing to him? It doesn't make sense!"

"He thought it would hurt Daddy," Sari replied. "Paul told me what he said. He thought Daddy treasured us, because he kept us so close to home and had bodyguards for us."

"And it was only because he wanted to marry us to rich men and make even more money," Merrie said sadly. "Like being sold into servitude."

"At least I escaped the prince," Sari said wistfully.

"What would you have done?" Merrie wanted to know.

"I'd have gone to Eb Scott and said, 'Make me a mercenary!'" she replied, grinning.

"I don't think he takes women, Sari," Merrie said.

"Sure he does," came a deep voice from the doorway. Eb Scott walked through it, along with his two men. He chuckled. "One of my best mercs is working for Wolf Patterson and his wife on their ranch. She's the best merc I ever trained."

"Wow," Sari said. She smiled. "But I think I'll make a better prosecutor than I would a professional soldier. Just between the two of us."

"Any coffee going?" Eb asked.

"You bet!" Mandy got up and went to get it. "Black, right?"

"How did you know that?" he called after her.

"Never met a lawman or a merc or an outlaw who ever wanted it any other way," she called back.

Eb just laughed.

"Have they found out anything?" Sari asked worriedly.

"They're running the tire-track pattern at the FBI office in Washington," he said. "Same with the shell casings. It shouldn't take too long."

Sari rubbed her arms. "It's so strange," she commented. "I mean, whoever shot at me did it twice and missed both times. I've never read about any contract killer who missed his target. Well, except the one who shot Sheriff Carson a couple of years ago, and that was only because the sheriff moved unexpectedly."

"Do you think they have a suspect?" Merrie asked.

Eb smiled. "It's too early for that. Evidence isn't gathered in a day."

"I suppose so," Merrie replied.

The front door opened. There was some murmured

conversation. Then Paul came in the door, looking out of sorts and coldly furious.

He shook hands with Eb. "Thanks for coming over," he told the older man. "We're going to need more eyes and ears than we can afford."

"Glad to help," Eb said. "What do you need?"

"We've got a suspect, but he skipped town before we could make an arrest."

"You do? Who is it?" Sari asked breathlessly.

"Somebody none of us would have guessed," Paul said, sounding disgusted.

"Oh, no. Morris!" Sari burst out. "It was Morris, wasn't it?"

CHAPTER FOURTEEN

"It makes sense," Merrie exclaimed. "Even if he would do anything for money, Morris has known us for years. He had to feel something for us."

"Enough to save my life. Twice, by missing the shots," Sari commented. She looked up at Paul. "He ran?"

He nodded. "But he won't run far enough," he added. "The fact that he even tried to take the shots, regardless of whether or not he missed on purpose, is enough to put him away for a long time."

"I won't feel too sorry for him," Sari said. She was sure that it was Morris who made Paul feel small, who played on his pride by mentioning how nice it would be for Paul to land a rich wife.

"Neither will I," Merrie said. "There was always something about him that I didn't like. I couldn't explain it. It was like that feeling you get when you walk into a house sometimes and the hairs on the back of your neck stand up."

"There goes my sister, the paranormalist," Sari teased affectionately.

"I'm just sensitive. I'm an artist," she reminded her sister. "We see everything!"

Paul smiled at her. "That's true." He glanced at Eb.

"You should see her paintings. She manages to capture the entire individual."

"You do portraits?" Eb asked.

"I do," she replied. "I'm not that good, though."

"Baloney," Paul interrupted. "She did a portrait of my cousin Mikey from a few photos I had. She painted him on a black background with a knife lying on a desk beside him."

"Is that relevant?" Eb wanted to know.

Paul chuckled. "Mikey is a minor local crime boss back home."

Eb pursed his lips and whistled, glancing at Merrie.

"Nobody hum the *Twilight Zone* theme, please," Merrie teased. She laughed. "I guess I am a little spooky."

Sari got up and hugged her. "You are not spooky. You have a gift for showing people the way they really are."

"A rare one," Eb said kindly, and smiled. "And I don't think you're spooky."

"Thanks," Merrie said.

"How did they nail Morris so fast?" Sari asked.

Paul looked sheepish. "I recognized the tire pattern," he said. "I drove the damned car every day to take you girls to school. When I was out of town, Morris drove it. Mr. Grayling liked a certain brand of tires and he bought it for every vehicle on the place, even the trucks. I told the FBI crime lab, they checked it and we had a winner. If it was the limo from here, it had to be Morris."

"Nice detecting!" Sari enthused.

"Yeah, thanks," Paul replied. "And now all we have to do is catch him." He shook his head. "Poor guy."

"Why do you say that?" Sari asked.

His eyes were tender. "Honey," he said gently, "you don't take a contract and then fail to fulfill it. There are consequences."

"Usually fatal ones," Eb agreed. "If Morris is smart, he'll turn himself in. With any luck, the guy who floated the contract won't have relatives inside prison who'll have him for breakfast." He hesitated. "But we have to remember, he's still on the loose, and we can't let our guard down." He glanced at Sari and Merrie.

"We've got better protection than Fort Knox," Sari said, with a wry look at Eb. "Those guys you sent over are really something."

"They are," Eb said. "The government keeps trying to lure them away from me, but considering all the budget cuts, I don't expect to lose them anytime soon. I pay well, and there are some really good perks."

"Apparently I'm in the wrong business," Paul joked.

"Well, you won't get rich in government service, but you have medical and dental and retirement," Eb reminded him.

Paul looked at Sari quietly. "Yeah. All the great perks." He smiled wistfully and turned away. "I'm heading back to San Antonio. I have a report to write. Several reports, in fact. That's in addition to the cases on my desk that I haven't had time to look at." He glanced at Sari and Merrie. "I'm glad you two are okay. Mandy, too." He frowned. "Where is Mandy?" he asked suddenly.

"In here, wearing my fingers to the bone, washing all the supper dishes by hand because the stupid dishwasher quit and I'll never find a repairman at this hour of the night!" Mandy wailed, covered up in soapsuds from fingers to elbows.

"I can fix a dishwasher." Eb chuckled. "Lead me to it."

"Can I watch? In case I have to do it one day." Merrie grinned.

"Come along."

Merrie shot her sister a speaking conspiratorial glance as she followed the other two into the kitchen.

Sari stared up at Paul with quiet misery. "I'm glad we know it was Morris. And I'm glad he missed."

"Leeds will pay for this, one way or another," he said. "Meanwhile, you and Merrie are safe enough. Eb's guys will take care of you."

She searched his eyes. "I'm so sorry about your family."

"I was eaten up with guilt, for years afterward," he confessed. "But when I got back into the Bureau, they set me up with this psychologist." He made a face. "Spiky hair, black lipstick, keeps snakes. I thought they were nuts. But she sure knows her business. I learned that life happens. That we can't control every minute of it. Sometimes we have to be leaves on the river."

She nodded, understanding exactly what he was saying.

He drew her to him. "You aren't going to be rich

anymore, right? I mean, not two hundred million dollars rich, right?"

"Right," she whispered, breathless at the contact with his tall, fit body.

"So since you're poor, like me, it's okay if I do this…"

He bent his head and nibbled softly at her mouth until he coaxed it to open. One hand came up behind her head to force her lips hard against his. In seconds, the contact went from teasing to passionate. He held her against him and wrapped her up tight, putting three years of loneliness into one long, deep, hard, anguished kiss.

She was floating. Drifting. Flying. She held on for dear life while her heart tried to escape from her chest. It was the closest to heaven she'd come since he walked out of her life. She moaned helplessly.

"Bad idea," he whispered unsteadily, his lips still touching hers.

"What is?"

"You. Moaning. They'll think you've been hurt."

"They will?"

"Probably."

She lifted closer to him. "Let's just say I'm drowning and you're giving me mouth-to-mouth resuscitation," she moaned against his mouth, coaxing it back to hers.

They were totally lost in each other when someone coughed. Loudly. Since they hadn't heard the first two coughs.

They burst apart. Eb and Merrie and Mandy were trying hard not to look amused.

"Okay, it's like this. She was drowning and I was giving her mouth-to-mouth resuscitation," Paul said. They all started laughing. "Everybody's a critic!" he muttered.

"I'd give you ten out of ten, myself," Eb teased.

"So would we," Mandy laughed. Merrie nodded.

"I'm going home," Paul said. He glanced at Sari with soft eyes. "Keep the doors locked. Scream if anybody tries to come in. And don't take candy from strangers," he added on the way out.

"What if it's peppermint?" Sari asked. "I love peppermint."

"Ignore her, she's daffy," Merrie said gleefully.

"Her feet aren't that big," Paul chided.

"Daffy. The adjective, not the duck!" she returned. He grinned at them and left them standing there.

SARI, PREDICTABLY, DIDN'T sleep all night. The way Paul had kissed her was like a promise. She knew that he'd been intimidated by her wealth, but after the will went through probate there wouldn't be any money left. Well, the house and its contents, but that wouldn't amount to much. And the government was certain to confiscate what her father had earned illegally. If she and Merrie were left with just the house and furniture, she had greater hope for the future than ever before. It was like a new beginning.

She went to work the next day floating on air, her mind barely on her caseload and the pressure of learning to participate at trial. The next session of superior court was a month away, so she and the other ADAs would be hard-pressed to get all the cases ready for

Kemp and Glory to argue, even with help from Tera researching decisions that might mean a win in the harder ones.

The problem was that there were too many cases for too few employees. It was the same story in any prosecutor's office, no matter the size. Some cases were plea-bargained, some were continued, many went to trial. Some were won, some were lost, superb arguments notwithstanding. It was a fascinating process to Sari, who'd only studied past cases up until now. The real thing was sometimes gut-wrenching.

They were prosecuting a case against a young offender who'd murdered his grandparents in a meth-induced haze. He didn't remember doing it, but his grandparents were still dead. His parents insisted that their son wasn't capable of murder. The public defender said he could produce witnesses who would swear the boy was with them at the time of the killings. It looked like a lost cause until an unexpected phone call informed the DA that ten thousand dollars had been taken from the old couple, who had hidden it in a shoebox in the closet. A few of the bills dated to the midfifties. Armed with that information, sheriff's deputies and investigators were sent out to area stores to ask about the odd denominations. Sure enough, a convenience store owner still had two of the bills. They were so unusual that he'd kept them and replaced the bills with newer ones. He gave them to police. He also described the young man who'd paid for a six-pack of beer with them. He matched the description of one of the witnesses who could provide the defendant with an alibi.

There were two other bills used to pay for a meal at the local fried chicken franchise, where an assistant manager had found the old bills suspicious and called authorities out to make sure they weren't counterfeit. The deputy who answered the call still had them in his evidence locker.

One chain linked to another to give the prosecution enough rope to hang the defendant, whose public defender agreed to plead him guilty rather than fight it out in court. Faced with the hard evidence, the witnesses turned state's evidence in return for reduced sentences. The perpetrator remembered very little of the crime, but his friends gave a complete account of what happened. The young man was distraught, his parents even more so. When he was sentenced, neither of his parents stood by him. His public defender discussed the sentencing with Glory and Sari. He'd been sure that the young man was innocent. It was another hard lesson learned in the public arena of law.

That case demonstrated to Sari the beauty of cooperation between law enforcement and prosecutors, because neither could have put together the winning case without the other. She learned that she would be required to go to crime scenes when she was prosecuting defendants. One of the local police officers provided her with her own personalized barf bag, to be kept for her first murder case. Considering the very small number of murders in Jacobsville, and Jacobs County itself, in a year, she was more likely to be prosecuting defendants charged with assault, battery, robbery, drug use and distribution, and passing false checks. It was unlikely she'd need a barf bag for those, she thought with a grin.

But you never knew. After all, there had been at least two notable murders in the past two years—a body found in deplorable condition near a local river, and the murder of the late Betty Leeds. With increased population came increased crime. Sure, she replied. But considering that only five new people had moved into Jacobsville in the past year, that statistic was just a little iffy. The policeman only grinned.

PAUL CAME TO supper that Sunday night. He brought a single red rose for Sari and handed it to her with a flourish while Mandy and Merrie hid out in the kitchen to get the meal on the table.

"It's lovely," Sari said, breathless.

He touched her soft cheek. "I thought one rose conveyed a meaning that was a little different than a huge bouquet."

Her heart ran away. "Did you?" she whispered. Her eyes were eating his strong, handsome face.

He drew her closer. "Yes." He sounded breathless, too. His eyes were on her softly parted lips. "I've missed you."

"I've missed you, too."

His hands came up to frame her oval face. He stared into her blue, blue eyes for a long time, until her heart threatened to beat her to death. He bent his head. His hard mouth brushed over hers slowly, tenderly, parting her lips even more. She heard the intake of his breath as his hands tightened and his mouth came closer, closer...

"Supper!" Mandy called from the kitchen without opening the door.

"Oh, damn," Sari groaned without thinking.

"Double damn," Paul added, catching his breath.

She searched his dark eyes. It was like a beginning, a new start. "I'm hungry," she managed to say, still vibrating with desire.

"Me, too." He drew in a steadying breath and caught her small hand tight in his big one. "I guess dessert has to wait for a bit, then," he mused, drawing her toward the kitchen.

She laughed. Life was sweet.

IT WAS A riotous meal. Mandy had fixed homemade chili and Mexican corn bread.

Paul hardly knew what he was eating. His eyes barely left Sari's flushed face for a single minute. He felt, as she did, the newness of a relationship based on truth, not secrets.

She smiled at him with her heart in her eyes. "Any luck tracking down Morris?" she asked.

He chuckled. "Just rumors. He went to Mexico to join the Zetas. He signed on with the revolutionaries in Syria. Stuff like that. If you want my guess," he added, sipping his second cup of coffee, "he's somewhere close by, hiding out from the people who hired him."

"You think he'll try again?" Merrie asked worriedly.

"He might," Paul said honestly. "But if he does, he'll be in custody before he raises the gun again. I'm not kidding. Eb Scott has some top secret surveillance equipment that his men are using. It's cutting-edge technology. Believe me, Morris won't get a third chance."

"That makes me feel so much better," Sari said. She smiled sheepishly. "I'm not usually a nervous person. But it's been a rough couple of weeks."

"I know it has," Paul said, his eyes encompassing all three women. "But the worst is over. I promise you." He looked straight at Sari. "Things are going to be sweet from now on."

"Sweet," Sari repeated, lost in his penetrating gaze.

"Very," he said huskily.

She nodded. "Very."

"Uh, Sari," Merrie said in a teasing tone, "that's the seventh teaspoon of sugar you've put in that coffee."

"Teaspoon," she parroted, still lost in Paul's eyes. Then she realized what her sister had said. She hesitated, glanced at her sister and then looked at her cup. She grimaced. "Mandy, do you think I could have a fresh cup of coffee?"

Mandy laughed. "Sure, if you promise to let me put the sugar in it."

Merrie grinned. Sari looked sheepish. Paul laughed.

"If you want to sweeten that coffee, just put a finger in it," Paul said softly. "You're so sweet you don't need extra."

"Awwwww," Mandy and Merrie said together.

"Cut it out," Sari muttered, flushing.

"Oh, someone called about the probate of the will," Mandy told Sari as she put the coffee at her place. "He says it will only take another week or so. He wants you to call him."

"Tomorrow," Sari said, distracted, her mind only on Paul.

"He appointed her executrix, since Mr. Darwin didn't specify one in his will," Mandy explained to Paul. "Since she's the eldest."

"Most of what he has will be impounded," Paul volunteered. He hated sounding so happy about it. He'd been beaming all day, since Jon had told him what the government intended to do about Grayling's money. "Sorry," he told the women. "He entered into a conspiracy with Betty Leeds to defraud a bank and use it to launder money from organized crime. The Treasury Department will be able to trace his transactions, and we'll be looking for links to organized crime contacts who participated in the money laundering. Hopefully, we'll be able to close down some of the illegal activities that provided the money."

"What sort of activities?" Merrie asked.

"The usual. Gambling, prostitution, extortion. There's a laundry list of crimes."

"I still don't understand why Daddy wasn't satisfied with what our mother left him," Sari said sadly. "He had more than enough already."

"Not quite enough to support his habit." Paul hesitated when they looked surprised. He hadn't shared this finding with them. He grimaced. "Okay. He was addicted to heroin. He used all the time. His habit amounted to thousands of dollars a day."

Sari gasped. So did Merrie.

"In addition to the narcotics use, there was a lesion in his brain," Paul added. "It was found during the autopsy. Dr. Coltrain said it helped explain, along with the narcotics addiction, his episodes of violence. But what killed him was a heart attack. Not really too surprising, considering the amount of drugs he was using," he added quietly.

Sari sipped her hot coffee quietly. "At least I don't feel so guilty anymore. We never knew that he used drugs," she said. "Neither Merrie nor I had ever been around people who were drunk or on drugs. We didn't even know the signs. When he hit us, we thought he was just angry at things we did. Like not straightening the towels on the racks in our bathrooms, or having the area rugs in our bedrooms less than parallel to the bed."

Paul was shocked. "What?"

Sari looked up. "He was a perfectionist," she said. "Everything had to be in perfect order, all the time. We were scared not to do what he said."

"He was using that belt on them, and I never knew," Mandy said heavily. "Even with the threats he made to my brother, I would have done something, if I'd known. He made sure I was out of town or away from the house when he did it."

"He knew you'd try to protect us," Merrie said gently.

"And we never told you, to protect you," Sari added. "I don't imagine he used drugs when you were around, either, Paul, because you'd have recognized the signs."

"I would have," he agreed. "Sadly, nobody can stop a madman," Paul said angrily. "At least, not without

the law behind them. And he was rich enough to by-
pass the law, apparently."

"He bought people," Sari said coldly. "If he
couldn't buy them, he threatened their families. It's
how he kept out of jail for so many years. But drugs...
We never knew!"

"I guess it explains the way he was," Merrie added.
"It doesn't excuse it, though."

"Not a bit," Mandy muttered. "I guess I was blind,
too. But, then, I'd only been around people who
smoked weed. My brother did, when I was in grammar school. I remember how he always smelled of it.
The smell made me sick." She smiled wanly. "I guess
that's all that kept me out of trying it, too. That, and
the way our mother took care of us. She never put a
foot wrong. But my brother stayed in trouble with the
law." She shrugged. "I always wondered if Mr. Darwin knew about him, and that's why he actually hired
me when his wife died. It was leverage he could use,
to keep me quiet about his private life."

"You didn't know what he did to us, but we all
knew what he did to the horses when he lost his temper with them," Merrie said, and shivered. "He killed
one. We didn't see it, but the trainer got drunk and told
us. It broke his heart. He loved his horses."

"After that, he was careful to make sure the horses
were put up when Mr. Darwin went to look at them,"
Mandy said. "And he made sure that there was no reason to bring one out, where Mr. Darwin might find a
reason to get angry and hurt it."

"We had a dog, when Merrie was very small," Sari

recalled, her face tautening. "Daddy got mad at us and slammed the dog's head into the front door." She closed her eyes in remembered pain. "He laughed."

"My God!" Paul burst out. "Why didn't you tell me about this?" he asked Sari.

"Because if I'd told you, you'd have said something to him and he'd have fired you," Sari said huskily. "Or he'd have done something worse. People didn't cross him without consequences, ever!"

"I had no damned idea!" Paul said angrily.

"We couldn't tell you," Merrie said, backing up her sister. "He'd have known who told you, Paul." She winced. "We had enough scars already."

Paul was remembering what Sari had told him, about the beating that had resulted when Paul resigned his job. He winced.

"Don't," Sari said softly. "It wasn't your fault, not really. I blamed you, but anything could have set him off."

"That's true," Merrie agreed. "I guess the drugs explain a lot that puzzled us before. We didn't know he had a habit."

"He never showed it," Sari said. "Except in sudden bursts of rage. He seemed perfectly sober, except for the headaches and the sweating. He always sweated when he'd used the belt on us. He was sweating the night he came home from Betty Leeds's house, the night she was killed."

"Killed." Merrie grimaced. "Our father was a murderer," she added. "What if we're like that? Like him?"

"We're not like that!" Sari interrupted. "He was high on drugs and he wasn't quite all there mentally, either. Maybe it was the lesion, maybe it was congenital, but he chose his own fate. We're not like him, Merrie. We'll *never* be like him."

"Maybe not," her sister replied, "but it's not exactly a recommendation, is it? Some nice man wants to marry us and we tell him about Daddy, and he worries that maybe he'll have children who have a tendency to kill people."

"Someone who loves you won't care about that, honey," Paul said softly. His eyes turned to Sari. "He won't care at all about what your father did."

Sari flushed with pleasure. The look was as intimate as a touch.

"He might have killed our mother, too," Merrie said quietly. "Dr. Coltrain thought he did. He wanted a thorough autopsy, but Daddy had him called out of town and a doctor appointed to do the autopsy who was in Daddy's pocket."

"The only way to find out for sure would be to order an exhumation," Paul said gently. "That's pretty drastic."

Sari drew in a breath. "Let's just get through with this investigation before we start looking for more tragedy," she suggested. "Whatever we do, it won't bring Mama back."

"No," Merrie agreed. "But the truth should be known."

Sari met her eyes. After a minute, she nodded. "Yes. It should."

AFTER SUPPER, MANDY and Merrie stayed in the kitchen to do the dishes. Or so they said. There were secret smiles as Paul led Sari out of the kitchen by the hand, past the living room and into the garden room. It was too dark to see outside, and the blinds were drawn. There was a love seat and a cushy chair and a coffee table.

Paul sat down in the cushy chair and pulled Sari gently down into his lap. "And now we can have dessert," he whispered as his lips parted hers.

She linked her arms around his neck and gave him her weight. Her eyes closed. Her head fell back against his shoulder with a long, shuddering sigh.

"Sometimes we get second chances," he bit off against her eager mouth. His big hands slid up and down her sides, barely brushing her breasts, testing the firm skin over her ribs. She caught her breath.

"Sometimes…we do," she said shakily.

"Slow down, tiger," he murmured softly as his hands grew bolder. "We've got all the time in the world."

"No, we haven't," she moaned. "They'll finish the dishes and fix dessert. And then they'll come looking for us." She was gasping because his hands had found soft mounded flesh with hard tips and they were busy taking possession of them.

"They'll go slow," he said into her mouth. "We'll go slow, too, baby. Slow, like honey trickling down a tree trunk… That's it. Lift up against my hands. I love the way your breasts feel, Isabel. They're like little apples, round and firm and delicious. I'd give anything to strip you out of that blouse and put my mouth right over the nipples and suckle you, hard."

She moaned out loud and arched her back, on fire with the mental images of what he wanted to do swirling in her head. She wanted it, too. Wanted it until it was like thirst after hiking miles and miles through a desert...

His warm, strong hands went under the blouse, under the lacy little bra. He pushed it up, raised his head to listen for a minute. His eyes slid down to the beautiful, freckled white skin, her rosy nipples pointing hungrily toward his face.

"Don't cry out," he whispered as he bent his head. "They'll hear."

She had to bite her lower lip almost hard enough to draw blood to obey his feverish whisper. Her body arched so violently that she wondered if her spine might snap as she tried to get even closer to that warm, devouring mouth as it began to draw the warm flesh hungrily inside it.

She whimpered helplessly, shuddering. The pleasure was overwhelming. Her nails dug into the back of his neck, into the thick hair at his nape, as she coaxed him, pleading for more.

One big hand was under her thigh. It clasped there, hard, and pulled her into the curve of his body, pressing her against a flat stomach with blatant evidence of his arousal.

"I want to," she breathed over his head. "I want to...so much!"

"Me, too," he murmured roughly against her soft, warm skin. He lifted his head. His dark eyes glittered up into hers as they hung there together in the warm semidarkness of the room. There was just enough light to let him see what he was touching, what he was kissing. "But we can't, baby," he added on a harsh breath. "We can't!"

"I'm twenty-five years old!"

His mouth covered hers hungrily for a few seconds. He lifted his head. "I don't carry anything in my wallet anymore," he ground out. "Do you understand?"

She just stared at him until she finally understood what he was saying. "Wallet?" She drew in a long breath. "Oh. Oh!"

"And I'd bet my government pension that you don't take anything to prevent pregnancy," he added with pursed lips.

She flushed and hoped it didn't show. She drew a soft little hand along his hard cheek. "I'd be too embarrassed to ask Dr. Coltrain for something like that," she confessed sheepishly. "Even if I wasn't, there's only one pharmacy in Jacobsville, and everybody would know."

He laughed softly. "Miss Purity," he chided. But it was tender teasing, and he loved that about her. He loved her innocence.

Suddenly there were noises coming from the general direction of the kitchen.

"They're discreetly letting us know that we'll have company soon," he whispered.

She linked her arms around his neck with a long, lazy sigh. "Then you'd better put my clothes back on, hadn't you?"

"Spoilsport." He bent and drew his lips lovingly

over her breasts once more before he put her bra and blouse back in place. "What a place to have freckles," he whispered wickedly.

She hit him and flushed. "Stop!"

He chuckled. "I'll bet they go all the way down, too."

"I'm not saying."

He traced her swollen lips with a long forefinger. "Very soon, I'm going to find out for myself. So, fair warning."

"Paul, I don't know," she began.

"I know you're still living next door to Queen Victoria, metaphorically speaking." He chuckled. "We'll take it slow and easy. Okay?"

She wanted to ask questions, to know what he expected of her. Surely he knew that she couldn't settle for just an affair. But it was too early in their renewed relationship to start setting limits and making demands. So she just said, "Okay," and smiled.

He drew her face into his throat and rocked her against him tenderly. "It's been a long three years, Isabel," he whispered into her ear.

She nuzzled closer. "Yes."

His arms contracted. "I'm not leaving you ever again."

Her heart jumped. She smiled against the warmth of his throat, smelling the aftershave she'd always loved because it was the only kind he ever wore. "If you leave, I'll go with you," she whispered.

His arms tightened and he groaned again.

A door opened. "Ice cream and vanilla cake with buttercream frosting!" Merric yelled across two rooms.

"The ice cream is now melting!" Mandy added.

Paul and Sari burst out laughing. He let her up and got up himself. He leaned down. "Well, well, we get dessert twice," he whispered into her ear.

She blushed even more. Mandy and Merrie were kind enough to pretend they didn't notice.

THE NEXT MORNING at work, Cash Grier and his wife, Tippy, came by the office to show off their new son in his carrier.

"We thought you might like to meet our new houseguest," Cash said amusedly, glancing around the office.

"He looks like both of you." Blake Kemp chuckled as he looked down at the little boy.

"Yours is growing like wildfire," Tippy commented. "We saw him this morning when we dropped Tris off at pre-K. Violet was there with him."

"I like the teachers," Blake commented.

"So do we," Cash agreed.

"He's such a little doll," Sari said. She moved closer. "Could I hold him?" she added.

"Of course," Tippy said with a smile. She extricated her son from the portable car seat and handed him to Sari, who was sitting in a chair beside the boss's desk.

Paul, who'd been in a conference with Kemp, was also in the office, watching. He smiled wistfully at the way Sari looked with a child in her arms.

"Careful," Cash cautioned. "He spits up a lot. Your suit will never be the same."

Sari made a face and didn't even look up from

thc little boy. "It's a thirty-dollar suit." She chuckled. "Like it would matter."

There was a sudden silence all around her. She looked up, puzzled.

"You ride around in a stretch limo," Paul commented quizzically. "What the hell are you doing in a thirty-dollar suit?"

CHAPTER FIFTEEN

SARI GLANCED AT Paul with wide eyes. "I get a salary, and it's a good one, but I can't really afford designer clothes on my paycheck," she laughed.

Paul scowled. "Your father was filthy rich," he began.

"Well, yes, but Merrie and I never had much to wear. He took us shopping in stores where he had credit, and he told us exactly what to buy. We had a very limited number of things we were allowed for school." She bit her lower lip. "When I was invited to join the chorus, I had to refuse, because Daddy wouldn't buy me a blazer. It was part of the uniform we were required to wear for performances. Merrie couldn't do theater, and she really wanted to. Because Daddy wouldn't let her have costumes. He also said he didn't want her exposed to people who cursed and had loose morals. But I think that was just an excuse not to have the expense."

Paul was lost for words. Now that he thought about it, when Isabel came and jumped on his bed at night to chat, she was always wearing one of two types of pajamas. He'd never connected the dots before. Her high school and college clothes were also mostly the same style and color. It had never dawned on him that she didn't wear designer clothes.

"It didn't matter," Sari said softly, when she realized how unsettled he was. "We never noticed. In fact, it helped, because we didn't stand out from the other kids. The girls knew about fashion, you see." She grimaced. "We got teased a lot because we were rich but we looked like we were dressed from yard sales."

"What a piece of work your father was," Paul gritted out. "You didn't have cars, either. He wouldn't even let you learn to drive. I thought he was just being overprotective." He shook his head. "I looked but I didn't see."

Sari's attention went back to the baby in her arms. She smiled down at him, playing with his tiny hands. "You lucky people. You actually have two of these. A matched set!"

"Pretty much," Cash agreed. He shook his head. "And I thought I had a bad childhood."

"Plenty of people have it way worse," Sari replied. She lifted the little boy in her arms and made faces at him. "Life has a way of evening things out, though. We have sad times. Then we have happy ones," she added, her heart in her eyes as she looked at Paul. He looked back, his eyes dropping to the child and back up to her radiant face.

"We do, indeed," he said huskily.

Cash took the child from her with a grin. "We're going to eat ice cream," he said. "None for you, yet," he added to the baby, and wrinkled his nose at the little boy.

"He's going to have dark eyes, I think," Sari said, watching him. "But I don't know about his hair. It has red highlights, and your daughter has hair like yours," she added to Tippy. "It's so beautiful."

"So is yours," Tippy said with a smile. "Red hair is the rarest color. Someone in your family must have had the recessive gene for red hair," she added to her husband.

"There are no recessive Genes in my family," Cash said haughtily. "We had a recessive Charles, though. And I think one of my uncles was a recessive Harry. Quit that, you'll give our son ideas!" he added haughtily when Tippy punched him in the arm.

"You and your recessives," Tippy teased, her eyes brimming with love when she looked at him.

He bent and brushed a kiss on her forehead. "Let's go. They have work to do."

"He's free today," Tippy explained.

"I am not!" Cash said emphatically. Then his dark eyes twinkled. "But I'm reasonable," he added.

Tippy laughed as they said their goodbyes and went out the door.

"Back to work, everybody," Blake mused. "You, too," he told Paul. "San Antonio is that way!" He pointed north. "You can malinger with my ADA when your boss gives you a day off."

"Malinger? I never malinger. That's something criminals do in dark corners," he added haughtily. Then he grinned at Sari. "I might vegetate in her direction, though. I do a great imitation of a potted plant. I could hold leaves and stand by her desk."

She laughed uproariously. "I'd really love to see that, but I have cases to write notes on," she told him.

"And I have crooks to catch. See you Friday night. Dinner and whatever's playing at the movies."

"I think it's a love story," Glory teased.

"It's a murder mystery," Sari corrected. "But it's a funny one, so it's okay. See you later, Special Agent Fiore," she added with a pert smile.

He winked at her and left.

THE NEXT DAY, it all went to pot. The family attorney in San Antonio called and asked Sari and Merrie to drive up to see him about the will.

Puzzled, Sari asked for time off from work, and had the driver—a new but trustworthy man—take them up to San Antonio.

The attorney, a droll, quiet man named Jack Daniels, ushered them into his expensive office and pulled up chairs for them. Then he sat down behind the desk, with a computer and a stack of files.

"Your father's estate—well, his liquefiable assets, at least—has been frozen by the federal government, as you know," he told them, looking over his glasses at both girls. "However, he had documents in his possession that pertained to monies your late mother had accrued in two Swiss bank accounts, which he was not permitted to touch due to a clause in her will. She left the savings accounts to her daughters, one account each, of the same amount of money."

"Savings accounts?" Sari said, reeling.

"Yes." He presented the records of the savings accounts to the girls.

Sari looked at hers and almost passed out.

Merrie had an equal reaction.

"Daddy never told us about these," Sari exclaimed, going pale. "I was with Mama when she died, and she said that Merrie and I would be taken care of. I thought she meant Daddy would take care of us."

"She knew your father quite well, which is why she left the money in such a way that it was impossible for him to touch it."

"And he never told us." Merrie sighed.

"He didn't want us to have money, because we could have gotten away from him," Sari added in a low, sad tone. She smiled at the attorney. "We never had many clothes, or any freedom at all. He had men watching us night and day. We can't drive, we don't own cars, we couldn't even buy clothes. All Merrie and I have…had…is my salary as an assistant district attorney. I gave our housekeeper some of that, too, for groceries." She sighed. "Our father was using drugs and dealing them, and we didn't even know." She drew in a breath. "I suppose we're pretty naive for women in our twenties."

"You'll catch up," the attorney assured them. "Now, let's go through some of the details. I'll need your signature on some documents, Miss Grayling," he added, speaking to Sari. "You realize, I'm sure, that probate in an estate this size could take from several months to a year, especially since the federal government must decide which percentage of your inheritance was garnered in illegal activities. In the meantime, I'm appointing you executrix and I'm readying papers to be filed in court which will notify the public of impending probate and solicit any unpaid or due bills." He smiled gently. "Your career in law will have already covered these subjects, of course."

"Of course."

THEY WERE IN the car, riding back home. Sari was silent. Her dreams of the future were going to go up in flames the minute Paul knew how much money was in those savings accounts.

"Maybe we could keep it a secret," Merrie said worriedly.

"And maybe whales will fly," Sari said philosophically.

"It was just a thought."

Sari looked out the window and tried not to think about what was ahead. Paul cared for her, she knew he did. But it would be the same old story. He wouldn't want a future with her because she was rich again. It would be too much of a blow to his pride.

She stared at her hands and wondered why she didn't just chuck it all and go to Australia, or New Guinea, or Africa or...

"It's Paul, isn't it?" Merrie asked softly. "You're worried about what he'll do."

"I know what he'll do," Sari returned. "He'll do exactly what he did before." She looked out the window again. "He'll leave, because I'm rich and he works for a living." A stray tear rolled down one pale cheek. She swiped at it angrily.

"Give him a chance," Merrie suggested softly. "He's a proud man, Sari, and he's had a hard life just being honest in a family of criminals. Remember his cousin Mikey?"

Sari had to swallow twice before she could answer without crying. "Yes. Mikey is more than just a small-time crook, you know. He was actually arrested in connection with a mob hit in Trenton, New Jersey. They couldn't prove he did it, but the witnesses swore it was him they saw with the deceased."

"Oh, my gosh!"

"Imagine having a hit man in your family and trying to work as an honest lawman," she added. "Surely there were times when they looked at Paul suspiciously just because of who he was related to. His father was one of the biggest mob bosses in town before he died violently."

Merrie's intake of breath was audible. "How do you know all this?"

Sari glanced at her. "You can't say."

"I won't. Who?"

"One of our bodyguards. The tall one, Rogers. He's related to somebody in the US Marshal's office in Trenton."

"Poor Paul," Merrie replied quietly. She looked at Sari worriedly. She didn't want to put into words what she was thinking.

Sari did it for her, wiping away a tear. "He's had to prove himself over and over again. He wouldn't want to be accused of marrying a woman for her fortune, but that's what it would look like to outsiders." She turned and saw the truth of the statement reflected in her sister's sympathetic face. "It would look like he was taking the easy way to big money, just like most of the members of his family have."

Merrie nodded. "I'm so sorry."

Sari drew in a long breath. "Well, I'll tell him and let him decide." She laughed. It had a hollow ring. "As if there's going to be any mystery about his choice."

"You never know. He might surprise you," Merrie said hopefully.

Sari raised both eyebrows over red, swollen eyelids. "And whales might fly," she repeated.

SARI WAS WAITING at the front door when Paul called for her that night, but she wasn't dressed for dinner and a movie.

"What's up?" he asked, because he could read the turmoil in her pretty face.

She took him by the hand and led him out to the glass room, with its easy chair and love seat. But this time she didn't sit in his lap. She sat on the edge of the love seat with her hands tightly clasped in her lap.

"Our family attorney had Merrie and me drive up to San Antonio to talk to him today."

"And?" His face was grim.

"And our mother left us money in two savings accounts in Switzerland. This is in addition to the house and furniture and a small trust that we get when we turn thirty," she began. "And pending any money that we inherit from our father after the government settles on what he got illegally. That will take months. But we get the savings accounts right now, because they were covered in our mother's will and already allocated at the time of her death."

"What sort of savings account?" he wanted to know.

She drew in a long breath. "Two hundred million. Each." She actually winced with each word.

Paul didn't say anything. He sat like a statue with his olive tan suddenly paler than it had ever been. His big hands were clasped together between his spread knees. He looked down and felt the agony all the way to his toes. It wasn't as bad as he'd expected. It was far worse. Two hundred million. And he worked for a living.

Sari didn't have to ask what he felt, or what he was going to do. His body language was very explicit.

"I could give it all to charity." She laughed bitterly.

He looked up. His face was resigned, his eyes dead in a drawn, taut face. "Honey, every member of my entire family took the easy way to wealth. They robbed, they intimidated, they broke the law coming and going to get big money. I'm the only one who went the honest route. Now you tell me what people are going to think if I..."

She stood up. Tears were threatening. Her heart was breaking. "I know what they'd think, Paul," she said in a husky, defeated tone. "I knew what you'd say before we got home this afternoon. You don't even need to put it into words."

He bit down hard on what he wanted to say. If she'd been poor, if he'd been rich, if, if, if...

She was weighing his reaction. It didn't take a mind reader to know that he wasn't that upset by the revelation. He seemed as calm as he did at her office when he came to talk to her boss. She couldn't know that it was training, half a lifetime in training in law enforcement, that produced that cool demeanor he showed when he was upset. Suck it up, in other words.

"You can marry some rich guy and have rich kids," he said, trying to make a joke of it.

"I won't marry anyone. And there will never be kids," she returned.

He scowled. "Why not?"

She lifted her face. "My father was a cold-blooded killer. I won't pass those genes along to a child." She moved toward the door.

"For God's sake, there are generations of people descended from killers who never break the law!"

She turned. "It doesn't matter. I like my job. I'll put away criminals and help keep the streets clean." She smiled sadly. "It's a dirty job, but somebody has to do it."

He grimaced. "Isabel," he said softly.

The tone of his voice was almost physically painful. "You don't want me because I'm rich," she said, and laughed helplessly. "I thought if you lo…if you cared about someone, nothing mattered."

He didn't let a glimmer of emotion show. "So they say."

She managed a jerky smile. He'd just admitted in a roundabout way that he didn't care for her. Certainly, he didn't love her. She had to accept that and learn to live with it. "I'll pass on the movie tonight, if you don't mind. I brought home a dozen case files that need looking through."

He only nodded. "I'll see you around, kid," he said, and forced a smile.

"Good night, Paul."

He watched her go, her back arrow straight, nothing of her internal agony on view. Well, she probably hadn't cared that much, anyway, he told himself. She was naive, for a woman her age. Maybe she'd only wanted him because he was familiar to her, because he'd been around so long.

There were plenty of rich guys in the world. She'd find one someday.

He wasn't going to care. He didn't dare care. His pride wouldn't let him marry her. He tamped down the anguish inside him. It was as hard as losing Lucy and little Marie. It was like losing them, all over again.

He went back to his apartment and finished off half a bottle of whiskey before bedtime, and hoped that he wouldn't get a call on his cell phone before it wore off. It didn't make him feel much better, but it numbed the hurt long enough to let him get some sleep. He was never going to get over Isabel, no matter how much alcohol he drank.

SARI WENT TO the kitchen to get a sandwich. Mandy had a nice spread laid out on the table, roast beef and herbed potatoes and homemade rolls, but suddenly Sari had no appetite.

Merrie exchanged glances with her. She knew without a word being spoken what had happened when Paul came to take Sari out.

"I feel absolutely wicked," Merrie said, trying to cheer up her sister. "We can buy clothes that don't fall apart after three washings. We can get new shoes that actually fit. We can take driving lessons and buy a real car!"

"I wouldn't mind learning to drive, I guess," Sari said blankly. "What will we do with the limo?"

"Give it and the driver to Mandy," Merrie said gleefully. "We can buy her designer clothes and when she goes shopping at Sav-A-Lot, she can wow all the customers."

"Too late, Tippy Grier already did that," Mandy teased. "But thanks for the thought, sweetie." She looked at Sari. "You need more than a peanut butter sandwich if you're going to stay up all night going through case files."

Sari made a face. "Sorry. I'm not hungry."

Mandy hugged her close. "You can't fool us. We love you. Paul walked away, didn't he?"

Sari broke down. Mandy held her closer while a sad Merrie looked on.

"There, there," Mandy said softly. "Some things take time. But it will all come right. You'll see."

IT DIDN'T COME RIGHT. Sari went through the motions of living while people searched for Morris. She was guarded like Fort Knox. But she didn't care about being watched anymore. She didn't care about anything. The love of her life didn't want her because she was wealthy. She didn't know how she was going to live without Paul, now that she knew what it was like to be held in his arms and have him cherish her. It had been bad enough three years earlier, when he'd just walked away without a word. At least he'd had the courtesy to say goodbye this time.

A week later, Blake Kemp called her into his office and closed the door.

"I know, I'm backsliding," Sari said before he could

open his mouth. "I'm…sort of going through a bad patch right now. I'll get through it."

"You need a week off. I've called in favors and borrowed an ADA from San Antonio. He'll be here first thing Monday morning. You go somewhere and deal with this. You're too valuable an asset to wither away."

She sat down and folded her hands in her lap. "I'm so sorry…"

"We've all been there," he said. "I know how it hurts to lose somebody you love." Shadows flowed through his eyes briefly. He'd been in love with a local girl who died, years before he married his wife, Violet, and had a child. Everybody knew about it.

Sari sighed. "Thanks, Mr. Kemp."

"They say your friend Paul is setting new records for sleepless nights up in San Antonio," he replied, watching her jump as she reacted to the words. "He's volunteered for every stakeout they've got. He says he can't sleep."

"He lost his family in a horrible way."

"Years ago," Blake returned. "He lost you this week. That's what's killing him."

Her pretty face contorted. "He doesn't want me because I'm worth two hundred million dollars," she bit off. "I only have value to him if I'm poor and people wouldn't accuse him of trying to get rich quick."

"You know why he's that way, don't you?"

"Yes." She sounded defeated. "I don't blame him. I really don't. But trying to get over him again is killing me. He just walked away last time. He didn't even say goodbye. I never knew why until he came back into my life." She looked up. "And now he's gone again."

She drew in a long, slow breath. "I think I'll go down to the Bahamas and live on the beach for a few days. Heaven knows I can afford it now."

"Your bodyguards will have to go along," he reminded her. "Remember, Morris is still on the loose."

"I'm not taking them along," she replied. "Merrie and Mandy are far more vulnerable than I am. I can take the corporate jet to Nassau. Nobody will even know I'm gone. I'll get Mandy to drive me to San Antonio, so even the chauffeur won't know that I left."

He tried to think of a way to stop her, but he couldn't. "It's hurricane season," he said finally. "Be careful you don't get blown out into the ocean."

She smiled. "Will do, boss."

He chuckled. "Life goes on, you know," he added when she was on her way out of the room. "It has to."

"I'll get my act together before I come back." She lowered her eyes. "Thanks. For the time off, I mean. I know I haven't been here that long…"

"You really are an asset," he interrupted. "I'm not losing you. Go have a holiday."

"Yes, sir. I will."

He smiled. "Have a safe trip."

"Thanks."

MERRIE AND MANDY ARGUED. So did the bodyguards. It did no good. After a brief shopping spree in San Antonio with some of her newly acquired wealth, Sari packed and had Mandy drive her to San Antonio, where the corporate jet picked her up. Her heart was breaking. She didn't know how she was going to go on. But she had to find a way to live without

Paul. Maybe a holiday was just the thing to start the healing process.

She checked in to one of the biggest hotels in Nassau, right on the beach. A gentleman in the lobby was hawking tours to some of the outer islands. It sounded like just the sort of thing she needed to get her mind off her problems. So she signed up.

She unpacked and hung her new wardrobe up in the closet. It had been fun to go shopping in San Antonio and buy clothes that actually fit and looked good. She'd enjoyed watching Merrie marvel over new styles with affectionate amusement. Neither of the women had ever had anything that wasn't cheap. Most of what their father insisted on buying for them was the same dull colors and styles year after year.

While they'd shopped, Sari had been looking around her, unconsciously hoping for a glimpse of Paul on the streets, in the restaurant where they had lunch with their two bodyguards. But he wasn't there. She hadn't really expected him to be. In a way, she wished he'd never gone back to the FBI, never been sent to San Antonio. Losing him for a second time in one lifetime was almost physically painful.

She had the television in her room turned on, but she wasn't really paying much attention to it. They were reporting on some unusual weather pattern developing in the Atlantic Ocean, a late-season tropical depression that might have the potential to become a hurricane very soon. They warned viewers to take precautions.

Sari didn't even watch it. She went out onto the patio and filled her eyes with the delight of the ocean

beyond the bay, the tall, limber casuarina trees dancing in the growing fever of the wind. She closed her
eyes and drew in the warm, moist, fragrant air through
her nostrils. She smiled. It brought back memories of
the only other time she'd been to the Bahamas, as a
small child, with her mother and sister. It had been the
sweetest vacation of her life. She remembered playing
in the sand on the beach, with her laughing mother
spread nearby on a colorful towel, amusing little Merrie with plastic toys. It was one of the only times they
had, away from her father, before their mother died.
It had been a happy time. There were so few of those
that Sari treasured each memory.

It was typical of their father that he'd hidden anything their mother had left them. There had been jewelry handed down in their family for over a hundred
years that Darwin Grayling had just sold. He told
the girls that possessions were only important if they
could be spent or traded for gold. He had no sentiment and he raised them not to have any. It backfired,
of course. Out of his sight, they were their mother's
daughters.

Their mother had been a gentle, sweet, kind woman
who loved to cook and do handiwork and listen to
classical music. Too soon, they'd lost her. Left with a
maniac who yelled and hit them if they dared to mix
colors of towels in their own bathrooms, if the towels weren't straight on their racks. Sari thought, not
for the first time, that there had been something seriously wrong with her father, even before he started
using drugs.

She was amazed that none of the women in the

household had ever noticed that the man had a drug habit at all. Not that they saw much of him. When he wasn't away on business, he was traveling with that Leeds woman.

One of the investigators who came to the house mentioned something about a sick racehorse that had been shipped north for a race. The horse had suddenly died. Darwin had shipped it back home, by train, to be buried because it was one of his favorites, he'd told the track owner. Odd, too, because he didn't like the horses. He liked the money they won. She recalled that he'd actually killed one of them in a violent temper, like the one he'd been in when he hit Merrie and Sari. Like the one that had resulted in Betty Leeds's death.

She frowned thoughtfully. She'd learned through her job that drug smugglers sometimes had cocaine in condoms that they swallowed or even had children swallow, so they could get them through customs. It had turned her stomach, to think a human being would ever endanger a helpless child in such a way.

But if they didn't hesitate to do it to small children, what about racehorses? She recalled the horse who'd gotten sick. He'd lost the last five races, and the trainer said he had a healed injury that might slow his time enough to disqualify him in future competitions. Her father didn't keep animals that didn't earn their keep. Had anyone bothered to look in the horse's stomach?

She got on the phone and called Mr. Kemp at once.

"I'm sure someone checked that out," Blake told her. But he frowned. "Bentley Rydel might have been called in to consult by the trainer. Let me call him. I'll get back to you. Just in case, do you know where they buried the horse?"

"Yes. There's a small hollow behind the barn, with a stand of mesquite trees and a big oak. It was somewhere in there. You could find it with ground-penetrating radar."

"I'll make sure they know. Thanks, Sari." He hesitated. "How's Nassau?"

"It's nice here," she said. "I'm going on a tour of the outer islands Friday. It sounds like fun."

"You do know that there's a tropical depression bearing down on the Bahamas?"

She laughed. "Yes, I know. But they're not sure it will develop into a hurricane, or that it's going to impact us here. In any case, they'll tell us how to stay safe." She paused. "Thanks for worrying, boss."

"I don't like breaking in new help," he said, tongue in cheek. "Have a good time. See you in a week."

"See you."

SHE WAS ABOUT to leave on the tour when her cell phone rang. She pushed the button and listened.

It was Blake Kemp. "You were right," he told her. "Apparently your father buried the horse with the idea of going back later to recover the stash. Hell of a way to smuggle drugs. The poor horse!"

"The trainer said that the sick horse was losing races," she replied. "Daddy never kept anything around that didn't pay its way." She hesitated. "I forgot to ask Mr. Abernathy what will happen to the racehorses," she added sadly.

"If they weren't used as collateral for loans or confiscated in some other way from the drug trade, you'll inherit them. You and Merrie," he added. "Meanwhile, your ranch manager will provide for them, right?"

"Right." She drew in a breath. "Of all the despicable ways to transport drugs. To kill a poor horse and use it like that!"

"Some people have no honor."

"I'm starting to notice that."

"Forget about crime and just focus on getting a suntan," he suggested. "Thanks again for the tip, Sari. I passed it along the chain of command."

Kindly, he wasn't mentioning the FBI, which would mean Paul, who was working the case. Or she thought he was.

"We had another bit of news," he added quietly. "Agent Fiore has submitted a request to try out for the FBI Hostage Rescue Team. If he's accepted, he'll be leaving San Antonio, I assume." He paused. "I'm sorry, but I thought it might be easier hearing it from me."

She fought the lump in her throat. "It is. Thanks, boss."

"Life happens," he said "But sometimes, unexpectedly, miracles happen. I'm qualified to know," he added.

She knew that he meant his Violet and their child. "I'm fresh out of those," she said sadly. "But life does go on. See you."

"Sure."

She hung up and cried her eyes out. It was what she'd expected, really. She didn't think Paul was the sort to settle down, and he certainly wouldn't want to risk running into Sari very often in the city. He knew how she felt about him. She couldn't hide it.

She packed a small bag to carry with her on the tour of the islands, which was to culminate overnight at a private resort. It also featured dinner on a three-masted schooner, which offered a meal fit for royalty.

She turned off the television and left. It was a shame that she hadn't left it on for just five minutes longer. A hurricane watch had just been issued for the outer islands.

CHAPTER SIXTEEN

PAUL WAS GOING through the process of applying to the FBI's elite Hostage Rescue Team. He had a friend who was a sniper in one of the two units, and he hoped that his skills and his physical condition would qualify him for one of the openings.

It was going to be a long shot. He was in his midthirties. He'd be competing against guys in their twenties, in much better physical shape than he was, with better weapon skills. But he couldn't stay in San Antonio and risk running into Isabel, as he certainly would if he continued as a special agent. It wasn't something that his heart could bear. The rigors of training, and the adrenaline rush of standing on ready night and day for assignments in the exclusive HRT would keep him from brooding too much.

Jon Blackhawk was less than enthusiastic about his plans.

"You're one of the best agents I've ever worked with," Jon told him with genuine feeling. "I hate to lose you."

"Hey, I might not even get to apply," Paul said, chuckling. "They don't pick just anybody for the application process."

"You'd have a good shot at it, if that's what you really want to do," he added. "You should talk to Garon Grier. He was with HRT for several years."

"I'd forgotten that," Paul said.

Jon nodded. "The guys who were on his former team came to the hospital when his wife was about to give birth. She had a leaky heart valve and didn't tell him. Her life was almost taken by a serial killer when she was a little over eight months pregnant. She lived against all the odds."

"I'd heard a little about him, but nothing that personal. Poor guy. He seems happy enough now."

"A wife, a son, a good job and a ranch in Jacobsville. Not bad at all."

Paul knew what the other man was saying. He pretended not to understand. "Anything else in the pipe about Morris?" he asked, changing the subject.

"We got a tip from a guy who thought he saw him in a restaurant here in the city," Jon replied. "All our violent-crime agents are leaning on their CIs to see if anybody knows anything."

Paul understood the reference to Confidential Informant very well. Every agent had several, usually ex-cons who could be persuaded to feed information back to the Bureau. They were invaluable in tight investigations.

He thought of Isabel, still under the gun, along with Merrie and Mandy, as long as Morris was on the loose. It unsettled him, thinking that Isabel could die. He'd gone through hell when he left Darwin Grayling's employ years before. He'd almost gone off the deep end, remembering Isabel's soft arms clinging to him, her mouth answering his in a hunger that eas-

ily equaled his own. She didn't know, but he'd tried
to hire back on two miserable weeks later. Darwin
Grayling had been polite and friendly, but he'd already
replaced Paul and there were no other positions. He
was sorry, but surely Paul would be happier closer to
his wife and child, Darwin had said. Paul had had to
agree. The lie had carried him too far already to turn
back. He just hadn't known it.

He'd agonized at the thought of Grayling telling
Isabel about his wife and child. Lucy and Marie were
long gone, of course, but nobody in Jacobsville knew
that. It must have been devastating for Isabel, thinking he'd cheated on his wife with her. He hated the
pain he must have caused her. He'd known nothing, of
course, about what Darwin Grayling had done to his
daughters after Paul's confession. He'd hired back on
with the Bureau with the help of a former colleague
now in high office. His beautiful, painful dreams of
Isabel had slowly faded into memories. He'd had to
let go or lose his mind.

Now here he was again. Same song, second chorus. He was going to lose her all over again, and for
the same damned stupid reason: money.

Another man might have gone ahead and said to
hell with pride. But Paul couldn't. He was the only
member of his family who'd managed to go straight
and stay honest. It mattered to him, what people
thought. It mattered too much, perhaps.

He'd pretended that it was easy to leave. Isabel obviously thought that he had no real emotion invested
in their relationship, that he could just walk away
without looking back.

It wasn't like that at all. He wanted her to the point of obsession. If they'd been equals, nothing short of death would ever have pried him from her side. But all that damned money. He drew in a long, sad breath. It was just too much to contend with.

Maybe they'd like him for the HRT. He knew the cutoff age. He was getting very close to it. There were older men on the team, of course, but they were agents who'd been with HRT for a long time. He'd be the FNG. The blankety-blank new guy. He'd run the gauntlet while he tried to endure the training. Later, if he managed to make the cut, he'd be assigned either to an assault team or a sniper team. The former was where all the real action was. Assault went in head-first. Snipers could lie around in a ghillie suit in some forsaken forest or jungle for days, dodging mosquitoes and poisonous snakes while some guy in a suit in DC decided whether or not they were going to see any action at all. You had no choice about which unit you joined. That was decided by higher-ups.

Assault was better suited to young guys, he conceded. Snipers could line up shots, take their time, be on their own. There were benefits to each group. The greatest thing about HRT was the comradeship, the sense of belonging, of family. Those guys were thick. During training, they learned to depend on each other and trust their comrades in close-quarter shoot-outs. They stood up for one another. Well, as best they could. If an inquiry followed an action, an agent was required to provide truthful information when asked for it in an administrative process, and everything he said would be discoverable to civil litigators if lawsuits ensued. It was part of the job.

He went back to work with his heart dragging on the floor. If he was chosen to go through the training—and if he didn't wash out, as many very physically fit guys did—it would mean moving to another place, somewhere without Isabel. He felt sick at the thought of never seeing her again. If he could stay in San Antonio, at least he could keep in touch with Mandy. He could make sure Isabel was safe, even if he was only saving her for some other man.

He hated the thought of Isabel marrying someone else. She said she didn't want marriage or kids, but he knew that was a lie. She loved kids. He ground his teeth together. He had to stop thinking about her or he was going to go crazy! Principles, he thought to himself, were unbearable sometimes.

ISABEL WAS WALKING on the beach on one of the outer islands when the wind suddenly picked up and black clouds surrounded the small island.

"It's a hurricane!" one of the elderly guests gasped. She held up her cell phone. "It's all over the news!"

"What are we going to do?" another guest asked the tour guide.

"We must not panic, that is the first thing," the guide replied in a crisp British accent. "We must get to cover. Please come with me. And hurry!"

He got them all into the big motorboat they'd arrived on, turned on the ignition and steered toward the main island as fast as he could go.

"We're not going to make it," a soft Southern-accented voice said beside Isabel. Pale blue eyes gazed wistfully. "It's too far, and the storm is too close."

"We'll make it," Isabel assured her. "Look!"

Sure enough, there was sudden calm and quiet. They were in the eye of the storm.

"With any luck, we can get to New Providence before it hits again!" the tour guide called from the front.

"With luck," Isabel echoed.

She was thinking of Paul. If they didn't make it, she'd never see him again. She lost herself in sweet memories of the brief time they'd had together before her inheritance ruined everything. If she died, she would carry those memories into the darkness with her. Even as the thought entered her mind, the black clouds began to catch up to the boat, looming over it like sudden death.

PAUL WAS WATCHING the news after a long and grueling shift trying to help the local PD run down a bank robber. They'd caught him, but it had taken time. He had his feet up and a beer in one hand while he listened to the day's events.

The robbery was in the news. There he was on the six o'clock news. Well, there was his back, with the big white FBI letters on it. The bank robber in handcuffs filled the screen. There was a voice-over telling viewers about the chase. He took a sip of beer. He hadn't listened to the news in three days. It wasn't really a priority, except because of the arrest today. He listened without much real interest as the news switched to a hurricane that had hit somewhere near New Providence, in the Bahamas, the day before. He paid no attention to it. Weather somewhere else wasn't his concern. He flipped off the television and went to riffle through the small freezer compartment of the fridge, looking for some sort of frozen meal he could nuke for supper. He didn't taste what he was eating, anyway. He missed Isabel too much. He was just going through the motions of living. It was an empty life.

The phone rang just as he put his hand on a beef Stroganoff dinner. He put it back in the freezer and picked up his cell phone from the coffee table. He frowned. Why would Mandy be calling him?

"What's up, beautiful?" he teased.

"Have you seen the news, about the hurricane in the Bahamas?" she asked, choked up.

"Sure. Why?" he added, with a sense of premonition.

"Sari's down there," she said.

He felt his heart seize up. "Isabel's in the Bahamas?" he exclaimed. "Why?"

"Her boss thought she needed a vacation. She was so upset over you…well, never mind. Anyway, I've tried to call her, over and over, and I can't get through to her." Her voice broke. "They say it hit the outer islands. That's where she was, on a tour. I spoke to her just before she left Nassau yesterday." She swallowed down the fear. "Communications were affected and the airport was closed down because of the storm. It took a day to get communications restored, they said, and to get the airport reopened. News crews are just now being allowed in, along with rescue people…"

He sat down. His whole life passed before his eyes.

He'd walked away from Isabel. She'd been so upset that her boss had sent her on a vacation. She'd pretended that it didn't matter that he didn't want her, because she was going to be rich again. But she cared about him. Of course she cared about him. She loved him. And he'd tossed her away, because she was rich and he wasn't. He closed his eyes on a groan.

"Paul?" Mandy prompted.

"Sorry," he said huskily. "I was just thrashing myself mentally. Listen, get them to fuel the baby jet, drag a pilot and copilot out of bed, and pack an overnight bag. I'll meet you at the Jacobsville airport after I try to explain to Jon Blackhawk why I'm going AWOL."

"He won't mind," Mandy said with a sigh of relief. "Thanks. I was so worried!"

"They still haven't caught Morris. You'll be safe enough with me, but Merrie should stay there. We can call her as soon as we know something. The bodyguards will look out for her."

"I already told her that," Mandy said. "I'll get packed and have the limo drop me at the airport."

"See you there."

He hung up and dialed Jon Blackhawk's unlisted number. A small voice came on the line.

"Do you want to talk to my daddy?" the small voice said.

"Yes, please," he said gently.

"Okay. He's not busy. He's just kissing my mommy. Daddy!" he called. "There's a man who wants to talk to you!"

Paul was chuckling when his boss came on. "He's already got a great phone personality," Paul said.

Jon laughed. "That's my boy. What's up?" he added.

"Isabel's in the Bahamas, on the outer islands that just got hit by a hurricane," he said in a tight voice, from which he was trying to purge emotion.

"And you've got the Grayling jet fueled and waiting at the airport with Mandy," came the soft reply.

"Yeah. Sorry…"

"If it was Joceline, I'd already be in the air," Jon said quietly. "Go get her."

"Thanks. I… They said the hurricane hit, where she was," he added heavily.

"Miracles happen when you least expect them. Go get on that jet."

"Thanks, boss. I'll make up my time."

"That's the last thing I'm worried about. I hope things go well, Paul. Let me know how it goes."

"I'll call you as soon as I know something."

Paul hung up. He was momentarily diverted, when he thought how easily Isabel could have died. He might not be in time. He'd sent her running…

He turned and went into his bedroom to pack.

It didn't take long. He was at the airport in scant minutes. Mandy was standing there, by the main desk, small overnight bag in hand. She was in jeans and a sweatshirt, her hair put up haphazardly, no makeup. She looked as haggard as he felt.

"Let's get moving," he said.

She fought tears as she smiled. "Thanks for coming along."

"We'll find her, honey. Okay?"

She swallowed down the fear. "Okay."

IT TOOK TIME to get to New Providence. The storm had subsided by the time they arrived, although there was some damage in Nassau. The brunt of the storm, however, had hit the outer islands. Paul cut through red tape by finding a special agent in Nassau who was kind enough to help him with inquiries about the tour group.

But that took time, too. Eventually, they had a general location. The agent wasn't forthcoming.

"The storm took out communications on Newport," he told Paul, naming the small island that the group had gone to. "All I could find out was that there were casualties. I'm so sorry."

Paul held on to his nerve. "Thanks. I'll get out there and see what I can find out."

"Tell them aid's on the way," the agent added. "Relief agencies are gearing up right now."

"I will."

Paul hung up and turned to a pale Mandy. "I'm going out there…"

"Don't bother trying to keep me here," she said simply. "My baby's there. I'm going, too."

He didn't try to argue with her. They hired a boat and started for Newport.

Mandy had the family credit card, backed by some of Isabel's fortune, and it made the process easier. Paul was amazed at how just the name Grayling opened doors, even here. The old man owned a lot of real estate in the islands. Whether or not the money he got from it was legal was something Justice would have to sort out. At the moment, Paul was just happy that Grayling's reputation cut through some of the red tape while they searched for Isabel.

The rumor that Newport had refugees was a false one, as so many rumors following disasters were. Even as they parked the boat at what was left of the marina, they saw white sheets covering three bodies.

"You stay here," Paul told Mandy firmly.

"I want to see…"

He caught her before she could run in that direction and held her close. "Mandy, I've seen drowning victims. You don't want your last memory of Isabel to be this one, if she's there."

She sobbed helplessly, but she gave in with a long, shuddering sigh. She stepped back and wiped at tears.

Her sad face lifted to his. "Poor Paul," she said, her voice breaking on his name. "Your last memory of her shouldn't be this one, either, if she's there."

He swallowed. His face was ashen. "I'll take my licks. She wouldn't have come here in the first place if I hadn't been such a fool. I let her think I didn't care." His eyes closed. "Damn money, Mandy. Damn all the money in the world! I should have said to hell with what people might think…!"

She touched his arm lightly. She forced a smile. "Go see," she said, nudging him forward. "We might get a miracle. God loves people who care about each other."

"Does He?" He let out a hollow laugh. "He and I haven't been on speaking terms for a while. I blamed Him. But it was me, all along. Me and my damned pride, that caused the two biggest tragedies of my whole life."

He turned and walked toward the sheets, flashing his credentials at a policeman who was overseeing the recovery operation.

"Any of them redheads?" Paul asked the man with assumed carelessness. He didn't want to give away that he had only a personal reason for being here, or he might get himself sent back to Nassau.

The man looked at him with a taut, drawn face. It hurt people to have to look at dead bodies, even tough cops. He nodded. "A woman. There," he said, indicating a sheet.

Paul had to steel himself to go toward it. His nerves were standing on edge. If she was there, he'd... God, he didn't know what he'd do! He'd go nuts!

He knelt beside the body, which was beginning to swell from the heat. With just two fingers, he lifted the sheet where the face was. He'd seen terrible things all during his career in law enforcement, but this was beyond most experiences. The body had obviously been in the water for a day, in the heat, and sea creatures had been at it. The face was ringed by soft, waving red hair.

He put the sheet back quickly. He had to fight not to throw up, to scream, to cry like a whipped child. Tears stung his eyes. He couldn't even get up.

"You know that one, yes?" the policeman said in a soft, gentle tone.

Paul got to his feet. "It's Miss Grayling," he said in a dead voice. "Isabel Grayling. She was down here on holiday. I'll have to…make arrangements…" His voice broke.

The policeman, a family man with children, pulled the FBI agent into his strong arms and rocked him like a child. "It's all right, sir," he said softly. "It's all right. I'm so sorry."

Mandy, looking on, was devastated. There was only one reason Paul would break down like that. She'd never seen him even shed a tear in all the years he worked for Mr. Darwin. Tears erupted from her own eyes, and she thought with horror that they'd have to tell Merrie. How could they do that on the phone? It would have to wait.

There would have to be an air evacuation of Isabel, and then a funeral would have to be planned.

She was openly sobbing when Paul pulled her against him and rocked her as she cried, giving back the comfort that the kind policeman had given him.

"They'll bring them over to New Providence shortly. We'll…make arrangements to have her flown home." He bit his lip to keep from breaking down all over again.

"There, there," Mandy said softly, reaching up to stroke his black hair. "We'll get through this, Mr. Paul."

"I never should have left," he choked out. "Not the first time, not a few days ago. I never should have left, Mandy. What the hell does money matter? I never even got to tell her…that I loved her!"

She hugged him, letting her own tears fall. There, in the clearing of the clouds, with the sun low on the horizon, they made a black silhouette against the sky.

Iᴛ ᴡᴀs ᴀ sad trip back to New Providence. The boat bearing the bodies would be along in another hour or so. Paul steeled himself to do what he had to. The pilot and copilot would have to be notified, there would be formalities and papers to sign before the body could be released. They wouldn't be able to go right home, under the best of circumstances.

Isabel was dead. She was gone. He'd never have a chance to make up for all the heartache he'd caused her. Deep down, he knew her feelings were as deep as his own. She'd been pretending, just pretending. The trip to the Bahamas was proof that she was mourning him, as he'd mourned her. As he'd mourn her now for the rest of his life, because he was a fool. Because he thought his pride was more important than she was. Because of money.

"You have to stop beating yourself up, Mr. Paul," Mandy said when they got in to the marina. "It won't help."

"She wouldn't have been here, but for me," he said quietly. "How do I live with that, Mandy? How do I…?"

They became aware of a noisy group nearby. Some people were just getting off a sailboat. They were wet and disheveled. Refugees, he thought, watching them disembark. They were a wretched-looking lot. Several men, two elderly women…and a red-haired woman.

"Isabel!" His voice could have been heard all the way to the middle of Nassau.

She turned, and looked, and there he was. There Mandy was. They'd come down here to look for her. He had to care, just a little!

She stopped in midthought because he gathered her up in his arms and he was kissing her as if he were going away to war and might never see her again. His arms hurt her, and she didn't care. His mouth hurt hers. She didn't care. She held on for dear life and kissed him back, her tears mingling with his as the sun set.

Mandy just watched, secure in the knowledge that her baby girl was alive, that they didn't have to go home and plan a funeral, that they didn't have to tell Merrie something that would break her heart. However it had happened, Sari was alive. She was alive!

"Paul…" Sari tried to speak.

"I love you," he ground out against her mouth. "I don't give a damn if you're worth two hundred million dollars. I am never leaving…you…again…as long… as I live!" he said between desperate kisses.

Sari just melted. "I love you, too, Paul," she whispered when he gave her a chance to catch her breath.

He smiled sheepishly. "You do? After all I've done?"

She clung to his hard neck as he held her in his arms, suspended off the ground. "I understood."

"You always did. I was such an idiot." He drew in a long breath and kissed her again, but more gently this time. "Oh, God, we were coming back to plan a funeral, and here you are, wet and tired and alive. Alive!"

She couldn't wrap her mind around what he was saying. "Plan a funeral?"

"One of the bodies had red hair," he explained heavily. "I wouldn't let Mandy look, but I had to. It was bad. I couldn't really identify her, but she had red hair..."

"Oh, the poor thing," Sari said, wincing. "She was with our group. She'd just lost her husband, and she went on the tour to try and keep her mind off her loss." She managed a sad smile. "She'll be with him, now."

"You're with me now," he whispered, searching her eyes. "Oh, God, honey, I'll never leave you again. Never, as long as there's a breath in my body!"

She snuggled close, burying her face in his throat, where the pulse beat madly.

Mandy came to join them, reaching up to smooth Sari's hair. "Thank God miracles still happen," she told the younger woman. "We were terrified that we'd lost you."

Sari smiled at her from the shelter of Paul's arms. "I was terrified that we'd all die," she said. "I'll tell you about it later. It was the worst thing I've ever seen. The others were swept right off the deck of the boat. Then the boat went down. There wasn't a life jacket among us. They drifted off when the boat sank. We weren't wearing them, idiots that we were. We treaded water, waiting to drown. There was a sailboat. It saw what happened and sent out a lifeboat for us. I owe that captain my life. We all do."

"We'll make sure we do something for him," Paul said softly.

"We'll buy him a bigger boat, is what we'll do." Mandy chuckled.

"Not a bad idea," Sari said with a mischievous grin. She searched Paul's dark, soft eyes. "A much bigger boat."

SARI PUT ON a pair of pajamas she'd purchased from the gift shop downstairs after a long, warm bath, while Paul dealt with the aftermath of the trip to Newport. He found out the name of the policeman who'd worked the rescue and requested a call from him, which came promptly. He apologized for the mistaken identification, but added that they'd found the woman they were looking for back in Nassau. The policeman was happy for Paul. And Paul decided that he was going to make sure the policeman and his family had a big Christmas present from Santa that year. Sari came into his room as he was finishing up the call. She and Mandy had moved into the big bedroom off the main sitting room of the penthouse suite. Paul took the smaller room. Sari perched on his bed, smiling at the picture he made in black silk pajama bottoms, with his broad, muscular hair-roughened chest bare.

"Just like old times, huh, honey?" he teased.

"Not quite." She searched his eyes. "Everything's changed. So what now?"

He was having second thoughts again, she knew it. He had a worried, harassed expression.

She wasn't having any more of that pride thing. She got up and locked both doors, walked back toward the bed and shed her pajama top.

Paul, predictably, reacted like any man who'd gone without sex for years. He fell on her like a starving lion.

"Oh," she gasped, arching off the bed as he worked his way down her now-nude body with his mouth.

"Didn't know guys did that to women?" he teased huskily. "You noob."

She gasped again. "All I ever knew was…what you taught me!" she protested.

He stilled and lifted his head. "What?"

"Daddy never let us date…"

"You've worked for the DA's office for months, out of Daddy's reach," he said. "What about that other lawyer Mandy said you dated?"

"The only man who ever touched me in any intimate way was you," she said simply. Tears stung her eyes as she met his. "How could I have done anything with someone else, when I loved you from the time I graduated high school?"

His eyes closed. He shivered. "I didn't realize." He drew in a breath and bent again to her soft, hungry body. "Isabel, I'm still not sure this is a good idea."

"It's a great idea." She arched up. "Oh, that feels good!"

He chuckled at her wide-eyed enthusiasm. "Okay. I think I still have something to use in my wallet."

"Don't you dare."

He scowled as he looked down into her eyes. "What?"

"Don't. You. Dare." She enunciated every single word. "I'm not losing you again. No more noble sacrifices because I'm rich. No more running away because you think people will accuse you of being a gold digger. No more, Paul."

He searched for words. "We could have an affair and get it out of our systems," he began.

She reached up and drew his body down on hers, smoothing her long legs around his with intent. "One thing I have learned about you," she whispered into his mouth as she undulated sensually under him. "You're as conventional as a short haircut. If I'm pregnant, you're not going anywhere."

"But, we…" He gasped. She moved and he gasped again.

"We…?" she teased breathlessly.

"The hell with it," he ground out. "I haven't had sex in so long, I'm not sure I remember how!"

He was moving now, touching and brushing, and making her feel sensations she'd never felt in her whole life. She shuddered and shuddered again as he found her with his hands, exploring, discovering. She bit her lip as one exploration went deeper.

"It's all right, honey," he whispered. "It won't hurt for long, okay?"

"Okay." She bit her lip harder, but the pain was gone suddenly as he touched a place that made her whole body tense and arch and shiver.

"There?" he whispered. "Yes. Right there!"

She was barely aware of anything except her own sensuality as he brought her to one peak after another. Finally, when she was almost out of her mind with the tension, he went into her with one long, smooth motion of his hips and her eyes flew open in wonder.

"That's how it feels," he whispered, smiling through the tension. "Lift up. Let me watch. Let me see…" His eyes closed and his face clenched, mirroring her tortured expression as his hips began to move down with a hard, quick, deep motion. "Sweet," he ground out. "Sweet…sweet…oh, God, so…sweet!"

She felt him lose control. But it was all right, because she'd already gone up so high that she barely registered the hot throb of him inside her before the tension finally snapped and he cried out in his ecstasy.

She cradled him on top of her as he shuddered and shuddered. She smiled with a new knowledge of men and lovemaking that felt like the sun bursting inside her.

She kissed his shoulder, noting the scar that ran across it where a bullet had made a path long ago. She kissed that, too.

"Now try to leave me," she murmured drowsily.

"Not after that, honey." He chuckled wearily. "I'd crawl to you on my knees to feel that surge of pleasure again, and that's no joke. Never like that, Isabel," he added, lifting his head to look down into her soft blue eyes. "Never in my whole life."

She touched his hard face, traced the chiseled mouth, the lips that were swollen from the long contact with hers. "I love you."

"Yes." He bent and brushed his mouth over her eyes. "And I love you. We'll deal with it. But you're marrying me the minute I can get a license," he added firmly. "I'm Italian," he told her. "We do things right. Even the worst people in my family got married before the kids came along."

She smiled lazily and moved, loving the sensations she felt, because he was still deep in her body. "I love kids."

"Me, too." He lifted his hips and pushed down softly. "Besides," he whispered as he moved from side to side and felt her body shiver, "making them is a hell of a lot of fun."

"Oh...yes!" she whispered shakily. She didn't say anything else for a very long time.

THEY FLEW BACK to the States the next day. Paul never let go of Isabel's hand, not even once. Mandy knew what was going on, because they were inseparable as soon as they came out of Paul's room.

"Now, don't look at me like that," Paul groaned when Mandy arched her eyebrows at them. "I'll get a marriage license today. I swear."

Mandy just burst out laughing and hugged them both.

The bodyguards were with the car when it came to pick them up at the airport in San Antonio.

"Merrie? How is she?" Paul asked when he saw them.

"She's at the house with two other guys from our unit," the tall one said immediately. "There have been some developments in the past day," he added. "We'll fill you in on the way back to the house."

"Oh, dear," Sari said worriedly.

"It's not all bad," the broader one assured her when they were in the car and leaving San Antonio for Jacobsville. "Morris confessed to taking the contract. But he said he couldn't do it," he added, smiling at Sari. "He'd been around you and Merrie too long to take your lives. He's turning state's evidence. Well, as much as he can. You see, there's a second shooter."

"What?" Sari and Paul burst out together.

"Yeah," the taller one said heavily. "Morris said Leeds told him that he'd hired somebody else to do

Merrie, somebody special. He figured that Merrie, being the youngest, was Grayling's favorite."

"Oh, my God," Sari gasped.

"We'll handle it," Paul said, pulling her close. "Don't panic."

"Grier's on it," the tall one told them. "He still has contacts who work as independent contractors and do sniping in black ops. Garon Grier got in touch with one of his old teammates who now heads HRT and asked about men who were kicked from the sniper program for certain reasons."

"The HRT. Oh, God!" Paul burst out.

"What?" Sari asked.

"I put in an application...well, I'm pulling it, right now." He pulled out his cell phone and made a call. He was grinning when he hung up. "They're sorry I'm not going to apply. But they sent congratulations anyway."

"Congratulations?" the tall bodyguard asked.

"Yeah," Paul said, looking down at Sari with his heart in his eyes. "I'm marrying Miss Millionaire here." He looked back up. "And no bull about how I'll never have to work another day. I'm not giving up my job. I'll just be the head of the household with the lesser income," he added, and mischief made his eyes glimmer as he looked at Sari.

She laughed and pressed close. "Nobody would ever think you were a gold digger."

"Damned straight," the tall one returned, smiling. "He's got too much pride."

Paul smiled back at him.

"You could give it all to Dandy, Sari," Mandy suggested, tongue in cheek.

"Who's Dandy?" the broad one asked.

Paul laughed. "He's a retired racehorse who lives in the stable. Thirty years old and swaybacked. Gosh, he could have all-gold feeding troughs and fourteen-karat hooves if you gave your fortune to him."

"What a story that would make," Mandy agreed.

Sari cocked her head and pursed her lips. "I've got some ideas. But they'll wait. Right now, I just want to go home!"

CHAPTER SEVENTEEN

MERRIE HUGGED SARI. "Oh, I'm so relieved!" she said. She glared at Paul and Mandy. "Mandy left me a note that you were in a hurricane in the Bahamas and the two of them were going to look for you. Then they never even called! I tried, but all the lines were busy. I never could get anybody to answer me!"

"We found a drowning victim that we thought was Isabel," Paul said softly. "It wasn't her, but we were too torn up to talk to you. And we didn't want to do it over the phone."

"Oh, gosh!" Merrie let go of Sari and hugged him. "I'm sorry. I'm so sorry."

He hugged her back. "We found Isabel coming off a sailboat with some other survivors when we got back to Nassau. It was a pretty intense reunion." He actually blushed.

Sari looked wicked. "Yes, it was extremely intense. And now he has to marry me." She blushed, too.

"Nobody's dragging me to any altar," Paul commented drily. "I'm running there, as fast as I can."

"You can be my maid of honor," Sari told her sister, who was gasping and crying and hugging them.

"But you'll need a dress," Mandy began.

"I'll get something very simple. We'll have a min-

ister perform the ceremony here, to keep the press out.
We can't have a big society wedding," Sari added.
"Not only because Merrie's in the crosshairs, but be-
cause of Daddy. We don't want a circus."

Paul agreed. He didn't add that there would also
be a danger of the contract killer finding a way in
through florists or caterers if there was a public ceremony. "We'll be just as married," he promised Sari.
"But you have to have a white gown with a veil,
honey. At least that."

"I know the owner of a little boutique right here
in Jacobsville," Sari said. "Marcella. She does beautiful work."

"We're getting married day after tomorrow," Paul
informed her. "How quick can she sew?"

Sari pulled out her cell phone. "Let's find out."

LUCKILY, MARCELLA HAD a gown in Sari's size that had
been returned by a customer who changed her mind
two days from her wedding. It was beautiful and it
fit like a dream. So they were married, by Jake Blair,
at the Grayling estate, with Merrie and Mandy; the
Grier brothers and their families; Jon Blackhawk and
his brother, McKuen Kilraven, and their families; and
Blake Kemp and Violet; Glory Ramirez and Rodrigo;
and Tera, Mr. Kemp's paralegal, for witnesses.

It was a short, beautiful ceremony. Paul lifted Sari's veil and smiled before he bent and kissed her
softly in front of the whole crowd. Showers of con-
fetti followed them back down the aisle, on the way to
a huge reception in the house itself. Of course, there
had been bodyguards every inch of the way. One of

the guests was a longtime friend of Merrie's, Randall Colter, who'd been in town on business when he heard about the wedding and called Merrie for an invitation.

Randall had a stepbrother named Ren who lived on a huge ranch in Wyoming. Ren oversaw a Fortune 500 company. He was wealthy and lived alone, and he had state-of-the-art surveillance and a dozen former mercs as security guards. Merrie would not only be safe up there, but if she took the corporate jet, nobody would know she was gone and she couldn't be traced easily.

Paul and Sari thought it was a good idea. Merrie was hesitant. She'd heard too much about Ren to feel comfortable with him, and she thought Randall was lying when he said she'd be welcome. But Randall convinced her. The Colters' housekeeper, Delsey, would treat her like a relative, he said, and Ren wasn't home much, anyway. He traveled a lot on business.

They convinced Merrie to go. Meanwhile, Paul ramped up the investigation into Darwin Grayling's illegal enterprises and went back to work after a feverish three-day honeymoon in Galveston, during which he and Sari saw very little outside their hotel room.

"I WANT TO talk to Timothy Leeds," Paul told Jon Blackhawk.

"He's in custody at San Antonio PD," Jon said. "I'll phone Lieutenant Rick Marquez and have him arrange it." He paused. "Why?"

"He hired someone else to kill Merrie," Paul said heavily, noting the other man's surprise. "I thought it was all over when Morris got nabbed. It's not. Leeds said he hired another guy, more professional, for Merrie. She was the youngest, so he thought Grayling would care more for her. Damned irony, isn't it?" he added coldly. "He sets up hits on both Grayling women to punish a man who was already dead."

"He didn't know it at the time," Jon replied. "He's tried to help. He did know where Morris hung out. We staked out the bar and caught him the morning after you and Mandy left for the Bahamas."

"That was a hell of a trip. I identified a corpse that I thought was Isabel." His eyes closed. "Funny, how quick you get your priorities in order when you think you've lost everything."

"You were lucky," Jon said, smiling. "She's a great catch. It never hurts to have an ADA in your corner when you're working a local case," he added before Paul could take offense at why she was a great catch.

"She's going to be a firecracker, all right." He grimaced. "The money still worries me, you know?"

"I do know. It was the opposite thing with Joceline and me. She was a step above the poverty level and I'm worth pretty much what the Graylings are," he added on a chuckle. "My brother and I own half a county back in Oklahoma."

"I heard that." He cocked his head. "You never thought she wanted you for what you had?"

Jon shook his head. "She had my son and never told me, because she was afraid I'd think she wanted to be kept up. I knew her better than that." He smiled sadly. "We had a rocky time of it before I knew the truth."

"I guess I blew the thing up until Isabel looked more like a bank account than a person."

"You came to your senses in time."

"Yeah." Paul grinned. "Lucky me. I'll drive over to SAPD and have a little talk with Leeds. Maybe he can remember something else that would help us find out who bought the contract on Merrie. If we know who he is, we can find out how he operates. Meanwhile, we're sending her to stay with the brother of a good friend, up in Wyoming. She'll go in the corporate jet and nobody will know the destination."

"Not a bad idea. But she'll need to be watched..."

"The man owns purebred Black Angus bulls worth millions," Paul said. "He's got state-of-the-art surveillance and half a dozen ex-mercs working security on his ranch. Merrie will be fine."

"At least we have Morris," Jon added.

"And at least Morris had a conscience," Paul agreed. "I never liked him. He was the old man's pet, because he'd do absolutely anything for money. He was a good choice, for a contract killer. Except he really hasn't got the killer instinct. Thank God."

"No argument there."

TIMOTHY LEEDS WAS nervous and he could hardly sit still in the interrogation room with Paul.

"I was so drunk, I don't remember much," Timothy protested weakly.

"You had to be sober enough for money to change hands," Paul replied. He didn't smile. He hesitated every time Leeds answered, just enough to make the man even jumpier. "You hired him in Brooklyn, in a bar."

"I remember that."

"What did he look like? Was there anything about him that stood out?" Paul persisted.

Timothy locked his hands together between his splayed legs and grimaced as he registered Paul's cold expression. He drew in a breath and tried to think, to picture the man he'd seen through a fog of alcohol. If he could help them find the man in time, before he killed the youngest Grayling daughter, he might escape life in prison. It was worth a try.

"He was tall and distinguished looking," Timothy began. "I remember it surprised me. I mean, Morris looked like a man who'd do anything. This guy—he stood out because he was so dignified. You know, as if he'd never soil his hands with a weapon. He had black wavy hair and his eyes were an odd color, they were almost amber. He never blinked. And he had this ring…"

"Ring?"

"It was gold, you could tell. It had a cobra coiled around it. The head had rubies for eyes. It was creepy. Sort of like him. He didn't ask for much in the way of identification at first, so I thought maybe he was going to pass on the deal. But then he said he knew how to find people, that he'd worked as a skip tracer once." He hesitated. "Will that help?"

"Hell, yes," Paul said. He got up. "If you remember anything else, have them get in touch with me and I'll come back."

"Will this help my case?" Timothy asked plaintively.

"It's not up to me. But I'd say, yes." His eyes narrowed as he contemplated how life would have been if Morris had taken the shot and made good on it, if the contract killer still on the loose got Merrie. "You caused two innocent women a hell of a lot of trouble."

"I know. I'm sorry. I loved my mother." His voice broke. "I was out of my mind with grief. I wanted to hurt Darwin Grayling the way he hurt my mother!"

Paul drew in a breath. He hated feeling sorry for the guy. He had mental issues, that was obvious from the few talks he'd already had with him. "Listen," he said gruffly, "things you do in the heat of the moment come under the heading of crimes of passion. You can ask your public defender to plea-bargain the charges down. You'll still serve time, I won't lie to you. But it's a chance for a lesser sentence."

Leeds looked up with his round face. His eyes were red and swollen. "I'm just so sorry," he said. His voice broke. "I hope Darwin Grayling burns in hell forever," he added on a sob. "My mother never hurt a soul." His head dropped. "She'd be ashamed of me, for what I did," he added in a whisper. "She'd be ashamed."

Paul couldn't find the words. He patted the other man awkwardly on the shoulder, called the guard and left.

"I HIT PAY DIRT," Paul told Jon when he got back to the office. "We're looking for a man who seems too dignified to lower himself to acting like a thug. He worked as a skip tracer once, and he wears a very distinctive ring. It's a golden cobra with ruby eyes."

"Nice," Jon said. "By the way, Rick Marquez is asking us for help investigating the case. I told him

I'd give it to you," he added with a grin. "So knock yourself out."

"Just what I had in mind," Paul said with a grin.

PAUL SPENT HOURS on the computer, more hours combing the city for his few CIs, plaguing other agents for information from theirs. A week later, they had something. All the digging turned up a contract killer who was known not only for his ruby ring, but for the elegance of his dress and the reputation he had for never missing a target. He'd been charged in two murders, but kind strangers had provided him with airtight alibis. The strangers had usually vanished, and the witnesses suddenly forgot what they saw. So neither of the cases ever went to trial. Simon Marcus was well-known in some law enforcement circles.

"At least we have a way to track him now," Paul told the women over supper. "Jon's got his best people looking. So does the sheriff down here."

"My office, too," Sari added, smiling at him with her whole heart. "We'll find him in time. I know we will."

Merrie drew in a long, wistful breath. "I don't want to go live in Wyoming," she said miserably. "Randall talks about his big brother from time to time. He sounds scary."

"You'll be safe there," Sari persisted. "Besides, Randall will be there to protect you."

"No, he won't," Merrie said miserably. "He's only going along to introduce me. Then he has to be on the road on ranch business for several weeks." She grimaced. "I'll never get through this!"

"You have to be somewhere safe," Paul empha-sized. "The man is methodical. He'll be looking for you here."

"He'll stand out," Sari added. "Once we know the way he operates, we can find a way to trap him."

"You hope," Merrie said, dejected.

"It's a big ranch, Randall said," Sari reminded her. "Big enough that you can keep out of big brother's way. Take your art stuff along and draw! Think of it as a vacation."

"Most vacations don't come with short-tempered cattlemen."

Paul pursed his lips. "You might grow to like him."

"What was it you used to say?" Merrie asked Sari. "I remember. You said, and whales might fly." She grinned.

Sari laughed. "Okay. I did say that. But give the man a chance."

"I don't seem to have a choice," Merrie agreed. "Randall's coming to get me this weekend."

"See?" Paul said. "It's all going to work out."

Merrie forced a smile. She didn't really believe it.

THAT NIGHT, LYING in Paul's warm, strong arms in bed, Sari believed that dreams came true.

"You're quiet tonight," he said, nudging her face with his. "What's going on in that quick, legal mind?"

"You'll find out tomorrow."

His eyebrows arched. "Tomorrow?"

She rolled over and brushed her mouth against his bare shoulder. "Mmm-hmm. Our attorney's talking to your attorney."

"What the hell for?"

"It seems you've been left a legacy."

He sat straight up in bed. "A what?"

"A legacy. Our father thought so much of you that he left you a hundred million dollars."

He stared at her. "Isabel…!"

She sat up, too. She put her fingers over his sensual mouth. "It's all quite legal. So now you don't have to worry that everyone will think you're only with me because I'm rich. You're rich, too." She grinned.

"Isabel." His brows met in the center of his forehead. "Honey."

She leaned forward and put her mouth against his. "We're the only two people who will know the truth. Publicly, you received an inheritance from my father, and it's money that never was touched by illegal activities. He loved you like a son." She grinned. "I should write novels."

Her lighthearted, generous nature overcame his protests. He searched her eyes. "Are you sure you want it this way?"

"I'm very sure."

"I'm not giving up my job," he said.

She kissed him softly. "I'm not giving up my job, either."

He chuckled. "Damn, I love you."

She bit his lower lip. "Just give in. It's nice being rich. You can afford a new car now."

"I'll get a new Ford SUV," he said stubbornly. "Nothing fancy."

"That's entirely up to you." She kissed him again. "What's mine is yours. Now we're equals and everybody will know it." She cocked her head. Her blue, blue eyes twinkled.

"Torment," he said tenderly. He kissed her softly, drawing her across his body so that she was lying in his lap. "I love you almost beyond bearing."

"I love you, too. So much!"

He sighed. "It wasn't only the money."

"What do you mean?"

He smoothed his hand down over her pert breasts, visible under the thin gown. "I went after a mob boss. He murdered my wife, Lucy, and our daughter, Marie. It took me a long time to get over losing them." His eyes searched hers. "I was afraid I'd lose you, too." His face contorted. "In the Bahamas, when I saw that body and thought it was you..." His arms tightened. He buried his face in her throat and rocked her. "Dear God, I thought, she's dead and it's my fault. I killed her! And I'd never even told you that I loved you. I let my pride stick it to me again." He lifted his head. "I can't...lose you, baby. I can't!"

She wrapped her arms around him and held on tight. "You won't lose me," she whispered. "I'm not going anywhere. We're married. We're going to live happily ever after. Period."

"Happily ever after?" he asked, searching her eyes.

"Ever after. I swear."

He relaxed, just a little.

"I swear!" He relaxed more. She reached up and kissed him hungrily. "Come down here," she whispered, easing onto her back on the mattress.

"Why?" he teased.

"It's the happily ever after part. I want to work on

it a little more," she said huskily. She laughed, deep in her throat. "Come on. Practice makes perfect, right?"

All at once, the money didn't matter, the past didn't matter, nothing mattered. Just this beautiful redhead with her laughing blue eyes. "I'll show you practice," he murmured, and he lowered his body onto hers.

MERRIE WAS PACKED and ready to leave the next morning. She looked like death warmed over as she hugged Mandy and Sari and Paul.

Randall Colter was tall and blond and devastating. Handsome, educated, charming. He collected women like some people collected books. He shook hands with Paul and hugged the women.

"Don't worry. She'll be safe with us," Randall assured them. "When I'm not around, my brother will be. He can wrestle grizzlies," he added. "Nobody's hurting my best friend on our place."

"You can call us any time you get homesick," Sari assured her sister. "On one of those six throwaway phones we bought you, so that the call can't be traced to you. You'll be safe."

"Meanwhile, we'll find the cleaner," Paul added. "Just watch your back."

"You know I will," Merrie replied. She looked from one of them to the other and smiled gently. "I should paint you two like that. You look… I don't know…completely connected."

Paul tugged Sari close. "That's us," he said, looking down at her warmly. "Connected!"

"Got your cell phones?" Sari asked.

Merrie nodded. "All six. Well, I guess we'd better go."

"I guess." Randall took her arm and picked up her suitcase. "See you."

"Bye," Merrie called as they stepped out the door.

"I̲t̲ w̲i̲l̲l̲ b̲e̲ all right," Paul assured his wife when they heard the limo drive away. "She'll be fine."

"It will be lonely without her," Sari said quietly. "Merrie and I have never been apart, except when I went to the Bahamas."

"It will only be until they catch the killer," Mandy reminded them. "And meanwhile, she'll be safe. Is anybody hungry?"

"I've got to interview a potential witness in a robbery," Sari said.

"I've got to pore over case files looking for a contract killer," Paul said.

"Well, I'm hungry, so I think I'll make myself a sandwich," Mandy replied.

They looked at each other. "We can't work on empty stomachs, right, honey?" Paul asked Sari.

She grinned up at him. "Not so much. What kind of sandwiches?" she asked Mandy, as they followed her into the kitchen.

"Something he'll like," she returned, winking at Paul. "Thick pastrami on rye with mustard."

"My favorite!" Paul exclaimed.

"You big-shot FBI agents aren't the only people who can find out things," Mandy told him.

"And who have you been talking to?" Paul wanted to know.

"Your cousin Mikey," she replied. "Did you know that he can make pizza from scratch, tomato sauce and all?"

"Since when do you know Mikey?" Paul asked.

"He's my brother's best friend." Mandy chuckled. "Well!"

She glanced at him. "He said he'll come down for the christening, by the way."

"What christening?" Paul asked absently as he poured coffee into a cup at the counter.

"Your child's."

He nodded. "My child's…" He stopped dead, with the coffee cup in midair. He turned and stared at Sari with his mouth open, his eyes wide, stunned.

"When we have one," Sari returned, laughing at his expression.

"Oh." He finished putting coffee into the cup and sat down beside her. He leaned over and kissed her tenderly. "Well, whenever you're ready," he told her with pursed lips and twinkling eyes. "I have no objection to boys or girls or both."

"Maybe a baseball team?" she teased.

"Sure. As long as they come along one at a time," he laughed. "And not all at once."

"Bite your tongue!" Sari shot back.

Mandy, watching them, thought how dreams sometimes came true. The two of them had been like two halves of a whole for years and years. Despite the tragedies, and the heartache, there they sat, with the future sitting bright and beautiful ahead and no more obstacles keeping them apart. Merrie would be all right. They'd find the man Leeds had sent after her.

And who knew, Merrie might actually like that tough Wyoming rancher once she got to know him.

Miracles happened when you least expected them, she mused. There would be no more tears shed because of that tortured man who'd lorded over everyone for so long. There would be laughter in this house again, now that it was free of Darwin Grayling's ominous, fearful presence. There would be children playing in the halls, their laughter like music. Happiness would radiate from every corner.

Sometimes, Mandy thought dreamily, life was sweeter than words could express. The two people at the table, oblivious to everything except each other, would surely agree with that sentiment. She smiled as she loaded pastrami onto thick slices of rye bread and reached for the mustard.

* * * * *

*Be sure to check out Diana Palmer's next book,
UNDAUNTED.*

*Falling in love with her boss's handsome
millionaire neighbor was easy for Kate Martin.
But will she ever reveal the secret that changed
Garrett Carlton's life forever?*

Turn the page to get a glimpse of UNDAUNTED.

CHAPTER ONE

KATE MARTIN WAS sitting on the end of the dock, dangling her bare feet in the water. Minnows came up and nibbled her toes, and she laughed. Her long, platinum blond hair fell around her shoulders like a silk curtain, windblown, beautiful. The face it framed wasn't beautiful. But it had soft features. Her nose was straight. She had high cheekbones and a rounded chin. Her best feature was her eyes, large and brown and gentle, much like Kate herself.

She grew up on a small ranch in Comanche Wells, Texas, where her father ran black baldies in a beef operation. She could ride and rope and knew how to pull a calf. But here, on Lake Lanier in north Georgia, she worked as an assistant to Mamie van Dyke, a famous and very wealthy writer of women's suspense novels. Mamie's books were always at the top of the *New York Times* bestseller list. That made Kate proud, because she helped with the research as well as the proofing of those novels in their raw form, long before they were turned over to editors and copyeditors.

She'd found the job online, of all places. A Facebook friend had mentioned that a friend of her mother's was looking for a private assistant, someone trustworthy and loyal to help her do research and typing. It wasn't until she'd applied and been accepted—after a thorough background check—that Kate had learned who her new boss was. Mamie was one of her favorite authors, and she had been a bit starstruck when she arrived with her sparse belongings at the door of Mamie's elaborate and luxurious two-story lake house in north Georgia.

Kate had worried that her cheap clothing and lack of social graces might put the older woman off. But Mamie had welcomed her like a lost child, taken her under her wing, bought her a proper wardrobe and taught her how to cope with the many wealthy and famous guests who sometimes attended parties here.

One of those guests was Garrett Carlton. Garrett was one of the ten wealthiest men in the country—some said, in the world. He was nearing forty, with wavy jet black hair that showed only a scattering of silver. He was big and broad and husky with a leonine face and chiseled, perfect lips. He had a light olive complexion with high cheekbones and deep-set eyes under a jutting brow. He was handsome and elegant in the dinner jacket he wore with a spotless white shirt and black tie. The creases in his pants were as perfect as the polish on his wing-tip shoes. He had beautiful hands, big and broad, with short fingers that looked as if they could crush bones. He wore a tiger's eye ring on his little finger. No other jewelry, save for a Rolex watch that looked more functional than elegant.

Kate, in her plain black cocktail dress, with silver stud earrings and a delicate silver necklace with a small inset turquoise, felt dowdy in the glittering company of so many rich people. She wore little makeup and her pale blond hair was in a thick bun atop her head. She held a champagne flute filled with ginger ale. She didn't drink, although at twenty-three, she could have done so legally.

She was miserable at the party, and wished she could go somewhere and hide. But Mamie was nearby and might need her phone or for Kate to write down something for her. So she couldn't leave.

From across the room, the big man was glaring at her. She squirmed under his look, wondering what she could have done to incur his anger. She'd never even seen him before.

Then she remembered. She'd been out on the lake in Mamie's speedboat once. She loved the fast boat. It made her feel free and happy. It was one of the few things that did. She'd been crazy about a boy in her class at the vocational school where she'd learned administrative skills. When he'd asked her out, all her dreams had come true. Until he'd learned that her father ran beef cattle. Unfortunately, he was a founding member of the local animal rights group, PETA. He'd told Kate that he found her father's profession disgusting and that he'd never have anything to do with a woman who had any part of it. He'd driven her home, all but thrown her out of his car, and rushed away. After that, he ignored her pointedly at school. Her heart was broken. It was one of the few times she'd even had a date. She went to church with her father, but it was a small congregation and there were no single men in it, except for a much older widower and a divorced man who was her father's age.

Her home life wasn't much better. She and her father lived in a ranch house that had been in the family for three generations and looked like it. The furniture didn't match. The dishes were old and many were cracked. Water came out of a well with an electric pump that stopped working every time there was a bad storm, and there were many storms in Texas. Her father was a rigid man, deeply religious, with a sterling character. He'd raised his daughter to be the same way. Her mother had died when she was eight years old, and she'd seen it happen. Her father had drawn into himself at a time when she needed him most. That was before he'd started drinking. He'd rarely been sober in recent years, leaving most of the work and decision making on the ranch to his foreman.

He'd never seemed to feel much for his only child. Of course, she wasn't a boy, and it was a son he'd desperately wanted, someone to inherit the ranch after him, to keep it in the family. Girls, he often said, were useless.

She'd dragged herself back from her memories to find the big man walking toward her. Something inside her wanted to run. But her ancestors had fought off floods and cattle rustlers and raiding war parties. She wasn't the type to run.

She bit her lower lip when Garrett Carlton stopped just in front of her. He wasn't sipping champagne. Unless she missed her guess, he held a large glass of whiskey, straight up, with just a cube of ice in the crystal glass.

He glared down at her from pale, glittery silver eyes. "I had a talk with the lake police about you," he said in a curt, blunt tone. "I told them who you worked for and where you lived. Pull another stunt like yesterday's on the lake, and you'll find out what happens to kids who take insane risks in speedboats. I've had a talk with Mamie as well."

She drew in a shaky breath. "I didn't see the jet ski…!"

"You weren't looking when you turned," he bit off. "You were going too fast to see it at all!"

She was almost drawing blood with her teeth. Her hand, holding the flute, was shaking. She put her other hand over it to steady it. "There was nobody out there when I started…"

"Your generation is a joke," he said coldly. "Unruly kids who have no manners, who think the world owes them everything, that they can do whatever the hell they please, do whatever they like, without consequences! You go through life causing tragedies and you don't care!"

She felt tears stinging her eyes. "Ex-excuse me," she said huskily, turning away.

But he took her firmly by one shoulder and turned her back around. "I never make threats," he said coldly. "You remember what I've told you."

Tears overflowed her eyes. She couldn't help it. And it shamed her, showing weakness before the enemy. She jerked away from him, white-faced and shaking.

He frowned, as if he hadn't expected her reaction. She turned and ran for the kitchen. She put the flute down on a counter and went out the back door into the cool night air, desperate to get away from him. Nobody knew where she was. Nobody cared. The tears tumbled down over her cold cheeks. She'd grown up without love, without the simplest display of affection after Dolores left the ranch, except for an occasional hug from the women in her church. She'd lived alone, had her dreams of romance shattered. And now here she was, her pride in shambles, hounded out of her home by a relentless enemy who seemed to think she was a juvenile delinquent bent on killing people. All that, because she went a little wild in the speedboat.

By the time she got herself together and snuck back in, Garrett Carlton was nowhere to be seen. She went back to Mamie's side and stayed there the rest of the night, hoping against hope that he wouldn't return.

IT HAD BEEN a sobering confrontation. She hoped she never had to see Garrett again. Sitting on the dock, she moved her toes in the cool water, laughing softly at the tiny fish still nibbling on them. The lake was glorious in autumn. Leaves were just beginning to turn, in every single shade of red and gold the mind could imagine. There was a soft breeze, lazy and warm, because autumn had come late to Georgia. Kate, in her long cotton dress, with its brown and yellow and green print, looked like part of the scenery in a postcard.

"What the hell are you doing on my dock?" a cold, angry voice growled from behind her.

She jumped up, startled, and grabbed her shoes, too unsettled to think of putting them on. "*Your* dock?" She'd thought the house was closed up. She hadn't seen any lights on in it for days and she'd never considered who might own it. The dock had always been deserted. She'd been coming here for several days to enjoy the minnows and the view of the lake.

"Yes, *my* dock," he said angrily. His hands were shoved deep in the pockets of his tan pants. He wore a brown designer polo shirt, which emphasized the muscles in his chest and arms.

"I'm sorry," she stammered, her face turning bright red. "I didn't think anybody lived here..."

"Funny girl," he shot back. "Mamie knows that I'm here three months of the year. You knew."

"I didn't," she bit off, feeling tears threaten all over again. She moved away from him. "Sorry," she added. "I'm sorry. I didn't know..."

"I come here to get away from people, reporters, telephones that never stop ringing. I don't want my privacy invaded by cheap little girls in cheap dresses," he added insolently, sneering at her off-the-rack dress.

Her lower lip trembled. Tears threatened. But her injured pride wouldn't let that insult go by unaddressed. "My dress may be cheap, Mr. Carlton, but *I* am not." She lifted her chin. "I go to church every Sunday!"

Something flashed in the eyes she could barely see. "Church!" he scoffed. "Religion is the big lie. Sin all week, then go to confession. Sit in a pew on Sunday and hop from one bed to another the rest of the week."

She just stared at him. "From what I hear, bed-hopping is your choice of hobbies. Not mine."

He laughed shortly. "Women will do anything for a price."

As if in answer to that cynical remark, a beautiful brunette in a fashionable dress stuck her head out the door of his lake house. "Garrett, do hurry," she fussed. "The soufflé is getting cold!"

"Coming." He gave Kate's dress a speaking look. "Did you get that from a thrift shop?" he asked insolently.

"Actually I bought it off a sale rack. And for a very good price."

"It looks cheap."

"It is cheap."

"Just stay off my dock," he said coldly.

"Don't worry, I'll never walk this way again," she murmured as she turned to leave.

"If you take that speedboat on the lake again, you pay attention to where you're driving it. The lake police will be watching."

She didn't turn around. Her stiff little back told its own story.

"Impudent upstart," he muttered.

"Overbearing pig."

She thought she heard amused laughter behind her, but she didn't turn around. She kept on walking.

MAMIE LOOKED UP as Kate walked into the room. She was smiling, but the smile faded when she saw the younger woman's face. It was flushed, and traces of tears marred her lovely complexion.

"What's wrong, sugar?" she asked gently.

Kate drew in a breath. "I didn't know Garrett Carlton owned the house down the shore," she said. "I've been sitting on the dock, dangling my feet off the edge. He caught me at it and ordered me off the property."

Mamie grimaced. "I'm sorry, I should have told you. He spoke to you at the party, about the boat, didn't he?"

"Yes, more like threatened and intimidated me," she replied with a wan smile. "I wasn't being reckless at all. I just didn't see the jet ski. It came out of nowhere."

"You have to anticipate that people on jet skis do crazy things. So do other motorboat drivers. We had a tragedy here on the lake a few years back. A speeding motorboat hit a houseboat and killed two people."

"How horrible!"

"The driver had been drinking. He was arrested and charged, but the passengers on the boat were still dead."

"I'll be more careful," Kate promised. She grimaced. "I don't understand why he dislikes me so much," she murmured absently. "He was horrible to me at the party. And he looks at me as if he hates me," she added.

Mamie had a feeling about that, but she wasn't going to say what it was. She only smiled. "I'll have a dock built on the lake, just for you, sweetheart, so you can dangle your little feet." Mamie's was one of the few homes on the lake that didn't boast a private dock. Kate had to drive Mamie's car over to the marina to use the boat. Or walk, if Mamie was away, as she often was. It wasn't that much of a walk for someone as young and athletic as Kate was.

Kate laughed. "You don't have to go to that trouble. I'll walk over to the marina and dangle my feet off the docks there. It isn't as if I can do it much longer, anyway. It's October already."

"With your luck, the dock you choose at the marina will be the one where Garrett keeps his sailboat," Mamie chuckled. "Docks don't cost that much, they're mostly empty drums with planking on top. I'll have Bill see about it next week." She waved Kate's protests away, then said, "Come on in here, will you, honey? I want to dictate some chaotic thoughts and see if you can inspire me to put them into an understandable form."

"I'll be happy to," Kate replied.

"Who was the girl on the dock?" Maria asked as she and Garrett shared the soggy, tasteless soufflé she'd taken out of the oven.

"Some millennial," he said coldly. "And that's all I want to say about her."

She sighed. "Whatever you say, darling. Are we going out tonight?"

"Where do you want to go?" he asked, giving up his hope of a quiet night with a good book and a whiskey sour.

"The Crystal Bear," she said at once, naming a new and trendy place on the outskirts of downtown Atlanta, where the main attraction was a huge bear carved from crystal and a house band that was the talk of the town. The food wasn't bad either. Not that he cared much for any of it. But he'd humor Maria. She was beginning to get on his nerves. He gave her slender body a brief appraisal and found himself uninterested. He'd felt that way for several days. Ever since that little blond pirate had almost run into him on the jet ski and he'd given her hell for it at Mamie's party.

The girl was unusual. Beautiful in a way that had little to do with her looks. He'd seen her, from the porch of his lake house, usually when she didn't see him. There had been a little girl who'd wandered up on the beach. The blond woman—what was the name Mamie had called her?—had seen her, bent to comfort her, taken the child up in her arms and cuddled her close, drying her tears. He'd seen her walking back down the beach, apparently in search of the missing parent.

The sight had disturbed him. He didn't want children, ever. Countless women had tried to convince him, practically trick him into it for a decade, but he was always careful. He used condoms, despite assurances that they were on the pill. He was always wary. Because he was filthy rich. Women were out to ensnare him. A child would be a responsibility that he didn't want, plus it also meant expensive support for the child's mother. He wasn't walking into that trap. He'd seen what had happened to his only brother, who lived in misery because of a greedy woman who'd gotten pregnant for no other reason than to trap him into a loveless marriage. That marriage had ended in death, on this very lake. It chilled him to remember the circumstances. The blond woman brought it all back.

Still, the sight of the woman with the child in her arms, her long, shiny hair wafting in the breeze, made him hungry for things he didn't understand. She had no money, and wasn't even that pretty. It puzzled him that he should have such an immediate response to her. That night, at the party, he'd stared at her, hungered for her, wanted her.

He'd frightened her with his reckless anger. He hadn't meant to. She didn't seem like other women he knew, who pretended tears to get things. Her tears had been genuine, like her fear of him. He'd been shocked when she backed away from him. It had been a long time—years—since anyone had done that. And never a woman.

Then he'd found her sitting on his dock, laughing as she dangled her feet in the water. The sight had hit him in the heart so hard that it had ignited his temper all over again. He had no need of this blond woman. He had Maria, bright and beautiful, who would do anything he asked, because he showered her with the expensive diamonds she loved.

The blond in the cheap dress had been wearing even cheaper jewelry. Her shoes had been scuffed and old. But she had a regal pride. It amused him to recall her cold defense of her morals. Which were of no concern to himself, he thought, and promptly shut her out of his mind.

MAMIE CALLED KATE to her office a few mornings later as she was sealing the last of several envelopes that contained the neat little notes Kate had typed and printed for her. Mamie had just finished signing them.

"I would have done that for you," Kate protested.

"Of course you would, but I had some time." She put the envelopes in a neat stack. "You can stamp them and put the address labels on. Here's the thing, sweetie, I'm going to be away for about two or three months. A sheik has invited me to stay at his palace and see the sights in Qawi with his family. We'll watch horse races, attend cultural events all over the Middle East, even spend some time on the Riviera in Monaco and Nice on the way home. Do you want to stay here or go home to your dad?"

Kate swallowed. "Well…"

"You're welcome to stay here," she said gently, because she knew how Kate's father treated her. Kate had often lived with another family in Texas, but she'd said often that she didn't want to impose on them. "You'd be doing me a favor, actually, because I wouldn't have to close up the lake house. What do you think?"

"I'd love that!"

Mamie smiled. "I thought you might. Okay. You know what to do. You can drive the speedboat, too, but no speeding," she added firmly. "You don't want to make Garrett angry. Really, you don't."

Kate frowned at her employer. There was something odd about the way she'd said it.

Mamie sat down and folded her hands in her lap. "I wasn't always a famous author," she began. "I started out as a newspaper reporter on a small weekly paper. From there I moved to entertainment magazines, doing feature stories on famous people." She grimaced. "One of them was Garrett Carlton. His best friend—who turned out to only be a distant acquaintance—had assured me that he had Garrett's permission to tell me things about his private life. So I quoted the man as my source and ran the story."

"This sounds as though it ended unhappily," Kate said when her companion was very quiet.

"It did. The man who gave me the quotes was a business rival who hated Garrett and saw an opportunity to get even for a business account he lost. Most of what he told me was true, but Garrett is fanatical about his privacy. I didn't know that until it was too late. Long story short, the magazine fired me to keep him from suing."

"Oh, no."

"It was a bad time," Mamie recalled quietly. "I was just divorced, with no money of my own. I depended on that job to keep my bills paid and a roof over my head. I landed another job, with a rival magazine, a couple of weeks later. Luckily for me, that publisher didn't like Garrett and wasn't going to be forced into putting me on the street for what another magazine printed."

"He tried to have you fired from that job, too?" Kate asked, aghast at the man's taste for vengeance.

"Yes, he did. So when I tell you to be careful about dealing with him, I'm not kidding," Mamie concluded. "I would never fire you, no matter what he threatened. But I still work for publishers who can be threatened."

"I see your point," she said quietly. "I won't make an enemy of him. I'll make sure I stay out of his way from now on."

"Good girl," Mamie said gently. "You're very special, Kate. I trust you, which is more than I can say about most people I know. I wanted children, but my husband didn't." She smiled sadly. "It's just as well, the way things turned out."

"Why is Mr. Carlton so bitter?" Kate asked suddenly. "I mean, he never smiles and he's always upset about something or someone. It just seems odd to me."

"He lost his brother, his only sibling, in an accident on this lake. A drunk boat driver hit him and Garrett's fiancée in their houseboat and left the scene. They both died." She swallowed. "Garrett spent a fortune, they say, searching for the man's location for the police. He was prosecuted and sent to prison. He's still there."

"Did the drunk man have family?"

Mamie nodded. "A wife and a little girl. They lost their home, their income...the child had to go to social services. The mother ended up dead of a drug overdose. It was a tragic story, all the way around."

"Life is so hard for children," Kate murmured, thinking of the poor little girl. Garrett Carlton was vindictive.

"It is." Mamie looked around. "Well, I'd better be on my way. Come help me pack, Kate. I have a couple of evening dresses I want to give you. They're too small for me, and they'll suit you very well."

"I never go anywhere to wear evening dresses," Kate laughed. "But thank you very much for the thought."

Mamie glanced at her. "You should be dating, meeting men, thinking about starting a family."

"I haven't met anyone I felt that way about, except Steven." She shuddered. "I thought he was the perfect man. Now I'm not sure I'll ever trust my judgment about a man ever again."

You'll get over it in time, honey," Mamie said, a

gentle smile on her face. There are plenty of handsome, eligible men in the world, and you have a kind heart. You don't think so right now, but men are going to want you, Kate. That nurturing nature is something most men can't resist. They don't care as much for physical beauty as they do for someone who's willing to sit up with them when they're sick and feed them cough syrup." She grinned.

Kate laughed, as she was meant to. "Well, one day. Maybe."

Mamie left in a whirlwind of activity, met by a stretch limousine with a stately driver in a suit and tie. She gave Kate a handful of last-minute chores, a research assignment to complete for her next book, and an admonition to be careful about going out after dark. Her parting shot was to stay off the lake in the speedboat until Garrett went to his home in the South of France as he did most years just before Christmas.

Kate promised to be careful, but no more. The speedboat had become her solace. When she was out on the lake, with the wind blowing through her long hair and the spray of the water on her face, she felt alive as she'd never felt before.

SHE HADN'T TOLD MAMIE, but she was still hurting from Steven's rejection. She'd felt close to him, felt a sense of belonging to someone for the first time in her young life. His rejection had been painful. Ideals were worthwhile, certainly, but it had been her father's choice of vocations that had alienated him. He hadn't considered that she might not feel as her father did. He simply walked away, without a backward glance.

For several weeks, she hoped that he might call or write, that he might apologize for making assumptions about her. But he hadn't. In desperation, she'd written to a former girlfriend in San Antonio, where Steven had moved to, a mutual friend from high school. The friend told her that Steven was involved with a new organization—a radical animal rights group, much larger than the one he'd belonged to when Kate knew him. That was when Kate finally gave up. She wasn't going to have that happy ending so beloved by tellers of fairy tales. Not with Steven, anyway.

She walked idly through the woods, a stick held loosely in her hand. She touched it to the tops of autumn weeds as she walked, lost in thought.

She almost walked straight into the big man before she saw him. She jumped back as though he'd struck out at her. Her heart was beating a mad rhythm. She felt breathless, frightened, heartsick. All those emotions vied for supremacy in her wide brown eyes.

She bit her lower lip. "I'm sorry," she said at once, almost cringing at the sudden fierce anger in his broad face.

His hands were jammed deep in his trouser pockets. He was wearing a beige shirt with tan slacks, and he looked, as usual, out of sorts.

He glared at her from pale glittering gray eyes, assessing her, finding her wanting. His opinion of her long brown checked cotton dress with its white tee shirt underneath was less than flattering.

"Well, we can't all afford Saks," she said defensively.

He lifted an eyebrow. "Some of us can't even afford a decent thrift shop, either, judging by appearances," he returned.

She stood on the narrow path through the woods that led to the lake. "I wasn't trespassing," she blurted out, reddening. "Mamie owns up to that colored ribbon on the stake, there." She pointed to the property line.

He cocked his head and stared at her. He hated her youth, her freshness, her lack of artifice. He hated her very innocence, because it was so obvious that it was unmistakable. His whole life had been one endless parade of perfumed, perfectly coifed women endlessly trying to get whatever they could out of him. Here was a stiff, upright little Puritan.

"You're always alone," he said absently.

"So are you," she blurted out, and then bit her tongue at her own forwardness.

Broad shoulders lifted and fell. "I got tired of eating soufflés, so I sent her home," he said coolly.

She frowned, searching his face. He showed his age in a way that many older men didn't. He pushed himself too hard. She knew without asking that he never took vacations, that he carried work home every night and stayed on the phone until he was finally weary enough to sleep. Business was his whole life. He might have women in his life, but their influence ended at the bedroom door. And nobody got close, ever.

"Can you cook?" he asked suddenly.

"Of course."

He raised an eyebrow.

"My father has a little cattle ranch in Texas," she

said hesitantly. "My mother died when I was only eight. I had to learn to cook."

"At the age of eight?" he asked, surprised.

She nodded. Suddenly she felt cold and wrapped her arms around her body. "I was taught that hard work drives out frivolous thoughts."

He scowled. "Any brothers, sisters?"

She shook her head.

"Just you and the rancher."

She nodded. "He wanted a boy," she blurted out. "He said girls were useless."

His hands, stuffed in his pockets, clenched. He was getting a picture he didn't like of her life. He didn't want to know anything about her. He found her distasteful, irritating. He should turn around and go back to his lake house.

"You had a little girl with you a few days ago," he said, startling her. "She was lost."

She smiled slowly, and it changed her. Those soft brown eyes almost glowed. "She belongs to a friend of Mamie's, a young woman from Provence who's over here with her husband on a business trip. They're staying at a friend's cabin. The little girl wandered over here, looking for Mamie."

"Provence? France?"

"Yes."

"And do you speak French, cowgirl?" he asked.

"*Je ne parle pas trés bien, mais, oui,*" she replied.

He cocked his head, and for a few seconds, his pale eyes were less hostile. "You studied it in high school, I suppose?"

"Yes. We had to take a foreign language. I already spoke Spanish, so French was something new."

"Spanish?"

"My father had several cowboys who were from Mexico. Their families were here before the first settlers made it to Texas," she said, absently defending them.

His pale eyes narrowed. "I didn't say a thing, but you don't like even the intimation of prejudice, do you?"

She shifted on her feet. "They were like family to me," she said. "My father was hard as nails. He wouldn't even give a man time off long enough to go to a funeral." She shifted again. "He said work came first, family second."

"Charming," he said.

"So all the affection I ever had was from people who worked for him." She smiled, reminiscing. "Dolores cooked for the bunkhouse crew. She taught me to cook and sew, she bought me the first dress I ever owned." Her face hardened. "My father threw it away. He said it was trashy, like Dolores. I said she was the least trashy person I knew and he…" She swallowed. "The next day, she was gone. Just like that."

He moved a step closer. "You hesitated. What did your father do?"

She bit her lower lip. "He said I deserved it…"

"What did he do?"

"He drew back his fist and knocked me down," she said, lowering her face in shame. "Dolores's husband saw it through the window. He came in to protect me.

He knocked my father down. So my father fired Dolores and him. Because of me."

He didn't move closer, but she felt the anger emanating from him. "He would have found another reason for doing it," he said after a minute.

"He didn't like them being friendly to me," she sighed. "I felt so bad. They had kids who were in school with me, and the kids had to go to another school where Pablo found work. Dolores tried to write to me, but my father tore up the letter and burned it, so I couldn't even see the return address."

"You should have gone with them," he said flatly.

She smiled sadly. "I tried to. He locked me in my room." She looked up with soft, sad eyes. "Mamie reminds me of Dolores. She has a kind heart, too."

There was an odd vibrating sound. She frowned, looking around.

He held up the cell phone he'd kept in his pocket. He glared at it, turned the vibrate function off, and put it back in his pocket. "If I answer it, there's a crisis I have to solve. If I don't answer it, there will be two crises that cost me a small fortune because I didn't answer it."

"I don't even own a cell phone," she said absently.

How would she pay for one? he almost said out loud. But he didn't want to hurt her. Life had done a good job of that, from what he'd heard.

He nodded toward the sky. "It will be dark soon," he said. "You shouldn't be out alone at night."

She managed a smile. "That's what Mamie says. I'm going in."

She turned, a little reluctantly, because he wasn't quite the ogre she thought he was.

All the way down the path, she felt his eyes on her. But he didn't say another word.

Don't miss UNDAUNTED
by New York Times *bestselling author*
Diana Palmer.
Available July 2017 wherever
HQN Books and ebooks are sold.

www.Harlequin.com

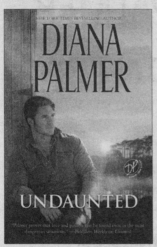

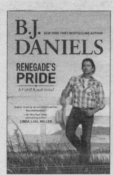  

 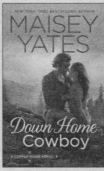 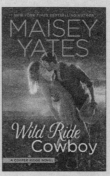

Get 2 Free Books,
Plus 2 Free Gifts -
just for trying the *Reader Service!*

DIANA PALMER

80183	FIRE BRAND	___ $7.99 U.S.	___ $9.99 CAN.
78994	WYOMING BRAVE	___ $7.99 U.S.	___ $9.99 CAN.
78940	UNTAMED	___ $7.99 U.S.	___ $9.99 CAN.
77976	LONG, TALL TEXANS VOLUME II: TYLER & SUTTON	___ $7.99 U.S.	___ $8.99 CAN.
77973	WYOMING RUGGED	___ $7.99 U.S.	___ $9.99 CAN.
77966	THE MORCAI BATTALION: INVICTUS	___ $7.99 U.S.	___ $9.99 CAN.
77570	DANGEROUS	___ $7.99 U.S.	___ $9.99 CAN.

(limited quantities available)

TOTAL AMOUNT	$_____
POSTAGE & HANDLING	$_____
($1.00 FOR 1 BOOK, 50¢ for each additional)	
APPLICABLE TAXES*	$_____
TOTAL PAYABLE	$_____

(check or money order—please do not send cash)

To order, complete this form and send it, along with a check or money order for the total above, payable to HQN Books, to: **In the U.S.:** 3010 Walden Avenue, P.O. Box 9077, Buffalo, NY 14269-9077; **In Canada:** P.O. Box 636, Fort Erie, Ontario, L2A 5X3.

Name: _____

Address: _____ City: _____

State/Prov.: _____ Zip/Postal Code: _____

Account Number (if applicable): _____

075 CSAS

*New York residents remit applicable sales taxes.
*Canadian residents remit applicable GST and provincial taxes.

H
HQN™
www.HQNBooks.com

PHDP0617BL